Other books by
Heather Justesen

Sweet Bites Mysteries
Brownies & Betrayal
Pistols & Pies
Muffins & Murder
Eggnog & Extortion

Carver Ranch romances
Second Chances
Identity
Safe Haven

Other Romances
The Ball's in Her Court
Rebound
Family by Design
Blank Slate
The Switch
Shear Luck
Dancing at the Flea Market
Homecoming

Books under the pen name Heather Tullis

The DiCarlo Brides
A Perfect Fit
SEALed with Love
Reclaiming his Bride
Family Matters
Wild Hearts
The Last Bride
Getting Her Groom

In The Garden
Hello Again
First Crush
Not in the Plans— Winter 2017
Last Chance—spring 2017

Echo Ridge Anthologies
Christmas Kisses
Kisses Between the Lines
Silver Screen Kisses—March 2017

HEATHER JUSTESEN

Published by Jelly Bean Press, PO Box 548, Osawatomie, KS 66064
ISBN: 978-1-63034-023-0

Image by Perkus iStock Photo ID 21954968
Cover design by Bill J. Justesen
Cover design © 2016 by Heather Justesen

Dedication

To Teresa K, for making an otherwise intensely difficult year a lot more fun, and to lava lamps and the sweet release they can bring.

Part 1

Chapter 1

"WHAT DO YOU THINK about the name Rogan?" Jimmy asked.

"No way. I'd sooner go with Grendle." Shelly turned to look out the window at the passing scenery, mostly to hide her smile. Snow adorned the trees and fence posts along the roadside. The headlights reflected off the ice, illuminating the creek bed below on their right and the rising hills on the left. She'd never liked driving through Nephi Canyon at night.

"Grendle wasn't even a real person—and you would never be so cruel." He nudged her with his elbow. "I know you better than that."

Her lips quirked, enjoying the banter. She caught his glance in her direction along with the flash of the dimple in his right cheek—it never had the decency to duplicate itself on his left side. "The whole discussion is academic, since we aren't even married yet—"

"The wedding is only five days away," he said, as if she needed reminding.

"—and I'm not going to try having children until you at least finish at Snow College—which is more than a year off."

He laughed. "It's never too early to discuss the future." An oncoming car's headlight glared through the windshield and made his tawny hair turn a ghostly silver.

She held in a chuckle as she watched the snow fall softly around them. It wasn't bad yet, but promised to grow heavier as the night progressed. She was grateful they'd finished their shopping early, but looking at the weather,

1

wished she hadn't dawdled over dinner. It had been so long since the two of them had been able to spend much time together, especially time alone. He'd been off his mission for over two months, but her final semester at Utah State University while he was living at home in Ephraim still kept them apart. "If you're looking for an argument, I'd rather discuss the Nuggets' chances against the Bulls." She picked a topic they could both discuss with gusto.

"Just because your brother-in-law plays for the Nuggets does not make his team inherently better."

"And your irrational preference for the Bulls won't improve their chances."

"It's about the team dynamics. Besides, loyalty's important."

"So if they were ranked last in the nation, you would still stick by their side?" She tried to make her voice sound scathing, but couldn't manage it. She loved his loyalty. In fact, she loved everything about Jimmy and had for as long as she could remember.

"Ranked last in the nation? As if that would happen with Cliff on the team." He snorted and took his eyes away from the winding pass between Nephi and Fountain Green.

"Eyes on the road. I'd prefer to arrive back home in one piece," she chided. The roads through the canyon could be nasty, even without fresh snowfall.

"It was barely a glance. Besides, I enjoy being with you. After all the time we spent apart, I still have a hard time believing you said yes."

"You worried that I wouldn't?" She kept her tone light but didn't look at him. The fact was, she'd very nearly told someone *else* yes. A few months earlier she'd found herself caught between her love for Rob, the man she'd been seeing casually for several months, and Jimmy, the one she'd loved since childhood and who would return from his mission in a matter of weeks. Jimmy had won, of course, as she had known he would long before she promised to wait for him, but it hadn't been an easy decision.

All throughout the past semester, she'd caught the edge of hurt and anger in Rob's demeanor every time their eyes met on campus. It was a relief to be done with school, knowing he would finish in the spring—long before Jimmy finished at Snow and they moved to Logan so Jimmy could earn his own degree.

"I know I shouldn't have doubted, but when your companion gets a Dear John, it can be hard to remind yourself your girlfriend would never do something like that to you." He reached over and gave her clasped hands a squeeze. "I couldn't ask for anyone better."

Guilt didn't creep over her this time—it flooded. Her mind raced as she tried to find the words to tell him the truth—he deserved that much. Though he'd known she dated occasionally, he had no idea how serious her relationship with Rob had become. It wasn't that she was trying to keep it a secret—she hadn't been able to get the words out. Maybe this was her chance. "Jimmy."

"Hold on!" His hand left hers and clasped the wheel.

Shelly looked through the windshield to see a huge elk turn to stare at them from its position in the middle of the road. She had barely enough time to take a deep breath and steel herself for impact before the car crunched against the animal, then spun and flipped end over end.

When the car stopped moving—she was fairly certain it was her head that was still spinning, and not the car—Shelly pried her eyes open. Her head pounded, and her chest heaved as she fought to breathe after the collision knocked the air from her lungs.

"Jimmy?" She looked to the left where she expected him to be, but didn't see him. Stiff and anxious, she searched the back seat, but didn't see him there, either. Had he been thrown out? Her heart rate ratcheted up and she looked around to see if she could tell where he'd gone. The side windows were all missing, the roof smashed several inches lower than it should have been in most places, and the front window was nothing but a mass of spider web cracks. "Jimmy!"

When she moved her right arm, pain lanced through her and she clutched it close to her chest, trying to ignore the way the skin poked out on the side. The bone had to be broken.

She looked around, but couldn't find her cell phone anywhere.

With her free hand, she shook her door, but it was too smashed to budge. She studied the window opening with its chunks of shattered glass. She used the snow scraper at her feet to clear the way, then, trusting her clothes to protect her, began pulling herself through—not an easy task one-handed.

It took more work than she expected as she discovered that she hurt all over. If she hadn't been so anxious to find Jimmy, she might have stayed put, but she had to find him.

"Jimmy!" Shelly called his name every few seconds, certain this time he would answer. Maybe he was only dazed from the jolt. She saw the headlights from another car parked up on the edge of the road. The car had rolled a lot further down the embankment than she had thought. A person walked in front of the headlights, and she could see them coming down into the creek bed. Shelly was about halfway out of the car window when a strong pair of arms grabbed her under the shoulders and helped her. She stifled a scream of pain as her right arm was jarred.

"Are you okay?" a man's voice asked. He helped her to her feet, but didn't let go until she felt steadier. "Is there anyone else in the car? Who are you looking for?"

"My fiancé. I don't know where he went. He's not in the car." Shelly took a step away, searching for a dark shape in the white snow while her head and muscles screamed at her to stop. Hysteria rose in her chest as she considered all the things that might have happened to Jimmy.

"I think you're bleeding." The man—somewhere in his forties—touched the side of her head and nodded, as if confirming the injury. "Is your arm hurt?"

"Yes, I think it's broken."

"We called 911, but we're not sure how much they understood. The signal's bad here."

Like she needed him to tell her that. She'd lived in the area all her life. "Thanks. Do you know where my fiancé is?" She tried to move through the deep snow, but sank nearly to her knee with every step.

"Hey, over here. I found someone," another male voice called out, rougher and lower-toned. "Come help me, Mark."

The man with Shelly turned to her. "You should stay here."

"Now, Mark. Hurry! He's in pretty bad shape," the man called again.

It was freezing and Shelly was in her shoes and shirtsleeves. She reached through the car window and pulled out her fluffy winter coat, struggling to wrap it around her one-handed. Then she moved as quickly as possible toward the two men. They were on their knees in the snow. There was no direct light around them and the reflections of headlights above them weren't enough to illuminate their actions.

More people arrived and began moving down the embankment, but Shelly ignored their calls, intent on the very still figure lying between the two strangers. Jimmy couldn't be hurt, not after everything they'd been through. She felt herself begin to hyperventilate and her head spun again when she saw the dark spots against the whiteness of snow around him. Maybe it wasn't blood, she told herself. It could be anything.

"I found a heartbeat. Hold pressure on that wound," one of the men said.

Shelly sobbed, trying to grab Jimmy's hand, but a woman held her back. Shelly tried to get away, to get back to Jimmy, but the woman pulled her further from the scene. "Miss, were you in the accident?" the woman asked.

"Yes."

"You need to sit. Come on, let's go up to the road. The police and paramedics will be here soon."

"I can't leave him. What if he needs me?" She struggled a little longer, then, too exhausted to fight, allowed herself to be led up to the road as the ambulance crew arrived. A Highway Patrol trooper came over and began asking her about the accident, and another EMT joined her, questioning and checking Shelly.

The next thing Shelly knew, an EMT was coaxing her onto a backboard. "Any time there's a roll over it's protocol to backboard patients," he explained when she resisted. "It's only a precaution."

"I've been walking around for a long time now," Shelly protested.

"And the adrenaline that's kept you moving will wear off soon. There might be something wrong and you don't even know it yet. Please? My partners are taking good care of the guy you were with."

Feeling light-headed and queasy all of a sudden, she consented and soon found herself strapped on and wearing a c-collar. They set her board on the bench seat in the back of the ambulance and strapped her in before they staunched the sluggish blood flow on her forehead. After that, the EMTs mostly focused on Jimmy, who had been loaded onto the wheeled gurney a couple feet away.

As soon as he was in the back, the ambulance headed for the hospital in Nephi. The EMTs said Jimmy needed help breathing, an IV, and various other things Shelly didn't understand. They checked her blood pressure, shone a bright light in her eyes, and asked her some of the same questions she had already answered. She wanted to ask why they kept repeating themselves, but didn't want to waste her breath as she heard the worry in the voices of the people working on Jimmy.

The twists and turns of the canyon nauseated Shelly and she wondered why the driver had to take the corners so fast, yet it seemed to take forever to get to the hospital in Nephi. With every bump or jolt or shift on the road, pain screamed through her arm.

"Sorry," one woman told her after a head-spinning turn. "An ambulance isn't exactly built like a race car. They don't corner very well, even when driven carefully."

"I think I figured that out." Shelly tried to smile, then asked for the hundredth time how Jimmy was doing. Still, she only got the answer that the others were taking care of him, and would do their best.

That wasn't very comforting, especially when one of the crew members asked about bringing in a helicopter to get Jimmy to Utah Valley Regional, and another said the copter would never travel through the storm.

Shelly's heart plummeted. It had been her idea to go to Provo earlier. Jimmy had protested that there was too much to do and the weather report wasn't good, but she insisted. She needed the time alone with him before she went crazy with preparations, time to reassure herself that she'd made the right decision. Now she wished she'd never thought of it. If Jimmy didn't make it—the thought was too awful to consider. She pushed it away and was grateful when one of the EMTs finally said they were pulling into the hospital parking lot.

The long night only got worse.

Shelly had been through x-ray and was released from the backboard before anyone would tell her anything about Jimmy. A man in a white coat, whose tag read Dr. Chung, came into her corner of the ER, clipboard in hand. "I hear you're engaged to the other patient, Jimmy Sorenson."

"Yes, we're getting married in five days. Is he doing all right?" Shelly huddled under the warm blanket the nursing staff had given her, but she continued to shiver. She couldn't seem to get warm.

The man frowned, a haggard look on his face. She wondered if he was old enough to be a doctor. He looked awfully young. "His injuries are extensive. The ambulance has already taken him to Provo for critical care treatment."

Her own injuries were forgotten as panic crowded into her chest. "I have to go. I need to call someone to get me. I've got to be with him."

"What you need to do," the doctor interjected, "is let me put a cast on that broken arm and take care of you. By the time you're finished, your parents should be here. They're already on their way. You can talk to them about taking you to Provo."

Though the pain medication the nurse had given her earlier was kicking in so she struggled to think, Shelly realized she was stranded and needed to be treated. Still, every minute crawled as she waited for them to finish the cast. Her mother arrived nearly an hour after Shelly reached the hospital and still the cast wasn't done.

When they finally climbed in the car, Shelly was forced to endure the endless drive to the trauma center. The falling snow only served to slow their progress. She leaned back in the seat and closed her eyes after fifteen minutes of the car crawling through the heavy storm. Cursing the pain medication, she fell asleep.

When they reached the emergency area at UVRMC, Jimmy was still in surgery. A nurse took them to a waiting room, where his parents already sat with a few of his siblings in a small alcove of chairs. Shelly and her mom joined them.

"Shelly, how are you?' Carol hugged her, clinging and shaking.

"I'm okay. It's just a broken arm."

Carol's eyes went to Shelly's forehead. "Looks like more than a broken arm to me."

"Oh, yeah," Shelly touched the head wound that had finally stopped bleeding after she got into the ambulance. It was still bandaged. "A few scrapes and bruises, possibly a concussion. Nothing that won't heal. Have you heard about Jimmy yet?"

"No." Carol turned to the nurse, her face white and older than Shelly ever remembered. "Will my son be all right?"

The nurse spoke in a reassuring tone, and Shelly pushed back the fear that stole over her. "He's still in surgery. They're doing the best they can for him. I'll send the doctor out to speak with you as soon as possible. It may be a while."

Shelly wanted to scream, to cry, anything. All she could do was hold her broken arm close, feeling frozen and silent. *This can't be happening.* She stared at the stark white walls and floor. Jimmy's siblings and their spouses asked her questions and she repeated the nights' events, trying to think of anything they could have done differently. Could they have stopped it? How long before Jimmy recovered? She couldn't think of any other outcome.

A couple of hospital workers in mint green scrubs walked past them, talking about a basketball game at one of the local high schools the previous night. A man strolled the halls with a young boy in a hospital gown, telling stories about the fun things they would do when the boy got out. A cell phone rang somewhere.

Somehow, none of it seemed real. It could all have been on a television screen and not have affected her less. *I wonder if this is what shock feels like.*

Hours passed before the doctor came in. His grim face said enough. Shelly didn't bother listening to his words. The edges of her vision began to turn fuzzy, then black and she gulped in air, even as her chest grew tight.

"Shelly, hey, are you okay?" Her mom's voice pierced her senses and Shelly felt herself being shaken. "Come on, we can see Jimmy soon. Deep breaths, honey."

Not sure if it was the stress, the medication, or both, Shelly fought to stay alert, and after a moment, started to feel better, though the lightheadedness lingered. "How is he?"

"Out of surgery. It's touch and go." Her mom put a hand to Shelly's forehead. "We have a little wait before they'll let us into his room."

Carol crouched beside her "Honey, are you sure they should have checked you out of the hospital? Are you okay?"

"I'm fine. I just need to see Jimmy." Despite more questions, Shelly stuck to her stance. Jimmy's sister-in-law brought her a soda and a grilled cheese sandwich from the café down the hall, and at her insistence, Shelly ate. Surprisingly, it did help her feel better.

When they were finally allowed into his room, Jimmy's father and a brother talked in low tones about giving a priesthood blessing. Jimmy's sister-in-law stood to the side of the doorway, hugging herself with her arms. Shelly found a seat and took Jimmy's hand gingerly in hers, but felt little warmth. Carol sat on the other side of the bed, taking her son's other hand.

The hospital staff only allowed everyone to stay long enough for Jimmy's dad and brother to give him the blessing. What she felt when they finished, however, was not the reassurance she sought, but disbelief as Jimmy's father, Allan, commended Jimmy's spirit back to his Father in Heaven. She wanted to scream in argument, but couldn't get out anything but a low moan.

When the prayer was over, Shelly glared at Allan and found her voice again. "You were supposed to make him better."

"I wish I could, but I'm only the mouthpiece of the Lord, and He wanted Jim to come home." His voice was raw and tears streaked his face, but it didn't make her less angry with him. How could he let Jimmy go without a fight?

Then everyone acted as if a sentence had been passed. Carol sobbed over her son's hand, his brothers took turns saying a few words and saying goodbye, and even Shelly's parents tried to pull her from his bedside. They were wrong. She and Jimmy were getting married. She knew it.

Shelly was so numb, the tears would not fall. Inside, she felt like she was dying, too.

After a while, everyone left her alone with him. She could hear Jimmy's labored breath as he struggled for air. He was so pale.

She stroked the matted hair on Jimmy's forehead. The sides of his face were streaked with blood. Her fingers caressed his right cheek, searching for his dimple. She thought of all the times she and Jimmy had driven around and talked in the evenings when they were teens. Sometimes he would tease her, and despite all he could do to keep a straight face, the dimple would always give him away. He had no poker face.

She'd always loved that about him.

"Jimmy, you wouldn't leave me now, would you? We have so many plans, a whole life together—at least six kids in that big house on Main Street. I love you." The last words were barely a whisper as a lump in her throat blocked them. Her long hair hung limply over his body as she leaned down to plant a kiss on his cheek.

Shelly whispered memories about things they had done together and plans for the future. She knew she had to keep talking, sure the effort would keep him alive.

Her eyes were dry as she played with his CTR ring, his constant reminder to Choose The Right, twisting it from side to side and chatting away. As she spoke to him, her heart filled with fervent prayer that he would be healed, despite what the doctor had said. Despite the blessing that told otherwise.

After a few minutes, his parents came back in with the doctor. A moment later, the steady, but slow, beeping on the heart monitor slowed even further and the machine set off a warning bell. The doctor told everyone to leave and called in a crew of hospital staff.

The wait in the hall took forever, and Shelly huddled into herself against one wall. She didn't acknowledge her mom's arm wrapped around her.

Eventually the doctor re-emerged, covered in sweat. "I'm sorry, there's nothing more we can do." He hesitated for a moment. "His records show he's an organ donor. There's never a good way to ask this, but would you give your consent for us to use this tragedy to help others?"

When Allan's rough voice whispered agreement, Shelly pulled away from her mother's embrace and hurried down the corridor, unable to stand it.

They were giving up.

She didn't know if she would ever forgive herself for how it had happened.

Chapter 2

SHELLY WOKE TO THE SEARING reminder that Jimmy was dead. She turned onto her side and squeezed her eyes closed again, fighting the tears and despair that tried to overtake her. Maybe if she tried hard enough, she could convince herself he was still on his mission. She'd waited patiently for him for two years. Surely she could manage to wait longer—at least until the pain didn't threaten to yank out all her internal organs and smash them to mush.

She knew she wasn't fooling herself, but thinking of him as only being away for a while helped quell the pain, if only a little. The fact was, between his mission and her last semester of school, it had been well over two years since they were able to spend any real time together. The regular emails and phone calls since he came home had been a big improvement, but were nothing like being near him.

That made her feel guilty. Then she felt guilty because she hadn't been fully faithful to him while he was on his mission. If she had been, she wouldn't have struggled so much over her relationship with Rob, even if it had been perfectly respectable.

She still felt a pang of sadness when she thought of Rob—the man she'd dated and sung duets with the previous school year. The one she had told about Jimmy, but then dated often anyway. When he'd proposed only days before Jimmy returned to Utah late in the summer, she had found herself far more tempted than she had expected.

It had been a near thing, that decision. She doubted Rob knew how narrow the margin had been between choosing him or choosing Jimmy. She'd loved them both so much.

Why had she felt so strongly that she should choose Jimmy if he was going to die five days before the wedding? *Why did that happen?* The confirmation of her decision had come again and again since then, yet here it was, her wedding day—and she would bury the man she had loved since she was fifteen.

There was a knock at the open door and Shelly checked the clock. Past time to get up—if she wanted to face the day, that was. "I'm awake," she called out.

Her older sister, Lily, came in, closing the door behind her. "If you're going to get to the viewing on time, you ought to leave now."

"I don't want to go." Shelly could barely get the words out through her parched throat.

"You didn't go last night, either." Lily's voice was soft, filled with compassion.

"So?"

Lily sat on the edge of the bed and studied her younger sister. "Not going won't stop it from being real."

"I know that," Shelly snapped. This was supposed to have been her wedding day.

There was a long moment of silence—long enough for Shelly to feel bad for being short-tempered. She knew her sister wanted what was best for her. Lily had been married only a few weeks earlier to her second husband, Denver Nuggets center, Curtis Werner. She'd taken several days to come home with her two young children to attend the wedding-turned-funeral. Lily had been a rock of support. Curtis had managed to stop in for the day between games.

"I'm sorry. I'm not trying to be difficult." Shelly closed her eyes so she wouldn't have to see the hurt on her sister's face. Being alone with her thoughts was terrible. But dealing with other people's sympathy was almost as bad.

"You know you'll regret it if you don't make it to at least a few minutes of the viewing."

Since she figured her sister was right, Shelly nodded. But there was no reason to get there early. Another glance at the clock told her that early wasn't an option anyway, not if she was going to shower and make herself presentable—a must after laying around in a funk since she returned from the hospital several days ago. "Fine. I'm getting up. Will you help me wrap my cast so it won't get wet?" She struggled to pull her broken arm out from under the covers, the cast making her movements awkward.

"Of course." Lily stood and Shelly pushed back the blankets. Her stomach complained at the lack of nourishment over the past few days, and she didn't know if her hair would ever comb out again. She almost didn't care.

❁ ❁ ❁

SHELLY HAD AGREED WITH her sister that she needed to go to the viewing— but she didn't want to arrive too soon. If she had to spend much time in there with the empty shell that used to be Jimmy, she thought she might crack.

Ten minutes before the viewing was supposed to end, she sidled into the room, keeping her gaze averted from the coffin that dominated one wall. Chrome gleamed from the handles along the sides, drawing her attention to the box as she avoided eye contact with everyone. The heavy smell of flowers filled the room.

Carol, Jimmy's mother, refused to be ignored, however. It took only seconds for the woman to cross the room and envelope Shelly in a hug. "Honey, I'm so sorry this happened!"

Suddenly Shelly felt too numb to cry. Everything seemed too unreal to be true. All she wanted to do now was to hang on, to get through this day. This minute. Then maybe she would be able to tackle the next one. "I know everyone will miss him. We had him back for such a short time." Her voice sounded wooden in her own ears.

"Yes. But now he's gone home to do more important work." Carol's voice caught on the last word, as if she were still trying to convince herself, while she wiped at the tears that trickled down her face.

Shelly only nodded, and allowed the woman, who should have become her mother-in-law that day, to lead her across the room to the coffin. With every step, she felt her heart sink more, and the bile in her stomach rose.

The unreality of the situation was even more pronounced as Shelly looked at the body that used to be Jimmy. She didn't know if it was the coloring, the effects of the accident, or simply her own detachment, but it was easy to convince herself it wasn't really him. He didn't look like that. Jimmy had a constant sparkle in his eye and a joke on his glib tongue every time he opened his mouth. He was energetic and sweet and loved her like no tomorrow.

Whomever it was lying in the coffin, it definitely wasn't the Jimmy she had loved so hopelessly as a preteen, and so giddily when he finally realized she was a girl and not just the irritating kid around the corner—then so deeply as they finished high school and he headed off for his mission.

She reached out and touched his arm, stiff beneath the white temple clothes. She didn't feel any emotions, really, but preferred numbness to the grinding pain she had carried over the past few days.

A moment later, she stepped back across the room so she couldn't see in the coffin anymore and stood, waiting for the family prayer. Carol hadn't said as much, but Shelly knew she was expected to stay, and then follow the family in and sit with them through the funeral.

While she waited, a long-time neighbor came through the room, stopping to speak to everyone and searched Shelly out. "Honey, I'm so sorry. What a terrible wedding day this has turned out to be."

Shelly's stomach twisted and she fought to keep her composure and not run from the room at the woman's insensitive comments. Instead, she hid the pain, murmuring something unintelligible and wishing the woman away.

She was grateful she hadn't been asked to speak, didn't have to participate in anything that happened through the rest of the day. She simply gave wan smiles and accepted hugs through the proceedings, then returned home and climbed in bed to shut everything out again.

❀ ❀ ❀

THE NEXT DAY, SHELLY got out of bed, showered, did her hair and makeup, and went down to breakfast. She played with her toddler nephew and infant niece, baked Christmas cookies to take to the neighbors, and tried to ignore the cheery sound of seasonal music as it played in the background.

She followed the holiday pattern, getting through one day, one hour at a time, though she pretended it wasn't real, that Jimmy would be back someday. Most of the time, she succeeded in convincing herself nothing was wrong—there was only a delay in timing. Shelly opened gifts, ate when she had to, and moved along automatically.

When school started up again after the holidays ended, she began work at the Institute of Religion across the street from the Snow College campus. Her temporary, part-time job was perfect, as the students distracted her and kept her busy every day. Though she got a lot of curious looks from locals, few asked her how she was doing—for which she was grateful. If she heard whispering behind her back from some of them, she did her best to ignore it.

She only wished her job was full-time to fill the extra hours. When she was offered a second job running the checkout at Kent's grocery store full-time in her free hours, she took it eagerly.

❀ ❀ ❀

"CURTIS AND I HAVE been talking about you," Lily said over the phone in late February. "Didn't you say once that you wanted to study abroad?"

Shelly rolled her eyes as she sorted dried silverware into the drawer. She was fairly sure she had said something like that, since the thought had crossed her mind several times over the years, but it hadn't fit with her plan—the plan to get through school before Jimmy returned from his mission. "I might have. I finished my degree, though."

"I did some research. There are schools in England that have a single-year master's program. Your grades were always excellent, so you could get admitted easily. Think—you've always been fascinated with England. This could be your chance to live there, and study history right where it happened. You could even dig around for the genealogy we haven't been able to track down from here. There's a great university only ten miles from where Great-great-grandma Florie was born."

It was almost tempting—except for one very important detail. "Um, hello, I work at Kent's. You can't think I've got that kind of cash." Shelly picked up a sauce pan next and wiped it down before setting it back in the drawer under the stove. She started to get a kink in her neck from holding the tiny cell phone between her shoulder and ear.

"Um, hello," Lily echoed Shelly. "Someone you know has plenty of money and can't think of a better way to spend it."

"Your kids are will need college tuition, too."

"We'll have that all set aside before Curtis finishes his contract here in Denver. No worries. Let us help you. You're doing nothing and going nowhere there in Ephraim."

"You loved living here." Shelly threaded the drying cloth through the handle of the fridge and grabbed the dish cloth to wipe down the table.

"Yes, I did. It's a great place to grow up and there are lots of possibilities for people to do something with their lives if they get the proper schooling—a bachelor's degree hardly prepares you for anything these days. Especially as it's not a teaching degree. I don't think you're even making plans for the future. If you don't want to study abroad, that's fine, but you need to do something, and staying there in Ephraim can't be good for your mental health. There are too many memories."

Lily was right about that. There *were* too many daily reminders of Jimmy. Shelly clung to them, even as she ignored the fact that she would never see him again. "I'm doing fine here. I'll move on."

"Mom said you work like crazy, read like a demon in your time off, and do nothing else. You don't go out with friends, and you don't even email or chat on the phone with Katie much anymore."

Shelly knew she hadn't spoken with her lifelong best friend lately. During their last phone call, Katie had encouraged Shelly to return to Logan to work or pursue her master's degree. There was no way Shelly wanted to run into Rob again, though. She had lost too much without reminders of his pain, on top of her own. "I spend a lot of time at the 'Tute. I meet people there, do things, get involved." She scrubbed extra hard at a dried spot of strawberry jam.

"Liar. You may be there, but Kellie said you never mix with the others, not really. And Danyelle said—"

"Do we need to hash this all out?" Shelly asked, not wanting to hear all of her shortcomings. It was a low blow to learn her younger sisters had been talking about her to Lily.

She looked up from the table and stared daggers at her sisters in the family picture that hung nearby. It was probably a good thing they were all out of the house at the moment.

"I sent you a packet with information from three or four universities. I think it'll interest you. You know you can't stay home forever, stagnating."

"Are you giving me an ultimatum? Pick something, or move out of Mom's house?" Shelly was pleased with her nonchalant tone.

"Don't be melodramatic. I only want you to look it over and see what you think. You may surprise yourself. If you have other plans, that's fine, but you need to do something about your future."

"You're pushy."

"I learned from the best. You are, if I remember correctly, the one who went out and found me an apartment in Logan before I even had a job, and despite the fact that I had no intention of moving there."

"I was right, too." Shelly couldn't help it—she had to smile to herself at the thought. If she hadn't been so helpful, Lily might not have moved to Logan, and she might not be married to Curtis now.

"Yes, you were. And I appreciate it. Please let me return the favor. You don't have to apply to any of the schools—just look at them."

Shelly knew she was beaten. "Fine, I'll look them over. I'm not promising anything else." But she felt the first stirrings of excitement in a long time. England did sound good. It would be a fresh start, something completely different to mirror the change in her life plans.

At least looking at the brochures would distract her for a while, even if she never took the next step.

❀ ❀ ❀

WORKING THE CASH REGISTER at Kent's kept Shelly busy, but the slow moments left too much time to think. All of the college students running through the store should have been a boon, but too often she'd catch a glimpse of light brown hair, or rolling laughter that was so much like Jimmy's. It fed the continuing nightmares she had of the crash, keeping them fresh in her mind.

She smiled as a local woman she knew only by sight came through her line. "How are you doing, Shelly?"

Though the look of compassion in the woman's eyes said she wondered how Shelly was coping, and that it wasn't simply a casual question, Shelly merely smiled and gave her the same answer she would give anyone. "Great. Keeping busy. How has your day been?"

"Life never stops, if you know what I mean." Then the woman's smile

17

faltered as if she realized what she was saying. "Well, spring sports are starting and James needs new cleats, Shaun has outgrown his school clothes and Lisa wants a prom dress, but we'll manage." The woman went on to talk about her son's batting average and expectations for playing college ball as Shelly rang her in.

Shelly glanced up when the doors slid open again and felt that familiar excitement, then devastation as a particular student came in with friends. He looked so much like Jimmy she was always fooled for a second before realizing it couldn't be him.

It must have shown on her face, because the woman turned from the credit card machine where she'd been signing her name and caught sight of the young men. "You poor thing. It must be difficult here with all the memories."

Shelly gritted her teeth, forced a smile, and handed her the receipt. "It's home to me."

When the woman left her counter with a sad face, then stopped to look back at Shelly as she chatted with another woman at the door, Shelly made a decision.

She had poured over the college brochures Lily sent her, read more on the school websites, and even played with admissions paperwork over the past six weeks, but hadn't made a decision one way or the other about going to England. She needed a change, though, and England sounded far enough away to find some peace.

Chapter 3

BY THE END OF APRIL, Shelly had been accepted at Hull University in Yorkshire, England—the school Lily had mentioned was near their ancestors' town. Her job at the Institute had ended with the close of the semester, and the Manti Pageant rehearsals were well underway. Shelly hadn't been able to participate while she was at USU, but now threw herself into preparations and helped with costumes in her spare time to fill the extra hours.

As the weeks continued to pass, Shelly grew more convinced that Lily was right. She needed a complete change of scene, and she wondered if getting involved in the pageant had been a mistake. Memories of warm June nights and practicing with Jimmy crowded her mind. The smell of grease paint and the familiar recordings of the narrator took her back to high school and the tingling excitement of a new relationship.

Once the show was underway, the bustle of people in downtown Manti reminded her of the past. She tried to remember her childhood—long before she had the slightest inkling of interest in Jimmy—as she walked past displays of books, trinkets, and pencil sketches of the prophets. She even offered to help serve at the annual turkey dinner with a high school friend.

That was how she ran into Rob again. She had been busy keeping an eye on the teens across the room between greeting people in line and hadn't looked to see who was coming. It wasn't until he was getting gravy from the woman standing next to her that Shelly saw him.

Rob had obviously seen her before he reached her station, where she scooped corn onto people's plates. "Hi, Shelly."

She swallowed in surprise and fought to put a pleasant smile on her face, even as emotions tumbled through her and her hands bobbled. "Hello, Rob. Did you come down for the pageant?"

"Yes. Lindsey hasn't been before, so I thought I'd bring her." The young Dean Cain look-alike gestured to a gorgeous raven-haired woman next to him. She stood several inches taller than Shelly's five-foot-three, had flawless skin, and was model-thin.

Wearing a decent, but well-loved tee and an old pair of jeans, Shelly felt dowdy by comparison. After a bad haircut, her hair was shorter than she liked, but if it hadn't been back in a net to keep it out of the food, it would at least look okay.

"That's great. I love the pageant. I've hardly missed a season since I was a toddler. I'm sure you'll love the show." Why did she have to sound like an idiot? What did he think about seeing her here, now? His number was still in her cell phone and she had thought about calling him several times over the past few months, but figured he had moved on. Apparently she had been right.

"Thank you. So how do you know each other?" Lindsey nudged Rob playfully with her elbow and sent him a flirty smile.

"Sorry. Lindsey, this is Shelly. We sang together quite a bit last year. Shelly, this is Lindsey, my new girlfriend." His expression was blank as he made the introductions.

Shelly was surprised by the knife of pain caused by his words—or rather, that the wound could get deeper than it had been a moment earlier. Still, she put on her best smile for them. "I hope you enjoy the evening. It looks like the weather will be perfect." She glanced down the line and realized there weren't many people behind them.

Lindsey put a hand on Rob's arm, but kept her gaze on Shelly. "So, do you get to eat once everyone is through?"

"Yes."

"Great—you'll have to join us. We'll save you a seat! I'd love to hear about Rob's life before we met. He's so closed-mouthed." She nudged Rob toward the peanut butter bars at the end of the table, and Shelly scooped corn onto the remaining plates.

She thought about skipping out. Soon she would need to get makeup and her costume on for the night, and the younger kids always needed extra help. She filled a plate for herself and turned to leave, but saw Lindsey gesturing her over. Shelly hesitated, but didn't want to be rude—or at least that's what she told herself—so she moved toward the couple.

They were a great pair, aesthetically speaking—two beautiful people with dark hair. Lindsey was already well tanned, while Rob's olive skin was only a shade or two darker than Shelly remembered from the previous December.

Feeling decidedly awkward, she slid into the seat across the table from Lindsey. "So, how long have you two been dating?"

"About a month," Lindsey said. "We're both working at Salt Lake Community College. I'm in admissions and he's in accounting."

"That's great." Shelly turned to Rob and sincerely told him, "I'm glad you got settled so quickly. I know how hard it is to get a job right now."

"Yeah." His mouth moved, like he was trying to figure out what to say next. He settled for, "And what are you doing now, besides serving dinner for the pageant?"

"I'm working at the grocery store in Ephraim. I've been busy with costumes and practices for the pageant, but after next week, I'll be getting ready to work on my master's."

"What are you studying? Which school will you attend?" Lindsey asked.

"History. I'm taking a one-year master's in England, actually. I won't leave until late August, and within a year, I'll be finished." Shelly carefully met Lindsey's eyes before turning to Rob.

"Isn't that where Rhett is?" Lindsey asked Rob. "Where is he serving, exactly?"

Shelly had forgotten that Rob's brother Rhett was on a mission in England. She quickly calculated and decided Rhett would be shortly past his hump day. "I'll be in Yorkshire."

"That's in his mission boundaries," Rob said. "It's the England Leeds Mission. You'll have to keep an eye out for Elder Durrant."

She'd been to Rhett's farewell as a 'friend' of Rob's, so she remembered they were actually half-brothers, thus the different last names. "I'll do that." Their gazes met, and she felt the zing of electricity that had been so strong between them the previous fall—until she'd chosen Jimmy over him. It shot down her spine and made a lump lodge in her throat. She missed spending time with Rob.

21

He'd sent her a condolence card shortly after the accident. Katie had spread the word on Facebook to all of their school friends long before spring semester began. She had appreciated his card, but been too numb to know how to respond. She still wasn't sure what to think. She caught his look at her left hand, where she still wore Jimmy's ring, and felt a pang of longing, even while she was torn by the feelings she had felt for both men. It was too late for her and Rob, though, even if she weren't leaving for England in a matter of weeks.

Lindsey broke the moment of silent understanding that passed between them, changing the subject to something funny that had happened to her brother on his mission. Shelly ate as quickly as she could without being impolite, and then excused herself to prepare for that night's show.

She wondered what would have happened if she'd chosen differently. Then she pushed that thought away. She still wasn't ready for a relationship, and she'd already hurt Rob once. There was no reason to believe he'd be willing to give her another chance.

Part II

Chapter 4

SHELLY WOKE TO LOOK OUT the airplane windows and find green hills racing below. She heard the soft, deep English accent of the old man behind her as he spoke to the children traveling with him. She pulled a long, gold chain from under her shirt and fingered the engagement ring on the end. Her hand didn't feel right without the ring—she'd worn it almost a full year.

There was a ding as the 'fasten seatbelt' sign flashed on and the pilot's voice blared from the loudspeaker. His deep voice resonated as he recited the time, temperature, and other pertinent information in British accents. The intercom squealed, and then clicked as he hung up.

Shelly tucked her book into the side pocket of her carryon and readied herself for disembarking the plane.

In only a few minutes, the plane landed and pulled up to the terminal. As she approached the baggage claim, Shelly worried about the time and whether she'd make all her trains that day. She'd never been in a foreign country before.

Crowds bustled around her and the loudspeakers blared. Two guys dressed punk-rocker style crossed her path with their many piercings and tattoos, and brightly dyed hair twisted in gravity-defying updos. In stark contrast, two old ladies strolled along, talking about knitting patterns. Hints of food from the airport vendors wafted though the air and Shelly caught the reek of cigarette smoke as someone walked past. She told herself it wasn't so different from walking through the airport in Salt Lake.

No matter how she tried, she couldn't believe her life. It was very different from Salt Lake, and ages apart from the sleepy town of Ephraim. She could swear the people around her didn't only look and sound foreign, but the air smelled different.

But maybe that *was* her imagination.

She found her bags quickly once they slid down the shoot. The first one was medium-sized and came away from the pile of luggage with no trouble. Other people bumped her on each side as they pulled their own luggage from the rotating system.

When her much-larger suitcase arrived, however, the process wasn't nearly so easy. She had packed her largest suitcase as full and tight as possible to avoid shipping charges, which made it rather heavy. Still, she hadn't thought much of that before now.

She yanked at the handle, and it rocked slightly, but still wouldn't clear the lip of the carousel. She dropped her other two bags, grabbed the large handle with both hands, and gave it another tug. It almost cleared the edge this time before slamming back down again. Shelly let out a huff of irritation as she followed the carousel further. She tripped over a small, bright pink suitcase and nearly fell on her face. This dislodged her grip.

Trying not to fall over, she reached out and was caught by a pair of very strong, very male arms. "Whoa, hold on there. Taking a face-plant here wouldn't be very good for the ego," a deep voice said. She looked up to see a tall, bleached-blond, blue-eyed Adonis in his early twenties smiling down at her, and exhaled in surprise. And she'd thought Rob was good-looking.

"Thanks."

"No problem." He released her once she'd steadied herself. "You don't want to lose track of your other bags there." He gestured behind her to where her things now sat on the floor. A teenaged girl watched Shelly and the man with amusement, then winked at the blond.

Shelly turned back in time to catch his return wink. Suddenly, his appearance didn't appeal so much after all. She grabbed her other luggage and stood out of the way while people snatched their own belongings. When the carousel brought her bag back around, the man pulled her suitcase from it before she could try again.

He set it beside her and grinned. "Anything else I can do for you?"

"No, this was it. But thank you." She smiled; both grateful for his help and embarrassed she'd needed it.

"My pleasure." His eyes slid down her form and returned to linger on her face.

Shelly became uncomfortable and tugged the luggage close. With another thank-you called over her shoulder, she hurried to the growing line at customs. After a brief word or two, the attendant told her to go on through.

A few minutes and some stairs later, Shelly found her platform. "Only five minutes." She rummaged through her purse for her ticket. Her hair fell over her face, blocking her view, and she blew a strand away, wishing it was long enough to braid or pull back in a pony tail. "There you are." She clutched her ticket for the Heathrow Express and searched for her train.

The air was filled with voices—almost all of them foreign. She still couldn't believe she was here—that she was doing this. What had she been thinking when she turned in the application? Sure, she'd thought about study abroad, dreamed about it long ago, but she hadn't seriously considered it.

Now she watched and waited for her first train to pull in, the next leg of her journey. Once it arrived, it didn't take long to get settled and pull out "Anne of Avonlea" for the hour-long ride.

The soft rocking of the train was relaxing, but she had slept on the plane and wasn't tired now. She also didn't want to risk having her belongings stolen while she slept.

When the train stopped, she hurried to transfer her luggage. Her stomach growled as she waited to board. She was glad this leg was only fifteen minutes long; maybe she'd be able to grab a bite soon. Shelly pulled out the rail guide and checked the schedule. *Rats, only five minutes between trips. I'll be lucky to make it at all.* The next train to Hull wouldn't go through there for another hour if she missed her connection.

In her hurry to exit, Shelly pulled too hard on one of the luggage handles and broke it. She stared at it for a few seconds in disbelief. "Great, exactly what I need," she muttered. She grasped the black corner ribbing and dragged the case out the door. The straps from her other two bags slipped from her shoulders, banging against the large bag, throwing her off balance for a moment, but she managed to keep from losing all of it. Her hair hung in her face again and she ignored it, irritated.

Why didn't I let Lily buy me the more expensive luggage? I'm such a penny pincher—and it wasn't even my money. Shelly hiked the straps of the carryon and other bag up on her shoulders again, then grabbed more tightly onto the ribbing on both sides of the large suitcase. She was glad it at least had wheels.

After finding where to go, Shelly hurried to the platform as the train came in. The doors opened and she tried to get on, but the wheels lodged in the crack between the train and the platform. She turned to get a better hold when someone else helped lift it. She looked up, surprised to find the same blond guy from the airport on the other end. He slid the bag to an empty row of seats and then flipped over the tag on the handle to look at it before he piled his bags on hers and sat beside her.

"Thank you," Shelly said.

"You're welcome. Are you going to Hull University this year?"

How did he know? It kind of creeped her out—even if he did seem friendly. "What makes you ask that?"

"You're not English and... I noticed the tag on your big bag has the International Office number on it." He shrugged.

If he'd recognized the number, he must be a student there as well, so she decided to admit it. "Yes." She had put the number on her bag in case it was lost in transit. She wouldn't have any other contact point until she got settled in her apartment in a few days. *No, it's a flat,* she reminded herself. *Call it a flat.*

"I'm Clay Fuller," he said. His ice blue eyes shone down at her. He had a perfect tan and gleaming white teeth. They were hard to miss when they were all on display.

"I'm Shelly," she said. "You must go to Hull too. You're not British, either." She saw, however, that he didn't have much luggage with him.

"Yeah, this is my last year, thankfully. But then, next year I'll have to find something to do with my life, so maybe that's not so exciting."

"You're from the U.S. aren't you? Back East, maybe?"

"Yeah, upper New York State. Where are you from?"

"Utah." She definitely wouldn't have placed his accent as New York. She wondered if she'd heard too many Brooklyn accents on TV.

"I've heard there's great skiing in Utah."

"So I'm told. I don't ski much, but I know a number of fanatics." Rob came to mind. He loved skiing. Jimmy had enjoyed it now and then too.

She was far happier curled in front of a fire with a mug of hot cocoa and a book, though. "Thanks again for your help. I was getting pretty frustrated."

"You're welcome. White knights are always ready to help a beautiful maiden in distress." He flashed her another grin, and she did her best to resist his charm.

The train pulled out of the station and Shelly leaned back into her seat, preparing for the two-hour ride. It was the last leg of her journey. Someone from the International Office was supposed to wait for her at the end. She hoped they weren't late.

"So where are you living?" he asked.

"I'm on campus."

He waited for her to continue, then prodded, "Dorm's or flats?"

"Flats."

His grin turned amused. "Secretive, aren't you?"

She shrugged. "So, tell me about Hull."

He gave her a few pointers of what to check out on campus, and mentioned he'd be helping with orientation that week. "So, are you getting maid service in your flat?"

Shelly held back a smile at his hunt for clues as to where she lived. "It surprised me to hear some of them had maid service—you never find that at a school in Utah. What's public transit like?"

"I wouldn't know—I have a car. Where do you live, anyway?" he went for directness.

"Do you think I tell every stranger I meet where I live, and give them my phone number?" A smile tugged at the edge of her lips.

Clay grinned and asked, "What are you studying?"

"History."

"Why come to England?"

"I'm studying the history of England. What better place is there?" She decided he'd asked enough questions. "So what about you? What are you studying?"

"Chemistry." He wiggled his eyebrow suggestively.

"Officially, or unofficially?" *Is this guy for real?*

He must have caught her eye-rolling because he lightened up on the suave affectation. "Both. I'll have my master's degree by the end of next summer. I want to do medical research."

"That sounds interesting." He didn't seem geeky enough to be a scientist. "Why are you here, then? Or does England have a corner on the sciences that I've been oblivious to?"

"My father met my English mum here, so this is where they paid for me to go."

"That's nice. Do you like it at Hull?"

"It's been fun," he said without much enthusiasm. "I've had lots of chances to see the world in the past five years. The International office hosts trips on all the long holidays, and short trips on some weekends." He studied her for a moment. "How about you? First trip to England?"

"First trip anywhere. I've never been outside the U.S. or even east of Colorado."

"This is a big step, then." He brushed his fingers over her wrist. "I'd be happy to help you out. You know, make sure you can find your classes, help you move into your apartment, take you out for dinner." A slow smile lit his face.

Oh, he's gorgeous, all right. Too bad his ego overshadows it. "Thanks, but I'm not interested." To reinforce her words, she picked up her book and opened it again.

Though he tried drawing her back into conversation, Shelly replied as briefly as possible. Eventually he opened his own magazine, though he didn't appear absorbed by it. Every time she snuck a peek over the top of her book, he was staring out the window, at her, or other passengers.

As they rode, she sized him up. He was quite tall and looked like he worked out regularly. His hair was obviously bleached, since the top was white while the closely cropped sides were light brown. His features were smooth and masculine; she imagined the word 'beautiful' was often applied to him. Shelly dropped her eyes when he looked up at her. Based on their previous talk, she guessed he was a pretty boy who liked to flirt and have fun. There was nothing especially wrong with that, but he'd never settle for one girl for more than a couple of weeks.

She knew his type.

And she wasn't interested anyway.

Eventually, the train pulled into the station at Kingston upon Hull—the city in which Hull University lay. "So, do you need a ride somewhere? My roommate's supposed to come get me in a bit," he offered.

"Someone from the International Office is coming for me." This had been the point of the trip that made her the most nervous—actually making it to campus without a problem. Planes and trains were simple, if you paid attention, but in a city of 300,000, it would be easy to get lost.

"Well, if they aren't here, the offer stands." He helped her pull her suitcase out of the train and onto the platform.

"Thank you." She had no intention of riding with him. She supposed there was always a taxi, but she wanted to make her money stretch as long as possible. Though Lily and Curtis offered her spending money if she needed it, she wouldn't take it unless she had no other option—they were already covering all of the expensive items like housing and tuition. Eight months' wages from her jobs should last most of the year if she was careful.

It was only a moment before she saw someone holding a sign that read: "Hull University International Students."

"Hi, I'm Shelly." She smiled with relief as she approached a woman with frizzy red hair.

"I'm Sasha, pleased to meet you. I was worried you wouldn't make the connection. I knew the timing would be close." She looked behind Shelly to where Clay stood, then commented as if he couldn't hear her, "I see you've already met Clay. He didn't waste much time, did he?"

"I don't believe in wasting time." He grabbed Shelly's bag again and tossed her a grin before heading out the door. "Where's your car, Sasha?"

She answered, then turned to Shelly. "Have any problems?" She asked as they stepped into the warm September day.

"The handle to my bag broke when I was getting on a train. Luckily, Clay was there to help me."

"He can be charming, can't he?" The redhead flashed him another smile.

After Clay deposited Shelly's things in the back seat, he said goodbye, throwing them both a wink before disappearing into the crowd. Shelly settled in while they discussed the events the International Student Office had set up for new students over the next few days.

When that wound down, Sasha turned the conversation again. "Looks like Clay's already picked his first conquest of the year."

"Not interested." The trip had been draining. All Shelly wanted to do now was flop onto a bed and sleep for the next decade. But she was used to feeling like that lately.

"Oh, come on—those eyes, that smile, the whole package—all the girls are crazy about him. You can't tell me you aren't the tiniest bit interested."

"He *is* good-looking," Shelly admitted. She caught Sasha's look. "Okay, so he's a total hottie, but he's *really* not my type."

"If you say so."

Chapter 5

ON THE FIRST DAY OF ORIENTATION, the new students learned about British lingo, how classes were conducted, and local customs. A panel of experienced international students answered questions about life in Hull. Clay was there, talking and flirting with every female in the room, so Shelly didn't think much of it when he approached her.

"Some of us are going out this evening after everything finishes up here. You want to join us? I'd be happy to pick you up." He reached out and slid a lock of hair back behind her ear.

Shelly pulled away automatically, though she stopped herself before she moved more than a few inches. She was uncomfortable with his familiarity, even if it didn't mean anything to him. "I don't think so. I'm still adjusting to the time change, but thanks for thinking of me."

"You're sure? It would be a great chance to sample local culture."

"I appreciate the offer, but that'll have to wait until another night."

"You'll adjust to the time change faster if you stay up all evening and go to bed at a more normal hour."

"Thanks for the advice. I'll keep it in mind." She moved away, raising a hand and claiming the attention of a Japanese student she'd met that morning at breakfast.

After lunch, more students took the new arrivals on a walking tour of campus. Five minutes into the circuit, the skies opened up and soaked them. At first, Shelly thought the storm was neat. Then it didn't stop and she became soggy and soaked through. She began to shiver, and her hair dripped and stuck to her face.

Though she may not have voiced her complaints aloud, she heartily agreed with the Italian guy at the back of her group who whined the last half of the trip. She made a mental note to buy an umbrella as soon as possible. When she returned to her temporary accommodations—she couldn't move into her flat yet—she hurried into a hot shower.

The next day, the group took a bus tour of the city to see some of the sights and get a feel for the way the city was laid out. She couldn't help but murmur to herself, "Toto, I don't think we're in Utah anymore." While everything at home had long-since turned brown from lack of rain and plenty of summer sun, England in comparison was richly colored with green leaves and grasses. Plants flourished everywhere.

Again she marveled that she was here, in England, of all places. This was her chance to explore a new world, if she could settle down enough to enjoy it.

She was determined to make the most of her stay—to study hard, delve into the culture, and see as much of the world as she could while she was here. She touched the ring where it hung around her neck, though hidden by her T-shirt, and wished instead for a future she would never have.

❀ ❀ ❀

"SHELLY COX," SHE SAID to the woman behind the table. After several days in temporary housing, Shelly was grateful to be allowed to check into her apartment building. The woman found Shelly's files and handed them over, pointing out Shelly's room on a drawing of her flat's layout.

Shelly had contacted the local LDS ward a couple of months before and found out there would be another member of the Church in her complex. Thanks to the bishop, she and El had traded a few emails over the past weeks and arranged to be roommates. It was nice to know she would have a way to get to church and activities, at least. Apparently they would be living with El's long-time friend, Andrea, as well.

"Thanks. Do you have a list of my flatmates?" Shelly was curious to know if she and El had been placed together, as they had requested. When the woman confirmed that as fact, Shelly took a moment to pray again that they would get along. She had never lived with anyone but Katie or her sisters, but knowing that at least one of her roommates would be LDS gave her a measure of comfort.

Soon she stepped back into the sunlight, dragging her large bag behind her. She was grateful the rollers were still good, despite the faulty handle.

She repeated the flat number in her mind as she wandered along the sidewalk between the street and caterpillar-like structure that contained her apartment. Each flat had a rounded wall with a window that stuck out like a little alcove with angled windows on the side. She wondered if that was to bring extra light into the rooms on gloomy winter days. White stone lintels finished off the tops of the windows and each doorway had a stone arch above it. This was far more charming than the dorms she had lived in at Utah State University.

She counted off the numbers on the building, searching for hers. "There we are." All the entryways were on the ground floor, but El had told her most of the bedrooms were upstairs. At least they were in this one—some of the other flats in the building had several more rooms, or so El had told her.

Her key worked in the lock of the freshly painted white door. She walked into a living area with a kitchen/dining room at the far end of the space. A set of stairs led up to the bedrooms and a door led to the one on the main floor. She was grateful to have been assigned this one, if only because it meant she didn't have to haul her bags up the stairs. They had communal bathrooms, but each girl had a private bedroom with a keyed lock. She had made sure she would be rooming only with girls, as most of the flats in the building were co-ed.

After she dragged her other bag into her room, Shelly returned to the front door to watch the others arrive. Some students greeted her as they walked past, headed for their flats. Others had been inside and were coming back out to chat with friends.

The weather was warmer than it had been since Shelly arrived in Hull a few days before, but she still pulled her sweatshirt tighter around her. She was beginning to doubt she would ever feel truly warm again—why hadn't she chosen to go to school in Hawaii instead? The lawns beckoned to her, but she knew she needed to put her things away before indulging in the afternoon air.

Finally, she fumbled with her key at the lock and stepped back inside.

"Oh, hello," a girl greeted her from one of the bedrooms. Shelly was surprised, as she'd thought she'd been the first to arrive. She recognized the girl from the other check-in line, though she had been quite a bit ahead. The girl wore a tan Hull T-shirt and blue jeans and ran around in bare feet as if it were her usual state. Her ragged-cut, light brown hair framed a pixie-shaped face.

"Hi, I'm Shelly."

"Hi, Shelly, I'm El. It's so good to finally meet you!" El bounced over and hugged her. "You have no idea how excited I am to have a member of the Church as my roommate. I can't believe they managed to switch us around to room together! I thought for sure they'd say it was too late."

"It's great to meet you, too." Shelly almost didn't know how to handle the bubbly girl. Was it back-to-school excitement, or was El always like this? She hadn't used nearly as many exclamation points in her emails as she did in her speech. Shelly looked at the person she'd been writing to for so long and decided to relieve her curiosity. "Now tell me—I've been dying to ask. Is your name really El?"

"Actually, my given name is Electra, but I hate that, so I go by El instead."

"Electra?" Shelly mulled it over. "That's kind of cool. I think there's a super hero with that name." She grinned, hoping it didn't sound as though she were mocking her new roommate. "Do you have super powers?"

"Yes. I can make Turkish delight disappear before your very eyes. And I'm good at it too, as you can see." She chuckled and patted her hips, which weren't at all over-large. "Other than that amazing skill, I'm pretty average."

Shelly wasn't sure if she was more amused or bemused. "So are your parents comic book fans?"

"My parents?" El's laugh was like ringing bells—loud, gut-bouncing ones. "Most people think my dad is stuffy and my mum incredibly proper." She tucked her hands into the back pockets of her jeans. "Actually, I'm convinced my dad must have stepped into the loo or something and my mum was still hallucinating from anesthesia when she named me. It's the only explanation."

"I think anesthesia must be responsible for a lot of names," Shelly said. "You should hear some of the ones I knew from college—I mean, uni—back home." It would be a struggle to use the local lingo, but Shelly was determined.

"I guess people are crazy everywhere." El looked back down at Shelly's suitcase. "That thing is huge. Still, you'll want a trip to the store once it's all unloaded. We could take the bus to Tony's if Brad doesn't get back with his car soon."

"That would be great. One of the other students pointed it out yesterday on our bus tour." She knew from the internet that Tony's was a local department store with almost everything she would need, other than food. Which, she reminded herself, she also needed to buy ASAP. "I could use a lot of things, since I definitely had to pack light." Towels and a local cell phone were high on her shopping list.

"How much time? An hour or so?"

"Perfect," Shelly agreed.

Shelly opened her bedroom door and took in the white walls, more brown carpeting, and a window. A desk flanked one wall, and a wardrobe stood along another with a small dresser.

The desk had a couple drawers for schoolbooks and supplies, and there was room under the bed to store suitcases. Shelly nodded in satisfaction as she unzipped her carryon, mentally comparing this room to her old one at Utah State University. "Better than Valley View." More private, too, since she would have her room to herself, even if she shared the rest of the place.

Shelly unloaded clothes onto the bed and began putting things away. She pulled pictures from the stack she had brought and put them up around the room.

The picture of her family went on a shelf above her bed. One of Lily and Curtis at the temple on their wedding day went next to the oak-framed one of Jimmy—which she laid on its back on the top shelf so it would be less noticeable. She couldn't put it in a drawer, but she didn't want to deal with curious questions yet, either.

Eventually El came to the door. "You ready?"

"Yeah." Shelly slid the empty suitcases under the bed. She grabbed her purse and checked it for her key and money before joining El. Though she looked forward to the experience, she hoped the trip wasn't too adventurous.

Chapter 6

THE GIRLS WERE EXHAUSTED as they returned to their flat. Shelly hadn't taken the time for more than a quick glance around the kitchen earlier. Now she looked closer. The kitchen was all white, or off-white, and had a small table with a Formica top and silver-scalloped edges. The four matching chairs were a bit worse for the wear. A window seat, large enough for three people, dominated one wall. She wondered how many decades the furniture had been there.

A fridge, stove, and a stainless steel sink took up most of the remaining wall space. Cupboards and a set of open shelves were squeezed into the corner.

As they finished putting away the food, a cute, dark-haired girl came through the front door and swallowed El in a hug.

"I wondered where you'd gone when I saw your stuff was here," she said. "It's good to see you. I missed you so much!"

"It's good to see you too, An. We were shopping."

The dark-haired girl turned, as if noticing Shelly for the first time. "Hi, I'm Andrea." Her brown eyes sparkled with excitement above a pert nose. She was even shorter than Shelly, close to five foot, and petite all the way around.

"It's good to meet you. I'm Shelly."

"El mentioned she'd heard from you weeks ago. Welcome to our corner of the world," Andrea said.

"Thanks. I'm looking forward to living here." Shelly turned and pointed to several boxes piled on the kitchen floor. "So, are these yours?"

"A couple of them are, but the others belong to Candy." Andrea glanced at El. "She's out with Eric *already*."

"Candy? *Please* tell me that's a nickname," Shelly said. It was bad enough she had a roommate named Electra—could any parent be cruel enough to name a kid Candy? The answer to that question, she realized, was yes. There were many worse names out there.

"It's a nickname. Her real name is Chandelle. Chandelle Lier, that is," El piped up.

Shelly winced. She wasn't sure if that was worse or not. "What were her parents thinking?"

"Her mum was probably under anesthesia, too," El said with a grin, then glanced at her watch. "I better ring my parents and let them know Brad and I got settled in all right. I'm actually surprised my mum hasn't already called, frantic." She pulled a cell phone from her pocket.

"I probably ought to make my bed." Shelly thought of the welcome pack that came with the apartment, which included all of her bedding. Once that was done, she would hook up the new laptop Curtis had picked out for her and send her family another email.

She was sending off the message to her family when she heard an insistent knock on the front door. Since her room was closest, Shelly hurried to open it.

"Hello, can I help you?" she asked as she peered up at a tall, tawny-haired guy. Dang, what was it with the hot guys around here?

He lifted an eyebrow. "Are you one of my sister's flatmates?"

Andrea joined in from behind Shelly before she could respond. "Brad, it's good to see you! How are you doing?"

Shelly moved out of the way as Andrea rushed past and threw her arms around him.

"I'm well, Andrea. It's good to see you, too." He released Andrea and turned back to Shelly. "And you are?"

"Shelly Cox. You must be El's brother. She mentioned you in her emails." He looked a lot like El around the eyes and mouth. She backed up in the hallway to let him in, and he brought a small box with him.

"She's excited about having a member of the Church for a flatmate. I've heard of little else the past few weeks."

"Git," El said as she came down the stairs, obviously catching her brother's comments.

"I'm sure she's sussed it out by now." He gave her a vaguely irritated look.

Shelly followed the conversation well enough, despite the British slang. She didn't think either sibling was actually mad. In fact, she almost expected Brad to reach out and ruffle his sister's hair, or for El to attack a ticklish spot under her brother's arm pit.

"What've you got there?" El asked.

"I found this in the boot with my stuff." He handed the box to her.

"I wondered where it went." She tucked it under her arm. "What else are you hiding? Some of my food?"

"If I had that, I'd never admit it." He turned his smile on Shelly. "How was your trip? Are you settling in all right?"

"Fine. El and I ran to Tony's earlier."

"She still needs groceries, though. We only picked up a couple necessities today," El added. "If I can borrow the car on Monday, that would be great. You can only carry so much on the bus."

"I'll probably be ready for a trip to the store by then, too." He leaned against the door jamb and smiled at Shelly. "If you ever need a ride, let me know. I'll be happy to help you out if El can't take you. I'm three doors down." He gestured to the left.

Feeling her face heat, Shelly smiled. "Thanks. I appreciate the offer. Maybe I'll have to take you up on it."

"Bye!" He waved and headed out the front door.

Shelly paused to watch the door swing closed behind him before turning back to her roommates. *Cute. Not an egomaniac like Clay, anyway.*

THAT NIGHT AFTER SHELLY returned from the banquet held for the international students, she pulled out her laptop and turned it on, grateful for the complimentary Internet service provided with her room. Though she didn't feel like writing a lengthy email, she popped onto her Facebook account and posted a quick note about her day.

Settled into my flat in England today. It'll be good not to live out of a suitcase anymore. My roommates seem nice. Can't wait for classes to start.

She didn't feel nearly as enthusiastic as she hoped she seemed. She was tired and more than ready for bed. It was only early afternoon in Utah, though, so she knew many of her friends and family would catch her note soon. She scrolled down to read a few other people's status updates and leave comments.

She had mostly stayed off social networks since the first of the year, but had been fairly active before that, so she had a large friend list. She felt a twinge of guilt when she saw one former neighbor mention his child's impending birth, and another announce an engagement. Too much time had passed without her checking in on people. She knew wallowing wasn't very attractive, but she'd needed the time. Now she was done with it, though. Time to really start over.

She paused when she got to Rob's latest status, which had been left only minutes earlier.

Meeting the girlfriend's parents tonight. Is it too cliché to bring flowers?

Shelly debated for a long moment, her fingers poised over the keyboard. Seeing him in June had been awkward and painful, and she wasn't sure if she ought to respond. On the other hand, though things had been uncomfortable when they last met, she hadn't sensed the deep bitterness from him anymore. She took a breath and started typing.

Flowers are never too cliché. Pick out a happy bouquet of Gerbera daisies or sunflowers to brighten the house. She'll love it.

She reread the post for punctuation and spelling, and hit 'share' before she could stop herself. Then she continued reading other people's posts. She saw he'd replied and clicked over to it. *Thanks, I'll do that. Glad you arrived safely. Keep an eye out for Elder Durrant.*

Her fingers itched with the desire to pop up a chat window and have a conversation with him. They had once been so close—it had been so easy between them. Instead, she posted back, *I will*, then closed the browser tab to prevent further temptation. He was dating someone else now and she would look forward, not backward.

A huge yawn attacked her and she shut down the computer. She had to get up early for church in her new ward.

MORNING DAWNED DRIZZLY. "A truly English September," Shelly muttered to herself as she pulled her head back under the covers. She peeked out from under the blankets again to glance at the clock. The warm bed teased and taunted, urging her to snuggle deeper into it, but she knew she had to get dressed for church and eat breakfast. With a groan, she gave the covers a final look of longing and stumbled to the dresser for clothes.

The shower water was warm and refreshing; its soothing power reached deep enough to improve her mood. Before she knew it, she was humming a favorite tune. She wanted to stay in the shower and enjoy the hot water, but hurried instead. Andrea and El had warned her it wouldn't last very long.

Soon she was ready for the day and stopped to pick up her scriptures from the desk drawer. Before walking away, she grabbed the picture of Jimmy from the top shelf and looked at it. She took a moment to caress the glass hovering over his face and blow a kiss. The picture was taken at a church activity the summer before he left for his mission. She could remember now when she and Katie had picked him up. The day had been sweltering.

Jimmy ambled over in a blue-and-white-striped shirt and tan jean shorts and slid into the back seat of Shelly's car. "Oh, goodies for me!" He slipped a chocolate chip cookie out from under the plastic wrap that kept the dessert on the plate.

Shelly shook her head with a smile as Katie answered, "Hey, those are for the activity. Leave them for dessert."

"But I've been lugging boxes all day. Besides, after dinner I'll only have room for watermelon." He ate half the cookie in one bite and chewed for a moment before continuing, "Are you coming with us? We'll catch the most."

"A bit overconfident, aren't you? Have you ever pulled a greased watermelon from the lake before?" Katie asked.

"No, but Luke's bringing a net, so we'll win!"

"Cheaters. You know we love watching you guys do things the hard way," Shelly said.

"You can do things the hard way if you like. I'm going to use a net."

She could still see the way he'd stuffed the rest of the cookie into his mouth and grinned before reaching for another. Chocolate chip had always been his favorite. She wondered if that was where her addiction to making them came from. Or was it the other way around? They'd known each other and dated for so long, it was hard to tell anymore.

Reigning in the emotions that the memories raised inside her, she put the picture back and turned to the kitchen. She couldn't afford to wallow any longer this morning.

El and Andrea greeted her in the kitchen. El ate an omelet with a side of sliced tomatoes and another of baked beans. Shelly found herself amused, as she'd heard about the English penchant for tomatoes, mushrooms, and baked beans as side dishes at breakfast. She hadn't figured out what the draw to the beans was—she liked them well enough in other ways, but wouldn't have thought to stack them alongside her eggs. Andrea was having cold cereal, which was more like Shelly's routine.

They greeted her and continued talking about some common acquaintance as Shelly collected her dishes and food and sat to eat. As she finished, there was a knock on the door and Brad entered. He had foregone the suit coat, but looked nice in his crisp white shirt and muted blue and green tie. She couldn't help but allow her gaze to linger a moment longer than was necessary.

"You're joining us?" Surprise tinged El's voice.

"Why wouldn't I?" His ears pinked up slightly, belying his tone, and he shot a furtive glance at Shelly. "You ladies about ready to go?"

"Have fun. Wish I were going with you instead of work," Andrea said as she snatched her purse and headed for the door.

When it closed behind her, Shelly asked, "Does she usually go to church with you guys? I thought she wasn't LDS."

"She's not, but she goes to activities and sometimes church with us," El explained. "She's been in pre-missionary investigation mode for a long time."

"Oh. Well, I'm going to go brush my teeth," Shelly said. She took care of that and grabbed her scriptures, telling herself it was only church. Nothing unusual would happen—it was a new ward, much like any other she'd known. Still, she couldn't help but be a tad nervous.

Chapter 7

DESPITE SHELLY'S RELUCTANCE to get out of bed, church had been nice. England was a bit of an adventure, so there had been some culture shock. At church, however, she knew what to expect and had been warmly welcomed.

"I get out of class at three o'clock tomorrow, so we can go grocery shopping any time after that," El said as they got out of the car back at their flats.

Brad answered, "Three will work for me."

Shelly agreed, and he went on. "So, is my sweetest sister going to feed me a nice Sunday dinner?"

"I'm your *only* sister! But if you bring those biscuits Mom sent us to *share*, I could arrange to do the rest. You want potatoes and corned beef hash, right?" Her eyes twinkled with mischief.

"*You* cook corned beef? I don't think so. You don't like it any more than I do," Brad said. "If you promise no corned beef, I'll bring some sodas, too."

"Great. You bring the easy things and I'll do all the cooking. As usual." El grumbled, but a smirk at the side of her mouth gave her away.

"You don't want to eat my cooking, anyway. It could be hazardous to your health." Brad flashed Shelly a smile. "Never learning to cook has its advantages."

"I've always heard it the other way around," she said.

"Depends on your perspective."

43

"My perspective says maybe you're eating cereal for lunch instead," El said.

"Come on, sis. Have a heart." He slung an arm around her shoulder. El rolled her eyes, but relented.

❁ ❁ ❁

WHEN SHELLY WALKED into the kitchen after changing out of her dress, she noted El had opted for sandwiches.

"Are you going to join us?" El asked.

"I don't have a lot to contribute." Shelly thought of her pitifully small stock of food in the fridge. Since they had been stuck on the bus for their shopping trip the previous day, she had been careful only to get the things she couldn't live without for the weekend. "I have bread and cheese."

"Eat with us today and you can help another time." El pointed to a bunch of lettuce that sat on the counter. "Could you help make the salad?"

"Thanks." She'd never seen college students make salad to go with an everyday meal before. Was El a health nut? "Do you make full meals often?"

"No, only a couple times a week. School keeps me busy. The rest of the time, I grab something quick or eat on campus."

"At Utah State I chose non-cooking dorms because I was too busy to use the kitchen much. I missed having access to one, though." Shelly finished rinsing the lettuce and started ripping it into pieces. "Still, I'll probably eat on campus a lot. I have a pretty heavy class load, and British schools are supposed to be harder than American ones."

"Oh, you'll be fine. You must be good if they accepted you." El glanced at her. "How old are you? Twenty-three, twenty-four? You Yanks don't graduate from high school until eighteen, right?"

Shelly chuckled, knowing her roommate started college at sixteen. "No, I'm only twenty-one."

"Did you graduate early?"

"I was eighteen like most people, but I had some credits from high school and I took summer classes to finish early. I finished last winter, before Christmas." Shelly tried to keep her voice level, though the words reminded her of the day she moved back home. "Only for two weeks," she'd told Danyelle, since she'd be sharing a home with Jimmy after that. Little had she known. "I worked in my hometown since then."

"What was the hurry to finish your bachelor degree if you were going to take so much time off?"

"There was an unavoidable change of plans. I was in an accident last winter." She was amazed she managed to keep her voice steady since overwhelming sadness spread through her chest. She'd been told it would get easier, but eight months later she'd noticed little difference.

The doorbell rang and El hurried to open it. She motioned for Brad to come in. "Go set the table, will you?"

Everyone sat when El brought the plate of cold cuts to the table.

"So, Shelly, you're here and you're set up for classes. What else do you like to do?" Brad asked, turning his green eyes on her. The saffron-colored shirt he wore showed off olive skin that matched his sister's. The shirt made his skin seem darker, like it had been bronzed in the summer sun, and it made his eyes stand out, green with hints of gold in them.

Shelly finished dishing herself some salad and passed it to him. "My classes should keep me busy. I expect to spend most of my free time studying."

"Do your plans include any fun?"

"Of course. I'll see the sights and go to activities. I came too far to sit in the library all the time, but my main reason for coming was to learn. We'll see if I can squeeze in anything more." She caught the look of interest in his eyes, but pretended she didn't. She wasn't anywhere near ready to deal with a new relationship.

A blonde woman with curly hair tumbling down her back and the most incredible blue eyes Shelly had ever seen came through the front door. She was thin and tall and her stark black blouse and leggings looked ultra-hip—like something you'd see on the runway.

"You must be Shelly," the woman greeted her. "I'm Candy. I saw your name on the list when I checked in. I tend to pop in and out a lot, so I probably won't be here much." She headed up the stairs without waiting for a response.

"Hello." Shelly watched the woman disappear.

"Don't mind her," Brad said. "She's always a whirlwind."

Candy came dancing down the stairs again, a purple lava lamp in her hands. "I know you'll love this as much as I do. Who could dislike such a pretty purple treasure?" She set it on an open shelf, petted it, talking to it in a low tone that Shelly couldn't understand. A moment later the light popped on as Candy plugged it in. "There you go, baby. You're all set." She turned back to her roommates. "I'm off for a date. Catch you all later!"

The door slammed shut behind her and silence prevailed in the room for a long moment while Shelly blinked in surprise.

"Hope you like lava lamps. I have the feeling we'll be seeing and hearing a lot about that one," El said.

Shelly had never been particularly partial to them, but she smiled anyway, infusing as much sarcasm into her voice as possible. "Oh, goody. I can hardly wait."

❁ ❁ ❁

THE NEXT MORNING, Shelly stopped into the International Office to sign up for a trip to Bath in a couple weeks.

Her first class was historiography, or the study of how history is recorded and later reconstructed by historians. It was one of the core modules required of all history majors. Later in the week she had her two other core classes: Europe imagined, and research design and strategy. She understood the reason she needed to get the core courses out of the way before she started the others, but hoped she wouldn't find the classes dull. She'd much rather be digging into what actually happened, rather than how that information was gathered.

Then again, if she was going to write that 15,000 word dissertation, along with all the other portfolio contents she had to put together this summer, she'd need the tools to do so.

Though she had picked up her books the previous week, and skimmed through the first chapter of this one, she hadn't had time for more than that, with all the orientation activities and moving in.

Lunch, studying, and a shopping trip later, she was putting away her groceries, pleased with having a few meal options now.

"I'm bringing some treats to family home evening tonight," El said when Shelly was done unpacking her food. "Do you have a minute to give me a hand?"

"Sure." There hadn't been much time at church the day before to meet most of the young adults in their ward. There was no singles ward or branch in their area, but apparently the single adults had family home evening activities together every week, and often hung out several more times each month. With all the drinking and partying Shelly had heard people in school talking about, she was glad to have a group where she knew she wouldn't have to face those issues. She looked at the collection of fruit El had spread across the counter and chuckled. "These are treats? Are you sure you're not a nutrition major?"

"Major?" El asked.

When she was a kid, Shelly had always thought English was English. Though she'd known better before her trip, she was still struggling to get the local lingo right. Apparently that one was different. "So, why aren't you studying nutrition?"

"That's no fun, not when there are so many other options. Don't worry—I bought a package of chocolate biscuits to share, too. There will be plenty of sugar to go around."

"Whew! I was worried about that," Shelly exaggerated as she picked up a knife and began slicing apples.

They worked side-by-side while Shelly told El a few basics about her family and background they hadn't already covered, leaving out any mention of Jimmy. In return, El told Shelly about her brother Kip and his wife and son, and a few more stories about growing up.

Andrea entered the kitchen, pushing her rumpled hair away from her face. "When did you two get back?"

"Almost half an hour ago. We made a lot of noise. I'm surprised you didn't hear us." Shelly threw a handful of apple cores into the garbage.

"I was taking a nap."

"She sleeps like the dead. Nothing wakes her up until she wants to get up," El told Shelly, putting orange sections into a bowl. "I don't know what it is with the two of you and naps. Lazy, that's what you are."

Andrea shook her head with an indulgent smile.

"Do you want to come with us to the activity tonight?" El asked.

"Sure, I was looking for an excuse to avoid my school work." Andrea picked up an apple slice. "Do you need some help?"

El directed her to prepare the pineapple leaning against the fridge.

full Circle

❀ ❀ ❀

CLASS THE NEXT DAY was overwhelming. When it was dismissed, Shelly numbly collected her things. Before shutting her notebook, she turned to a new page and started a list of what she needed to do to complete her assignment. She always knew it would be difficult here, and wanted it that way—less time to think about other things. *I can handle anything if I plan it out—I've done it before.* She left the classroom with new determination.

She could see that three classes a week would keep her every bit as busy as six had back in Utah. After her second class that day, Shelly stepped out into the billowing wind and shivered. Didn't it ever warm up here? The sky looked like the rain would start pouring on her any minute. She pulled her light blue jacket more tightly around her as she turned toward the library.

"Hey, you never called me." A male voice startled her from her thoughts.

Shelly turned to find Clay approaching her. "No, I've been busy, and I haven't needed you for anything." She seen the confused look on his face. "You told me to call if I needed anything. I didn't." When he came up beside her, she continued toward the library.

"I've been waiting for your call."

With baited breath, I'm sure. Aloud, she responded, "I do appreciate your help at the train station. It was very kind of you."

"That's more like it." His eyes twinkled as he spoke, and he poured on the charm. "A pretty thing like you is probably used to being swamped with calls from guys. Just promise to save a slice of your time for me."

Shelly stopped and turned to him, giving him an incredulous look. Sure, she'd dated from time to time in college. But the guys hadn't exactly been breaking down her door. And she'd never met anyone quite so arrogant. "I don't want to burst your bubble or anything, but I'm here to study, not to date. Guys who tell me what they think I want to hear don't impress me. Besides, I know you're far too busy with your other lady friends to miss me." She wondered where her gall had come from—she'd seldom been so outspoken before.

"Are you jealous?" His intrigue obviously deepened—she could practically see it go up a notch.

"I'd have to want a relationship to be jealous. You seem nice, but I'm not interested. Thanks again for your help." She turned and walked quickly away. She knew his type. If she didn't tell him no right now, he would never leave her alone.

She meant what she had said about not planning to date while she was in England. She didn't want to make any ties beyond friendship here. The idea of romance did not appeal. Mostly. Okay, she admitted to herself, she liked the idea of being in love again, but she couldn't imagine going there right now.

She pushed thoughts of guys out of her head and returned her focus to school work. She had another six days before this class again, but knew there was no time to spare if she was going to get through her assignments and reading by then.

Chapter 8

TIME FLEW DURING THE next week. Shelly hung out with her roommates, got involved at church, and spent hours writing emails and letters back home, all in addition to the time she spent studying. After she finished at the library Friday, she hurried to the flat for dinner. They had plans to see a movie that was being released that weekend.

"Candy will drive us over, and Andrea will meet us there in about forty-five minutes," El said as Shelly came in the front door.

"Great, I'll grab some dinner first." Shelly put her bag away, then went to the kitchen to eat. Soon there was a knock out front and El answered it. Shelly looked up in time to see Brad glancing toward her open bedroom door before he entered the kitchen.

A smile broke out on his face when he saw her "How are you ladies tonight?"

"Great," Shelly answered. "I'm starting to narrow down topics for my thesis."

"You don't even have to pick a thesis for months yet. What kind of overachiever are you?" he teased.

"I had some ideas rolling around in my head before I got here." She put away the sandwich ingredients in the fridge and sat at the table with her dinner.

Candy rushed in, stopped to pet her lava lamp, and then turned to the others. "Let's leave in fifteen minutes. I want to get a good seat."

"Where are you going?" Brad asked.

"To the cinema," El told him. "We're having a girls' night out—that means *just* girls."

"Oh, come on. You can always make it a friends' night instead."

Brad's arm came across the back of Shelly's seat, and she stiffened. It took a moment for her to debate whether to ignore his arm or shift away. Was it a casual gesture, or did he mean something by it? After several seconds, she leaned forward for her glass of milk, and didn't move back again. "We'll have to do that another time. Tonight it's just girls."

"Spoilsports."

El mentioned she'd heard from a friend back home, and she and Brad talked about the latest news through the rest of Shelly's meal.

After finishing her dinner, Shelly stood. "I'm going to get ready." Before she could reach her room, Brad was fast on her heels.

He walked to her doorway and stopped to look around. "So, are there more of you back home?"

She picked up her hairbrush and started using it, turning slightly away from him. "Of me, no. I'm an original, but I have three sisters."

"Is that your family?" He pointed to the picture over her dresser.

"Yeah." She felt a tug of homesickness. "I miss them." She had been in such a hurry to leave town by the time September had rolled around, anxious to leave all the memories that haunted her on every street corner. Now she wished her family was close enough to visit—and she hadn't been in England for two weeks yet.

Brad looked around the room at her other pictures and knickknacks. He stepped in and picked up the oak-framed snapshot of Jimmy, which she'd set on her desk earlier. "Who's this guy?"

Shelly set down her brush and took the picture from his hands. She looked at the photo again. Jimmy wore his favorite blue-and-white-striped shirt and several greasy watermelons from their earlier 'fishing' expedition in the lake sat on the table next to him—his catch of the day. She remembered how his biceps had bulged through the shirt as he brought a heavy melon up into the boat. He'd never been a serious athlete, but lifting boxes at the grocery store hadn't hurt his physique any.

Brad leaned against the desk and watched her. She felt his gaze on her face.

Her voice was soft, barely more than a sigh. "What I always wanted."

51

Longing filled her chest as she thought of him. She missed so many things: the feel of his comforting arms around her, the sound of his voice as they talked and joked. The sight of a fresh letter, detailing his missionary activities for the week, his cramped scrawl on the envelope and paper.

She missed the excitement she used to feel when she found one of his letters in her mailbox, and even the confusion that started to rise during the last few months of Jimmy's mission when she'd been seeing Rob and her heart had begun to tangle. When she felt her eyes prickle with tears, she shut off that line of thinking and set the frame back down.

With a glance, she noticed El standing in the doorway, a surprised look on her face. Putting on a fake smile, Shelly snatched up her purse from the bed. "If Brad would vacate, I can lock up here."

Looking a little stunned, he immediately acquiesced.

Shelly managed to put the scene behind her by the time they reached the cinema. However, a lingering sadness still hovered over her.

⚜ ⚜ ⚜

"HEY, LADIES. CARE for some company?"

Shelly turned, already knowing it would be Clay. He had a couple of friends with him and they all greeted Candy by name. Clay took the last step to Shelly's side.

"Sorry, guys. This is a girls' night. No men allowed." Shelly smiled to soften the blow, but had no intention of backing down.

"Harsh." His smile belied the word as he reached out and tugged on a lock of her hair. "Are you sure? I'd be happy to share my popcorn with you."

"I don't make the rules."

"Well, we might—" Candy's words were cut off with a sound that indicated she'd gotten an elbow in her ribs.

"It really is just girls tonight. You'll have to try another time," El interjected.

Candy gave El a dirty look, but Andrea arrived and backed El up.

Clay smiled. "Another day, then. Catch you later."

"See you." Shelly turned to her roommates.

Candy rubbed her ribs and grumbled, "I don't know why we couldn't sit with them, at least. Clay is a total hottie." She eyed Shelly. "I don't think he's used to being turned down."

"I'm sure his ego can take it," Shelly said, and smiled as the way cleared for her to order her ticket.

❀ ❀ ❀

EXHAUSTED AFTER THE MOVIE, Shelly returned to her room. She put on a pair of sweats and a T-shirt and washed her face.

As she returned to her bedroom, El came down the stairs. She followed Shelly into her room. "It was fun tonight, wasn't it?"

"Yeah. It was good to get out. I feel like I've done nothing but study since I got here. But I have that trip to Bath next weekend with the international students. I'm so excited."

"You think Clay will be on the trip?" El sent her a sideways look.

Shelly considered, then shook her head. "I don't know. If the International Student office goes every year, he's probably been before. This is his fifth year here, after all."

"He seems interested. He didn't flirt with the rest of us." El picked up the brush Shelly had set on the bed before they left earlier. "You didn't seem so interested, though. You could always tell him you've got someone back home."

Shelly followed El's gaze to the picture of Jimmy and pushed back the sadness welling inside her. "I don't have anyone waiting for me back home." Her mind strayed to the memory of Rob and his new girlfriend when she saw them together in June. Her heart clenched. Had it only been a year since she'd had two wonderful guys who wanted to marry her? She still wasn't sure she had made the right decision, and that thought made guilt claw in her gut. "I don't have anyone." She intended to keep it that way for a while longer.

Though she'd always been told that practice made perfect, it was getting harder and harder to stay in control of her emotions. Pain and sadness, and even a bit of anger at Jimmy for dying, roiled inside her and she fought to stay calm. She waited a moment to be certain she could keep her voice even. "It should be enough that I'm not interested in dating him. I don't have time to get entangled in anything. Besides, would my having someone back home stop him?"

"Good point." El rolled her eyes.

53

"You don't seem to be dating anyone." Shelly was curious about that. Andrea had gone out the previous weekend, and they'd only been able to get Candy to the theater without Eric because he worked that night, but El hadn't appeared overly interested in anyone. *Of course, the year was still young.*

"I agree with you about not having time for entanglements. It's easier that way." She didn't meet Shelly's gaze, but fiddled with the brush.

Though Shelly thought a story lurked behind El's blank expression, she didn't ask. She wasn't about to push for answers when she wasn't ready to talk about her own issues. She changed the subject, and a few minutes later El returned to her room upstairs. Shelly shut her door so the others wouldn't disturb her in the morning.

She pulled the long necklace out from under her pajama top and caressed the ring hanging on it. How could she tell anyone without gaining their pity? There had been enough of that back home. Leaving Jimmy's picture out that morning had been a mistake. She didn't know anyone well enough to confide in them about what had happened.

A long moment passed as she toyed with the ring. Finally she slid it back under her shirt, turned off the light, and blew the picture a kiss goodnight.

She ached as she lay in bed, not daring to cry out her pain. She prayed the dreams wouldn't come that night.

❀ ❀ ❀

A COUPLE OF DAYS later, Shelly rushed home from class, angry with herself and upset with the world.

"Hey, is everything all right?" Brad asked, breathing hard. He must have sprinted to catch her.

"What am I doing here? I'm wasting my time and my sister's money." Anger churned in her stomach, her back straight.

Brad took her arm and pulled her to a stop in front of him. "Hey, what's wrong?"

She fumbled through her bag. The paper was well crumpled from the way she had shoved it in. "This is what's wrong." She gave it to him and then started walking again, but more slowly this time. It took considerable effort to hold back the tears. The last thing she wanted to do was to start crying on campus. She worried that if she started crying, she wouldn't stop for hours, if ever. It had been so long since she'd last let go.

Everything was getting out of control. An ironic turn of events—last winter she wanted to cry, but couldn't. Now she didn't want to, and didn't know how long she would be able to hold it all back. If she walked fast enough, she could work off her frustration and she would be okay. She veered away from the flats and picked up speed.

Brad put a restraining hand on her arm. "Whoa, slow down. So, you got lower marks than you'd like. It happens to all of us sometimes." He returned the paper. "Besides, it's not *that* bad. They're decent scores, and it's only your first paper."

She put the essay back inside her bag, zipped it, and started walking again. "It doesn't happen to *me*. I worked too hard on it."

"You'll kill yourself running around campus with that bag. It must weigh 20 kilos." He steered her back to the flats. "Dump it, change your shoes, and we'll go for a run or something."

Shelly wanted to argue. But knowing he was right, she agreed, and walked back in silence. They both changed their clothes, and in five minutes were back out in front of their building. The exercise helped. After nearly an hour of fast walking with as much jogging as an out-of-shape Shelly could stand, she began to feel better.

That evening she was able to focus on her schoolwork, and though she was tired, she popped onto Facebook to see what her friends back home were doing. Katie was in love again, as she often was. Shelly congratulated her, and vented some of her frustration about school in a private message, then headed to bed.

Chapter 9

ROB WALKED UP THE STEPS to his apartment, exhausted after a long day at work, followed by loads of laundry and a shopping trip to fill his nearly empty cupboards. His feet rang on the metal steps as he brought in the last bags from his car, and he was glad to duck under the overhang, getting out of the drizzle. He'd had to tell Lindsey he couldn't make it when she'd invited him to a party, and she was not very happy about it.

He sighed and pushed through the doorway, dropping the last of the groceries on the counter before stopping to add fish food to the aquarium and to watch them swim for a minute. One of the angel fish had been looking a bit sluggish that morning, but it was zipping along fine now.

Leftover pizza from the previous night greeted him from the fridge—a sure sign that his roommate, Garrett, was on call at the firehouse. If he hadn't been in the middle of a twenty-four-hour shift, there was no way something as tasty as meat lovers, with extra cheese, would have made it through the day. Rob loaded up his plate and set it in the microwave to heat, then reached for his laptop.

Things had been hectic enough that he hadn't checked his email all day, and he turned straight to his Facebook account while his email logged in. He retrieved his pizza, took a large bite, and smiled at the cheesy goodness.

Then he slid back onto the chair and looked to see what was up.

He posted a new status, then read through others', leaving comments at a few. When he reached Shelly's status, he paused. It had been left hours earlier. *I heard schools here were supposed to be tougher, but I had no idea. I'm not sure I'm up to the challenge.*

They had dated for almost a year, and he knew what a brain she was. She took her schoolwork very seriously. He clicked to leave a comment and started to type. *So they have different expectations than you're used to. You're smart and flexible—you'll figure them out. Go get 'em, brainiac.*

He sent it, closed the window down for the night, and checked out his email. He had made great strides toward forgiving Shelly since she broke his heart a year earlier. Despite that, he was still angry that she turned away from their relationship to marry her missionary when he returned home. Rob had known about her relationship with Jimmy, but somehow he had never believed Shelly would choose someone else, not when they had grown so close.

Still, he'd been sorry to hear about the car accident, and he did still care about Shelly. She hadn't turned back to him, though, and maybe that was a good thing. Second-best to a dead man wasn't any better than second-best to a live one.

He pushed the thoughts from his head. He was with Lindsey now, and they had a great relationship. She was warm and bubbly and a lot of fun. Lindsey made him forget the sting of rejection, and gave him ample reason to go out and socialize. He grew fonder of her every day and had every intention of seeing the relationship through—at least, as far as it went. Whether that was marriage, he didn't know, but he wouldn't worry about it right now. Now was about moving on.

BATH WAS EVEN MORE amazing than Shelly had expected. There was so much to see—old buildings, the history, the whole feel of the older parts of town. She wandered with the other students into the shops, around the museum, and onto campus, thrilled by every echoing step as she imagined all her favorite heroines from Austen's novels walking where she now walked.

"So, this is where you've been hiding out," Clay said, coming up behind her in a gift shop. He stepped into her personal space, hovering only inches from her elbow.

She was looking at a display of Bath-themed items with her mind on her younger sister's Christmas gift. "Yeah, isn't it great? My sister Kellie will love this." She picked up a sachet filled with potpourri and trimmed with hand-crocheted lace. "Can't you see Eleanor or Marianne Dashwood keeping it in their drawer?" She held it between them while casually taking a step away.

"I'm afraid you've lost me." He sent her an indulgent smile.

"*Sense and Sensibility* by Jane Austen. It's a good book." Shelly turned her attention back to the shelves. "You should read more."

"I read plenty."

"I'm talking about literature, Clay, not magazines and comic books." She glanced at him from under her eyelashes and held back a grin when he scowled.

"I read books."

"Ones that don't have mathematical formulas and a periodic table?" She gave him her best innocent look.

He leaned toward her, his blue eyes piercing hers. "Ever heard of James Joyce, Mark Twain, and Ernest Hemingway?"

Her eyebrows rose and she tried not to blink in surprise at this revelation. She was impressed despite herself. "Yes."

He pretended to study a shelf of porcelain souvenirs. Then he let a smile slide onto his face. "Yeah, me too, but I don't read their books. I'm rather fond of James Dashner and Dan Wells, though."

Shelly couldn't help laughing. "That's almost more surprising than you reading the classics. I never would have seen you delving into dystopian YA or sociopaths."

"I think you'll find I'm full of surprises."

"I'm sure you are." She muttered the words under her breath as she moved on to a rack of postcards, looking for one to send to her parents, and another to send to Lily and Curtis.

He must have heard, however, because he chuckled. He let the silence flow between them for a few minutes before he brought up a new subject. "I found out where you live the other day." He stepped closer, his voice low and sultry. "Would you kick me out if I stopped by some time?"

Shelly thought of the cute waitress she'd seen him flirting with the previous night. He was one smooth character. She wasn't entirely unaffected by his smile and attention, but she wasn't fooled by them, either. "Let it go, Clay. You know you're not really interested in me."

He picked up her hand, played with her fingers. "If you think that, I'm losing my touch. Maybe I can make it more obvious."

"If you were any more obvious, you'd be a twenty-foot neon sign." She pulled her hand away. "Trust me when I say I'm not your type—and that goes both ways."

"Ouch." Still, he was undaunted. "What exactly do you think is my type?"

She looked around the crowded shop, searching for the kind of woman she could see Clay dating. When she saw a willowy blonde across the room, Shelly gestured in her direction. "Great figure, time-consuming hair and makeup, the latest fashion, and oh, look at the Gucci purse." As if to cement it, the woman lifted her eyes and took a long, appraising look at Clay. Her smile said she liked what she saw. "She's definitely interested. Why don't you go get her number? Your luck is bound to be better there."

She glanced back at him and saw appreciation in his eyes as he looked at the woman, then he returned his gaze to Shelly. "I'm not interested in her."

"Your loss." She turned and moved to another display.

Clay tagged along the rest of the afternoon, but to Shelly's relief, he didn't bring up dating again, and he didn't crowd her personal space. To her surprise, he was actually kind of funny and could even be charming when he wasn't obnoxious. She decided that when he was just a pal, he wasn't so bad to be around.

※ ※ ※

AFTER SPENDING MOST of the day in class and the library Monday, Shelly settled down at the kitchen table with the postcards she'd purchased on her trip, a pen, and a roll of stamps. She needed to get the cards sent out, and the other postcards she'd chosen to keep needed to be catalogued for scrapbooking later.

That done, she set them aside and pulled out her laptop. She had been very good that day, staying away from her email and social networks while she focused on homework. Now that dinner was behind her and she had a break before family home evening, she figured she had some time to play around and check up on people back home.

A while later, she looked up when the front door opened and Brad sauntered into the kitchen. El called out from upstairs that she was nearly ready.

"Hey, did you go running without me today?" he asked Shelly. "I popped by earlier, but you were out." Since the first time they'd jogged together he'd accompanied her on most of her daily runs, but there had been a few times their schedules didn't mesh.

"Yeah, sorry, I went early this afternoon. I couldn't wait." She had needed time to unwind after class so she could settle in to study again. "What's going on?"

"Not much." He took the chair beside her. "What are you doing? Not more research for the thesis you shouldn't even have a topic for yet?" he teased.

"I'm just sending my sister a card and checking my email. How're your classes?"

"I'm keeping up." He paused for a moment. "You look pretty tired. Are you all right?"

"I'll be fine, but I need to go to bed earlier than usual." She wasn't sure if it would help, though, as she wasn't sleeping well. Her dreams the past few nights had all been replays of the nightmarish accident the previous winter. It was coming up on Jimmy's birthday, and he was on her mind more than ever. She realized she was touching the engagement ring tucked beneath her shirt and shifted her hand back to the keyboard.

"I'll make sure we don't linger too late, then." He pushed a lock of hair away from her face and slid it behind her ear. "Are you about ready?"

Shelly felt her cheek tingle as he brushed his finger against it. She liked him, but found herself drawing away, turning back to the screen as an excuse to move out of range. When he kept his hands to himself, she was grateful, and a bit confused. "I only have this last email from my older sister."

Hey Shelly,

There's nothing too exciting going on here. Curtis has been called to be Scoutmaster for the Varsities. On top of that, he's been gearing up for the new season. The house is so big and quiet when he isn't here, we finally decided to get a dog.

The dog's a mutt, part Pekinese, that Stephen insisted we name Bark. Yes, that's right. We tried to convince him that Spot would be better, but he pointed out that the dog doesn't have any spots. Okay, I admit, he won't protect me from anything in the event of an emergency, but he does 'Bark' up a storm every time someone approaches the front door. At least I won't be surprised by an intruder. Lol

So, almost six weeks in England already. Amazing. I keep waiting to hear if you've gone out with anyone. Shelly, it's been almost a year since Jimmy died. Don't you think you should start dating again? You know he wouldn't have wanted you to sit around for the rest of your life. It's time for you to do something. I don't want to preach to you, don't get me wrong, but I worry about you. We just want what's best for you. We love you!

Lily

Shelly scrolled to the bottom to look at a couple pictures of Lily's kids. Brad asked her about them, and she caught him glancing at the text still showing on her screen. Shelly scrolled further down so he could only see the pictures, hoping he hadn't read any of the letter, especially the part about Jimmy. She loved her sister dearly—they had been through so much together—but Lily didn't understand. The thought of moving on the way Lily meant hurt too much to consider.

She knew Jimmy wouldn't want her to punish herself forever—he'd want her to be happy. They had seldom argued or had the minor disagreements she noticed in most of her friends' relationships. Still, she wasn't ready to get involved with anyone romantically.

She glanced over at Brad and saw the curiosity in his eyes as he looked back. She thought he'd probably seen too much of the letter. He didn't ask, though, and she appreciated it. She thought of the way he had touched her cheek. It had been a casual gesture, but at the same time, more than friendly.

El and Andrea came down the stairs and into the room, breaking Shelly's line of thought. "You ready to go?" Andrea asked.

"Sure. Let me put this away." She put the computer into hibernation and scooped it up, along with her postcards, carrying them to her room. There would be plenty of time to worry about all of that another day.

Chapter 10

INTERNATIONAL STUDENT ACTIVITIES, young adult church gatherings, and homework made the time zoom. Shelly accompanied her roommates, Brad, and a couple of his friends to her first rugby match in early October. Brad spent half the game explaining the positions and rules to her, ever patient of her ignorance. She focused on the game, the nippy air, and Brad's eager face in an attempt to blot out the pain that rode her every time she thought about the date—Jimmy's birthday. He would have been twenty-two if he'd lived, and he would have graduated from Snow College in a couple of months. She pushed the fleeting thought away again and focused on her surroundings.

After the game, they went to a local pub for dinner. Though she'd grown used to the different atmosphere, she kept close to the others, uncomfortable with all the drinking. Everyone else appeared perfectly comfortable, however, so she forced herself to act unconcerned. She was glad only Brad's friends had any alcohol at their table, and they both limited themselves to one.

"So, how did you like your first Rugby match?" Brad asked as they finished up their food.

"It was fun. I'll have to catch another one some time."

"Let me know when you have a free night and I'll see about getting tickets." He glanced over her head and smiled. "A snooker table just came open. Anyone interested?" Though the offer was made to everyone, he looked back at Shelly.

On the one hand, she didn't want to encourage him too much. On the other, she enjoyed his company, and had been watching the snooker players, trying to figure out the differences between it and pool. "I could use another British experience, if you're willing to teach me how it's played."

"I'd be happy to." He slid off the bench, and she followed him to the table.

Brad explained the rules and took her through one practice game before they settled in for an actual match. Partway through the second set, Shelly swore she heard Jimmy's laughter and looked up from the green-covered table. She knew it wasn't true, but had to look anyway. A local rock band played in the corner, ale flowed freely, and there was a constant stream of smokers going outside to get their fix between rounds. Calling herself an idiot since her heart was still racing, she turned her attention back to the table and sank her last ball.

"...then you would be the winner," Brad said with a grin.

"You totally let me win!" She laughed.

"Let you? I call that beginner's luck." He returned the balls to the table. "Would you like to play again?"

"The rest of us are ready to go. If you want to stay, I can get a ride with Andrea," El said, joining them at the snooker table.

"What do you think?" he asked Shelly.

"I ought to get back to my homework," she said after pausing to think about it. She wanted to stay, to be distracted a little longer. Being left alone in her room, with nothing but her thoughts would drive her crazy. Still, school work called to her, and she had already wasted most of the night. And the look in Brad's eyes told her she'd be better off keeping some distance between them.

"Oh, stay and play—you study too hard. Your homework can wait an extra thirty minutes," El said.

Shelly took a breath and then smiled, nodding. "I think I will."

"I'll see you at home." El returned to the group at the table.

The game was over too quickly, especially since Brad won, and he and Shelly walked back out to his car.

"Brr, it's cold out here." Shelly wrapped her arms around herself. Even in a thick coat, the wet cold sliced into her. She wondered if it ever really warmed up in Hull—she certainly hadn't experienced an overly warm day.

"So, how are your studies coming?" Brad asked.

"Better. I guess I needed more time to get used to the style the professor wanted. I did great on my last paper." There was a lot of satisfaction in that. School was something she had always done well.

"Glad to hear it." He sent her a side-long glance. "You could take better care of yourself, though."

"Do you think I need someone to check up on me?" She found his interest endearing. He was awfully sweet.

"No, but you've been tired lately," he said.

She brushed off his concern. "I have a lot on my plate. I like it that way, though. Busy is good."

He paused on the sidewalk and turned to face her. "Sometimes... it seems you're trying to keep busy with whatever you can find. It's like you can't stand to have time to think."

"What do you mean?" She hadn't thought she was that transparent. Or was he more observant than she expected?

He took a deep breath and started slowly, as though choosing his words with care. "Occasionally when I have something on my mind that I don't want to think about, I try to fill up my time with other things, to crowd out the unwanted thought. Maybe I'm homesick, or my roommates are driving me crazy. Maybe I'm trying to push away painful memories."

Shelly went from annoyed, to ready to cry, to angry in an instant. How had he known how to push her buttons?

She started to shake as emotions rolled over her. Shelly knew her runs, her activities—she had been volunteering on committees for the international center activities a lot lately—it was all to keep her mind and body occupied because Jimmy's birthday was today and she didn't want to think about it. She wanted to forget that a year before, she had been planning a wedding, juggling school with her relationship with Jimmy, and feeling guilty about Rob's broken heart. The guilt had lessened a lot, especially after she ran into Rob with his girlfriend. He had moved on, but the sting still returned whenever he came to mind—which was far too often.

Shelly crossed her arms in front of her chest in subconscious defense. They were approaching the car. Her lip trembled silently as he opened the door.

She sat, and he went around to his own side and let himself in.

After a minute, he spoke. "I'm sorry—it's none of my business. If you don't want to talk, I shouldn't push you. I could be way off-base."

"No, I shouldn't be so sensitive, and you're not *entirely* wrong." Shelly turned her head toward the window and closed her eyes, pushing away the tears that prickled and burned there. She made it sound like he had only hit on a grain of truth, when she knew he had caught the whole silo. They sat in silence for the rest of the trip home. She wanted to move past her pain, but she didn't think she was ready.

For so many years, even for most of his mission, Jimmy had been the center of her universe. Everything else in life was just preparation so they could be together, or fillers to while away the time. At least, that was what she had told herself when she started seeing Rob. He had become something far more important to her, but even when she started hanging out with him, her heart had clung to Jimmy.

She wasn't sure how Rob had insinuated himself in her heart as well, wiggled in to take up residence, but when she finally admitted he had declared a corner of it for himself, she still couldn't let go of Jimmy. Inside, she now still thought of herself as having that future with the man she had loved so long, despite knowing better.

The worst thing was not knowing how to change her mindset to include someone else, someone new—not while the guilt and pain of losing Jimmy still crushed her.

Brad parked and Shelly bolted from the car before he could turn it off.

She heard him hurry up behind her, reaching her as she opened the door. She didn't acknowledge his presence, but left the door ajar when she went in. It clicked closed as she saw the large arrangement of yellow roses dominating the kitchen table. The air backed up in her chest and she stopped to stare at the bouquet half wondering if she'd imagined it into being.

A small part of her relaxed, as if she had been waiting for the flowers, had known they were coming, as they had on this day for the past several years. The rest of her was flabbergasted.

Brad put a hand on her shoulder as if to prevent himself from running into her. It remained there for the briefest moment before he took a step back. She catalogued the way El smiled at her, and Candy stood by her lava lamp, fiddling with the cord, even Andrea's grinding rock music that filtered down the stairwell, but her eyes never left the flower arrangement. She could almost swear her heart stopped.

"They're for you. Yellow's the color for secret admirers, isn't it?" Candy asked.

"No, that's white." Shelly's voice was low and throaty as she stepped slowly over to the flowers. She stared at them while she drew a ragged breath. Her fingers hovered over the card for a moment, afraid to touch it. How could the flowers be here? She felt her pulse race, her hands shake with the adrenalin. Jimmy was dead. How could the roses be real?

El added, "It must be Clay trying to soften you up for his next try." He'd stopped by, looking for her a couple of times that week, though he'd missed her. El hadn't stopped teasing Shelly about it.

"They're not from Clay," Shelly said, almost in a whisper. They couldn't be—the thought was too unsettling.

"Who're they from, then? You must have another admirer, if you're sure they can't be Clay's." Candy slid a knowing glance at Brad. "And how do you know who they're from if you haven't opened the card?"

Shelly's fingers trembled as she finally pulled the card from the envelope and read it.

Dear Shelly,
I know Jimmy would have wanted you to have these today. We miss you.
Love, Carol

Unable to staunch the flow any longer, Shelly started sobbing. The card fell from her fingers onto the tabletop. She turned and ran to her room, dodging the mystified spectators.

Chapter 11

SHELLY LAY ACROSS THE BED, sobbing harder than she ever had, when El called through the closed door, "Can I come in?"

Shelly took a deep, painful breath and managed to speak, though her voice sounded like sandpaper. "Yes."

Entering, El set the vase of roses on the corner of the desk. "Would you like to talk?"

Though she wished she could, Shelly shook her head. She didn't think she could speak in complete sentences.

"Do you mind if I stay here for a few minutes?"

"No." Maybe she would be able to pull herself back together if someone was with her. How could Carol have sent those flowers? Didn't she know how hard it would make things? It only underscored that Jimmy was gone. If his mother had to send the roses instead, then he wasn't coming back.

El sat next to her on the bed and placed her hand on Shelly's back. In response, Shelly curled in on herself even more and buried her face in her pillow.

They sat like that for a long time, neither talking and El not trying to calm her like so many would have done. She was just there, a calm presence, willing to listen whenever Shelly was ready. After a long while, Shelly sat up, pulling her legs in front of her. She hugged her pillow tightly, but still didn't speak. She knew her face was red and her eyes puffy from the tears.

El retrieved a tissue and wordlessly handed it to Shelly. Finally she picked up the picture on the desk and brought it over, sitting next to Shelly again. "Is this Jimmy?"

Shelly nodded.

"And he died?"

Surprised at El's question, Shelly nodded and tears began flowing again. "How'd you know?"

"Brad and I put it together from an email he saw, and things you've said." El brushed hair out of Shelly's face. "What was special about today?"

Finally, Shelly felt able to speak. "It's his birthday. He always... gave me yellow roses... on his birthday."

"He gave *you* roses for *his* birthday? Now, there's a man," El said with a smile of admiration. Shelly smiled back weakly. "How long did you date?"

"Since I was sixteen."

"And how did he..." She stopped.

"A car accident, last December the sixteenth." Shelly pulled the necklace out from under her blouse and removed the ring, handing it to El.

"You were engaged?" she asked, raising her eyebrows as she looked at the miniscule diamond. "When was this?"

"We were supposed to be married December twenty-first."

El handed back the ring, but stared at her roommate. "Why didn't you tell any of us? You could have had our support all this time."

Shelly laughed low. "Yeah, like I needed someone fawning over me as if I were a broken child. I love my family and friends back home, but I felt suffocated sometimes. Everyone kept asking how I was, if I was going to be all right, whispering behind my back. I wanted to be a normal person again and move on with my life." Tears poured down her cheeks as she spoke. The dam had been broken and, as she feared, she couldn't stop the flood. "Even now, I get a long letter a couple times a week, asking how I am, if I'm okay, how I'm settling in. It's so frustrating. As if I haven't been here long enough to be 'settled in' by now."

"But you haven't been feeling like a normal person, or acting like one, either. You go out in public, but even then you keep to yourself, and you always avoid answering whenever someone asks about this guy." She tapped a finger on the picture. "You know everyone else will want to know now. I can tell them you've only had a bad day, but I don't think they'll buy it."

"What a joke, me thinking I could make it on my own," Shelly said ruefully. Tears still poured down her cheeks. She'd thought she had been in pain since the accident, that she missed Jimmy, but now that she was letting it loose, she wasn't just numb—the pain was worse than ever.

"What a joke, you thinking you should *have* to make it on your own. The Lord didn't put us on this earth to work out our problems by ourselves. He put us here to help one another. I might not know this guy, but I think I know you, and I want to help. I'm here if you need to talk, *anytime*, all right?" She touched Shelly's chin with a finger and guided her face up so their eyes met.

"Okay."

There was a knock on the bedroom door, and El answered it.

Candy stood on the other side, two mugs in her hands. "I thought you could use some hot cocoa." She turned to Shelly and shot her a sympathetic look. "I hope you're feeling better." She handed the mugs to El and shut the door again.

Shelly looked at El in surprise as she accepted the drink. "Was that Candy? Or did one of the body snatchers get her?"

El sat on the edge of the bed. "Search me."

They smiled over their drinks. Candy wasn't a bad person, but she was usually kind of self-involved. It was nice to see another side of her.

When they finished, El took Shelly's cup and walked to the door. "I'll let you get some sleep."

"El, thanks. It helped to talk about it."

She turned around and smiled, tears in her eyes. "You're welcome."

IN THE FOLLOWING DAYS, Shelly spent a lot of time remembering—no more trying to drown out her feelings by staying too busy to think. She spent hours curled up on her bed, writing in her journal, and reflecting on her emotions.

Amazingly enough, school got easier as she lived *through* her pain instead of pushing it away. She was finally starting to sleep better, so she was more alert in class and less stressed. When she was alone, she was often in tears, but it was a relief after the months of holding back. Little by little, she started to feel more like herself.

She didn't avoid social interaction, but she did cut back. Wednesday night after meeting with the single adults from church, she returned to her room to study.

A few minutes later, there was a knock at her door. "Shelly?"

"Come in, El, Andrea. What's up?"

"We didn't want to get back to studying yet and wondered how you were doing. You seem to be doing better."

It was obvious what they meant. "I'm starting to feel better." Shelly picked at her blanket. "I think Jimmy would've been ashamed of the way I've acted since he died. He wouldn't have wallowed all these months if things had been reversed."

"Ashamed?" El slid closer on the bed. "Don't you think you're being too hard on yourself?"

"Why would you have to be ashamed?" Andrea asked.

"Well, perhaps 'ashamed' is the wrong word. 'Sad' might be better. I can hear him—'Shelly, you're better than this. You know the Lord's directing our lives. This is what He wanted for us; we must accept it.' And I know he's right. He always had such unwavering faith." Tears dripped off her face. She reached up with the back of her hand and wiped her cheeks.

"I'm sure Jimmy, and the Lord, understand. You'll get through this, and they'll be proud of you for dealing with it." El grabbed a tissue and wiped at her sympathetic tears. "You're doing well. I can see a difference in you already."

Shelly chuckled. "You mean, besides the fact that my eyes are permanently puffy from crying?"

"Like either of us blame you for that." Andrea tipped her head. "You really believe he's up there watching you, then?"

"Yeah." Shelly smiled as she imagined it. "I don't think he spends all his time watching me, there's a lot of work to be done on the other side, but I know he checks in on me from time to time. That's the kind of guy he was."

"You really believe that? What do you think he's doing up there, besides playing a harp?" Andrea asked.

Shelly laughed before she could stop herself. "Sorry, the image of Jimmy—the most tone-deaf person I ever met—playing a harp is hilarious. No, he was an awesome missionary. I'm sure that's what he's doing now.

There are a lot of people who never heard of the gospel during their lives—they need a chance to hear it too."

Andrea didn't look completely convinced of that, but she didn't disagree, either.

El smiled. "So, stop me if I'm snooping, but you don't usually talk about Jimmy. How did you two get together? What was he like—besides totally gorgeous?"

A smile played across Shelly's lips as she tipped her head back and reviewed her memories. "Everybody said it couldn't last—puppy love, that's all. We're talking about high school love here. I was sixteen—what could I know? But by the time he kissed me, I knew it could last forever." She couldn't help sliding into story-telling mode—it all seemed fairy-tale-ish to her now.

"Jimmy and I grew up together, around the corner from each other." She looked back at her roommates. "I remember the city children's parade for the Fourth of July when I was nine and he was ten. I had decked out my faded pink bike. It was this 1960s hand-me-down from a cousin, and I decorated it with red, white, and blue streamers. A few silver strips from some old Christmas icicles were thrown in for good measure. I was so proud." She laughed, remembering the scene all too well. "When the parade ended, Jimmy blasted me and the bike with his squirt gun, destroying it all. All that work went down the tubes in seconds. I was devastated. I had hoped to keep the decorations on for a few more days."

"Boys that age are so insensitive." El folded her tissue.

"Yes." Shelly chuckled at the memory. "That incident seared into my memory, causing loathing every time I saw him clear until I turned ten, two months later. Since my mom insisted he be invited to the party, I relented. He brought me a truly cool new Cinderella Barbie, and I forgave him. Of course, back then I didn't think about the fact that his mother picked it out and he had only had to hand it to me as he walked in the door, heading for the goodie table."

Tears slid down Shelly's face, but she ignored them. She focused instead on the happiness of her memories, at the warm way they made her feel. Andrea passed over a box of tissues from the desk.

Shelly blew her nose and gathered her thoughts again. "After I graduated from high school, I took classes at Snow College for the summer.

My father worked on campus, so I got a partial tuition waiver. Jimmy and I had it all worked out—he would go on his mission in the fall, and I'd go to Utah State University to get my degree. Then, when he got home, we would get married and I'd be done with school, or almost, and would work while he studied."

She grabbed another tissue, but instead of using it, she played with it, flattening it out on the blanket, smoothing all the wrinkles. "He already had his mission call by then, Chicago Vietnamese-speaking, and he was stoked, or as you all would say, chuffed. I was, of course, happy for him, but dreaded spending the two years alone. I rushed through school as quickly as I could, desperate to finish before he got home."

"Like you do now." El rearranged herself on the bed.

"Yeah."

"What about you? Did you date anyone while he was gone?" El asked.

"Some, here and there." Shelly felt her face burn from embarrassment and chastised herself for being less than forthcoming. She had to stop doing that. "Okay, I saw a lot of this one other guy that last school year. We sang together, studied together, and occasionally went out on dates. Things grew more serious than I planned. I think I broke his heart when I chose Jimmy instead of him, but he seems to have bounced back. He's been dating someone else for months now." She took a deep breath and gazed out the window, remembering the way she had felt when she and Rob dated, and their final kiss before she'd turned him away. He hadn't made the choice easy for her.

"So there was someone else, once, and there can be again," Andrea said.

Maybe someday, but not yet. Shelly decided she needed to get back on track. "Anyway, Jimmy came home, made a big show with this tiny diamond, and I was thrilled. We had nine weeks after he came home to put the wedding together. Everything moved like clockwork until the accident. I'd just finished my degree and had a job lined up at the Institute."

The smile left her face and sadness took over as she continued, a fire burning in her chest. "For a long time after the accident, I felt like I was stranded. Like being the last rider on a Ferris wheel that the operator left. I was stopped at the top of the ride as a heavy wind and rain pelted down on me. I felt helpless.

"Unable to deal with reality, I went to work, wearing myself out so I wouldn't have to think or feel, not looking down into the abyss of metal pipes below me. I hoped that eventually the dawn would come and I'd be saved. The night seemed to last forever." She sat, tucked her head against her legs. Her arms encircled her head, closing her off from them. Tears streamed down her cheeks and dripped off her nose. Her shoulders heaved in silent sobs. She wasn't sure that night was truly over yet, but she thought she might see a light edge on the horizon—the harbinger of dawn.

"I'm sorry, I shouldn't have asked," El said after an awkward moment.

Shelly lifted her tear-stained face. "No, I needed to say it." She wiped at her cheeks, ineffectively, since the tears were still coming down. "Thanks for listening. Both of you. I guess I went off on a tangent, didn't I?"

"I'm glad you trust us with your memories," El said.

Andrea took on a sneaky grin. "Did Jimmy send you roses while he was on his mission, too?"

Shelly smiled. "He never missed, not in the five years we were together. Of course, it was a significantly smaller arrangement when he was on a missionary's income. I think he might have begged money from his mom to buy them."

"What a man." Andrea sighed, and El nodded her agreement.

Shelly decided to change the subject. She was done with this one for a while, all wrung out and exhausted, but somehow felt lighter. "Are you planning to go to the bonfire? It's Guy Fawkes Day tomorrow."

"How could I miss Bonny Night? Your stay in England would not be complete without it." El grinned back at Shelly.

Shelly cleared her lungs with a deep breath and smiled. Though she still had some grieving to do, she knew it would be okay.

Chapter 12

THE FIRST SNOW ALWAYS filled Rob's heart with joy. The official start of ski season was only a few weeks away, and he had his equipment ready to go. Reports said the rainstorm that had drenched downtown the previous night had deposited another eight inches on the slopes. He looked forward to taking Lindsey with him, shocked that she'd never been on skis. How could anyone who grew up in Utah not have skied before? It was simply wrong.

"Time to check the ski report?" Stu, his thirty-something co-worker asked.

"Yes. I can't wait for the big storm next week. Swooshing down the mountainside, cold air on my face." He loved the pump of adrenaline that came with it, and the thrill of movement. "How about you?"

"Nah, I'd rather stay inside and stay warm. I'll stick to skiing on the Wii." Stu's addiction to Wii Fit was legendary in their department.

Rob laughed as his work phone rang and he lifted the receiver. "Accounting—this is Rob."

"Rob, this is your father."

Rob's excitement vanished. How was it possible that you could go eight years without hearing a voice, yet still recognize it the first time you heard it again? Though anger and irritation filled him, he fought to make his voice unconcerned. "What do you want?" He pitched his voice low, trying not to draw Stu's notice. The man was a gossip of the worst sort.

"Son—"

"Don't call me that," Rob snapped, then clenched his teeth as Stu glanced in his direction.

"You *are* my son."

"Yeah, whenever you find it convenient." Though he wished he could make the words sound as if he didn't care, his throat tightened and his hands curled into fists until his knuckles turned white. Why was he still letting this man get to him? He'd thought he was over this, had put it behind him, but it hadn't taken much to pull it out of his past.

Several beats of silence passed over the line. "I'd like to talk to you."

Rob felt the familiar tug of pain in his chest, the longing to believe in the man who had let him down so many times. He couldn't do it, though. Only a fool kept putting himself out there when he knew his hopes would be quashed like a bug. "You're really good at talk. It's the follow-through that always tripped you up. Forgive me for not wanting to go through that again." He hung up the phone and sucked in a breath, fighting his emotions. No one had been able to tie him up in knots like his father did. When he felt level again, he turned his attention back to his ski plans, but the excitement had disappeared.

He tried to focus on work for the next half an hour, but wasn't able to accomplish anything, so he popped online to Facebook for something to shift his train of thought. He smiled when he saw Shelly's pictures posted only minutes earlier. She stood in front of a bonfire between two other women. The tag read, *Guy Fawkes bonfires in England have nothing on my high school bonfires for festivity or size—but an excess of alcohol appears to make up the difference for many of the revelers. Here I am with my roommates er, flatmates, El and Andrea.*

Rob did a quick online search to learn what Guy Fawkes Day was all about. He read an account of the failed attempt to blow up King James I and the members of parliament. The planned attack was in protest of the religious persecution of Catholics; he couldn't blame them. Rob popped back and left a response. *As long as there were no big explosions. On second thought, explosions can be fun.*

He checked out a few other posts in his quest for distraction and smiled when he was alerted that Shelly had responded to his comment.

There were fireworks afterward, if that counts. How many weeks until ski season starts? Have your skis been waxed and ready since Halloween?

He laughed—she knew him so well—and hit reply. *Halloween? Since when did I wait that long? They were ready by Labor Day.*

They shared a couple more comments before he signed off. When he closed down the website, he was feeling better again. He hoped Lindsey enjoyed skiing more than Shelly had the one time he'd talked her into going with him.

He sent Lindsey a text message asking if she'd like to join him soon.

❁ ❁ ❁

THOUGH SHE'D ALWAYS PLANNED to visit the city of Bradford about an hour away, it was mid-November before Shelly decided to squeeze a day into her schedule to make the trip. Her family genealogy only went back so far, and she'd hoped to be able to poke around and find a few more answers. She spent her Saturday sightseeing, learning a bit more history than she'd picked up online, and pinpointing the places where she might dig up information. Though the cool breeze tugged at her scarf and blew down her neck, at least it was the time of year for it to be cold. Shelly shivered and tucked her neck deeper into the knitted scarf as she opened the door to her flat.

"How was the trip?" Andrea asked when Shelly settled at the kitchen table with her laptop and camera. It was well after dark, but Shelly had gotten lost in the maze of bus schedules and it took longer to get home than she'd planned on.

"Great, minus transportation. It's a fascinating city, and I know I barely covered any of it." Shelly pulled the memory card from her camera and slid it into the special drive in her laptop. "I bet I took a hundred pictures today."

"Did you do any actual family history work?"

"Was I supposed to?" Shelly asked with a chuckle. "Oh, yeah, that. Well, I did ask about churches that have been around long enough to have records from the eighteen hundreds, but I spent too much time at museums and walking along the areas where the textile mills used to run—my great-great-great-grandfather worked there in the 1880s. Did you know there was a salt plant there once, too?"

"I believe I've heard that before." Andrea never lifted her eyes from her homework. "I'm sure if you spent three months combing the city, you'd still find new and fascinating facts about it."

"I'm sure that's true." Shelly pulled up the Internet and began uploading her pictures to the photo-sharing site she used. They would no doubt take hours to catalogue, but the next day was Sunday, so she should have time to make a dent. This was the easiest way to let her family see the pictures without having to send out multiple emails or bomb Facebook with shots.

"When will you go back?" Andrea asked.

There was a knock at the door and Shelly stood to answer it. "Not next weekend. I have a trip to London with the international students. Probably the following Saturday." She opened the door as she said this to find Brad on the other side.

"Probably *what* the following Saturday?" he asked.

"Go back to Bradford." She laughed as she heard the words in her head and teased him. "Hey, Brad, have you ever been to Bradford?"

"Cute. Too bad there aren't any towns called Shellyford. Shellyville? Shellytown?"

She gave his arm a playful nudge. "Those are truly horrid names for a town. Everyone is lucky no such place exists."

He chuckled with her and took the seat at the table beside hers. "What are you doing in Bradford?"

"Looking for my roots, and some sightseeing." She tucked one leg beneath her on the chair. "My great-great-grandma was born there before she immigrated to Canada—can't blame her for that after hearing what a sickly place the city was at the time. Years later she continued on down to Utah."

"If you decide you'd like some company, I could probably arrange my work schedule so I can tag along." He stood back up and began to rummage through El's cupboards, always making himself at home. "Where's El?"

"She had a date," Andrea said.

He whirled around to face her, shock registering on his face. "El had a date? My sister, El? What is this world coming to?" He tried to pass off the shock as a joke, but didn't do a very good job. "Who'd she go with?"

"Some guy from the family home evening group. If you'd been there lately, you'd have seen the way Chet's been cozying up to her." Andrea looked up from her book to give him a hard glare. "Do you have a problem with her dating?"

Shelly watched in fascination. There was obviously something more going on. The undercurrents and tones made that clear, but she wasn't about to ask.

He paused, as if uncertain of the ground beneath his feet. "No, I don't have a problem with her dating." He turned back to the cupboards, removing a sleeve of crackers and a tin of hot cocoa mix. "I've been working a lot. I go to family home evening with you when I can."

Andrea didn't respond, but bent her head over her homework again and started writing.

Brad pulled two mugs from the cupboard and filled them with water. He popped them in the microwave before turning back to Shelly. "Will you join me for an evening snack? Though, I apologize, it's not exactly high tea."

"It's not yours to offer, either," she pointed out. "But I'll work that out with El later. I'd love some. It's been a couple of hours since I ate."

He joined her again after pulling the mugs from the microwave. Steam rose from the hot water and Shelly already anticipated wrapping her hands around the mug, soaking up the heat. Her hands were always icy here and the cold wind she had experienced outside hadn't helped. Not that she didn't have the same problem in Ephraim in the winter, but she was usually safe in September, which hadn't been the case in Hull.

"Thanks." She added cocoa mix and stirred. When she glanced back at Brad and caught him looking at her, she felt herself blush. He was so sweet and not the least bit pushy. She wasn't sure what to do about him. Surely his interest wasn't a figment of her imagination, yet she enjoyed their easy friendship, and didn't want to read too much into it. Besides, she wasn't ready to date again. Not quite yet.

Brad asked her about her photos, and she added dates and locations to them as she told about her experiences that day. More than an hour passed before the front door opened again and El walked in.

"About time you came home. Where have you been, young lady?" Brad asked in mock censure as his sister all but skipped into the room.

"As if it's any of your business." She surveyed the nearly empty sleeve of crackers and the tin of cocoa mix and put her hands on her hips. "And would you please stop raiding my cupboards? There are stores, you know. You could always buy your own food."

"I'll replace it. Quit being so stingy." He glanced behind her. "Didn't invite him in?"

"Don't see him, do you?" She pulled a third mug from the cupboard. "He's a nice guy, but it was only a date."

"Have fun?" Andrea set down her pen and watched El move around the room.

"Yeah. It was great." El slid her mug into the microwave and started it up. "He mentioned a movie next weekend. Maybe."

Shelly smiled when she saw the glimmer of excitement in El's eyes. Then she glanced over and saw the concern in Brad's. It puzzled her. Was he playing the usual protective big brother role, or was there more to it?

"If I'd known you had a date, I'd have been here when he picked you up," he said.

El glared at him. "Now you know why I didn't tell you." She took the last few crackers and tossed the empty package in the garbage. "You can clear off if you don't like it."

"She's a big girl, Brad. You can trust her to make a few decisions," Andrea said.

His jaw tightened. "Of course she is." But the steel in his voice implied he didn't believe it. He stood and turned back to Shelly. "If you'd like some company when you return to Bradford, my offer stands."

"I'll keep that in mind." Mystified, Shelly stared as he said goodbye and stalked out.

After the door slammed behind him, El pulled her hot water from the microwave and set it on the table hard enough that it sloshed over the top and onto her skin. She shook her hand to flip off the water, looking like she wanted to swear.

What was that all about? Shaking her head, she shunted it aside and asked the others about what she should look for in London. The change of subject soon calmed all of them.

Chapter 13

BETWEEN SHELLY'S TRIP, school work, and activities, the next weeks were busy. She managed to avoid two more visits from Clay, but he had popped up all over the place on the trip to London. Though she was having a great time in England, she counted down the days until she finished finals and could fly back home for the month-long Christmas break.

Shelly, El, and Andrea walked out of family home evening the week of Thanksgiving after an especially good lesson about faith. Andrea turned to them. "Don't get too excited, only, I think I'm ready to talk to the missionaries."

"What?" El asked in surprise. She turned to stare, her eyes nearly popping out of their sockets. "Really?" She grabbed Andrea around the waist in a big hug.

"I'm not saying I'll be baptized," Andrea cautioned, though a huge smile split her face. "I know almost everything about your church anyway; I've been going with you for two and a half years now. I feel good there and everything I've learned so far makes sense."

Shelly was thrilled. "As soon as we get home, we'll call the missionaries to make an appointment." Andrea seemed to soak up everything she and El had taught her, and had asked questions about the lessons at church and FHE several times. Shelly had hoped Andrea would take the discussions before school ended, but until now, Andrea had rebuffed them whenever they hinted at the subject.

When they arrived back at their flat, El went directly to the phone to make the call.

THE ELDERS WERE ABLE to meet with them the next night. Chet picked them up and brought them to the girls' flat. "Hi, I'm Elder O'Brien, and this is my companion, Elder Durrant," a ginger-haired missionary said when the girls let them in. He had an Irish accent and a wide face covered in freckles.

Elder Durrant's name caught Shelly's attention and she studied the dark-haired young man. There was a definite family resemblance. "Elder Durrant, I've been watching out for you. Did you just get transferred into the area?" She'd seen a different man with Elder O'Brien last time he'd visited their ward.

"Yes, last week." A grin broadened on his face and Shelly felt a pang in her chest at the similarity to Rob's smile. She hadn't realized how much she missed Rob. Her thoughts were derailed when he continued speaking. "You're familiar. And American. Wait, didn't you sing at my farewell with Rob?"

"I did. You gave a great talk about enduring to the end. I imagine you've had to put it into practice a few times." Tears prickled at her eyes as she thought of that day, of the warm welcome his family had offered her. There hadn't been much chance to speak with the new elder—Rhett, she remembered—but he had seemed nice. She blinked back the tears and fought to maintain a smile. This was not the time to dredge up the past.

"I've reviewed my notes from that talk a few times, yes, and shared them with a couple of my companions. Overall, it's been great here, though." He took her hand for a shake. "Rob mentioned you were in the area. I've wondered if I'd run into you."

"Wait. You two know each other?" El asked.

Shelly smiled. "Yes, Elder Durrant's brother and I knew each other in college."

"That's funny. Do they look alike?" El studied Elder Durrant, who began to turn red.

"Quite a bit, even though they are only half-brothers." Shelly decided it was time to turn the conversation in another direction. Though El appeared to be merely curious rather than noticing anything odd about

Shelly's reaction, the questions were obviously making the man uncomfortable, and Chet appeared a bit wary as well. Shelly smiled at both missionaries. "As you can see, we don't have a living room, but we can all gather around the table."

The first discussion went well and after a long dialogue, Andrea agreed to another meeting. They scheduled another discussion for Thursday before Chet and the elders left.

Shelly excused herself to her room to get over the feelings of homesickness and what-ifs that circulated through her brain the whole discussion. If she had accepted Rob's proposal of marriage instead of Jimmy's she would be married now, and Elder Durrant would be her brother-in-law. But then she wouldn't have been here.

She wondered if Jimmy would have still died in some kind of accident, or if he would be alive and well if it hadn't been for her.

Her religious training suggested that it was Jimmy's time, that he had other work to do beyond the veil, but there were moments when she wondered about it. Shelly wondered if part of her would always feel responsible for what had happened, despite the fact that the road conditions had been worse than either of them had expected.

She remembered the previous summer, seeing Rob lean in to talk to the beautiful dark-haired woman he'd been dating. His Facebook profile indicated he was still in a relationship.

As tears of regret and loneliness slid down her cheeks, Shelly gave into the emotions—she would give herself a few minutes to cry it out, then move on. That's what she told herself. Sometimes she wasn't sure she believed it.

※ ※ ※

SHELLY SET A PUMPKIN pie on the table along with some whipped topping. "Happy Thanksgiving." The second missionary discussion was over and had gone quite well, though Andrea wouldn't commit to baptism when asked. That was fine, in Shelly's book—better that her roommate be completely sure.

Brad looked at her, teasing. "You missed it. Thanksgiving was ages ago."

"You're thinking of the Canadian Thanksgiving. In the U.S. we celebrate it on the fourth Thursday of November." Shelly dug plates from the cupboard, grateful they had enough for everyone. "I can't have turkey dinner with all the trimmings, so I decided pie would have to do."

"I miss Thanksgiving dinner." Elder Durrant patted his stomach as if it were empty. "Stuffing, turkey, cranberry sauce, gelatin with vegetables in it." He sighed longingly.

"Gelatin with vegetables in it? You Yanks are a weird lot," Elder O'Brien said, shaking his head as he accepted the first piece of pie and reached for the whipped cream. "There isn't anything odd in here we should worry about, is there?"

"Not unless you object to chili powder in your pumpkin pie," Shelly said, straight-faced.

The elder dropped his fork and looked at Shelly, appalled. "Are you serious?"

Elder Durrant burst into laughter. "No, she's joking. No one puts chili powder in their pumpkin pie." Then he poked searchingly with a fork at the piece Shelly handed him, his actions exaggerated. "At least, I think she's joking." He arched a single brow over his left eye.

Shelly stared at him. "Holy cow, how do you do that?" She put a finger over her right brow and held it in place while she lifted her left one. Then she switched eyes. Nope, even with help, she couldn't make her brows work independent of each other.

"I've been practicing since I was eight." He plopped a dollop of whipped cream on his dessert and passed the rest to Chet. "I nearly gave up before I managed it the first time. Rob was always jealous, but he could never do it." He licked his fork, then plunged it into the pie. Anticipation filled his face.

Shelly finished passing out the refreshments and took the chair she'd brought from her room. She closed her eyes and enjoyed the taste and texture of the spiced custard. No, it wouldn't make up for missing the big family reunion being held at her aunt's house at that exact moment, but it soothed her homesickness a little.

"You look too excited about that pie," Brad said.

"Sorry, I can't talk right now. I'm savoring." She forked up another bite and closed her eyes again, more to tease him than anything.

"So I see."

Though she wanted the last piece, Shelly let the elders split it a few minutes later; sacrifices had to be made sometimes.

❁ ❁ ❁

LATER THAT NIGHT, SHELLY posted a note on Facebook about her Thanksgiving celebration, such as it was, and included pictures of the missionaries. She saw lots of comments from friends about the football game that was still in progress in the U.S. and the copious amounts of turkey and pie they'd eaten or were planning to devour later that day. She enjoyed the pictures Lily posted of her little girl, Sophie, her face smeared with whipped topping. Sophie was almost two now, a fact that never ceased to amaze Shelly.

There was a tug of homesickness in Shelly's chest. "Hold on. Only three more weeks," she told herself. The last week would be finals, and she had a lot of studying and a couple of big projects to finish up before then.

Her eyes strayed to the list of friends who were online and she opened it up. When she saw Rob's name, she clicked on it and started to type. *Guess who I met this week? He's tall, dark, and wears a black name tag.*

Did you run into Rhett? He popped back a moment later.

Yes. My roommate decided to start taking the discussions. We're excited, but trying not to scare her away. I posted a picture and tagged you. Make sure to tag your mom, will you? The sound of drums pumped through the wall. The neighbor was home.

I hope it goes well. How are you doing? Missing home today?

Terribly. The elders were over to teach Andrea, though, so I made pumpkin pie. Your brother seemed especially pleased. His comp was disgusted by the thought of carrots in Jell-O, however. It's a good thing I didn't make that particular delicacy. She chuckled to herself.

I'm not sure I'm in love with the combination myself.

She couldn't help laughing—she remembered his look of derision when someone had brought it to a church potluck when they had been dating. *Have you been skiing yet?*

They bantered back and forth for a bit about his skiing addiction, debated if Utah or Yorkshire were colder—she figured she had a decisive victory there if you counted the average annual temperature and not just the winter ones—and then they circled back to pies so they could discuss the relative merits of pumpkin, apple, and pudding-filled varieties.

When she signed off half an hour later, Shelly felt as though they had managed to bring their relationship back to the easy camaraderie of old times. She had always been able to talk nonsense with him for hours as easily as more serious subjects. And when they were together, they could also stay silent without any strain between them.

He had mentioned his girlfriend near the end of their chat, and that brought an ache to her chest. She took a deep breath and pushed it away. Thousands of miles separated her from Rob, and she was happy to be where she was, in her current circumstances, regardless of other factors. Still, after she climbed into bed and turned off the light, she allowed a few tears to slip out, aching for home and her lost dreams.

Chapter 14

THOUGH ROB KNEW he ought to be thinking about Lindsey, his mind was on Shelly when he walked into his apartment after work. Her latest comment about life in England still made him smile. He could hear the hum of his aquarium in the background as he dropped his keys and the stack of mail onto the kitchen table. The bag of tacos he'd picked up on his way home joined the keys, and he walked over to the fridge to grab his jug of milk, which was lighter than it had been in the morning. The joys of having a roommate. He'd had a long day of sitting in front of a computer and was exhausted.

He settled into a chair, emptied the fast food bag onto the wooden tabletop, and twisted the cap off the nearly empty jug, tipping it to guzzle straight from the container.

The silence echoed around him. His roommate was getting married in February, so even when Garrett wasn't at work, he was rarely home. Rob's thoughts turned to Lindsey. She was expecting a proposal soon, he knew she was because she had brought up marriage in an off-hand way several times now—no way had it been random conversation. What was it they said about weddings multiplying? Maybe that only applied to singles wards.

Over the past month or two, he'd thought about asking Lindsey to marry him, even slowed down as he walked past the jewelers in the mall, but though he was starting to get pressure from several sides—one of which being his mom—he just couldn't do it. Not yet. They'd been dating for seven months, which should have been ample time to decide if the two of them would suit, but even though he cared about her, he couldn't bring himself to commit.

He took a final bite of the first taco and scrunched the wrapping into a ball, then threw it at the garbage can, missing by feet. He couldn't figure out why he was sitting on the fence—and apparently neither could Lindsey. He wondered how much longer she would put up with waiting for him to get serious about their relationship. He *wanted* to get serious, to get past whatever it was that held him back—he hadn't been shy about proposing to Shelly.

But he was over that whole relationship now. Completely over it—they were back to being friends again in the long-distance way that meant nothing. It was perfect, so it couldn't be what was causing him problems now. "Get a grip," he muttered to himself before taking a final bite of the second taco.

Irritated with himself, he sorted through the mail which had piled up in his box over the past several days. One stack was ads, the other bills. He paused as his eyes stopped on the return address in the corner of the bottom letter. L. Michael, his biological father—great. Disgusted, he scooped it up with the stack of ads and tossed them into the garbage can.

He returned to his seat and finished his dinner, then cleared away the wrappers and cleaned the kitchen, which had been teetering on the verge of disaster for several days now. When it was back under control, Rob sorted through his bills and paid them. He tried to ignore the tug at his mind as he stacked his bills on the end of the counter, ready to be sent back. What did Leland want? Why the letter? Why wouldn't he leave Rob alone?

Rob wandered into the living room and fed his tropical fish, checking the temperature and tank chemistry. He glanced at the television in the living room and considered looking for a game, then decided he wasn't in the mood. Likewise, when he looked over his movie collection. For something to do, he cleaned the room and pulled out the old vacuum. Still, the thought of the letter refused to shake loose.

It was time he should have been in bed, but he didn't think he could settle down. He told himself it was because of his relationship with Lindsey, but he couldn't fool himself—it was the letter all the way.

In disgust, he fished the envelope from the bottom of the garbage can. It was splattered with hot sauce on one side, but he opened it anyway, hating himself for not being able to leave it alone.

His stomach clenched. He already had more than enough on his mind, and now Leland had to write. Again.

Still, there was a bit of anticipation as he unfolded the slip of paper and scanned it. The words filled the page, chatty, but stilted. Questions about how Rob was doing, how he liked his job. Leland mentioned the events in his own life. It barely registered.

Rob thought it over as he crumpled the letter and tossed it back into the garbage can. Once he would've been thrilled to get a letter like that. He'd dreamed about the possibility so many times as a kid. Now, however, it seemed pointless. Leland had taken little interest in his son over the years, and there was no reason for him to play the doting father now.

Rob had written Leland faithfully every week while he was on his mission, like a good little missionary was supposed to. It had been one of the hardest things he'd ever done. What did get in return? One lousy Christmas card. After all the disappointments and broken promises, Rob wouldn't risk rejection again.

❁ ❁ ❁

CLASSES FINISHED, SHELLY'S final exams were only days away, and the elders came over for the last missionary discussion. She would finish her exams Wednesday, but wouldn't head home until Thursday evening. As she handed Elder Durrant a piece of the cake she had made earlier, she thought of his brother, as she found herself doing with increasing frequency of late.

"Are you going home for the holiday break?" he asked.

"Yes. I'll leave on Thursday." She already had one bag half-filled with mementos to give to her family. She glanced at him again. "Is there anything you'd like me to take home for you? Nothing big, but a few keepsakes? I'm sure I could squeeze in a surprise for your parents."

As soon as the words were out of her mouth, she wondered if her offer was a mistake. Why was she torturing herself by arranging an excuse to see Rob when she knew he was dating someone else? Still, she had suggested it, and the thought of the smile a surprise package would bring to his mom was reason enough. She had been very kind to Shelly when they met at Rhett's farewell, though there had been so many people around, there hadn't been much time to talk.

"Seriously? That would be great." A smile stretched across Rhett's face and his eyes danced. "My parents would love it. You live in Ephraim, though, don't you?"

"Yes, but we can make arrangements." She nearly stopped, but continued, wanting to follow through with her offer, now it was made. "I could arrange to meet Rob. He lives in Salt Lake, right?"

Again Elder Durrant lifted his right eyebrow, his expression saying he remembered her relationship with Rob. "That would be brilliant. How much space do you have?"

"Maybe the size of a basketball?" she suggested. "I'll have to weigh my bag and see where it comes out, but I can probably carry another ten pounds."

"All right. I really do appreciate it. Mom will be thrilled." He ate a couple bites of cake before turning his attention to Andrea. "So, you want to meet with us again after the holidays?"

"Yes." Andrea had eaten some of her cake, but mostly poked at it, nibbling on her bottom lip. Though she had admitted to believing the gospel was true, she'd hesitated to accept the call to baptism without speaking with her family first, even if only as a formality. When she had expressed her concerns of angering her parents even more if she was baptized without discussing it with them first, everyone agreed she should go home for the holidays and try to make her parents understand her feelings about it first.

Shelly hoped Andrea's family wouldn't talk her out of becoming a member, but knew it could happen. On the other hand, Andrea had been considering and praying about whether to join the Church for a long time, so maybe she would have the strength to make the choice she believed in, even without her family's support.

SHELLY'S FLIGHT ARRIVED in Salt Lake City a little before seven p.m. It had been a long trip—she'd taken a train to London the previous evening, then sat at the airport for several hours before her plane left early in the morning. After she met up with Lily, they would still have over two hours of driving to get to their parents' home in Ephraim—not counting the stop at Rob's to drop off the things Rhett sent back with her. Adding in the seven-hour time difference, she had been traveling for almost thirty hours.

She looked at her visit home with a mixture of excitement and dread and was almost glad for the long trek from the gate to baggage claim, tired passengers streaming up and down the terminal. She saw a mixture of emotions and exhaustion on their faces.

She was excited to be with her family and spend time with friends, but she also dreaded the memories her home town would bring up of her and Jimmy, and worried she might feel guilt again for finding a life without him, for wanting to make something special out of what she had.

The guilt had clung to her like a second skin until after the yellow roses arrived on his birthday and she had truly begun to mourn, but though it had mostly faded, she was concerned it wasn't gone forever. She also worried her friends and family might watch her every step, wondering if she would revert to the introverted, near-silent girl who had inhabited her body for months after Jimmy's death.

"Shelly, it's so good to see you!" Lily said as Shelly stepped off the escalator with her carryon.

Shelly threw her arms around her older sister and they hugged tight, rocking slightly from right to left. They both teared up, and when they finally released each other, they had to pause to wipe away the evidence, laughing.

"It's good to be back," Shelly said, glad she could mean it for the moment. "Thanks for picking me up. I'm sure the extra drive with the kiddos wasn't fun." People streamed past them as they met those waiting for them. Steven called out greetings to her from the back of the double stroller. His younger sister waved and chatted from the front seat. She wondered how unhappy they had been to get back in the car after the long drive from Denver a couple days earlier.

Lily brushed back her brown hair, which was longer than Shelly had seen it in years. "Day or night, I'd be here. I had a hard time convincing Mom not to come, even though she's already stressed to the max without losing half a day. She has so much to prepare for the church Christmas party next week, but she would've been here if I hadn't insisted on doing it myself. Curtis said he's sorry to miss you today. But he'll fly in after the game Tuesday night." Lily looked Shelly over.

"I can't say you look tanner."

Shelly laughed out loud as the kids started clamoring for food. "It's no wonder the English are so pale—it never gets warm enough to swim outside or sunbathe—well, not warm enough for my liking, anyway."

"As long as paleness doesn't mean you've been working too hard to venture out of your apartment." Lily handed each of her kids a cracker. "Let's go."

Shelly leaned over her niece and nephew in the stroller and gave them kisses. Stephen's light brown hair curled around his face. It was sticky on one side from a sucker wrapped in his grip. He hurried to tell her all about his dog, Bark. Sophie talked alongside him at top speed, though Shelly only understood a little of what she said.

"How's everything going?" Shelly asked Lily as she plucked her suitcase from the baggage carousel.

"Busy, busy. Of course, Curtis's schedule is always insane. I haven't had a lot of time to take things easy, with Steven in preschool and me getting ready for the new baby." She placed her hand on her stomach, which was starting to swell. They headed for the elevator to the parking garage.

"You look happy." Actually, Shelly thought her sister practically glowed. Curtis must be doing a lot of things right, despite his hectic basketball schedule. Of course, with what she now knew about Lily's first marriage, Curtis was practically guaranteed to make her happier than she had been before.

Lily smiled as they navigated through the crowd. "I am. I like Denver, I'm thrilled about our new little one, and Curtis is a great husband. Sometimes I have to stop and think to myself, wow, is this what other people's marriages are like? Is it really supposed to be this good? Not that it's perfect, but it's so much better than when I was married to John."

"I'm so, so glad. You've had enough problems, you deserve to be happy." Shelly had watched the fallout from Lily's first marriage first-hand, so she knew it had been pretty nightmarish.

The elevator doors opened as they reached them, so they walked right in and rode up to the parking lot. "Are you hungry?" Lily asked. "It's past dinnertime for us, and Steven's been begging for a hamburger since five minutes after lunch."

"Yeah, I could eat, even if my body does think it's after midnight. I also need to drop a package off for a missionary whose family lives around here. His brother's apartment is just off Bangerter Highway." Shelly wasn't ready to answer question about Rob—she was nervous enough as it was.

She thought about seeing him again, and about the way she felt when she talked to him during the pageant. Their chats on Facebook made it clear they were finally friends again, though they had kept things very light and not too personal. Would that connection she'd felt before still linger between them? *It doesn't matter,* she reminded herself. *He's still dating Lindsey. You have your friendship back. Be satisfied with that.*

She could try, anyway.

It was a beautiful winter night as they headed south. The mountains towered over the valley, rugged and covered in pristine snow. There was nothing like them in the UK, and they were an awesome sight under the nearly full moon, their majesty brought a lump to Shelly's throat. The stars were well hidden by the city lights, but once they got onto Highway 6 she should be able to see them well. It seemed like it was almost always cloudy in Hull, so she enjoyed the clear sky, even if the air was breath-stealingly cold.

"So, where does this guy live?" Lily asked once they were headed south on Bangerter.

"Turn right at 76th." She pulled out the directions Elder Durrant had given her, and before long they parked in front of a three-story apartment complex. Cars were parked shoulder to shoulder in the lot, and Shelly was grateful for the section marked Visitor Parking or Lily would have to drop her off and circle the block.

"Number thirty-six, up there on the top floor. I'll only be a couple of minutes." Shelly pulled out the plastic bag and headed up the walk, glad it had been cleared since there was easily more than a foot of snow on either side. She'd messaged Rob that she would stop by with something from his brother and the approximate time, so he knew to expect her. Her hands shook and her stomach was full of butterflies. What would he think? What should she say? Her thoughts were all jumbled together and she was abnormally aware of the sound of her shoes grinding against the rock salt someone had spread on the pavement

Shelly scaled the metal steps to the third floor and turned left. She touched her hair, hoping it wasn't a mess. It hung down her back in a virtual avalanche and she wondered if she should have combed it out. All of those hours of travel could not have been nice to her appearance—and why didn't she think about it before this moment?

She knocked on the door and waited while she heard someone moving around inside. A man wearing only faded blue jeans and a dingy muscle shirt opened the door and peered out at her. His dishwater blond hair was ruffled and he had a few days' growth on his chin, as if she'd awoken him.

"Yeah?"

Shelly tried not to laugh. "Hello, is Rob in?"

He turned his head inside and called out. "Hey, Rob, some foreign chick is here to see you." The guy stood back, opening the door for her.

"Chick," Shelly muttered in disgust as she stepped inside. His comment about her being foreign surprised her, had she picked up a slight English accent?

Surprisingly, the apartment wasn't as messy as the man. There were a few dirty dishes on the table and a couple of jackets lay on the floor inside the door. On one wall was a large fish tank—probably about thirty gallons, she guessed. It held a variety of tropical fish and reminded her vividly of the tank Rob had owned in college—though it had been much smaller.

"What?" Rob emerged from a door in the hallway, pulling off his tie.

The breath caught in her throat when Shelly saw him. *How could he possibly be better-looking than I remember?* "Hi, Rob."

"Hi, Shelly." Rob crossed the living room in two long strides. His hand lifted to hug her, a gesture that once would have been natural between them once. But he pulled it back before he got too far sliding his hand into his pocket. "How was your trip?"

She felt an almost visceral response to the lack of hug, but she tried to hold it back. No way could she still love him after so long—they had both changed. It wasn't reasonable.

She spoke over the lump in her throat. "Long, and not over yet. I love England, but I'm excited to be home for a while." As if drawn toward him by a magnet, Shelly took one step closer.

"It's so good to see you." He took the final step that separated them and, after another moments' hesitation, pulled her into the tight hug she had been craving.

Shelly smelled the familiar fragrance of his aftershave, lingering faintly, though he must have put it on many hours earlier. She smiled as the scent took her back in time to her days at USU. "It's good to see you too." She peeled back reluctantly and handed him the plastic shopping bag Rhett had given her. "If you or your parents want to send anything back to Rhett, I'll be happy to take it for you."

"I know my mom'll be thrilled to get this. It's very thoughtful of you." He gestured with the bag. "Thanks, I'll pass on the message."

Emotions swirled through her and she had to take a deep breath in an attempt to quell them. "Now, how are you doing?"

"I'm great, staying busy. Skiing regularly now. And yourself? How's school in England?"

"School's going really well. I feel good about my exams and I'm looking forward to next semester's classes." After standing there for a long moment, unsure what else to say, her heart full of the million things she wished she could talk to him about, Shelly pulled a paper from her pocket. "Here's my parents' phone number in Ephraim. If you have something for me to take back, just ring me and I'll be happy to stop by."

"Ring you? You even sound British." He took the paper. "Thanks again. It's good to see you." He pulled out his wallet and placed the note in one of the compartments.

She wanted to say a hundred things, but decided it would be best for both of them if she took off. "Lily's waiting for me in the car. I better go, but it was nice to see you again. Have a good weekend."

"I will, and I'll call you to pick something up. I'm sure my mom will want to send a few things back." His eyes bored into hers as they stared at each other for a long moment. "Bye."

"Goodbye." Shelly opened the door and stepped onto the balcony, feeling off balance.

The door shut behind her, but the window must not have been very good because she could hear Rob's roommate tease him. "What was that?"

"What do you mean?"

"If I didn't know you were set to marry Lindsey, I'd say like, four alarm fire, man. You're totally into her."

He's getting married. Shelly's heart dropped and her confusion doubled. She told herself she hadn't expected him to stay single forever, but she knew part of her had.

Shelly shook her head as she returned to the car. Her pulse raced and her hands trembled slightly, as they often did when she was nervous or upset. She pushed away her errant thoughts and slid back into the car. It was ridiculous to think of Rob as anything besides a friend now or ever again. He was taken. She had missed her chance.

Why did that make her want to cry?

"What?" Lily asked as she maneuvered the car out onto the road. "Was he acting weird or something?"

"No. He was... exactly the way I remember him." Shelly rubbed a hand over her aching heart as Lily pulled up to the light at the highway. "Only even better-looking, if that's possible."

"Come again?"

"I didn't mention it was Rob Michaels. I brought the package home from his brother." *And he's engaged to someone else.*

"Wait. Rob—Superman Rob? The guy you were dating when Jimmy came home?"

"That's him." Shelly had gone crying to Lily when Rob had proposed, unsure which direction she should take. The sisters had cried together over their romantic entanglements, and then both were engaged within a couple of weeks.

"Oh. So, who you were seeing wasn't an important detail for you to share with me? Just a *little* thing?" Lily shot her an incredulous look. "You didn't tell me you were still in touch with him."

"Not still, more like again, and only on Facebook, and nothing much, occasional comments on each other's posts is all. And maybe a little chatting, but we keep it casual." Shelly felt her face heat and knew she was blushing, which made her grateful for the darkness. "He's been dating someone since last spring, so it hardly matters that we've managed to re-establish our friendship."

"Your *friendship?* Of course. Nothing more ever existed between the two of you." Lily voice dripped sarcasm. "And you just happened to run into his brother, and just happened to think to drop off a package to Rob."

"Running into Rhett *was* a coincidence. I didn't know he was serving in our area when my roommate decided to take the discussions." Shelly smiled, though she fought to hold back tears. "And, yes, I wanted an excuse to see Rob again. I'm glad I brought the package, but he's getting married, so that'll be the end of it. I'm happy for him." She turned her head to stare out the window, surreptitiously wiping at a tear. She *would be* happy for him. Eventually.

If Lily disagreed with Shelly's comment, she didn't say anything more about it.

Chapter 15

SHELLY'S FIRST DAY HOME had been full of visits with family and friends. She loved seeing everyone again, the decorated store fronts, light-pole decorations and general happiness that came with the season. There was so much to do, so many people to visit, she didn't have any time to think—she even wondered if that had been everyone's intention.

The day after she arrived marked one year since the horrible accident that had killed Jimmy, and she didn't have a chance to brood over it. The dreams of the accident had returned the night before, stronger than ever after driving through the similar canyon to come home from the airport. Still, she managed to put on a smile and fake her way through things when the memories overwhelmed her, and she snuck away to put flowers on his grave. She hadn't been to the cemetery on the north end of town very many times growing up, and she wished it had more trees to block off the noise of cars passing between town to the south and Walmart directly to the north.

Still, as she set the yellow roses next to the bright lilies someone else had delivered earlier in the day, she turned her back to the shopping behemoth and focused on Jimmy for a few minutes. "Hey, there, it's me. I know, I haven't visited for a long time. England has been great, such a nice change of pace and new experiences. I'm sorry that I wasted so much time moping here when I know you would have wanted me to get on with my life. I still miss you every day, though. I hope you find a moment to think of me with everything you're busy doing up there. I like to think you peek down now and then to see what I'm up to, so you probably already know about El and Andrea." Still, she took some time to tell him about her roommates and how great they had been for her.

She also told him about Rob, and apologized for not telling him before. Though she still felt a little guilty about that, she was glad she had chosen Jimmy in the end, if only so he would die knowing she loved him.

Then she told him about how she wanted to be able to move on; but that she wasn't quite ready yet, but she hoped it wouldn't be too much longer. She ended by telling him she would always love him.

By the time she turned to leave, the cold winter breeze had nearly frozen the tear-trails she had been wiping off her face, her nose was running, and her toes were going numb.

It had been worth it though, even though she knew he wasn't here in this cemetery—he was somewhere better and happy.

As she prepared for bed that night—hours after her body had started complaining that it was ready for sleep—she realized she should have visited Jimmy's family. The day would have been as tough for Carol, Jimmy's mother, as it had been for Shelly. Though she knew the next few weeks were packed with parties, she promised herself to make it to Carol's soon.

When she woke in the wee hours of the night, her body refusing to go back to sleep, and her mind too wound up from nightmares, she spent the extra time digging through a box of keepsakes from high school, then paged through her scrapbooks. She cried off and on through the whole thing as she flipped the pages and read the notes she'd made about the activities she and Jimmy had enjoyed. The pages were covered in a light coating of dust—or maybe it only seemed that way.

She pulled out the box of letters she'd kept from his mission and cried over a few more of them, even as they gave her comfort. Then, exhausted, she crawled into bed with the stuffed purple puppy Jimmy had given her for her eighteenth birthday tucked under the covers with her.

Being home was tough, but she hoped it would also be healing.

WHEN JIMMY'S MOTHER, Carol, approached her in church the next day, Shelly felt a pang of guilt, but she offered a smile to the woman who had always treated her as a beloved daughter.

"Shelly, your mom said you'd be here today. How are things going in England?" Carol pulled her into a tight hug, then released Shelly and studied her face.

Shelly knew the woman was looking for the dead look in her eye that plagued her the previous summer. "It's been great. I'm learning so much and seeing all kinds of places around the country. When I go back next month, I'll take a trip across the channel with some of the international students to visit France. I'm very excited."

"That sounds wonderful. I'm glad you're having such a fun time there."

"I really am. I do get homesick a lot, and I have to work my tail off to keep up in school, but it's been so great. I'm making so many friends."

Carol squeezed Shelly's arm. "I know everyone here is thrilled to have you home."

Shelly laughed. "You don't have to tell me! It seems like everyone has stopped me to ask about England. It's almost a shame the bishop didn't ask me to speak so I could give an accounting to the whole ward at once!"

"I'll bet you're feeling loved right now though, aren't you?"

"Of course I am. This is the best place on earth." Shelly took a deep breath and met Carol's gaze. She tried to fight back the tears welling in her eyes. "I should have stopped by yesterday. I'm sorry I didn't think about it until it was too late, they kept me busy most of the day. It must have been very hard for you."

"It was, but I've felt—not happy, because I'll never stop missing him— but *okay* about Jimmy's death for a good while now. I know there was a reason he had to go Home, even if the accident seemed senseless to us." She dabbed at her eyes and they shared a commiserating smile. "I have something for you at my place. I'd appreciate it if you stopped by so we can talk more. There's so much to say, and I want to hear all about England."

"I'll make the time to come by. I promise." Shelly gave her another hug and took a deep breath to bring her emotions back in check.

THE WEEK FLEW BY in a flurry of activity as everyone pitched in to make holiday treats, wrap last-minute gifts, and take care of all the other little details that were part of the Christmas season. Her best friend, Katie, stopped by, and they spent an afternoon catching up, making Shelly long for her days at USU.

On several occasions, Shelly took to wandering the neighborhood, reliving memories. Every corner, street, and landmark held memories of Jimmy, and Shelly revisited them all as she walked. She still couldn't make sense of his death, but though she would always love and miss him, it was becoming easier to deal with.

Christmas Day, after all the presents had been opened and the wrapping paper cleared away, Shelly slid the homemade rolls into the oven for their big family dinner that night. It had been nice having Lily and Curtis with them, and her younger sister Kellie got an engagement ring for Christmas and was almost unbearably happy.

Shelly was thrilled for her, but found herself on the cusp of tears all day. She set the oven timer. The phone rang down the hall, quickly followed by the youngest Cox, her sister Danyelle, hollering that the phone was for Shelly.

"Hello, this is Shelly," she said when she'd lifted the phone to her ear.

"Hi, this is Rob. How are you enjoying your break?" he asked.

A burst of happiness filled her as she recognized the voice. It was ludicrous for her to be so happy, especially since she'd been on the verge of tears minutes earlier, but she couldn't help it. "Really well—everything's set. How are you?"

"I'm well. I just pulled out the package you brought us. My mom was giddy with excitement."

She slid down the wall and hugged her knees to her, feeling like a silly teenager talking to the boy she'd had a crush on for ages. "How's your family doing?"

"Great. My sister Michelle graduates from the U in a couple weeks. Natalie loved USU. My mom got a promotion to head librarian. She says thank you for the package. She thinks you're an angel, and wants to know how much room you have to take something back to Rhett."

"A little more room than what I brought home for you, but it needs to be in a bag that can be easily opened. And don't wrap anything, or I could have problems in customs." She loved knowing how happy the package had made his mom. It made Christmas seem more real.

"I'll let her know." He paused for a moment and she could hear voices in the background. "When are you planning on heading back through here?"

"In two weeks, on the ninth. I don't go back to school until January seventeenth, but I have a trip across the channel to France with a group of international students. I'm very excited. I'll probably go up to Orem the night before my flight and stay with my cousin, so I'll stop by sometime that Sunday to pick up Rhett's package. I fly out very early Monday." She clamped her mouth shut, realizing she had gotten too wordy. She was letting her excitement to be talking to him get to her—which was stupid. Beyond stupid.

"Great."

"So, what have you been doing to stay busy, besides work?" She twirled a lock of hair in her left hand, wrapping a ringlet around her first finger, her bare feet sunk into the long carpet fibers. When she sniffed, she could almost taste the yeasty scent of the rolls baking, even though they hadn't been in there long enough to smell them yet. She loved being home.

"Skiing, naturally."

"Naturally," she agreed. "Has your new ward roped you into any solos in church yet?"

"No. I'm hiding that particular talent. I'm much better at duets, anyway."

She felt warmth grow inside her chest at his words. They had sung so many duets together. "You only need someone to hold your hand when you get stage fright," she teased.

"Exactly. You haven't mentioned anything about *you* singing lately."

She chuckled. "Guilty as charged. I've been too busy to join the ward choir and haven't caught anyone's notice yet, I guess."

"How about you? Anything exciting going on in England?"

"I've taken a few trips with the international students, I'm staying busy with the young adults in my ward, and school's pretty crazy. That seems to be enough." She closed her eyes, and saw scenes of the times she and Rob spent together in college flashing through her mind—memories of sand volleyball, water fights, and hanging out, usually with a crowd of roommates, filled her head.

Another image of moonlight and damp grass snuck in, one with a kiss that haunted her for weeks, leaving her shaky and wishing she could have given him any answer but no. She pushed that memory away, remembering Rob's roommate's words. He was engaged. Off limits. Her throat closed off and she found it difficult to speak, though she wasn't sure what to say.

"Well, I probably better let you go," he said after a long, silent moment. "But it was good to talk to you again. I'll see you in a few days."

"I'll call first so we can meet up."

"Sounds good. Bye."

"Goodbye." She sat on the line for a few seconds after he hung up, wondering where the time had gone. Wondering why the pain of losing Jimmy was crashing down on her again. Was it guilt because of her call from Rob? Why would that make her feel guilty now?

THOUGH SHE'D HAD the best of intentions, Shelly's three-week visit home was more than half over before she made it to visit Jimmy's mom. Carol greeted her with another hug. "Shelly, it's so good to see you!" She led Shelly into the family room

They chatted about things in town, at school, their families, everything imaginable—except for Jimmy. Nearly an hour passed before they broached anything near the subject. "I've wondered for a while now," Carol began hesitantly.

"Yes?" Shelly prompted when she didn't continue.

"When I sent you the flowers in October, did it feel cruel? At the time I felt so strongly that Jimmy wanted you to have them, but afterward I wondered if it was harder on you to get them."

Shelly smiled weakly, unable to force a laugh. "It was hard on me, but," she stopped Carol before she could start to apologize, "I think I needed them. The flowers were what pushed me to start healing instead of walking around like a zombie, pretending to live. It was hard, but I think you did the right thing. It *was* necessary." She covered the woman's hand with hers. "I appreciate it."

"I'm so glad to hear that. I worried I'd made a huge mistake and made things worse for you." Carol blew her nose into a tissue and blotted at her eyes. "You were kind of zombie-ish for a long time. We all worried about you."

"Thanks. It's still not easy, you know it's not, but it's getting better every day. Thanks for your support."

"And now, I remember how upset you were when we announced we were going to take Jimmy off the machines and allow his organs to be donated to help others."

Shelly rubbed her face. That had been such a nightmare. She'd been far beyond capability of rational thought, so she'd overreacted, even knowing he couldn't be helped and wouldn't survive. "I'm so embarrassed by the way I acted. You made the right decision, of course. I know there was nothing else they could do for him."

"I'm glad you see that now. It turns out his liver and kidneys were damaged too much in the accident to be used, but the doctors were able to use his heart, lungs, corneas, and many other parts to help people. I'm told twenty-five people were taken off the organ, eye, and tissue lists because of Jimmy." She picked up a piece of paper and handed it to Shelly. "I thought you might like to read this."

Shelly's hands trembled as she accepted the single-spaced page, which was signed only with initials. Taking a fortifying breath, she started reading from the beginning.

Hello, I find myself struggling for the words to express my feelings, knowing the blessing I received was brought about by your loss. I'm a twenty-seven-year-old wife and mother. I have two young children, and due to an accident when I was thirteen, had never seen their faces.

The gift you gave me last December has changed all of that, however, and I'll never be able to thank you enough for the ability to see my son's eyes brighten with delight or the dimples in my daughter's cheeks. The terror that one of them would get into trouble and I wouldn't be able to stop them has come to an end. My life may not have literally been saved by the transplants I received, but it has been forever changed for the better.

The letter went on, but Shelly's eyes were unable to focus through the tears that flowed down her face. This was one woman—only one of the twenty-five people who benefited from Jimmy's death. While the thought of anyone benefitting would have caused a huge wave of anger the previous summer, now it filled her with peace. She wiped her eyes and struggled through the rest of the letter, before returning it to Carol. "Thank you. That was beautiful, and I know Jimmy is so happy to have helped this family."

"I needed to share it with you. I hoped it would make a difference." Carol took the letter and folded it back up.

"I'm sure it will. I've found my feet this semester, but I appreciate you sharing it with me. It does make me feel better." Shelly took the tissue Carol offered and wiped her eyes, sure her makeup would be a streaky mess by now. "I ought to head home."

"Yes, of course, but first," Carol picked up a small gift bag that had been sitting beside the table. "I didn't get around to cleaning out his room until a few weeks ago, getting it ready for Craig, who came home from Japan last month. It was too painful before." Shelly nodded in understanding. "This was down in a drawer. I wish I'd looked sooner."

Shelly took the bag and peeked in. It contained a letter and a wrapped box with her name scribbled on it in Jimmy's handwriting.

"I remember him talking about getting you something special for a wedding gift, now that I think about it," Carol said as Shelly pulled the box from the bag.

Shelly's hands trembled and she wasn't certain if she dared open it. Though it had been a great trip home, it had been hard dealing with the memories, forcing her to cope when she hadn't before moving to England. This was another hard step, knowing Jimmy had wrapped this for her before he died. In the box was a layer of tissue paper, and Shelly uncovered a beautiful silver locket. It was heart-shaped, with roses and ivy engraved on the front. When she opened it, she found a picture of him on one side, and a picture of her on the other. She didn't know where he'd gotten them.

She handed it to his mother, and then noticed the back was engraved. Carol returned it and Shelly flipped it over. It read, *"To my love, forever in my heart."* Shelly had to cover her mouth to stop the cry she knew was about to escape. A few tears escaped onto her cheeks as she dealt with the wave of grief and love that swept over her. It was so like him. "Thank you, Carol. I'll head home now, if you don't mind. I could use some fresh air."

"Of course. Drop in again if you have time before you return to school." She pulled Shelly into a tight hug.

Before she could make her escape, Craig, Jimmy's younger brother, walked in the front door. A smile spread on his face when he saw her and he crossed the room in two quick strides. "Shelly, it's so good to see you again." He wrapped her in a hug, and she appreciated his sibling-like embrace.

"Hey, Craig. Welcome home. How was the mission?"

"It was awesome, but it's great to be back." He released her, then took a closer look at her face. "Did I come at a bad time?" He reached out and wiped a tear from her cheek.

"No, you came at a great time. I was about to go, actually, and I'm glad we got a chance to talk." She shook her head, marveling at how tall he'd grown, and that he'd added a few inches between his shoulders too. "If you don't stop growing or filling out, we'll have to start calling you Paul Bunyan."

"Other than the red nose, you're looking pretty good too," he teased. "I meant to catch you in church the other day, but you're too sneaky for me. How are things in England?"

They talked for ten minutes before Shelly felt she could get away. She was glad to have had a chance to speak with Craig—he and Jimmy had been close and it was good to see him doing so well.

When she left, Shelly decided she needed time to think, so she took the long way home.

She wandered slowly down the quiet streets of Ephraim. A dog barked in a backyard and she passed young children playing in the fresh snowfall, though it was too dry for packing. If it hadn't been for the newer cars, she could have believed herself to be back in the seventies or eighties. Coming home again had brought a sense of timelessness. Change was hard to believe when she was surrounded by all of this sameness.

Reaching home, she knew everyone would be in the living room talking, or sitting down to lunch. Not ready to face them, Shelly went into the backyard and cleared off a swing, sitting even though she was already shivering and she knew she would be wet when she stood again. She pulled the locket out to look at it and put it on. Then she grabbed the letter she had stuck in her pocket in her hurry to leave. It was dated December 15th— the day before the accident.

Dear Shelly,

I can hardly tell you the joy I feel as I write you this letter. I have waited so long to make you mine and to have you with me always. I want you to know that I love you and always will, no matter what the future holds for us. I love you for your goodness, your sweet heart, and kindness. I know you will make a wonderful wife and mother because you love so well. You were meant to share that love with those around you.

Shelly, the Lord has plans for us, and we need to remember that His plans are not always our plans. There will be disappointments and setbacks in our marriage, but no matter what, He will be there for us, if we try to live for Him. He'll not lead us astray or forget us, even in the midst of pain. This locket says it all. Regardless of what life brings us, whatever the trials, you are my love, forever in my heart,

Jimmy

A cold breeze cut through her coat, chilling her bones as if trying to fight the warmth in her chest. She lingered over the words, hearing him say them in her head. She'd known his inflection so well, the cadence of every sentence on his tongue. She closed her eyes and pictured his face, and peace washed over her. *It's okay. This is how it was supposed to be.* The words were soft, as if whispered in her ear. She opened her eyes quickly, wondering if someone was nearby. Then she realized the words hadn't come from around her. The voice had been Jimmy's.

Was he really there, or had she imagined it? *Does it matter?*

Suddenly she knew it was all right. The Lord was in control, and Jimmy had been needed on the other side of the veil. Indescribable peace filled her heart as she recalled the words she had heard. She reread the letter, proof of his love for her, and wept tears of relief.

Chapter 16

THE SECOND HALF OF her holidays at home flew by. Since the locket and letter, Shelly hadn't felt as sad as before. The long walks ended, unless she was walking with Danyelle, and the issues that had been plaguing her felt far less serious. The nightmares had even lightened in severity and regularity. She still missed Jimmy, and probably always would, but finally felt as though she had closure.

Before Shelly knew it, she was driving north to catch her plane back to England. She had made arrangements to meet Rob at his apartment to pick up the items for his brother and would then continue on to Rich and Denise's house for the night.

She lifted her hand to knock on Rob's door with nerves tingling through her veins. She reminded herself that she was happy to have his friendship back, but knew when he opened the door that she didn't really believe it. She missed the *something more* they had shared from the very beginning.

Rob smiled as he motioned her in. "Come in. How was the visit home?"

"It was wonderful. I've missed everyone so much." She looked into his eyes and their gaze held. *You're near the top of that list.*

"I'm sure the feeling was mutual." His eyes shifted to focus on something else, and he led her over to the couch. "So you'll have your master's when you're done. Any idea what you'll do?"

"Not really. I'll be able to teach lower-level history classes at junior colleges. Maybe I can work on a PhD, but then, that leaves me with teaching or doing research." She wanted to kick off her shoes and tuck one leg under her, but decided that presumed she'd be there for more than five minutes, so she crossed her ankles instead. "I'm looking forward to this semester, though. I get to dig into history, not just learn how to study it. I've been jotting down notes all week about things I want to check on and possibilities for my thesis. I also have more family history research to do while I'm over there." She glanced around a bit. "You're spending Sunday afternoon alone?"

"Yeah, Lindsey's gone home to see her parents. I guess the Christmas break wasn't long enough." His smile was weak.

"It seems like we spend weeks preparing for Christmas, then it's over in a matter of hours," Shelly said. "Do you think maybe we've got it all backwards? Perhaps we should spend an afternoon preparing, and then enjoy ourselves for the rest of the holiday season."

"We could skip the extensive decorating and treat-making and sit around lazy instead." His grin brightened the room.

"But then I would miss my mom's famous Christmas cookies."

"Who says they can only be made for Christmas, anyway?"

"Good point. Maybe I'll make them for Valentine's and Easter too." The thought was enough to make her mouth water, and she decided she'd do that.

"And you can ship me a few, so I can give them a try."

Shelly laughed and leaned back into her seat, settling in for an interesting chat. If only they didn't live so far apart.

Oh yeah, and then there was Lindsey.

❁ ❁ ❁

THE MORNING AFTER SHELLY'S late arrival in England, she got on a boat to cross the channel to France. The trip acted like a buffer for Shelly, separating her life in Utah and everything she had learned on her trip home, from life at school. When she wasn't completely wrapped up in her adventures visiting the Eiffel Tower or strolling along the River Seine, she took a few moments to close up and put away the parts of her past she couldn't relive. Jimmy was gone, and Rob was getting married—as much as she wished it wasn't true.

It was time to look forward.

When she returned to her flat in England, all her roommates, Brad, and Chet were squeezed around the kitchen table playing a card game and eating junk food. Classes would resume in the morning, and Shelly was exhausted. What she wanted most was a hot shower and to tuck herself into bed.

Brad looked up at her entrance, a bright smile welcoming her into the room. "Come join us, Shelly. We'll start another round in a bit." His eyes studied her, lingering longer than necessary.

She took the moment to reevaluate as well. He was such a nice guy—not to mention good looking—and the invitation he extended seemed to be for more than cards. She felt torn, but then smiled in return. "Let me drop off my stuff and change." She often slept in a pair of sweat pants and a T-shirt—perfectly acceptable for mixed company. She told herself she was only going to play with them for a half an hour, catch up with everyone's holiday adventures, and then go to bed.

When she got back out to the kitchen, there was an empty chair for her between Brad and Andrea. A cup of hot cocoa sat on the table, putting off a wonderful aroma of chocolate and cinnamon. "Whose is this?" she asked as she sat.

Brad studied his cards, moving a few around in his hand, though Chet was taking his turn on the other side of the table. "Thought you might be thirsty. And cold. You're always complaining about it."

Surprised by the thoughtfulness, Shelly wrapped her hands around the steaming mug, pulling it close. "Thanks. I appreciate it." Did she whine that much, or did he pay more attention than she thought? She sent a sideways look at El, and caught the knowing expression on her face.

Shelly returned her gaze to Brad as she took a sip of the cocoa. He glanced her way. "Have a good trip to France?"

"Yeah. It was fascinating, and the trip home was good. You?"

"It went well. We went to France too—my parents took us to Nice to see my grandparents. I always enjoy it there. It's been quiet here since we came back for work, though." He tossed down a few cards and drank the end of his cocoa. "It's good to have you back."

She smiled, feeling her cheeks heat with his words, and turned her attention to Andrea, who called out that she was the winner.

109

As she climbed into bed almost two hours later, Shelly wondered how she had missed that Brad was so thoughtful and fun. Was she so stupid that she hadn't seen it earlier?

Maybe, she thought as she drifted into sleep, she hadn't been ready to act on it before.

❀ ❀ ❀

AS THE WEEK PROGRESSED, Shelly started noticing all the clues she'd missed about Brad. He was always offering to take her shopping, sharing a treat, or making her a cup of cocoa or the herbal tea he stocked in his sister's cupboard. He made sure they got out to run regularly and pulled her away from school work when she would otherwise hole up without coming up for air. In every little action, he offered her friendship without strings—but now that she was in a place where she could consider something more, she saw indications that he'd be happy to alter their relationship if she gave him some encouragement.

She could warn him up front that she was going home soon and not to get any ideas, but there were two problems with that: First, it assumed something serious would develop between them and that was stupid—it was just interest, maybe even curiosity, so why was she looking ahead to the future?

Second, knowing that Jimmy was coming home, and that Shelly was serious about him, hadn't stopped Rob from falling in love with her, or her from falling for him. She'd learned the hard way that things didn't always turn out the way you planned, and when they didn't, you were bound to get hurt.

Then she wondered if she was avoiding things with Brad because she was scared rather than for the reasons she had been giving herself. Was she comparing him to Rob, or considering him on his own merit? Thoughts tumbled through her head as she tried to separate her feelings for the two men.

She couldn't deny that Brad was a great guy, and that he had been a wonderful friend. She even felt attracted to him—a feeling which was growing stronger every day. But she didn't know what she really thought about *him*.

After coming back from one of their afternoon runs, she went through the motions of cooking dinner while she considered everything.

The big question still hung over her—would it be fair to Brad to get involved in something she knew could only last a few months? Was the possibility of being hurt a good enough reason not to get involved any deeper? Was there ever a relationship that wasn't a risk?

"Hey, Shelly, how was your day?" Brad came in carrying a cake from the bakery down the street.

"Great, how was work?" She looked up from stirring the pan of noodles. She leaned over it, tasted the tomato sauce, and added a couple more shakes of basil.

"It was all right—for work."

"That should do it," she said to herself and put the lid back on the pot. When she turned around to face him, Brad watched her from the table. His gaze seemed to cut through her, analyzing her actions, expression, and mood. She realized she'd seen that look before.

"What?" she asked self-consciously.

"You just seem different. Did you have a good day?"

"I did. Class was fascinating, and I'm looking forward to this semester."

"Andrea will be home in a few minutes. She bought rolls," El said as she joined them, pulling a fruit salad from the fridge.

Brad talked about his coworker pulling pranks, and Shelly noticed the way his eyes crinkled at the corners when he smiled. His expression was emphasized by his thin, dark eyebrows.

After dinner, they sat to watch a movie in El's room. They clustered together on the bed, pillows propped behind them, sharing a bowl of popcorn.

"You don't laugh much," Brad said in a whisper. He sat between Shelly and El, Andrea on El's far side.

"Sorry, I guess my mind's somewhere else." Shelly turned toward him. Her blue eyes looked into his green ones, and the moment stretched between them. She could swear their eyes said so much more than words ever could. A shiver ran down her back and she had trouble breathing, but neither of them looked away.

"Where's that?" he asked softly after a long moment.

"Where's what?" She had lost the thread of conversation, too distracted by his angular cheekbones and the softness of his lips.

111

A smile crept onto his mouth. "Your mind. You said it was somewhere else."

She wasn't ready to admit the truth—that she'd been thinking of him, of the wisdom of encouraging his interest in her. Of acting on her interest in him. "Russia. Siberia, really. It's an intriguing place, don't you think?"

"Mmmm, especially at this time of year. All that... snow." The glint in his eye said he didn't believe of word of it.

"Imagine how popular cross-country skiing must be. And snow shoeing. And... ice skating."

"You think that might be why they always do so well at the Olympics? In figure skating, I mean?"

"I'm sure that's it." Shelly felt the heat rising in her cheeks and was glad the room was lit only by the television screen.

"Shhhh. If you're going to talk, you can go out to the kitchen," El said with a scowl.

Brad flinched, giving Shelly the impression that he got an elbow in the ribs. "Sorry," he muttered to El. He shot Shelly a long-suffering look. She fought back a smile and turned her eyes to the TV again.

Her determination to focus on the show—or anything besides Brad—wavered after only a few minutes, and she felt her attention drawn to him again. She didn't turn to gaze at him, but she was acutely aware of how close he was. She held in a sigh and wondered for the hundredth time if she had any business getting involved with someone she would say goodbye to in a matter of months.

She smiled shyly and tried to focus on the TV. Eventually she found herself wrapped up in the show.

Chapter 17

THEY HAD BEEN BACK to school for almost a week before Shelly, El, and Andrea were alone together to talk about Andrea's trip home. "So how did it go?" Shelly asked. She had expected Andrea to say something that first night, but with the guys there, she hadn't seemed comfortable. They all sat on El's bed, munching on a bag of cookies Shelly had brought.

"Did you tell your parents about wanting to be baptized?" El asked.

"I did. I waited until after Christmas, because I knew they wouldn't be happy about it." Andrea chewed on her bottom lip and pulled her legs up to her chest.

"And?' Shelly prompted when Andrea didn't continue.

"After the new year, I sat down with my parents and told them that I wanted to join the Church." She sighed loudly. "They were *not* thrilled. My mom tried to talk me out of being baptized. She's heard so many lies about the Church; I had quite a time explaining the truth. When I offered to call the missionaries so they could answer the rest of her questions, my dad put his foot down." She seemed to smile only to cover her desire to cry.

Several seconds passed before Andrea continued, but her voice sounded stronger when she did. "They didn't forbid me to get baptized, but they weren't happy about it." She laughed lightly. "The funny thing is, I don't think they would have minded if I had converted to almost any other religion—they just don't like the idea of me being a Mormon."

"I'm sorry you're having so much trouble," Shelly said, resting a hand on her friend's knee. "I'm sure in time they'll see how happy you are, and realize that it was a good decision." She paused. "You *are* still going to be baptized, aren't you?"

"Yes." Andrea sniffed and grabbed a tissue from the box beside the bed. "Yes, I'm still going through with it. I want to be a member. There were a few bad days after I spoke with my parents, but after a lot of prayer I realized I knew what I had to do. If this is right, then I can't turn my back on it. And I know it's right." She made a fist with her left hand and pressed it to her chest. Her voice broke, and tears made her eyes glisten, but conviction rang in her voice.

Shelly and El both hugged their roommate, and they called the missionaries to set up the baptismal interview.

❀ ❀ ❀

AFTER TWO WEEKS of thinking about her developing feelings for Brad, Shelly still didn't know what she wanted. It was early February, and in her preoccupied state, she had gotten far less studying done than she'd hoped. Andrea's baptism had been beautiful and perfect, and scads of ward members showed up to offer their support.

Shelly was keeping up with her classes, but just barely, and there was so much still coming up to distract her further. Like the trip to the Lake District that weekend.

Shelly sighed, enjoying the silence that hung comfortingly around her despite the late-morning hour. Finally, she arose from bed. She was so glad her peace in the morning solitude had returned. After Jimmy died, she had grown to hate solitude and quiet. It had become a time of torment. To be able to enjoy moments without noise and distraction was a balm to her soul.

As she moved around her room getting ready, she began planning her day. Her classes were finished for the week, even though it was only Friday, but Shelly had notes to review and organize, and she'd finally selected her thesis topic, so she needed to get permission to use it. She also hadn't been shopping in well over a week and had been without milk for several days—which had made breakfast difficult.

In the kitchen, she was surprised to see El packing a lunch. "I thought you had the day off."

"I was supposed to, but they called and asked me to fill in for Carry.

Brad planned to ring me this afternoon to go grocery shopping. I made a list, if you'd grab a few things for me." She gestured to a page she had attached to the fridge. "Or you can give it to Brad, if you don't need to go."

"No, I definitely need to go. I'll be happy to pick up a few things for you." Shelly tried not to roll her eyes when she saw the list of at least twenty items.

"Here's some money. If it isn't enough, let me know and I'll pay you back."

"Sure. Have a good day," Shelly said as El hurried out of the room, carrying her lunch bag.

Shelly looked at the clock on the wall. "Now, what do I do first?" She put a pan on the stove to start some hot cereal, and gathered her notes from the past couple days. Pulling up a chair, she sat at the table, one leg beneath her. She tugged her blue, oversized shirt down over her too-loose sweatpants and began sorting things out. She had lost weight since she started running regularly, and needed to replace a few items that no longer fit well.

For now she was more interested in her research. She had picked up a few things while in Bradford that could be used for her thesis. Most of it, however, was family group sheets. She had spent hours poring over parish records, trying to locate family members whose remains had long ago turned to dust.

She had searched online for records when she was a teenager, but she hit a brick wall. Now she hoped to find more in person; the search was not going as well as she'd hoped.

On the other hand, she had taken pictures of the ancient house her great-great grandmother had lived in as a child, as well as a number of other places around the area, and she'd visited a number of museums, which had given her interesting tidbits about what their lives may have been like.

She set aside the family history and focused on her thesis instead. Several hours passed and she was enjoying an apple to curb the hunger gnawing at her stomach when there was a knock at the front door.

"Did I wake you?" Brad grinned at her when she answered the knock.

"What? Oh, I forgot." Her hand wandered to her unruly hair, pulling the ponytail out of the elastic. "I was having some lunch," she said as they stepped into the kitchen. She gathered her hair into a more presentable arrangement. She really did need to get in the shower today—an hour ago would have been nice, she thought as she wondered if there were mascara streaks under her eyes.

"And doing homework again, I see. Have you finished your mid-term assignments yet?" he teased, though they were only a couple of weeks into the semester. He opened his sister's cupboard and pulled out a toaster pastry, then sat next to Shelly. "I rang El, but she's not answering. I thought maybe she left her phone in her room."

"No, she got called in to work." Shelly took another bite from her apple.

"Ah. They have a tendency to do that." He studied her oatmeal, empty yogurt cup, and apple core. "Tasty meal."

"I enjoyed it—and at least it's healthy." She sent a pointed look at his pastry. She didn't need to tell him the oatmeal was from breakfast. She had lost track of time.

He shrugged with a smile. "So, how's the data search going for your thesis?"

"I have tons of information, but I'm not sure how much of it is useable. It all depends on what else I find to bring it together." She saved the notes on her laptop. "El said something about going shopping. Are you still interested?"

"I have the rest of the day free. I'm at your service, ma'am," he answered with a formal bow of the head.

Shelly grinned in response.

Forty-five minutes later, Shelly was showered and dressed to go. She rang the doorbell at Brad's apartment, and Terrell answered.

"Here you are, once again. Don't you ever get sick of this guy? I mean, seriously, you could do so much better than a git like him. There's me, for example." He leaned languidly against the door jam. His long, ruddy hair fell down over his eyes, matching the light freckles that dotted his face. He wore tan corduroys and a dark blue polo shirt, managing to look preppy and comfortable at the same time. It was so Terrell.

Shelly chuckled despite herself. "Come on, Terrell, what would your girlfriend say?"

"Hey, back off, man. She has better taste than to go out with you." Brad pushed past him to join Shelly on the front walk.

"I'm concerned that her view of better taste than me is *you*... But there's no accounting," Terrell said.

Shelly laughed at the roommates' antics. It was kind of embarrassing, but she knew Brad teased Terrell's girlfriend about dating a loser sometimes.

"So," Brad changed the subject. "Are we buying out the store?"

"Yes, if El has anything to do with it. She asked me to pick a 'few' things up for her, and then gave me this list." She pulled it out of her pocket and opened it with a flourish.

He groaned, but took it to look over, then refolded and stuffed it in his shirt pocket.

AFTER THEY FINISHED SHOPPING and had put the food away in their own flats, Brad came back over.

"So, any plans for the evening—beside doing all your homework before it's assigned?" He noticed the stack of papers Shelly had been going over again on the kitchen table.

"I don't have anything in mind. How about you?"

"Would you like to go to the UCI? I understand there's a good film playing."

"Yeah, I'd like that." A smile crept across her face at the thought—she hadn't been to the movie theater in ages.

The movie turned out to be a good one—plenty of action, a little love, and no bedroom scenes, thank heavens.

They shared some popcorn between them and Shelly was acutely aware that their hands kept bumping into each other as they reached into the container. She shook her head, chiding herself for acting sixteen again.

When they came out of the cinema, it had snowed icy crystals that made everything glisten in the street lights, as if lit by a thousand miniature candles. The air was cold and nipped at their exposed hands and faces, taking her breath away. She realized she had chosen the wrong shoes when she started sliding all over the parking lot. It had been packed in the cinema lot, and Brad had to park on the far end.

"Careful, we don't want you breaking a leg. Casts are so inconvenient for running." He steadied her by the arm. Soon Shelly regained her footing and held onto his hand for extra help.

"Your hands are warm," she said as they sat in the car. "How is it that mine got so cold in the theater?" She wondered when she had gotten bold; it was so out of character for her.

"Let's see if we can rectify that situation." He reached over and took her hand.

She felt a thrill of hope and excitement run through her chest at his actions. She loved this part of relationships, the newness and anticipation of what might be around the corner. The fact that she and Brad had been dancing around, not acknowledging whatever this was between them for so long made it all the more interesting.

"Will you need a ride to where you're leaving for your trip in the morning?" Brad asked as they stood in her apartment entry a while later.

His offer was definitely welcome. "I had planned to take the bus, but would be eternally grateful if you could give me a ride over. I have to be there at seven."

"No problem. I'll see you in the morning." He brought the hand that he was still 'warming up' for her to his lips. He brushed his mouth along the backs of her fingers. She trembled as he looked into her eyes, and a silent bolt of understanding passed between them. Reluctantly he let go of her hand and broke the gaze, opening the outer door. "See you in the morning."

"See you." Hoping that moment hadn't been all in her head, he floated into her room and prepared for bed on autopilot.

After reading her scriptures that night, Shelly removed the chain and ring from where they had hung under her clothes since she left home. The nearly microscopic diamond sparkled in the lamplight as she studied it. So many chapters of the past lay recorded in the ring, even things that had happened long before she received it. She fingered the gold band for a long moment, then set it away in a drawer.

It was time to move on.

Chapter 18

WINTER WAS NOT THE BEST time of year to visit the Lake District, Shelly thought as she burrowed deeper into her coat. There was barely a skiff of snow across the ground, left behind from a light storm the previous day, but the air was damp and cold and a soft breeze teased the exposed skin along her neck and face.

The area was beautiful, though. Small lakes nestled in the valleys between ancient mounds of black rock. Quaint towns tucked at the foot of the hills and farmlands bordered by rock walls, created a picturesque view. She made a promise to herself to come back when everything was green and wild flowers would be out.

After a long day of sightseeing, Shelly and some of the other international students picked a restaurant a couple blocks away from the motel for dinner. Clay had been part of their group, and paid more attention to Shelly than to any of the other women in his sight line—though he didn't restrict himself to flirting with only her. He'd never struck her as the kind of man who would follow at a woman's heels, like some dedicated puppy, but his attention had been rather too focused.

"Why do you keep coming on these weekend trips?" Shelly asked him as they crossed the street to the pub where they would all eat dinner.

"There's so much world out there to see." He eyed her, his lips tipped up at the ends, though Shelly wouldn't have called it a smile. "Would you rather I stayed home?"

Yes. No. It confused her. He definitely added humor to the day, full of witty remarks, and coming up with random facts about their locations. He didn't spout off a full history, as a tour guide would have done, but he still shared insights. The day was always more interesting when he was around, but his attention was too pointed for her taste.

She couldn't believe he was as fascinated in her as he claimed to be, or as the message in his eyes said he was. In fact, she had been hard-pressed to figure out what his real reason was—thus her question. "It's generally nice having you around," she admitted. "You seem to know your way, and you do tend to entertain. On the other hand, if you've been here four times already, I have to wonder why you came again. I'm sure the lakes are nicer in the summer."

His lips tipped up even more. "You're right. You should come back in the summer when it's almost warm and everything's green." He reached out and pushed the hair back from her face. "I'd be happy to bring you."

She moved away from his hand, feeling a blush rise at the intent look in his eyes. She honestly didn't know what to make of him, but didn't have a chance to tell him thanks, but no, as someone else from their group opened the pub door and they all hurried in.

There was some jostling and laughter as they squeezed around a table, and Shelly wasn't surprised when she ended up wedged into the spot beside Clay. She was, predictably, the only one in the group who didn't order alcohol. After an hour or so, she wished she had chosen to eat at the restaurant attached to their motel. The group grew more boisterous as the pints were refreshed again, but she didn't want to walk the two blocks back to her motel alone in the dark.

The evening stretched and she played a couple of pathetic games of snooker, then was grateful when one of the other girls suggested returning to their rooms. She pushed her chair away from the table. "I'll come too. Anyone else ready to go back?"

"I'll come with you." Clay stood, threw a few pound notes on the table, and grabbed his coat. A few others joined them, but half the group opted to stay.

As the cold air rushed over them, slipping into every empty air pocket between her and her coat, Shelly snuggled in as deep as possible. She wished she hadn't forgotten her scarf when a breeze slid across her neck.

"Cold?" Clay put an arm around her shoulders and pulled her close.

"You always are, aren't you? I could warm you up, if you'd like. My roommate is still back at the pub."

Shelly shivered again, but this time she didn't think it was from the cold. She pulled out of his embrace, keeping her voice low so the others wouldn't hear. "Clay, I thought I made it clear that I'm not interested in dating you."

"I never called it a date." His grin made it clear he was thinking more along the lines of a one-night stand.

"And that's supposed to make me feel better?" She glared up at him. "The answer is 'no,' and that won't change. I wish you'd let it go."

They trudged on in silence for a nearly a block before he spoke again. "You keep sending me mixed signals." He stepped closer to her and set a hand on her shoulder. "It's like you're playing games with me."

"That's not true. I've never once hinted that I want anything romantic or intimate with you. The fact is, you won't take no for an answer." She stopped on the steps of the motel while the others went in, leaving them alone. "You need to let it go, Clay. It's not going to happen, and the way you keep bringing it up will only irritate me more. You're a nice guy, but I have no interest in a relationship, or whatever else you imagine happening between us."

"Fine. Sorry." He held up his hands as if to ward off her anger. "That's the end of it. I promise."

"It better be." Shelly clamped her jaw closed and hurried to her room. The worst of it was that she did like him. He was a nice guy, not to mention totally gorgeous. She could almost shrug her shoulders and go out with him—if she trusted him to keep his hands to himself—but she had promised herself never to get involved with someone who didn't share her values, and he definitely didn't. Not planning to get serious with anyone in England made little difference. If things developed with Brad, it would only be a few months of fun, but he shared her values, so it wouldn't be a problem. But she couldn't go against everything she believed to date someone who would push her to do things she didn't agree with.

When she reached her room, Shelly took advantage of the solitude to warm up in a hot shower before her roommate returned, then she fell into bed and slept.

THE REST OF THE TRIP finished without incident. Shelly hung out with some of the other students and Clay avoided them. When the bus pulled in the drive at the university, however, he approached her again.

As they got off the bus, he stopped her and guided her away from the others.

"Clay," Shelly said with a note of warning in her voice.

"I wanted to apologize for my behavior last night. You're right, I have been a *bit* persistent and I want to start over. Would you accept my apology?"

Shelly looked at him, her arms crossed in front of her chest. She studied his face for a long moment. *That sounded sincere enough, but I don't buy it,* she thought Still, she decided to give him a chance to prove he meant what he said. "See that it doesn't happen again."

He smiled as if she had given him absolution. "Would you like a ride home? There's plenty of room in my car."

"That won't be necessary." Shelly felt relief as she heard Brad's voice. She turned to look at him as he stopped beside her. She couldn't help but grin back at him when she saw his smile. She'd called him as they drew close to the city, but hadn't expected him so soon.

"I was afraid I wouldn't get here before your bus arrived," he said as he took her overnight bag. "Did you have a nice trip?"

"I did. Thanks for coming to get me." Shelly smiled, then turned to Clay. "As you can see, I've got it covered. Have a good week." She turned away and accompanied Brad to his car.

She didn't look back.

Chapter 19

BRAD DIDN'T BRING UP her private conversation with Clay until they reached the parking lot behind their building. "So what was that all about? I saw Fuller pull you aside to chat."

Shelly shook her head as they walked around the corner of the building. "I told him he needed to back off last night. He was apologizing."

"You didn't believe him, did you?" Brad looked a bit nervous about how she'd respond.

"I accepted it verbally. He sounded sincere enough, but I don't expect him to change." She sighed. "He's a nice guy, just not what I'm looking for."

Three beats passed in silence between them, and when Brad spoke again, his voice had dropped a few notes. "And what *are* you looking for?"

She felt a zing of excitement in her chest at his tone. She tipped her head to the side and looked up at him, and an embarrassed smile took over her mouth. His gaze was direct, but teasing and it cause heat to flood her face. "Someone who understands what's important to me."

"I'll bet that person's not so far away." Brad winked, then opened the door to her flat.

The zing increased to a trill and Shelly wondered if she'd be able to pass the extreme heat of her blush off as a reaction to the cold.

Brad dropped her bag at the door, and they joined everyone in the kitchen.

"Shelly, we expected you to call for a ride," El said.

"I called Brad, and he was able to pick me up." She tossed a smile in his direction, then took a chair across from Andrea. "Anything interesting happen while I was gone?"

"Not much. Last night we met at Sarah's to hang out." She mentioned one of the other single adults in their ward.

The front door opened and Candy came in, shopping bags hanging from each hand. "Hi, all. Have a good weekend? I found the best sales! Wait until you see the new skirts I picked up!" She breezed through and deposited the bags on the floor, then inspected her lava lamp. "How are you doing, baby?" She touched the glass and tipped her head, then spun to face them. When she spoke again, her voice was icy. "Who bumped her?" She stared at each of their faces. "The lava is all broken up. Who bumped her?"

"No one touched the thing," Andrea said.

When Candy gave Shelly a suspicious glare, she held up her hands. "Don't look at me—I've only been home two minutes."

No one claimed responsibility, and Candy let out an irritated huff. "Don't do it again. She needs tender loving care." She stroked the glass again, then snatched up her bags and stormed upstairs.

Everyone at the table shared an incredulous look, then burst into smothered giggles.

"I can hear you laughing!" Candy yelled.

Shelly covered her face with her hands, trying to hold it in.

"Is she for real?" Brad asked in a whisper.

"Don't ask. None of us understand." Andrea gulped in a couple of breaths.

"Would you like some hot cocoa?" Brad asked Shelly, as he stood and pulled a tin from his sister's cupboard.

"Yes, please," she answered. His thoughtfulness softened her a little more.

A moment later he joined them at the table with two cups.

She thanked him and he winked in reply as Andrea went off on a story about her own shopping trip. The conversation wandered on. Eventually Shelly excused herself to bed, glancing back for a last glimpse of Brad.

A COUPLE OF NIGHTS later, Shelly sat at the kitchen table studying when Brad came over after work. Shelly was surprised when she looked up and saw textbooks under his arm as he followed El into the kitchen.

"You're always sloggin' away at that homework. Do you ever stop?" he asked as he sat in the chair next to hers and spread out his own papers.

"Nope, I'm thinking about being a student for life. If I stop going to school, I have to get a job and pay my own bills." Shelly settled her book on her lap so she could see him. She loved that he would tease her about studying, despite the fact that he had obviously come with the same purpose in mind. "Did you have fun with your roommates last night?"

"Yes, it was good." A funny expression appeared on his face, but it disappeared in an instant. "How about family home evening? Anything interesting happen?"

"Interesting as in unusual or exciting? Then, no, but it was fun. We wrote our testimonies in copies of The Book of Mormon for the missionaries to give away, then hung out for a while."

They sat up for a couple of hours working on assignments before El stood and stretched. "If I'm going to get to work in the morning, I better head to bed. Don't stay up too late." She wagged her finger in Brad's face.

"Yes, ma'am." He saluted before she went upstairs to her room.

Shelly gave up on the book that still sat open on her lap. "Clearly I'm not studying this anymore." She closed it, making sure the paper stuck out to mark her place for the next day. She was getting tired and her brain was on overload. Time to go to sleep and let her mind straighten it out and slot it into some kind of order so she could start over the next day.

Brad took the book from her and set it on the table.

Shelly pulled out the leg she'd been sitting on and winced at the pins and needles that shot down to her toes. "If I read one more history date tonight, my eyes will start swimming."

"You look tired." Brad pushed a few strands of hair away from her face and tucked them behind her ear. "Like you should have gone to bed hours ago. Trouble sleeping?"

"No, just staying up studying." She tipped her head to the side and smiled at him. She liked having him so near, more or less alone with her. Every moment they spent together, she liked him better. "Waking up early to get back to work. It's the social life, stealing my study hours from me, that's the problem."

His eyes focused on hers and his voice dropped, both in pitch and volume. "Is that so? Do we need to cut a few extra people from your schedule so there's room for the rest of us?"

She sucked in an uneven breath. "I could think of a few I wouldn't mind trimming out." She was mesmerized, and felt a shiver slide down her spine.

"Not me?"

Her voice was barely more than a whisper when she returned, "No. Never you."

Then his mouth was on hers and she leaned into him, enjoying the moment, testing the waters of this new relationship. He threaded his fingers into her hair, holding her there while he tasted her mouth. Though passionate, the kiss was sweet, gentle, and all too brief.

As he moved away, Brad emitted a low chuckle. "Do you know how long I've wanted to do that?"

"Oh? Tell me."

"Since the moment we met."

Shelly smiled, wondering why she'd made him wait so long. She hadn't been ready for a relationship in September, but that kiss—she could have handled that weeks ago.

His fingers caressed her cheek until she clasped them and held them in her lap, wanting to keep him close. "I'm sorry I've taken so long to come around. You must have the patience of Job."

He chuckled. "You're worth the wait." He squeezed her hands. "So, do you think I could get some time with you tomorrow night, say, dinner? Just the two of us?"

"I'd love that."

A few minutes later Shelly walked Brad to the front door to say goodnight. Before stepping out into the cold, he leaned down and kissed her goodbye. Shelly's heart soared. It had been so long since she had felt this way.

"See you tomorrow," she told him.

"Tomorrow," he echoed back as he shut the door behind him.

Shelly took a deep, satisfied breath, and turned to go to her room.

She stopped short when she found her roommate staring back at her. El held her arms folded in front of her as she stood halfway down the stairs. Shelly waited for a reaction, but El only stared expectantly.

"What?" Shelly broke the silence. She tried to drop her smile, but couldn't manage it.

"What? What do you mean 'what?' I'm gobsmacked. When did this happen?" A huge grin split El's face.

"It's been coming on for long enough. Don't you think?" Shelly asked. "But in the past couple of weeks, things have kind of developed."

"Yes, I see that. And I couldn't be happier." El came the rest of the way down the stairs and wrapped Shelly in a hug. "You're exactly what that boy needs."

Instead of sleeping, Shelly found herself curled up on El's bed talking well into the night.

Chapter 20

VALENTINE'S DAY WAS a week away when Rob walked into the mall again. He made a beeline to the jewelers, having every intention of buying a ring. His roommate's statement about him being engaged had been a bit premature, though the thought had been creeping into his mind more and more often. Rob knew Lindsey waited in expectation of a proposal, and spoke as if everything was already settled between them.

He'd planned to fulfill that expectation, but every step he took toward the long bank of windows and shiny glass counters full of glittering stones and gold settings grew harder. He stopped at one of the windows and peered in at the display, feeling his throat tighten at the thought of walking inside.

For months now, Lindsey had talked about the future, their home, and kids, though she had been careful to couch the discussions in general terms, rather than specifics of the two of them. Until recently.

When he thought that far ahead, Rob couldn't see it. The two of them had fun together and the relationship had been important to him—what he'd needed to get over Shelly after graduation. He cared about Lindsey, really *wanted* it to be more, to be everything—he wanted to be married—but now, staring at the display of rings and facing that very permanent option, he couldn't walk into the store.

He'd thought he could, but finally admitted to himself that after seeing Shelly again, the doubts had grown. Now he wondered if he had been fooling himself all along.

He'd been attracted to Shelly Cox from the first moment they'd met.

She had never made a secret of the fact that she planned to marry Jimmy, but he hadn't worried much about that. Instead, he looked for ways to spend time with her. Their duets grew out of that, and they had practiced together far more than necessary—he'd made sure of it.

When she had finally agreed to go on a date with him, he'd been thrilled, and everything continued to progress beautifully. That is, everything was great until a week before her missionary was scheduled to return, and Rob told Shelly he wanted to marry her. He couldn't exactly call it a proposal—there had been no ring or getting down on one knee, but he'd laid his feelings on the line.

He'd been certain she shared his feelings, that she loved him in return. However, once she got past the shock of his announcement—which he thought shouldn't have surprised her in the least, all things considered—and their mind-blowing kiss had ended, she'd had no trouble at all turning him down.

She'd never looked back. That fact had hurt the most.

He shoved his hands in his pockets and turned away from the jeweler's. Thinking about the past few months, Rob realized he'd known for a while now that his current relationship wasn't going anywhere, but he'd *wanted* Lindsey to be the one. Wanted to put the pain of losing Shelly behind him, to look forward to the future with a woman who loved him. It had made him hold on to the wrong relationship too long, which hadn't been fair to Lindsey.

He walked through the mall for a long time, circling the halls as he tried to make a decision. Could he break up with Lindsey so close to Valentine's Day? Wouldn't that be cruel? But how much more cruel would it be to string her along when he now knew things would not end the way she wanted?

People rushed past him, their arms laden with packages. He wandered into Dillard's and picked out a bottle of nice perfume instead of the ring. Lindsey would love it, as it was just the kind of thing she'd wear. Now he had to figure out how to break it to her gently.

PERHAPS GENTLY WASN'T in Lindsey's vocabulary, Rob thought as he climbed out of his newly pungent car. He had shown up for their dinner date and took her to her favorite Mexican restaurant. She talked about work, he talked about his ski trip the next day, and they left the restaurant side by side. He had thought he'd covered his nerves okay, had worked at it the whole time.

After he helped her into the car, she turned to him. "What's going on?"

He glanced at her in surprise. She knew something was wrong? How should he start this conversation? "I've had something on my mind for a while, and I've been trying to figure out how to bring it up."

"Well, what is it? If we're going to have any kind of future together, communication is important, don't you think? It's the keystone to a strong marriage."

Rob felt his throat close up and fought for a lungful of air as he pulled onto the road. "Yes," he managed, then sucked in another breath. "Communication is completely important."

"That's what I think. We were talking about that at work the other day when Maria said she'd lied to her boyfriend. I knew you'd agree that there's nothing so freeing as the truth."

He felt his eyes open wide as she seemed to have hit the subject on her own. Only she still had no idea. "Yes, exactly."

"So, what was it?" she asked. She opened the console between the seats to look for a stick of gum. He'd been stocking her favorite flavor there since he had taken her to the Manti Pageant. "What's this?" Lindsey held up the little white gift bag the department store used. He'd stashed it away for the date.

"I got it for you for Valentine's Day, but I thought maybe I'd better give it to you early." His heart constricted when he saw her excitement.

"Really?" She flashed him a wide smile.

Suddenly he realized what she thought it was. He watched as she hurried to open the bag and dipped her hand inside. Her face fell as she removed the perfume. "Wow. This is, um, nice." Her disappointment was palpable.

Rob pulled in front of her apartment and parked the car as she began to open the bottle to sniff. "It's great perfume, Rob. Thanks."

There was no good way to say this, so he decided he best get to it. "Lindsey, we've been going out for a long time, and you're a special woman to me."

She turned to him, all smiles. "Oh, you're special to me, too, Rob. I can't imagine loving anyone the way I love you." She went to put the lid back on the perfume, but as she wasn't looking at it, she missed.

He felt like his shirt collar was too tight, but didn't tug at it. He deserved to be uncomfortable. "Yes, well, that makes this harder. You see, I don't think this is working." He winced as soon as the words left his mouth, but there was no calling them back.

"What's not working?" Her hands frozen in midair.

"Us." He felt like the biggest jerk, looking at her open mouth. "I know you were hoping maybe we could become... more than we are now, I'd thought we would too, but it's not—"

Her left hand, holding the perfume, hit the console and some of the perfume splashed out. "Hold on. We've been talking marriage, and now, out of the blue, you think we've made a mistake? What about our June wedding? I have my dress picked out. The temple's reserved. The reception center, the photographer—nearly everything's in place."

His heart clenched at the raw pain in her eyes, then her words registered. She already had her dress, and reservations at the temple for the ceremony, not to mention all those other things, and he hadn't even asked her? They hadn't even had a specific talk about their timing and expectations. Obviously he'd missed something important in those conversations and communication she was talking about. "You reserved the temple and a photographer?"

"Yes, June is a busy month and I have a large family. If I was going to get the right room on the nineteenth; I knew I'd have to make the reservations early. We talked about getting married. You knew I was thinking June." She gestured with the still lidless perfume bottle.

"And you didn't think to discuss a date with me, or wait until I actually proposed, to set everything up?" He was incredulous. He knew she tended to plan ahead, but this was crazy.

"You're blaming me when you never told me that you didn't want to marry me? You have the nerve, after all this time, to break up with me? Seriously? What kind of jerk are you?" She looked at the bottle in her hand,

131

then doused him and the upholstery with the contents, giving it a good swing so it splashed across the back seat of the car as well. "I never want to see you again." She snatched her purse and slammed out of the car.

Rob wiped away the perfume that streamed down his face, stunned at what she'd done. "That went well." He started the car and left the parking lot, feeling the perfume trickle down his back. Perhaps he should have bypassed the consolation gift. He couldn't entirely blame her... well, he could. It was a dirty trick, after all, but he hadn't been fair to her.

Still, how could she have scheduled a sealing room in the temple without even talking about a wedding date with him? Or which temple they should be married at? He wracked his brains, trying to remember if the two of them had ever discussed it, but couldn't remember a conversation that would have given her a reason to start making decisions. When he pulled into his own parking spot ten minutes later, he ran his hands through his damp hair and groaned. He was bound to smell like a woman for weeks.

Now he better understood how Shelly had justified letting their relationship ride for so long. It didn't stop the pain losing her had caused him, but it made things easier to understand—and made him feel even worse about doing the same thing to Lindsey.

He rolled his window up and headed in to change his clothes. And shower. Maybe twice. Next, he needed to visit his sister's to use her steam cleaner. As he jogged up the front steps to his apartment, he wondered if it was even possible to get all the perfume out of his car.

Chapter 21

SHELLY SPENT AN HOUR getting ready for her first official date with Brad. She wasn't counting the movie they'd seen together a couple of weeks earlier as a date. That was just two friends hanging out. This was different. She knew the distinction was thin, but was nervous all the same.

"You look nice," El said as she came to stand in the bathroom doorway. "I don't know why you're so worried about every hair being in place, though. It's just Brad."

Just Brad. Only my first official date in over a year. Shelly didn't bother to explain. "Are you and Chet doing anything this weekend? Maybe the four of us could get together. You know, if tonight goes all right." There had been a noticeable lack of Chet in their apartment over the past week, though Shelly had been sure something was brewing between them, but El hadn't said anything about it.

"No. Nothing coming up any time soon." El avoided Shelly's gaze, and tweaked a lock of her hair instead.

Unconvinced by the nonchalant way her roommate answered, Shelly watched El's face in the mirror. There was a knock at the front door and El made excuses to answer it. Though Shelly wanted to press her to find out what happened between her and Chet, she didn't have time for it now, as she heard Brad's greeting.

"Is Shelly ready?" he asked.

Shelly emerged from the bathroom, melting a bit when he turned his bright smile on her and passed over a florist bundle of pink roses and white daisies. "Thank you." She buried her face into the blooms and took a deep sniff of the barely unfurling rose buds. "They're beautiful."

"It's only fitting," he answered easily, and leaned in to press a kiss to her cheek. "Though I couldn't find anything as beautiful as you."

El made gagging noises as she walked into the kitchen.

"She can't help herself," Shelly told him when he looked daggers in his sister's direction. "She's your sister. It's her job to do that." She turned and followed El into the kitchen. Shelly pulled out the vase her flowers had arrived in the previous fall. It felt kind of funny—wrong, almost, to use the vase that came with Jimmy's flowers for a bouquet from another guy. She knew that was all in her head, and the previous bouquet hadn't even been from Jimmy, anyway, so she swallowed back the emotion and took a moment to arrange the new buds while she came to terms with the change.

When she turned back to Brad, she had gotten her nerves mostly under control. He helped her put her coat on and she took his offered hand, snatching up her purse on the way out the door. "So where are we going?" she asked when they stepped into the cold.

"Hull New Theatre has a group of Scottish dancers performing tonight, if you're interested. I thought we could grab some dinner first."

"That sounds great." She'd love to take in traditional dancing, and Shelly could feel her stomach rejoicing at the suggestion of a meal—between studying and getting ready for their date, she hadn't taken time to eat anything.

Ten minutes later she slid next to him in a booth at the Gardner's Arms—one of his favorite pubs. "You don't mind, do you?" he asked. "We can eat somewhere else if you'd prefer."

"No, of course not. It's a sight better than McDonald's."

He chuckled at that. "Is that where your dates usually take you?" He picked up her hand again and began twisting her CTR ring.

"Not if I can help it. There weren't a lot of options for students on a budget in Ephraim, though, so I've had my share of their burgers and fries. I much prefer fish and chips."

"Aren't you sick of them yet?" he asked, leaning toward her. His eyes sparkled with teasing laughter.

She moved toward him and tipped her head to the side, putting on her most flirty smile. "Not even close."

The waitress came over and asked what they'd like. Brad requested sodas and two orders of fish and chips. The waitress gave him a sideways glance, scratched something off her pad, then repeated the order and returned to the kitchen.

"Not your usual fare?" Shelly asked, wondering what had been scratched over. "You prefer the corned beef hash, I understand?"

He nudged her with his shoulder. "I thought we already established my long and abiding hatred of corned beef. Thank goodness my mum is French, and doesn't try to foist the stuff on us at every turn like so many of my friends have had to endure growing up."

"Yes, but don't they like it?" Shelly asked.

"I can't help it if they have no working taste buds." He ran a finger down her cheek. "Perhaps it's past time I got a new set of friends."

Shelly laughed and they settled back as he began a rousing tale from his childhood.

"SHE'S IN A RELATIONSHIP?" Rob's stomach plummeted as he saw the latest status change on Shelly's Facebook account. He hadn't expected her to stay home and never date for the next six months, but neither had he expected her to rush into a new relationship.

Well, hardly rush, Jimmy had been dead over a year now, but still—he had just broken things off with Lindsey.

"What was that?" his co-worker, Stu, asked.

"Nothing, talking to myself." Rob closed the Internet window and turned back to the spreadsheet in front of him. A thread of regret over breaking up with Lindsey entered his mind, but he pushed that away. He hadn't split with Lindsey so that he and Shelly could get together. Spending time with Shelly had underscored how little he and Lindsey had in common. The breakup was way overdue. Still, he wondered what would have happened if he'd made that move sooner. If he'd split with Lindsey the previous fall, he would have been free to spend more time with Shelly while she was home for the holidays. Then maybe...

There was no use in this train of thought. Anything could happen in six months. There was no reason to believe Shelly's newest relationship would get serious. And if she didn't come back to Utah available, well, he'd have to deal with that—he'd done it before and more painfully. "Did you get the monthly numbers from food services yet?" he asked Stu.

When Stu passed them over, Rob pushed the pain and worry from his mind.

※ ※ ※

WEDNESDAY WAS VALENTINE'S Day, and Brad arranged to take Shelly out to dinner. When he greeted her with a kiss, Shelly's heart beat fast and the breath caught in her throat. It had been so long since she had been with someone on Valentine's Day. The previous year she had spent the evening alone with a sappy movie.

The two years before that, Jimmy had been on his mission, so she'd spent them with the girls on her dorm floor, watching chick flicks. *Mostly* just girls, anyway. Rob and one of the other guys from his floor had shown up with cupcakes and popcorn to share with the half-dozen women gathered around the television. The guys hadn't even complained about the movies. She smiled at the memory, then nudged it away. She was going to focus on where she was now, not what had once been.

Brad's hand wrapped around hers and he pulled her out through the door as she called goodbye to El. The air was crisp and cold, biting at her nose and cheeks. It invigorated her, making her glad to be alive.

Shelly enjoyed every minute she spent with Brad. Her sisters and friends back home seemed thrilled she was dating someone again. Her mom, however, was concerned about her getting too involved with a guy who lived in another country. Shelly wondered if there was any right answer for her mom. Either Shelly dated someone, or she didn't. She was living *in another country*, after all, so it was likely that she would date someone who was *from* a country other than her own. She had plenty of opportunities to date Clay, who was at least American, but Shelly seriously doubted her mom would consider him an improvement despite the relative proximity.

They took a meandering drive to the shore and Brad pulled up to a cozy restaurant on the edge of the water. The sky was covered with clouds, and only the palest hint of light from the moon peeked through. "It's a beautiful night," Shelly observed as he helped her from the car. "It's been a while since I've seen the stars."

"An unfortunate side effect of living in Britain—not nearly enough clear nights to star gaze," he agreed as he took her hand again. "I hope you like this place. Andrea suggested it."

"I'm sure I'll like it, then." They followed the sidewalk to the door of the restaurant. The building was covered in light gray clapboard and the roof was shingled with well-weathered shakes. It was so charming; she couldn't wait to see inside.

She entered the restaurant to find lights dim and soft music emanating from hidden speakers. Potted plants dotted the dining room, offering extra privacy to patrons. Shelly smiled. She had never been anywhere more perfect for the most romantic night of the year—the place fairly oozed ambience. The waiter showed them to a table at the end of the room, against a bank of windows overlooking the water. They had a clear view of the waves as they rolled in, crashing against the rocky shoreline. "This is so beautiful," she said when they were seated across from each other and the waiter left menus with them.

Brad took her hand across the small table. "I'm glad you like it. I wanted to take you somewhere as special as you are."

Shelly felt herself blush. He always knew exactly what to say. "Well, thank you." She squeezed his hand and took a look at her menu.

The evening was everything she had ever dreamed: a quiet table, romance, good food, and great company. As they talked, Shelly peered out the window at the lights dancing on the ocean. She wondered if she would be able to see France on a really clear night. The thought was so ridiculous, she found herself inhaling a swallow of water.

"What are you laughing about?" Brad asked.

Shelly cleared her lungs and smiled when she stopped coughing. "I had this notion that we could see to the continent from here. France, in fact—which we most certainly could not. What's closest over the water? Brussels, the Netherlands?"

"The Netherlands. However, while one can see the shore of France across the channel if you stand on the Cliffs of Dover, the distance from here to the Netherlands is something like two-hundred miles, so I doubt even your eagle eyes could manage it."

Shelly laughed again and took his hand on the table. *Oh, well. I didn't expect the night to be that perfect, anyway.*

full Circle

IT HAD NOT PASSED Shelly's notice that she returned from her date to find El still sitting at home in the same sweats she'd been wearing hours earlier. After kissing Brad goodbye at the door, she stalked into the kitchen and faced her roommate. "You said you had plans tonight."

"I did. Work has been eating up all my study time lately. I had to focus on a paper that's due soon." El didn't lift her eyes from the book.

Shelly sighed and took the chair across the table. "What happened with you and Chet?"

"We broke up."

"So I noticed. How long ago, exactly, was that? And why didn't you mention things had gone south between you?" When El acted as though nothing had been said, Shelly reached out and put her hand over the page El was reading. "Come on. I blubbered all over you, didn't I? Let me return the favor."

El ceased writing and set down her pen. When she peered up at Shelly, her eyes looked helpless. "He's a great guy. Too great to keep stringing him along. There was no future for us, and I preferred not to pretend there was."

Shelly studied El for a long moment. "Do you mean there's no future because you don't feel anything for him? It looked to me like you clicked fine."

"We did click. Like a door slamming." El shrugged helplessly. "He's wonderful and had all these ideas about seeing us together for the long haul, and... I couldn't do it."

"I see." But Shelly didn't see. She considered El's words for a long moment, trying to read between the lines. She knew there was something more there. The subtext practically screamed—unfortunately, it seemed to be speaking in a foreign language. "So, the two of you hit it off, you were totally into him, he was totally into you, you have all the important things in common, but there's no future?"

El looked down at her paper. "Er, yes?"

"You want to try again?" Shelly gave her a hard stare.

"No. I'm sticking with that."

"I think you're making a mistake, but I guess it's your life." Shelly stood, frustrated with her friend, and wishing she could pick away at El's psyche until she figured out the real problem. "I'm headed to bed. Have a good night."

"Good night." El's voice was small, hurt.

Shelly felt bad and wanted to poke and cajole El into talking, but didn't see that it would do any good. Better to let her stew for a while, then try again later. After she washed her face and brushed her teeth, Shelly shut herself in her room for the night. When she lay down, she realized she wasn't ready to sleep yet, so she hauled out her laptop and checked her Facebook account. It was only four o'clock in Utah, so most of her friends and family were still getting ready for their Valentine's Day activities. She posted her own note.

Had a great date with Brad. Beautiful restaurant, good food, great company. Best V-Day in years. Thanks, Brad!

She scrolled down the list, making comments on friends' posts, checking the pictures her sister Kellie had posted of her wedding bouquet, and learning Katie had broken up with the guy she had been dating at Christmas. She paused when she got to Rob's status. *Grabbing a bite and heading to the slopes tonight.*

Shelly wondered if Lindsey thought of skiing as a romantic date. Then she read the comment from Lindsey under his status: *At least you'll have a pleasant-smelling trip up the mountain. I've got a date.*

"That's interesting," Shelly muttered under her breath. Had she misunderstood Rob's roommate at Christmas? She wondered when Rob and Lindsey had broken up, so she followed the trail on his electronic wall and realized it had only been about a week. "Ouch. That had to hurt, one way or the other. And Lindsey doesn't sound happy."

Though she noticed he was online, she talked herself out of bringing up a chat window. If he was sensitive about the failed relationship, it might not be the best time to talk. And she didn't know what to think, except to feel a tiny twist of satisfaction that he wasn't getting married after all.

Chapter 22

THE WEEKS RUSHED BY, one practically running over the next, as if in a race to see which could reach the finish line first. Before Shelly knew it, March was nearly over and the three-week Easter break was before her. She packed her bags to go on another trip with the international students, excited to spend the next ten days touring Portugal, Spain, rushing across France, and into Italy. She was sure she could spend ten times as long at any of the individual countries without coming close to being satisfied, but was excited to see more of the world.

Brad took her to the drop-off point at the train station and stayed to keep her company until some of the others arrived.

"I wish I were going with you," Brad said as he pulled her close.

"So do I. Are you sure you have to work?" She slid her hands around his waist. She felt almost guilty about taking the trip since she already felt so indebted to Lily and Curtis, but when they insisted on making it a Christmas gift, how could she turn them down?

"Maybe we'll have another chance to do some sightseeing together. When you get back, we'll take a couple of day trips."

"That sounds great." Shelly pulled him closer and buzzed her lips over his cheek.

His face darkened as he looked over her shoulder. "Fuller's going too? I don't like him. Not trustworthy, that one."

"Don't worry. I'm all yours." She touched his cheek and turned him back to face her, then pressed her lips to his. He must have decided she had the right idea, because he drew her closer and lingered over the kiss.

Shelly pulled back and smiled up at him. "I'll keep in touch. Have a good week."

"You too." He kissed her again quickly, then released her, and she boarded the train with a carryon and the one suitcase that still had a handle.

The week was not exactly relaxing. Shelly realized later she should have expected as much. Walking all day from place to place and staying up late to see regional dances and shows or hanging out with the others in her group kept her low on sleep and in constant need of refueling—which was fine by her, since the food was fabulous and she wanted to try it all.

The trip was wonderful, amazing, and exhausting. On the return flight, Shelly settled into her seat on the plane next to an Australian student and drifted off to sleep. She was brought out of her stupor some time later by someone tapping on her shoulder.

"Good morning, sunshine. The airplane will touch down any second. You'll probably want to get your carryon ready," Clay said from the next seat.

Shelly stretched and looked around, realizing where she was. "Where's Carla?"

"She got up to use the restroom about an hour ago, and I took over her seat. You were out of it a *long* time." He flashed that charming grin that would have made most women melt. "You're pretty cute when you're asleep."

"You're pretty cute when you're quiet," Shelly shot back and stretched her arms out in front of her. Why couldn't he accept that she wasn't interested? What was his problem?

"Touché." He didn't seem the least concerned about her comment, however. "We both know you like the way I look all the time."

"Of course," she said sweetly. "I just like *you* a whole lot less when you're talking."

"So, do you have plans Tuesday night?" he asked as the plane taxied to their gate at the Humberside International Airport—which was only about twenty miles from Hull.

"Clay, I'm not interested in going out with you, and I'm dating Brad."

"I know. But you've never really given me a chance." He smiled, unfazed by her refusal. "I saw you first."

"This might surprise you, but you're no longer in second grade, and

I'm not the last sticky bun in the bakery box." She didn't have the patience for this. "Seriously, Clay, hasn't the thrill of the chase gotten a bit old yet? Why don't you focus on some girl who's interested instead of wasting your time with me?"

Clay studied her for a moment, and the engaging smile slid from his face as a more serious expression appeared. "There's something about you that I've never seen before. You're all lit up inside. I don't understand it. I'd like to learn more about whatever it is that makes you that way."

Should she believe him? She didn't know. She paused before she answered him, wanting him to understand. "Religion makes me that way."

"I'd like to understand why." He placed a hand on her arm.

Shelly moved away and considered her options. *I can always act like I believe him. Of course, that doesn't change anything—hold on.* The merest trickle of an idea took root, sprouted, and grew leaves and flowers in a matter of seconds. The idea was too perfect. Trying to hold back the glee that burned through her, Shelly turned back to him. "Do you really want to know what I've got that makes me so happy? What is it that draws you to me?"

"Of course. I've been badgering you all year, haven't I?" A sly smile formed on his lips.

The flight attendant announced that they were at the gate, and everyone stood to gather their bags and disembark the plane.

"Are you free Tuesday night, say, about seven?" she asked before he could head down the aisle without her.

"I'm free anytime you want me to be," he said, wiggling his brows.

"All right, be at home Tuesday night. Once I've checked the schedule, I'll let you know if you should plan a different time."

He seemed a little too pleased with himself as they walked down the terminal to gather their luggage and go through customs.

He caught up with her before they reached Brad, who waited to pick her up. "Hold on, do you need my address? Or I could pick you up instead."

"I believe you added it to our phone list in the kitchen, didn't you?" She remembered him looking at the list on the side of the refrigerator and picking up a nearby pen. He was unbelievable sometimes.

"See you Tuesday." He grinned and took off before they reached Brad.

"Hey, have a good trip?" Brad greeted her with a quick kiss.

"Yes, it was great. I took about a zillion pictures and wrote copious notes. It'll take me weeks to sort out the photo file."

He picked up her bag and moved toward the outside door, catching her hand with his free one. "What was all that buddy, buddy with Clay about?"

She held in a tiny grin. "Remind me to explain when we get back to my flat. I have to take care of something." The glow of anticipation simmered inside her. "So, how was your week?"

He gave her a side-long glance, but allowed her to change the subject.

When they got back to the flat, Brad stood at her bedroom door and talked to her as she unpacked her bags and showed him the trinkets she'd bought.

Finally he reminded her, "You had to tell me something about Clay?"

"Oh, yeah." The grin she had held back so carefully on the plane stole over her. "It's not something I really have to tell you—although I have every intention of explaining—but I do need to make a phone call first." She stood and wrote down Clay's address from the board on the fridge, along with another number they had jotted down there.

Then she returned to the table and pulled out her cell phone. Brad waited quietly, though the impatience showed on his face.

"Hi, Elder Durrant? This is Shelly Cox. It's good to talk to you, too. Listen, I'm calling because I have a referral for you. Are you available Tuesday at seven o'clock?"

Chapter 23

TUESDAY EVENING, SHELLY holed up in the library to study. She kept a close eye on the clock, knowing Clay wouldn't be happy about the visitors she'd arranged for him in her place. She had to hold back a smile when she thought of his reaction. Around eight o'clock, she took a break from studying and decided to work on her pictures.

Though she had uploaded all the photos from her trip to her online file, there were hours of cataloguing left to do before she got through half of them. At an hour or so a day, she figured she might finish by the end of August—if she didn't take any more picture between now and then, an unlikely scenario at best.

She checked her inbox while she was online. Her mother had sent a collection of excerpts from her great-great-grandmother's journals. Shelly didn't have time to read them right away, so she saved them for later. Finals were only a month off and she wondered if she'd get everything done in time.

At nine, she decided she couldn't put it off any longer and headed home. She found Clay leaning against her building by the front door, scowling deeply. She wondered how long he'd been there and if the extra wait had improved his temper or worsened it. She didn't particularly like dealing with angry people, but she took a deep breath and pushed ahead.

"Oh, hi, Clay. How are you?" she asked nonchalantly.

His eyes nearly bugged out of his head. "How am I? A girl sets up a date with me, sends the Mormon missionaries instead, and then calmly asks how I am?" He took three ground-eating steps to stand in front of her.

She gave him a cool appraisal, ignoring the way the nerves fluttered in her stomach at the look in his eyes. "I never said I'd go out with you. I never even said I'd be there tonight. I only told you that if you wanted answers to your questions, you should be home at seven."

"We had a date." He pointed his finger at her for emphasis.

"No, Clay." She pushed his hand out of her face and stood strong, trying not to be intimidated by the extra foot of height he had on her. "Did you, or did you *not*, say you wanted to know what makes me special?"

"You know I did."

"That's why I sent the missionaries. That's what they do. They teach people how to be happy. They have a message about the thing that makes me what I am." She folded her arms in front of her. "If those are the answers you're seeking, there's no one better to help you find them than the missionaries."

His anger seemed to lower a notch, but he didn't back off. "You tricked me."

"You *never give up*. Look, Clay, it's really time to stop. No more requests for dates, or uninvited visits to my flat. No more flirty conversations or playful comments. This has to end. Seriously." She looked at him firmly. "Do you understand, Mr. Fuller?"

A long moment passed while his expression went from hard, to irritated, to accepting. Finally, he nodded. "Yes, I understand." She could see the resignation in his eyes, though he was still upset. She couldn't blame him. She would've been unhappy too, but enough was enough.

"Goodnight." She passed him and continued down the sidewalk to her flat, relieved to shut the door between them. The confrontation had actually gone much better than she'd expected.

"Shelly," Candy greeted her from the kitchen. "Clay was here to talk to you a while ago." She took another wipe at her lava lamp with a soft cloth. It left behind a streak, which dried quickly on the hot glass. Apparently it was bath time, Shelly thought as she watched Candy rub at non-existent specks.

"He seemed kind of upset." Candy gave her lamp a satisfied pat and returned it to the shelf, taking a moment to make sure it was exactly centered.

"Yes, I know. He waited outside for me." Shelly got a glass of water and tried to sort out the relief, weariness, and guilt that vied for supremacy inside her. She'd expected to feel smug about her accomplishment, but somehow did not.

"Why was he so mad?"

She took a long drink, then smiled with less satisfaction than she had expected. "He lost."

THE NEXT FEW WEEKS were hectic as everyone prepared for exams. Even Candy decided studying was important. Despite the fact that they each had a private room with a desk, she often sat at the kitchen table, muttering over her class notes. She got annoyed if anyone interrupted or distracted her, flew off the handle at trivial things, and then went out partying every night. She set herself up for a bad day after too much to drink and not enough sleep, then did the whole thing over again.

Shelly couldn't figure out why Candy didn't simply study in her room or go to the library. Despite the fact that Shelly used these two options a lot, she was ready to strangle her roommate long before the week of exams was over.

Thursday, with only one test left, Shelly decided she'd studied enough and began cleaning up the kitchen. No one had done much to keep the place livable that week, so it was a mess. Their flat did have maid service for the kitchen and dining area on Saturdays, but Shelly hated to leave such a disaster for the poor student to clean up, and she didn't want to wait two more days for it to get some attention. She threw out the moldy leftovers from the fridge, scrubbed the counters, and pulled the knickknacks off the shelves to dust. She set Candy's precious lava lamp on the counter and began cleaning the shelf where it normally sat.

"Shelly, take a break. Who cares if the ruddy lamp has a clean shelf? We all hate it," Andrea said from the table where she studied while she ate.

"I know, I just–" Shelly's elbow bumped the lamp as she turned to speak to Andrea, and the lamp tipped. She had to hurry to catch it before it fell. With both hands on the top, a sudden impulse seized her. Without taking a moment to consider her actions, she gave it a whirl, rotating it around the edge of the base, causing a swirling motion to the liquid inside, then did it again. A burst of surprised laughter escaped her lips as she felt euphoria take over her. The 'lava' liquid separated into tiny balls that began floating, suspended in the clear fluids.

She giggled uncontrollably, letting out some of the tension that had been building inside her all week.

"Shelly! What brought that on?" Andrea asked, her question both shocked and amused.

Shelly looked down at the lamp in her hands and couldn't believe what she'd done. She let go, backed away, and covered her nose and mouth with her hands almost in embarrassment. "I can't believe I did that!" She knew she ought to feel bad. Candy would not be happy when she saw the lamp.

"Me neither. She'll have a fit!"

"It felt really good." Shelly giggled some more, and then carefully returned the lamp to its normal spot. She turned and sat at the table, placing her hands on top. "I should have done that months ago." She covered her mouth as if to stop the words. "Oh, I didn't just say that!"

The two of them dissolved into laughter.

After a few minutes, Shelly got up and finished cleaning, avoiding even looking at the lamp. She hoped it would settle before Candy returned home, but knew it would take a miracle.

El came home for dinner a few minutes later and after asking what happened to the lamp, heard the story and was thoroughly entertained by it. Candy entered the flat an hour later, arms lifted in exultation. "All done. I'm heading right out to the pub for dinner and a few rounds of drinks. Anyone care to join me?"

Shelly looked up as Candy passed her—making a beeline for the lava lamp for her ritual hello, as if the thing were a pet. "No, thanks," Shelly said. "I still have one test left, and a thesis to work on." Her premise had been cleared and she had already begun collecting data for it.

El and Andrea made similar comments. The three of them shared discreet looks and tried not to appear too interested in what Candy was doing.

"Better you than me." Candy peered at her lava lamp and gasped. "What happened to her?" She whirled around and faced the other girls. "What did you do?"

"What do you mean?" Andrea asked, a convincing look of puzzlement on her face. "It looks fine to me."

"She is not fine! Someone bumped her. Or maybe you've taken to shaking her up as soon as my back is turned." Candy leveled a gaze at her roommates.

"I shifted it to clean the shelf underneath, but I certainly didn't lift and shake it," Shelly said. "First of all, it's too hot when it's been on for a while."

"I don't believe you!" Candy grabbed the lamp by the base and put her free hand on top—the only parts of the lamp that wouldn't burn her. "If you can't appreciate a work of art like this, maybe I better keep her in my bedroom where she'll be safe!" She stomped up the stairs and slammed her bedroom door behind her.

"We should have done that in September," El muttered. The remaining roommates suppressed their giggles and returned to their dinners.

Chapter 24

SHELLY HAD NEVER KNOWN sixty degrees to feel so balmy and beautiful. Though it was still cool, she was grateful for the vast improvement over the cold, wet months of winter. When she came out of sacrament meeting on Sunday, she was thinking about the possibility of convincing Brad to take a long walk with her that afternoon.

Apparently he'd had another late night with his friends and hadn't ventured out of bed in time for church that morning—an event that had grown more common since the summer term had begun and the weather continued to warm. He also made it to fewer and fewer of the single adults activities held each week. He seemed available enough on other nights, however, and she found him on her doorstep more evenings than not. Things were going well between them, though she wished he'd joined them at church. His laxness in worship bugged her, but since they weren't getting serious, and she wasn't staying in England, she let it go.

Shelly stopped to talk to one of the other sisters in the ward, clarifying plans for their activity the next night, when a pair of large hands slid over her eyes.

"Guess who," a man said in a low, gravelly voice that was obviously disguised.

"Andrea, I don't have time for games today." Shelly smiled, wondering which of the guys it was.

"Andrea?" The hands lifted from her face. "Now I sound like a girl?"

Shelly's heart stopped and the air rushed out of her lungs as she recognized the voice. She would know it anywhere. She had to gasp as she spun to face him so she would have enough air to speak. "Rob! What are you doing here?" She couldn't believe her eyes, even as she wondered if they were deceiving her.

"What? No hug?" He spread his arms in invitation.

"Of course." She hugged him tightly, breathing in the familiar cologne and feeling his warm arms wrapped around her. She was stunned, thrilled to see him. She finally let go so she could look at him. He still made her knees melt and her heart yearn. "What are you doing here?"

"Well, my brother is a missionary in the area." His dark brows lifted over his chocolate eyes. "He's been around for a while. Have you had a chance to meet him?"

Happy to see him, and feeling a little goofy with excitement, she joined his silliness. "You know, I think I might have spotted him across a room once or twice."

"Oh, good. I was worried you hadn't. He can be really quiet and reclusive."

He managed to hold in a snort in response—his brother was a great missionary, but reclusive...not so much. She bumped his shoulder with her fist. "Come on."

He laughed. "Sorry, I couldn't help myself. We came out to pick him up."

"You didn't mention you planned to come when I saw you in January." Shelly put her hands on her hips, giving him her sternest look as she tried to keep her delight from overpowering him. "He never mentioned it, either."

"We're good at secrets." His lips tipped up into a smile, making her melt a little more.

"Actually," Rob's college-aged sister Natalie said as she joined the conversation, "Rob came in late to the game. He only decided to join us a couple of months ago."

"And still, you never mentioned it when we chatted online."

"I like to be mysterious," he answered.

"He thinks he can pull off mysterious," an older woman said as she stepped into the group. "We humor him from time to time."

"Hey!" Rob protested, even as he put his arm around his mother.

"Hello, Mrs. Durrant." Shelly had only met the woman once before, but remembered her well.

"Hello, Shelly. It's been a long time, hasn't it? Thank you so much for carrying those packages for us at Christmas. You can't imagine what a nice surprise it was." She hugged Shelly.

"You're certainly welcome. I'm glad I could help." She glanced back at Rob and caught his eye. He winked at her, filling her chest with flutters of confusion.

Mrs. Durrant patted Shelly on the arm. "I wondered if we could entice you to join us for dinner tomorrow night. Our treat. As a thank-you for everything. It was so thoughtful."

"I'd be happy to join you for dinner."

Elder Durrant and joined them and everyone headed into Sunday school. By the time Shelly and El left the church that afternoon, all the arrangements had been made. Shelly would eat with the family, and then take Rob and Natalie to family home evening with her.

"Wow, that was some reception from Elder Durrant's mom. Did you know her before?" El asked when they finally got in the car on the way home. "Because Rob sure seemed to know you." She sent Shelly an arch look. "And I don't mean in the casual way you indicated when you mentioned to Elder Durrant last fall that you knew his brother."

Shelly hadn't talked about everything that had happened with Rob, and she wasn't ready to dig into it now, either. What she felt most of all was confusion. "We dated some when I was at Utah State University."

"Ooooh." El stopped at the light and turned to Shelly. "Woah, wait. Is it *him*?"

"*Him*, who?" Andrea asked, looking between the two of them.

Shelly felt her face grow warm even as she marveled that El remembered the brief mention of Rob months earlier. "I don't know what she's talking about."

"Liar." El laughed and started the car moving again with the light change. "He's the other guy, the one you dumped when you chose your missionary. The other man you loved." She pounded her hand on the steering wheel. "He's here to see you. He came all this way—"

"He came to pick up his brother from his mission," Shelly interrupted, "Not to be with me."

"He wanted to marry you once," Andrea added, "He did look interested in you. In fact, I'd say he's still got strong feelings."

"Hello, dating Brad here." Shelly waved her hand. "Let's remember that fact, shall we?" She made a promise to herself that she wouldn't forget it, either.

"I'm just sayin'." Andrea gave her a knowing look before she changed the subject.

THE NEXT NIGHT, SHELLY showed up a few minutes early to the Durrants' hotel room.

"Shelly, please come in," Sister Durrant said, opening the door wider.

"Sorry if I'm early. My roommate had to drop me off on her way to work." Shelly stepped inside.

"Oh, I didn't think of that. I probably should have suggested we pick you up. But we're ready now, anyway."

Natalie, who was nineteen and had long hair the same dark brown as her brothers, greeted Shelly. When her mom stepped away, Natalie said in a loud stage whisper, "We're waiting for Rob to finish getting ready. He's such a primper. He takes *forever*."

"You twerp. I do not." Rob entered from the adjoining room. "I didn't take nearly as long as you."

"You say that, but you were wearing a different shirt a few minutes ago," Natalie pointed out.

"It had a stain," Rob protested.

Their father entered the room. "The car's ready. I managed to get some gas without any trouble. Hello, Shelly. Glad you're here. Are we all set?"

They stepped into the cool May evening, made cooler than the previous day because of the late afternoon rain that had since blown away. The car was small, but Shelly didn't complain about being crammed into the back seat next to Rob. Their proximity made it easy to carry on a conversation about people they both knew.

They met the missionaries for dinner, and Shelly felt completely comfortable with everyone. The meal was good, and afterwards, Mr. Durrant dropped off his kids to go to FHE with Shelly and the other singles.

To Shelly's surprise, Brad was waiting when they joined the group at a local park. "Hey, honey." He leaned in and gave her a brief kiss when she walked over.

"Hi. I didn't think you'd make it." Shelly turned to Rob and Natalie, and felt every bit as uncomfortable as she had when Jimmy came home and she'd been faced with introducing *him* to Rob. Awkward didn't even begin to cover it. "Let me introduce Elder Durrant's brother and sister. This is Rob and Natalie." She gestured back to Brad. "This is Brad. You met his sister El yesterday. She's my roommate."

"Nice to meet you." Rob shook Brad's hand, his face inscrutable. Natalie smiled and turned her eyes away, as if she were curious about what was going on around them, and not the least interested about the weird triangle in front of her. But the sidelong glances she snuck every few seconds belied her apparent disinterest.

"Likewise," Brad said to Rob with a hard smile on his face. "Any friend of Shelly's, and all that. How long will you be in the area?"

"They'll be having transfers in a couple of days, so we'll stay until then and move along on Thursday when Rhett's free." The twitch in Rob's cheek was the only outward sign that he was less than comfortable in the conversation. "What are you studying here?"

"Engineering. My master's. And you've got a degree, I take it, since you met Shelly at school?"

"Yes, I have a master's in accounting. I work at a college now."

Shelly thought she might go mad at the stilted, polite conversation. Thankfully, the leaders decided it was time to start the evening activity. The group had a prayer and short lesson, then everyone split into two teams so they could play Frisbee baseball. Shelly liked this. Baseball she could never play well, but Frisbee baseball—that she could handle. She was satisfied with her three runs at the end of the game, though she would have been a great deal more comfortable if Brad and Rob hadn't both been on her team.

"You didn't join us much when we were in college," Rob said as they munched on cookies a while later.

"I know. I was so busy, and I'm a terrible athlete," Shelly said.

"Terrible, huh? You ran in from the farthest corner of the field and weren't even breathing heavily."

"It's not that big of a field," she said, then caught sight of the smile tugging at his mouth. "I've been running a lot lately, every afternoon. It's amazing how much it helps with the stress of school and everything. Plus it's easier on the waistline, and budget, than making copious amounts of chocolate chip cookies." She averted her eyes and forced a smile when Brad joined them.

"You stay pretty busy still, don't you?" Rob asked.

"Let me tell you about Shelly and being busy," Brad said, sliding a proprietary arm around her waist. "She's with this group a couple evenings a week and with the international students far too often, so I'm lucky to get study time with her, never mind regular dates."

"Sounds familiar," Rob teased. "Haven't changed your tune at all since Utah State?"

Shelly rolled her eyes. "I like being busy."

"I wouldn't have you any other way." Brad leaned in to kiss her, and she turned her head to take it on the cheek. They had never kissed much in public, especially at church functions, which made his actions in front of Rob even more pointed.

After FHE, Rob and Natalie rode home with Shelly, Brad, and El in Brad's car. Though Shelly had looked forward to showing them around her flat and campus, the possessive way Brad had acted all evening made her wish they'd arranged to drop the Americans back at their hotel.

Instead, she invited them in for lemonade and a quick turn around her flat—which took about five seconds, though she made Natalie jealous by mentioning they had maid service on Saturdays. They sat around the table talking about college classes and teachers. Natalie attended USU, so Shelly was able to get the latest scoop on campus happenings and news on some people she knew the previous school year.

Brad stayed close by, glowering, until the older Durrants came for their children. Shelly was grateful when El started questioning her brother about a birthday gift for their mom, allowing Shelly to walk out with her guests.

With an unhappy look, Brad allowed Shelly to walk Rob and Natalie out to the car to say goodbye without hanging onto her.

"Thanks so much for dinner," Shelly said to Mrs. Durrant. She accepted their goodbyes, then stood to face Rob as everyone else piled into the car. She felt the sweet ache of loss when she caught his gaze. "It was good seeing you again." She searched for the right words. "Sorry about..." she looked back at her flat.

"No problem. I can't blame him. If roles had been reversed..." His shrug completed the sentence for him. "I'm glad we had a chance to chat. You're obviously thriving here." He paused and brushed his index finger over her cheek. "I can't tell you how happy I am to know that. I only want what's best for you."

His gaze pierced her right to the heart. Her tongue felt thick, and though a dozen sentence beginnings attacked her at once, none felt right. So she settled for "Thanks." Another moment of silence ensued, and then she reached out and hugged him tight, catching a last sniff of his cologne and fighting the emotions rising inside her. "Have a great trip. This is an amazing area, and I'm sure you'll enjoy it."

His smile bloomed and he stepped back, opening the car door. "Bye."

"Bye." She stood there, waving as they drove away, then put on a happy face and went back in to her flat—where Brad waited for her.

"So," Brad started when Shelly sat with everyone. "Do you have plans to see them tomorrow?" He reached out and played with the ends of her hair.

Did he have to act like that? The protective boyfriend act was amusing, and even a little sweet when it was about Clay. Now it was just plain irritating. "No, I understand they have a very full schedule over the next few days. I don't expect I'll see them again before they go home." Shelly changed the subject to the next singles' activity, and Brad didn't steer the conversation back. She was glad as she was still trying to sort out her feelings.

Chapter 25

THE NEXT AFTERNOON, Shelly sat at her desk working on the outline for her thesis. She'd done a fair amount of research already, but there was still so much to do.

Andrea appeared at her bedroom door. "Shelly, there's a call for you on my phone."

"What?" Shelly looked at her roommate in surprise. "On *your* phone?"

"Yeah, Rob's mom." Her brows lifted and a knowing smile filled her face.

Shelly accepted the cell from Andrea. "Hello?"

"Hi, Shelly, this is Marilyn Durrant. This was the only number Rhett had for your apartment"

"That's fine. What can I do for you?"

"Actually, it's more what I can do for you. We'll be returning home tomorrow and I wondered if there was anything you'd like us to take back for you. I'm sure your parents would appreciate the surprise as much as we did."

Shelly was floored, and more than a little excited about the idea of surprising her family. "That's very sweet of you. I'm sure my mom would be thrilled, and I do have a few things I'd like to send."

"We can swing by later if you'd like, or you can come here. We have a short break before dinner."

Shelly didn't want them back at her place. If Brad caught sight of Rob again the glowering might never stop. "That's fine. I can get Andrea to drop me off downtown. Will you be there around five-thirty?" She thought of what items to pack, and what to ship instead.

"Yes, that would work for us."

"How much space do you have?"

"Probably about the same amount of space as what you carried for us, perhaps a bit more."

"That will be perfect. Thank you," Shelly said.

"You're welcome. See you later, dear."

Shelly handed the phone back to Andrea. "They're returning the favor."

"So I gathered." Andrea's eyes sparkled. "And?"

"And, what?"

"And, are you excited to see Rob again?"

She was, but she didn't have to admit it. "I'm dating Brad."

"I know that." Andrea settled on the edge of the bed. "I also know you and Brad aren't serious, that you intend to go home in a few months, and that you and Rob have some major chemistry. You said you almost married him once."

Shelly slumped against the wall. Normally she would have discussed this with El—she was Shelly's main confidant. But since Brad was El's brother, it did make things awkward. "Rob and I...we have a great and messy past and I'm not sure what might be ahead for us, if anything. But Brad's important to me. So while I'll be happy if I see Rob again, I know nothing will happen between us." She couldn't afford to let herself go there right now.

"For as long as you've got an ocean and half a continent between you, you mean."

"For as long as Brad and I continue to be an item." At the look on Andrea's face, Shelly relented. "And the whole distance thing doesn't help."

Honestly, she didn't know what she thought about the electricity that practically sparked off her and Rob, but after almost four months of dating, she would see where things with Brad led her before looking anywhere else.

❧ ❧ ❧

ANDREA DROPPED SHELLY off in front of the inn where the Durrants were staying. Shelly knocked on the door of their room and waited to hear footsteps.

"Hi, Shelly, come on in," Rob greeted her.

Her smile widened. She reminded herself again that she was otherwise involved at the moment. "Hello. This was so kind of your mother."

"She was more than happy to reciprocate." He motioned her in.

Shelly saw the room was empty. "Where is everyone?" The two of them alone in a room together might not be the best thing ever.

"Mom said to apologize for her. They had to stop and buy a few things before we head out tomorrow. I volunteered to wait for you. The bag is over here." He motioned to the bed. "They should be back any minute."

Shelly glanced back at him and noticed he left the door wide open, as if welcoming the rest of his family. She was grateful he was careful about appearances. She totally trusted the two of them to behave, but it didn't hurt to ensure that they wouldn't be totally private. "I'd like a chance to say goodbye to them again." She set her bag on the bed. "I was so surprised to see you on Sunday."

"Mission accomplished, then." His gaze skittered away from hers.

Shelly turned back to the bag and packed her things.

He continued after a moment. "So Rhett told me how you used him to deflect a guy who's been bothering you."

Shelly flushed at the memory and wished Rhett had kept that to himself. "I never apologized to him about that. It seemed like an ideal solution at the time. I'm kind of embarrassed now, even though it worked beautifully."

Rob chuckled. "Don't be—it was brilliant. Rhett said it was all he could do not to burst out laughing when the guy realized Rhett and Elder Allen were his 'date.' He said they only stayed a little while and then left him with a Book of Mormon and their card."

Shelly became redder, but smiled. "I wouldn't normally have done that. But I'm telling you, when a guy uses a line like, 'I want to know what makes you all lit up inside,' you have to give him what he wants."

Rob laughed. "So, what are you going to do when you finish up here in a couple months?" He fiddled with a stack of brochures on a table a few feet away.

"Look for a job in Utah. I've already started, but so far nothing sounds promising. I keep hoping something will open up at a junior college for fall semester, though it'll make the timing awfully tight, and they've probably already finished hiring for next year."

"Good luck." He turned to face her. "I'm sure things are competitive, but you're one of the brightest people I know. Hopefully it won't be too hard."

"Thanks." She looked up at him, and as their gazes locked, she felt a longing for what they once had. Though she wanted to cross the room to him, she couldn't. She wouldn't do that to Brad, or to Rob. Or to herself. "I guess there's nothing I can do but hope, pray, and continue to put in applications."

Rob also seemed glued to his spot on the floor, though his hand lifted partway before he balled it and stuffed it in his pocket.

Natalie came in, lugging a grocery bag, breaking up the private moment. "Oh good, you're still here. Mom was afraid we might have missed you."

Shelly smiled, somewhat relieved to have company. She greeted the rest of Rob's family. Within fifteen minutes she was headed back out to the bus stop. She could have gotten a ride to her flat, but needed the breathing time to put the encounter behind her.

Unfortunately, the trip home took longer than she'd planned, and when she reached her flat, Brad was waiting in the kitchen while El puttered at the stove.

"Hey, beautiful, where've you been?" Brad stood and came over to her, giving her a casual kiss and sliding his arms around her.

She wouldn't lie, had nothing to hide, but still braced herself for his reaction. "Elder Durrant's mom offered to take a few things home for me, as a surprise for my parents. I've just been to their inn to drop things off."

His chin firmed and the glint in his eye turned cool, though he managed to keep his voice calm enough. "I'd have taken you if you'd asked. Did they bring you home?"

"No, Andrea dropped me off and I rode the bus back." She moved toward her cupboard, rooting around for ingredients for dinner, as well as an excuse to put some space between them.

She caught El's eye, and El mumbled something and headed upstairs. Shelly wasn't certain if she was glad to be left alone with Brad or not. Considering the way he'd acted the previous evening, and his current attitude, she was leaning toward 'or not.'

159

"Did you and Rob have a chance for another tender goodbye, then?" His voice was icy cold.

Shelly closed her eyes for a couple of seconds, then took a deep breath and faced him. "Why are you acting like this?"

"I saw the way he looked at you. He wants to be more than your buddy. He acted as though you had a long and *friendly* past." Brad crossed his arms over his chest. "I don't like sharing."

"I don't blame you." Shelly sat and motioned Brad to the chair beside her, turning to face him. He deserved at least some truth, though telling him all of it would be counterproductive. "Look, Rob and I knew each other for a long time, and yes, we dated for a while. That doesn't mean that I'm going to drop you because he shows some interest. He's going home. I'm staying here. If you want to keep dating me, you have to stop acting like a jealous git. It's not like we made plans for after I go home in a couple months. I'm dating *you*."

His expression went flat for several long seconds, though neither of them said anything. Finally, his face softened and when he spoke, his voice was calm again. "I'm sorry I'm acting like such an idiot. You're important to me and I could tell the two of you had a history you hadn't mentioned." He took her hand in his. "I don't want to lose you."

She smiled, reassured by his apology. "I'm not about to walk away from this relationship over another guy."

He leaned in and pressed a lingering kiss to her mouth, holding her tight. "Thank you."

Chapter 26

As SHELLY WALKED HAND-in-hand down the sidewalk with Brad in the evening air a few weeks later, she reflected that Rob's visit may have been just what her new relationship had needed. Ever since the Durrants had been in town, Brad managed to get to church every week and made it to more of the singles' activities than before. Of course, she admitted to herself, that could have been because his work schedule had changed and most of his friends had left town.

"What are you thinking?" Brad asked her as they rounded the corner to their street.

"About how nice it is to be with you like this. No plans, no stress—just you, me, and the busy traffic." He didn't need to know the direction her mind had taken. She was afraid her words would come across judgmental or nagging and that was the last thing she wanted to do. They only had a few months left together and she intended to enjoy them.

He chuckled. "If you ignore the honking horns and roaring motors, it's practically idyllic."

"Complete peace, if you forget the blaring stereos." Shelly motioned to the flat they were passing, which had music pouring from all the windows.

He dropped her hand and slid his arm around her shoulder instead, pulling her closer. "I have a couple of companies asking me to come in for interviews."

"That's wonderful! You're ridiculously brilliant, so I'm sure you'll be hired soon." She reached up and pressed a kiss to his cheek, enjoying the faint rasp of two days' beard growth against her fingers. "Now if only I could be so lucky. Where are the companies located?"

"There's one here in the city, and another in London." His voice was almost detached as he spoke. "The one in London has an office in the States. I understand they occasionally send people there to oversee projects."

"Wow. Sounds like you might have a chance to travel. That would be great. I know you said you'd like to." Shelly thought of the opportunity that would present for them to possibly see each other again, after she'd gone home. She quickly dismissed the thought, though. The U.S. was certainly harder to cross than England, and the chances of him being sent anywhere within six hours' drive of her were nil. "Whatever happens, it sounds like you'll land on your feet. But then, was there any question?"

He stopped in front of her flat and pulled her close. "Your faith in me means more than I can say." He dropped a lingering kiss on her mouth, and she readily reciprocated.

WEEKS PASSED AND SHELLY found the Fourth of July was not a terribly exciting day in England. Because she missed home, the parades, and fireworks, Brad took her to the seashore for a picnic and bonfire.

It was a perfect night. The air was warm—for Hull—and the breeze was light, staying comfortable until the sun went down. They talked and walked along the water's edge and then sat, enjoying the fire's crackling, roasting marshmallows and hotdogs while they watched the sunset. Streaks of orange and gold highlighted the clouds as they faced east looking over the North Sea.

"What a beautiful night." Shelly sighed, leaning her head on Brad's shoulder.

"It would probably be more spectacular if we were overlooking the Atlantic," he reminded her. The way they sat now, the sunset was actually behind them.

"True enough." She snuggled in closer. "You know, if I were home today, I'd be in Moroni watching the fireworks with my family. They have an amazingly nice show, considering the town is so tiny."

He brought his arm around her in a hug. "Well, it's not exactly fireworks, but we do have a fire."

"I could almost forget about books and research. I wish this night could go on forever." She rubbed her cheek against his nubby sweater and inhaled his scent mixed with wood smoke. This was one of the moments she wanted to remember even when she was old and gray. She had thought they weren't getting serious, but it was going to be very hard to say goodbye to him at the end of the summer.

He hesitated for a moment and then ran a hand down the length of her hair. "It could... well, not literally, but..." She glanced up and gave him a curious look. His chin firmed and he asked, "Shelly, when you think about us, where do you think we're headed?"

She wasn't sure how to answer. A few weeks before, she would have told him they were only friends having a great time, but she needed to go home. Now, though, she was confused. Her feelings for him had grown, and saying goodbye would be hard.

After waiting a moment for her response, he spoke again. "*Do* you think about us?"

Nerves jumped in her stomach. "I guess my feelings on that point are... in flux. I've always known I'd be going home next month, but it won't be easy." She bit her bottom lip. "What do you think?"

He moved a few inches away so they could see each other better. "Shelly, I love you. I want to spend the rest of my life with you." He touched her chin with his forefinger and his thumb grazed her cheek. "I want to marry you."

Her throat seized and she could feel her pulse race at his words. *Marry? Like temples and flowers and forever?* The thought had flitted across her mind once or twice, but she hadn't given it any real consideration.

"You don't need to give me an answer yet, but I want you to think about it. I need to have you by my side, always." He pressed his lips to hers, soft, sweet. "Shelly, when I look at my future, it doesn't look right without you. I see you in every scene."

His words jolted her and a pure shock of déjà vu hit her. She held her breath while she came back down to earth. It was so much like the proposal—or *almost* proposal—she'd received nearly two years earlier.

From Rob.

Shelly pushed the memory back, not wanting it to interfere. She had feelings for Brad, but was it love—and if it was, did she love him enough to stay in England forever? She forced herself to breathe. "I'll have to think about it."

"You can have all the time you want," he promised, then smothered her whirling thoughts with another kiss.

"SO, DID YOU HAVE a nice date last night?" El asked Shelly when she emerged from her room late the next morning.

"Yes, the weather was perfect, the sunset was breathtaking." Shelly pulled the cereal from the cupboard and said offhandedly, "Oh, and your brother asked me to marry him." She'd stayed up half the night thinking about it, which was why she'd slept so late.

"What?" El's hands fumbled on her cup of juice and sloshed some over the rim.

"Didn't you know? I thought he'd have mentioned to you that he was thinking about it." Shelly could see from the surprise in El's eyes that he hadn't said a word. She wondered if there had been signs that marriage was on his mind, ones she'd missed. If so, his sister obviously hadn't caught them either.

"Anyway," Shelly continued, "I guess he didn't exactly propose. It was more like, 'hey, have you thought about our future? I'd like to marry you,' and he left it at that." She retrieved a purple bowl from the cupboard and poured in some cereal. The parallels between this sort-of proposal and the previous one from Rob were driving her crazy. It made it even harder to keep her feelings for the two men straight, especially as her online conversations with Rob hadn't diminished.

"I guess I knew he was headed there, though we never talked about it. And what did you tell him?" El sat beside Shelly at the table. "I'd like to have you as a sister."

"I told him I'd have to think about it." Shelly smiled at the thought of being related to El.

"You haven't thought about it already?" El asked with a sly smile. "Not even a little?"

"It never entered my thoughts." Shelly saw her roommate's disbelief and reconsidered. "Okay, yeah, it has. But it didn't seem... rational. I mean,

I live in Utah, and I haven't gotten my head around the idea of living here forever. I've been so focused on going home again in six weeks and finding a job, even though I'll miss all of you," Shelly admitted. "I suppose I didn't let myself consider it, but I do care about him. I'll mull it over carefully."

"The change that's come over Brad in the past year is amazing. He's much more involved at church than he used to be, and I love having him around. You're a good influence on him."

Shelly smiled and considered for a moment what her life would be like as Brad's wife. There would be visits to Dover to see his parents, grandkids running through the house, and sitting with his family on Christmas Eve talking about silly things their kids had done that week. It was a nice picture.

Chapter 27

LATER, SHELLY SAT ON her bed and thought about the decision she had to make, and soon. Wasn't this why she'd struggled over whether to get involved with Brad in the first place? A big part of her wanted to marry him. It made sense. They loved each other, and he'd never been anything but sweet to her. He was thoughtful and caring. This had to be what the Lord wanted. Right? So why was she still confused?

She thought and prayed about little else, her mind filled only with the decision that would change her whole life—even more than the one she'd made to marry Jimmy. Marrying Brad would mean living in a different country, but even that wouldn't be a deal breaker. Not if this was the right choice.

The week went by quickly with studying and activities, but Shelly had a hard time concentrating on her paper and found herself staring into space far too often. As the week waned, she didn't seem to come any closer to an answer. She lay on her bed trying to study and heard someone come in the front door. When Andrea's familiar grumble reached her a moment later, Shelly got up from the desk and walked into the kitchen.

"How was work?" Shelly asked.

"Great. Fabulous. I can't wait to get a job where I don't come home smelling like grease." Andrea dumped her backpack on the table. "I am so glad to have a couple of days off."

Shelly leaned against the door jam, watching Andrea move around the room. Finally, Andrea stopped what she was doing and looked up at Shelly.

"What's going on? Did you put Brad out of his misery and agree to marry him yet?"

"No. I'm trying to decide if I dare ask you something, because it's a big favor."

"Spit it out. I'm too tired to play games tonight." Andrea winced, then set her jug of milk on the table. "Sorry I'm being so short-tempered. I need my bed. You know you can ask me anything. I might not give you what you want, but you're free to ask."

Shelly managed a smile and sat in one of the chairs. "I think I need to make a trip to the temple. I haven't been since I was home, and I could certainly use some guidance about now."

"The closest one's in Preston, right? That's only about a hundred miles. I could take you tomorrow, if you'd like." Andrea grabbed a bowl of cereal and sat at the table.

And that was why Shelly knew she could ask Andrea. "Bless you. I really appreciate it."

"No problem. I need a break from everything." She ran a hand through her dark hair, weariness plain on her face. "I'll see if I can go down to the baptistery."

Shelly reached out and put a hand on Andrea's wrist. "Thanks."

"You've been a great support for me this year. That's what friends are for." Andrea patted Shelly's arm, then returned to her dinner. "We could leave around nine. That should get us there plenty early."

"Nine sounds perfect." Shelly smiled in relief, already feeling better as she headed back to her bedroom.

THE NEXT MORNING went smoothly. Shelly was ready when Andrea came down for breakfast, and they left a little earlier than they'd planned. Later, she sat in the chapel before the session started and prayed long and hard that she would know what to do. Brad was so good to her, and she even thought she loved him, but she didn't feel right about marrying him. She didn't know if it was nerves, or an answer, so she prayed some more.

The Spirit was strong in the temple and Shelly felt peace. Afterward, she prayed in the celestial room for a long time. She wondered again if Brad was the right one. She wasn't sure if it was nerves after losing Jimmy, or if she was getting the right answer. As she prayed, an image flashed into her mind. Rob Michaels.

Shelly pushed away the image and refocused her mind. She had tried so hard not to let her feelings for Rob mix up her feelings for Brad. It wasn't fair to Brad, and she *wanted* to be fair to him.

But the feeling inside came strong to her that Brad was not the one. She reminded herself that didn't mean things would work out with Rob. There was a certain something between them even now, but that was far from a sure thing. It was possible she and Rob might never get back together—he could be dating someone already and she wouldn't know.

She shook her head to clear it again, but no matter how she tried to get a different answer, she realized she couldn't marry Brad. Tears poured down her face, but as she tried to figure out why she couldn't stay in this easy, sweet relationship, she had an epiphany.

Maybe the problem wasn't that she kept letting her feelings for Rob interfere with her relationship with Brad. Maybe it was the other way around. Her heart quavered when she thought of taking another chance with the man she had never completely stopped loving. Sure they were friends, but would he let her into his heart again?

Then she wondered if that was just mixed-up emotions left over from two years earlier when it had been a question of Rob or Jimmy.

Trying to sort it out was giving her a headache.

She put a hand on her forehead and sent another petition winging toward heaven for clarity, peace, and the courage to give Brad an answer he wouldn't want to hear.

Finally she stood and made her way to the women's changing room.

When she showed up at the visitors' center where Andrea sat quietly reading from her textbook in a corner, Shelly felt peace. She held tightly to it, knowing from experience that pain would encroach soon enough.

Andrea lifted her head when Shelly approached and smiled. "So, you decided to come out?"

"I was using up all the air, so they asked me to leave."

"I can see how that would be a problem." Andrea's lips twitched. "You want to grab a bite before we head back?"

"Yeah. I'm starving." Shelly had gone to the temple fasting, but closed her fast through prayer before she left the dressing room.

Andrea gathered her things and they walked out to the car. "It looks like you got your answer," she said casually.

Shelly nodded. "I made the decision. Now I have to tell him."

"You want to talk about it?" Andrea asked.

They walked up to the car and Andrea unlocked it remotely. As Shelly grabbed the handle, she shook her head. "Not yet. I'll tell you and El about it tonight. She'll want to hear every gory detail."

"True enough."

WHEN SHELLY GOT BACK to the flat, El was studying at the kitchen table. "Hey, did you have a nice trip?"

Shelly set her purse inside her bedroom door, then joined her roommates in the kitchen. "Yes, it was really good. I'll be glad to get home where I can go more regularly."

El closed her text book and looked up at Shelly; a hurt look filled her face. "So the answer's no. That's it, isn't it? You're going home?"

Shelly pulled out a chair and sat. "I guess I've known all week. I wanted so badly to stay that I wasn't listening." She closed her eyes as tears began to prickle. "Are you angry?"

"Angry? Are you crazy?" El bumped Shelly's arm. "I'm disappointed, but I understand. I love Brad, but sometimes I don't get him... Anyway, I guess I feel like we were meant to be sisters, beyond sisters in Zion." She offered an awkward laugh.

"Yeah. But now comes the hard part." Shelly slumped in the chair. "How do I tell *him*?"

Chapter 28

AFTER WORK THAT EVENING, Brad went out with his roommates and played some snooker. Shelly didn't see him until morning when he stopped by to pick them up for church.

"You don't look so great," Shelly said when he leaned down to kiss her hello. She ran a finger over his brow with concern.

"I have a bit of a headache," he admitted.

"If you went to bed at a reasonable hour..." she teased him. He merely smiled and led her out to the car.

Brad was going to join them for lunch after church and Shelly planned to pull him away for a talk after they ate. However, when he arrived at his flat to change, he received a phone call from work asking him to come in and help on an emergency. He went in, so the time of reckoning was pushed back. The next day by the time she got out of class, he was already at work for the afternoon and evening.

"I wonder if I'm ever going to get him alone again," Shelly told El in frustration when she realized he wouldn't be home until late.

Her chance finally came Tuesday afternoon when Brad joined her for their daily run.

They jogged in silence for most of the distance and then walked the last few blocks to cool down.

Brad took her hand as they walked. "I feel like I never get to see you anymore."

"I know. We've both been so busy." Shelly had been preparing herself for the inevitable conversation, but she still wasn't sure how to tell him her decision.

"Did you have a nice trip to the temple?" he asked.

"Yeah, it was beautiful, exactly what I needed." She wiped a trickle of sweat that slid down her cheek. "It's been too long since I went last. I used to go often when I was home."

He gave her hand a squeeze. "Shelly, have you thought about it enough yet?" he asked as they approached their building.

She took a breath and led him across the grass away from the apartments. "I have, and I've prayed. A lot." She sat under a remote group of trees and turned to him. "Brad, you're a wonderful guy, and I love you." His eyes glowed with delight. "But I can't marry you."

His face fell, but he took both her hands in his. "I know we could make it work. We love each other—that's what matters."

Her heart broke all over again as she saw the confusion on his face. "No, Brad, if love were all that mattered..." She stopped that line of thought because it could take them in circles for hours. "I'm really sorry. I wish the answer could be different. I tried so hard to *make* it be different, but I couldn't."

He was already shaking his head. "I understand if you're still having problems because of Jimmy, but honey, I know we're supposed to be together, I feel it down to my core." His eyes bored into hers. "No one else could make me as happy as you do."

"This isn't about Jimmy."

"What's it about, then? I can be anything you need. Give me a chance." Naked despair filled his eyes and his hands grasped hers even tighter than before.

"Brad, don't make this any harder than it already is." Shelly closed her eyes as tears threatened. Why had she dated him in the first place? Hadn't she known this might happen?

"Why? Why can't you marry me?" He released her hands and stood, towering over her.

She stood also and crossed her arms over her stomach. "I don't know why. I just can't."

"You said you love me. How can you say that but turn me down? What—what kind of answer is that?" His face was starting to turn red and his jaw tightened.

"I don't know!" She blew up. "I prayed about it and received an answer. That's how it *works*. We don't have to understand why we do, or *don't* do something. We do it because that's what the Lord wants, because it *feels* like the right decision or the wrong one." Her voice rose in frustration. "That's why it's called faith."

They stood for several long heartbeats, and she saw the rigidity leave his body as he relaxed. Soon the sadness in his eyes filled her heart with sorrow.

His arms slid around her sweaty back, pulling her close to him. His lips found hers and his kiss was sweet and full of longing. Shelly felt that strong yearning to stay in his arms, reveled in it for a few seconds before she broke away. "Brad, this isn't helping. The answer won't change." Tears filled her eyes and she turned back to her flat.

He took a couple quick steps and grabbed her elbow, stopping her from moving on. "Shelly, wait. What is it? I know you love me." He lifted her chin gently so she met his gaze.

"I'm sorry." There was no other answer she could give him. She turned around again and continued back toward the building. When she heard his footsteps moving away, she looked over her shoulder to see him stalk off.

How come love always seemed to end in heartbreak?

TIRED, ROB WALKED back out into the hot night air carrying his basket of clothes from the dryer downstairs. Too bad it was the height of summer. He could use a snow-covered slope whooshing below his skis about now.

His cell phone started to ring before he opened the door. He tried to pull it from his pocket while juggling the laundry basket at his doorstep. The caller ID showed it was Rhett. Seriously, the kid had the worst timing ever. Invariably, when Rhett called, Rob had his hands in something gross or his arms full of bags—it was like he had ESP for causing trouble. "Yeah?"

"Have you heated anything up yet? I thought I'd stop for a pizza on the way home."

"Fine, great. You know you'll eat most of it anyway."

"It's my metabolism. See you in a bit."

Rob heard a click on the line and shook his head. Sometimes it was hard to believe Rhett was already home from his mission. He still thought of him as that gangly thirteen-year-old, too tall for his skin, that Rob had left behind when he'd gone on his own mission. It was kind of fun sharing an apartment with him, though. Most of the time.

While he waited for dinner to arrive, he popped online and sent Shelly a note about a job opening on campus. He'd seen the proprietary way Brad had treated her, so he didn't know if she would even come home to stay. She might end up marrying the Brit. The idea churned in his stomach and he had to push it away. He thought he made his feelings clear when he saw her last. If she married Brad, there was nothing Rob could do about it. But hope made him send the link.

It didn't take long for Rhett to show up at the door with two five-dollar pizzas. He took a look around and set the boxes on the counter. "You've been cleaning." His eyes zeroed in on the laundry Rob was folding. "And you did laundry." He gasped dramatically. "And did you pull out a *vacuum?*" He turned accusing eyes on his brother. "What's her name? And how long have you been holding out on me?"

"Leland." Rob gestured to the counter where the newest letter lay unopened. "I couldn't settle down. I wish he'd leave me alone." He took a slice of pizza and bit into it.

Rhett nodded and finished off his own bite. "He is your dad, you know—"

That was as far as he got before Rob cut him off. "No, Marc is my dad." He chewed and swallowed. "I don't want to talk about it."

Silence echoed for thirty long seconds, then Rob heard Rhett open a drawer, and he turned his head to see his brother put the letter with the other unopened letters from Leland. Rob had told him to toss the lot of them more than once, but neither of them did.

"Okay, want to hear about the girl who just got hired at work? She's a dance major." Rhett wiggled his eyebrows, getting Rob to laugh despite himself. Once in a while Rhett was great to have around.

Chapter 29

"I'M GOING TO TALK to Brad," Shelly said as she and El ate breakfast one morning.

"Are you sure you want to do that? It might make things worse." El scooped up a bite of cereal.

"Can it get worse? It's been two weeks and he's still hiding away." Shelly finished her toast, not hungry. "Sometimes I catch him watching me through the window when I walk back home at night, but he ignores me on the street." She ran her fingertip through the crumbs on her plate. "I miss him."

"You expect him to magically become your friend again?" El's voice was edged with irritation.

"No, of course not." Shelly pushed back from the table and carried her dishes to the sink to wash them. "I know it won't be all hearts and flowers again. I just..." She shrugged, knowing it would sound lame to say she wanted him not to be hurting anymore.

"If you're asking for my advice, leave well enough alone. But you have to decide for yourself." El rinsed her dishes and returned to her room.

Shelly decided El was right and not to do anything, but when she came home that afternoon, she saw movement behind Brad's bedroom curtains. They closed when she glanced his way. Making up her mind, she dropped off her books and hurried over to his flat.

George answered the front door and when she said she wanted to talk to Brad, he shot her a look of disbelief. "I don't know if he'll talk to you, but you can try." He led her down the hall to Brad's room.

174

Shelly knocked. "Brad, we need to talk." She waited in silence for a long moment. She could hear sounds in the room, but he didn't say anything.

"Let him go, or come back tomorrow. If he's aled up again, he's not going to talk anyway," George said from behind her.

"If he's what?" Shelly wasn't sure she heard that right. She couldn't have.

Brad must have been standing on the other side of the door because it opened suddenly and his stony red face peered out. "Thanks, you're helping a lot," he shot at George's retreating figure. He turned and pulled Shelly into the room, shutting the door behind them.

He backed her up against the door, penning her in with one hand on each side of her shoulders.

How could his proximity have felt great a few weeks ago, but make her claustrophobic now? "Maybe we should step outside to talk," she suggested. *This* scenario hadn't been what she had planned.

His green eyes stared into hers. "Have you changed your mind?" His tone and expression made it clear he knew she hadn't.

She could hardly breathe. "No," she managed to croak out. *What was I thinking?*

"So, what are you doing here?" he asked.

"I hate this—you sulking, ignoring me unless you can peek through your drapes. I understand that you're mad. I'm *sorry* if you feel like I led you on. I didn't mean to. I thought you understood..." She wished she had somewhere to go, and could put some space between them instead of being stuck between him and the door.

"Understood what? That we were *just friends*, while you kissed me..." His voice resonated through the silence of the room, and she had no doubt George was catching the whole conversation. "That you wouldn't date anyone but me, but wouldn't get serious?" He stepped closer to her, his eyes changed, softening, and he lifted his right hand off the door to touch her face. His look was intent and her discomfort multiplied. As he leaned in to kiss her, she felt his breath fan her face. Her stomach constricted as she caught the smell of alcohol.

Whoa, how had she missed that before?

Shelly pushed him away and he stumbled back, reaching down to steady himself on his desk. Her eyes took in a collection of empty beer bottles littering the top and down onto the floor. She felt sick. Had he started drinking the moment they broke up? Had he been drinking all along? He was Mormon too, he didn't drink. Did he?

Brad looked at the bottles and his eyes widened as if he'd forgotten about them. He reached out and caught her upper arm as she spun to grab the door handle.

"No, Shelly, wait."

"I'm sorry I bothered you. You were obviously *busy* in here, spending your time on something more important." She tried shaking his hand off and moved to leave, but he held tight.

"Wait!" Brad seemed to search for a reason she should stay. He stumbled over his words in his haste. "It's not—I mean, you don't..."

She could hardly speak around the hot lump of pain in her throat. "I think it is, and I do. Let go of me." She opened the door, though she couldn't walk through it.

He paused for a moment, then slowly released her arm.

She hurried out of there.

Shelly made it to her room dry-eyed and stared out the window numbly. *How could I have been so wrong?*

Half an hour later, El appeared at Shelly's bedroom door. She stood for a long moment, then came in and sat on the bed. "Did you talk to Brad, then?"

"I'm such a fool. Why couldn't I see it?" Shelly asked, her eyes still staring through the glass. She felt empty. All those nights he'd been out with his friends. The ensuing headaches, lack of sleep and general grouchiness. Was he using hanging with the guys as an excuse to go drinking without letting her know about it? Had some of those times he'd been 'called in to work' actually been an excuse to go drinking?

El put her hand on Shelly's knee. "See what?"

"I went to his flat to talk. When he finally let me in, there were loads of empty beer bottles on his desk. He was totally ripped, and I didn't even realize at first." She rubbed her forehead, trying to makes sense of it. "When I look back, I can see he must've been drinking all along. It's like he's been lying to me and I believed it, all of it, without question. He knows how I feel about alcohol. I told him, and he agreed with me that it was stupid and led only to badness. Then he snuck around behind my back."

"I'm sorry. I thought that ended last fall. I mean, I worried when he was out with his chums, but—"

"You knew he drank, even after he was baptized?" Shelly asked in surprise.

"Yeah. Hang on," El said as if the realization had just hit her. "You didn't?"

"No," Shelly replied as if it should have been obvious. "I guess I'm this eternally naïve idiot who thinks people are what they appear to be. I thought he gave it all up."

"I'm sorry. I knew that he used to go out drinking with his buddies. Remember, Brad had been drinking with his friends for over three years when he was baptized." El tipped her head in acknowledgment. "Well, drinking *legally* for three years. He stopped for a long time after that, but—I don't know, maybe he didn't care so much anymore." El leaned against the wall. "I thought things had changed. I told you, you were a good influence on him."

"Maybe he was only putting on a good front. He has such potential, if he would just..." Shelly couldn't finish the thought—it wasn't necessary anyway. She and El had practically been completing each other's sentences for months now. Besides, she wasn't dating him anymore—talking it to death wouldn't change anything.

After a few minutes of silence, El asked, "So, does that mean I'll never see you again?"

Shelly smiled weakly. "You could come visit me sometime. You'll always have a place on my couch. Assuming I have a couch." She was glad when that brought a fleeting smile to El's lips, even though she couldn't manage one herself.

The silence lingered for several minutes before El broke it. "Have you heard on any of the jobs yet?"

Shelly was grateful for the change in topics; forward thinking was what she needed, not looking back. No doubt she would do plenty of that later. "Not yet, but I still have a few weeks left here before I go back. I'll probably find something soon. I heard about a teaching position at Salt Lake Community College and I think I'll apply for it, but they may hire before I get home." She hoped not, gainful employment could be an issue if she didn't get a job this semester.

"I wish you luck."

Shelly nodded. "I'd be teaching freshman-level U.S. and world history. At least, that's what the ad said."

"You'll make a great teacher." El gave Shelly a hug.

Shelly hoped so.

※ ※ ※

BRAD LEFT SHELLY A NOTE of apology the next morning. She was glad he didn't try to talk to her. She wasn't ready to discuss it yet—she felt so betrayed. At the same time, she tried very hard not to bring it up anymore with El. It was too easy to get her stuck in the middle, and Shelly didn't want to do that.

The good thing about the break-up was that Shelly didn't feel bad about keeping in touch with Rob online, or about wearing the locket Jimmy had given her. She'd barely had a chance to wear it last winter before depositing it in a safe place with the engagement ring.

Now she pulled it out and remembered that there was a plan, a reason for everything that happened. She just had to figure out what it was.

Chapter 30

THOUGH SHE WORKED like a demon during the week, Shelly spent the rest of her weekends on side trips all over the country—sometimes with Andrea, sometimes with El, and once on her own. She wished she had time and money enough to see every inch of the island from the northern tip of Scotland, to the famous White Cliffs of Dover, and over to the western edge of Wales. Then she would take several more months to investigate every hill and borough in Ireland.

She thought she might manage to finish out her time in England without speaking with Brad again, though she wasn't sure if that was good or not. That was, until she came home and found him standing in front of her apartment, in the same place Clay had waited for her months earlier.

He leaned against the door jamb, fidgeting with his keys. "Hey, Shelly, I know my timing stinks, but can we talk?"

She stopped and looked at him, unsure what to think. They hadn't spoken in weeks. She knew there was nothing he could say that would make her feel better about him, or them. He had pretended for so long to be something he wasn't. How could she ever trust him now? "I don't think that's a good idea."

"Please, for a few minutes. I know you're swamped with your thesis."

Actually, she'd turned it in already, but didn't feel a need to explain. "Do you really think hashing it out will make any difference?"

"Look, I know you go home soon and I have to talk to you first."

Despite her frustration, Shelly took a deep breath and nodded, then led him away from her apartment, back to the grassy spot where she'd refused to marry him before. When she sat on the grass, she wondered if it was a bad choice to return to that place, but she didn't want to take the conversation inside.

Brad sat across from her and looked at her intently. "I know I screwed up. I've been confused, not knowing what was most important. After we split up, my whole life went pear shaped. I made a right mess of everything." He plucked at the grass. "When you told me no it about killed me. And then you couldn't even give me a good reason why not."

Shelly couldn't help feeling a tad of irritation. "Obviously my decision was justified."

He held up his hand to stop her. "Agreed. I know how you feel about... some of my actions. I admit, I haven't been perfect this year. But I was doing so much better than I used to. In time I could become what you really want." He grabbed her hand and held it tightly.

What you really want. Shelly momentarily closed her eyes in pain as she heard those words. Obviously he didn't get it. "Brad, I don't want you to become what I want."

His stared at her, looking confused and disappointed.

Sometimes her mouth didn't wait for her brain to catch up. "I mean, I don't want you to become what *I* want for you, I want you to become what *you* want for you. It doesn't matter what I want." Suddenly she felt tired. Her emotions had already been stretched, but she couldn't muster more than a sigh now. "If you change for me, you'll be miserable. Who knows how long you'll stay my prince before you decide it isn't worth it, and take your horse back to the pub again?"

"But—"

"No but," Shelly cut him off. "It doesn't matter what I want from you. Trust me. I have friends who are married. I've worked with married women. I can't tell you how many times I've heard the phrase 'boys will be boys.' It was with more than a tinge of bitterness at times. I don't want that. If you change to make me happy, it won't last. I hope someday you decide you're ready to make that change because it'll make *you* happy. Then it might stick," her voice softening with intensity.

"But I love you! These past few weeks have been bad, real bad, without you. I need you with me. I know you love me too," he finished, pleading with his eyes as well as his words.

With a flash of insight, Shelly shook her head, knowing he was wrong. Peace filled her as she gently pulled her hands from his grasp. "My love for you isn't what you think." It all seemed so clear now. "I care about you because you've been so good for me, a great friend, a fun boyfriend, and I do feel love, but it's not enough."

"Shelly!"

"No." She stood and hitched her backpack onto her shoulders again. "You're a special guy, Brad. You have so much to give, but you and I aren't right for each other. And no," she cut him off before he could start to protest, "it isn't just about the drinking." She'd known love. With two men. This wasn't nearly as strong. Not strong enough to last. She didn't think she could be bold enough to use those words, though. She didn't want to make this harder for him than it already was. "I need to go home, and I need... for you to stay here."

Her mouth was dry, her hands shook, but her heart was strong. "Make something great of yourself. The woman you marry will be extremely lucky to have you."

This time his voice was low, the hope gone. "Shelly, please."

She shook her head. "I need to go." She turned away, a tear slipping down her face. Why was the right thing always so hard?

THE NEXT DAY SHELLY lay on her bed studying rail guides and maps with her dwindling bank balance in mind as she considered where to spend her last week.

She propped her head up with her hand, flipping pages and poring over numbers. She pursed her lips as she tried to decide whether to go north or southwest. Despite all her trips, she still hadn't been into Scotland or Wales and couldn't imagine going home without setting foot in at least one of them.

El came in and sat beside her. "So, I've been thinking. I've turned in all my assignments for the semester and I don't have anything else to do until final exams. My job is done. I wondered if you want to take a trip with me to my aunt's cabin at the lakes."

"The lakes. Like, Lake District?" Shelly had wanted to go back when she could scale the hills and sit on the shore without utterly freezing.

"Yeah, Cora isn't there right now. She offered to lend it to me anytime I wanted to go and take a friend. I can call her neighbor who has the key and let her know we'll be coming. We could stay all week and you can poke your head into every shop and museum while I study."

Shelly looked at her, feeling a tingle of excitement. It sounded perfect. There would be the issue of transportation, but El must have ideas about how to get there if she was making the suggestion.

"How quickly can you pack?" El asked.

"Give me an hour." Shelly laughed and jumped off the bed, scattering her maps onto the floor.

"Pack for a whole week. I don't have finals until Tuesday, and I'm not coming back a minute early." El rushed down the hallway to her room.

❀ ❀ ❀

AS USUAL, THE DRIVE through the English countryside proved green and rich with life. Shelly contrasted it to the scrub oak and June rye grass that grew sparsely along the roadsides where she was from. It was beautiful in Utah, but it was different. This was vibrant—and not only in the spring. She loved the rolling hills here, and didn't miss the mountains as much as she had thought she would.

She was sorry she would have to leave soon, even though she was excited to see her family again.

The girls arrived at the cottage in time to crash for the night. Somehow El had persuaded Brad to let her borrow his car. They investigated every shop, eatery, and history site within ten miles, and then took a day trip into Scotland. Shelly checked out all the tourist traps in Gretna Green before they detoured to nearby Caerlaverock and Lochmaben castles. Many afternoons, they stretched out on the beach. Unfortunately, the lake was way too cold to actually swim in, but the days were warmer than usual for this time of year and watching the water lap at the shore was well worth the time. It was the best holiday Shelly had enjoyed in ages.

Monday morning before they had to return to Hull, she and El sat on the shore, watching the water lap just beyond their toes. "You know, I would never use your brother or mean to lead him on," Shelly said. It had been on her mind so much lately as she tried to reason out all of her twisted and messed up relationships. This could be one of the last chances she and El had to talk about it, and Shelly needed to get it off her chest.

"I know you wouldn't. I'd never accuse you of being intentionally insensitive."

"Ah, there's that word—*intentionally.*" Shelly was disgusted for the necessity of it. "Well, as long as I didn't *mean* to break anyone's heart, then I'm okay."

El put down her book and sent Shelly an exasperated look. "That's not what I meant, and you know it."

"I deserve it. I knew I shouldn't have dated him. Apparently, I have a talent for making guys care about me and then *squashing* them."

"*Wow*, you do have a high opinion of yourself."

Shelly sighed. "You know what I mean."

"Yes, I do, and you're wrong." El tipped her head. "Well, *sort of* wrong."

"Sort of. That makes me feel so much better." Shelly picked up a pebble from the ground beside her and tossed it into the lake.

"I don't know all the whys and wherefores of your relationship with Rob before Jimmy came home, so I'm not exactly an expert on what went wrong."

"Did you know *wherefore* actually means *why*? Why do you suppose people use that word, anyway?"

El huffed. "Forget it. If you're going to be flippant, I'm not going to try." She turned back to her textbook, opening it again to the place she'd marked with her finger.

"I'm sorry." Shelly threw a few more pebbles into the lake, irritated with herself. "I think I was actually quite open with Rob. I told him about Jimmy the first time we had a real conversation that didn't revolve around classes, and it took months of friendship before I broke down and agreed to a date. That doesn't mean I should have pursued the relationship—or rather, allowed him to pursue it, knowing I'd marry Jimmy in the end."

"And Rob obviously has no responsibility for continuing to chase you when he knew you planned to marry your missionary." El's sarcasm oozed. "Give me a break—and don't beat yourself up over Brad, either. He knew you planned to go home, he knew what your standards were, and what you wanted in a relationship. If he chose to date you, knowing he wasn't living those standards, and that he was lying every time he pretended he *was* living them, that's his problem."

Shelly rubbed a hand over her face, breathing deeply a couple of times to stave off the tears she did not want to let loose. "I know you're hurting because he's hurting."

"Yes, but that doesn't make him any less responsible for his actions. I love him, and I wish the two of you had a fabulous romance that ended in wedding bells and you living down the street from me for the rest of our lives. It didn't happen that way. Guys are gits. Move on."

A moment of silence passed as Shelly tried to decide how to broach the subject that comment left. "All guys are gits? So you dumped sweet, heart-over-bucket Chet because he was a git?"

"What makes you think I dumped him? Maybe he dumped me. Did that ever occur to you?" El wrote in a notebook on her lap, her attention fixed on the paper, but Shelly could see she was doodling more than making notes.

"Yes. And then I talked to Andrea, who had talked to Chet's roommate and learned it was otherwise. And what about Adam and John?"

"All right, so I have a commitment issue!" El threw up her hands.

"An issue? It's more like a subscription." Shelly kept her voice low and casual, not wanting to push El too far, but needing to get this all out in the air. She didn't understand El's problem.

"What's it to you?" Now El's voice was more sulky than angry.

"You're my friend—a friend, I might add, who told me that I shouldn't have to bear the burden of mourning alone. One who told me I could talk to you about my problems anytime, and who actually got a bit teed off that I kept it to myself. Yet you keep plenty of your own problems close to your chest and don't share." Shelly let that soak in for a long moment. "I care about you, and I want you to know I'll be there for you, like you've been there for me, whether that's now or after we have an ocean between us."

It was a long time before El's voice broke into the sound of bird calls and the lapping of water against the shore. "I'm not all that great when it comes to trusting men, all right? They're lots of fun now and then, but I'm not walking off into the sunset with anyone."

Shelly swallowed, hearing the pain in El's voice. "What happened?" She waited, then prompted further. "When you first went out with Chet,

Brad appeared surprised, like you never dated. There was all this subtext between Andrea and Brad, but I couldn't figure it out."

"Call me a hypocrite and get it over with, will you?" El set her book aside. She rolled her eyes. "Fine. My first year of college, I went out with a guy named Alex. He was in his last year and getting ready for grad school. We dated about six months and he was talking about engagement rings, and I was seeing orange blossoms and white doves in my dreams."

"You were in love?"

"Heart over bucket." El picked up her own handful of rocks and tossed them into the water one by one. "My grades slipped because I was paying more attention to him than my studies, and I quit my job to spend more time with him, so my bank account got extremely low. My parents were not impressed. Then spring term started to wind down and finals were upon us and I was sure every time he took me out that 'tonight would be the night' for me to get a ring. Then one day he took me to a sweet restaurant where we talked and laughed in the firelight, the place smelled of delicious food and the bouquet of roses in the middle of the table. I had dressed up in my newest dress, sure this would be the time."

"He dumped you?" Shelly asked.

"Wait for it. He walked me to the front door and I had stars in my eyes." She placed a hand over her chest and sighed dramatically. "I knew I would never know another love like this. Then he told me he was engaged, had been since Christmas to a woman he knew growing up, and that he'd be married in a matter of weeks. He thanked me for the fun we had together and with a kiss on the cheek, breezed away."

"What a jerk!"

El nodded in agreement. "At least." She rubbed her hands together to remove the last bit of sand. "I'd put my personal standards aside to be with him. I'm not saying I had to go talk to my bishop afterwards and make a confession, but he wasn't a member, didn't share my values, and I knew he couldn't take me to the temple, but I figured, hey, maybe someday he'd come around—I was an idiot, I know. The next fall, I found out I wasn't the only one he'd been dating at school. I haven't gone out much at all since then. This year was a change for me, but I'm still not ready to trust myself, or a guy, to put me in the position of having my heart broken again."

"Right, Chet was obviously dating all the other girls in our singles group." Shelly infused her voice with sarcasm. "Maybe I should feel left out. He never got around to me." She couldn't help but poke at her friend a little, even though she did understand where El was coming from.

"You berk."

"I try."

"You know Chet wasn't seeing anyone else."

Shelly studied El's face. "So you dumped him for only dating you?"

"You make me sound like a total git when you say that." El huffed. "I got scared, all right? I liked him too much, and I just... got scared."

"What about Adam and John?"

"I didn't like them enough, actually. They were fun, but there wasn't a spark."

"Well, that's another story, then." Shelly watched a bird skim across the surface of the lake, then come up with a fish in its mouth. "I don't mean to make light of your experience, but eventually you'll have to trust again. You won't be happy if you don't."

"I know." El stared ahead, brushing a tendril of hair away from her face.

Shelly sent up a prayer that her friend would soon find that peace she sought.

Chapter 31

ON SHELLY'S FINAL NIGHT in Hull, she, El, and Andrea ordered pizza and took it to a park to eat in the open air as twilight fell. They would all move out of the flat the next day, though Candy had already left. Shelly took a deep breath, sad about all she would leave behind. She'd grown and changed so much in the past year, she hardly recognized herself.

"You start work on Monday," she said to Andrea, then turned to El. "And you start looking for a job on Monday."

"And you, the ever-efficient one, will start following up your applications the second your plane touches the tarmac," El teased.

"That *would* be efficient, wouldn't it?" Shelly laughed at the thought.

"I'll be moved into my new flat in Bath, setting out my things, making you two jealous 'cause you have to move home with your families," Andrea said. Despite the way she tried to sound excited, Shelly saw the sadness in her eyes. Andrea's parents had told her they didn't want her *corrupting influence* at home. They allowed her to come for visits, but she couldn't move home unless she left the church.

"I'll be following your example quickly, I hope. Too bad we'll be living on different continents, or we could be roommates." Shelly finished off the last bite of her pizza. She wiped her hands on a napkin, then leaned back on her elbows to look at the stars that had sparkled to life—what few they could see through the light pollution. "I'm scared to go home."

"Why would that scare you? You've been so excited for weeks," El protested.

Shelly smiled. "I'm totally happy to see my family again, but moving home, not knowing how long it'll be before I get out on my own, makes me nervous. Things were better at Christmas than they were last summer, but I worry I'll go back to being that weepy, whiny female that I was before I moved here, moping around. I don't want to be sucked into that black hole."

"So move out and start digging for a job," Andrea suggested.

"I would, but I'm tapped out." Shelly laughed at herself—she'd always been so sensible, she never allowed her bank balance to get so low before. "I've got enough cash to pay my train fare back to London tomorrow and buy a few meals to get me home. I'd planned to keep some in reserve, but I couldn't help myself—I wanted to see everything while I had the chance. I'll have to borrow money to get into a flat, and I refuse to do that until I have a way to repay it—which means a job." She sighed. "So I have to move home for a while."

"You know, you're a different person than you were at the first of the year," El pointed out. "You're not going to become weepy or whiny this time. You're doing great."

Shelly nodded and remembered the angry, confused person she'd been then. "Thanks to some nosy roommates who wouldn't let me get away with keeping it to myself."

"What can we say, we're real pains in the... Oh, I'm not allowed to say that anymore, am I?" Andrea pulled a face as the other two laughed.

SHELLY GOT TO THE TRAIN station in plenty of time the next day. El and Andrea had left hours earlier and it was too lonely to sit at the flat alone. Of course, her train arrived late, because it would when she was anxious to get moving. As she loaded her bags into the car, she turned to wrestle her large bag into the train behind her—she hadn't fixed the handle properly.

Instead, she peered up into Clay's eyes.

"I always wanted to be a white knight," he said as he picked up her large bag and lugged it, with his own, onto the train.

The man had some serious muscles. Still, she didn't want him getting any ideas. "Clay," she said warningly.

"Don't worry, I'm not going to ask you out—I'm just making sure you get on the train and home again. Wouldn't want you to get stuck on this rock." He set her bag next to an open seat. He looked at her for a long moment. "So, how was your year in England, all things considered?"

Already feeling a touch of wistfulness, she smiled. "All in all, I'd have to say it was brilliant."

"I'm glad. You're a nice girl." He reached out, offering his hand for a shake. "It was good getting to know you."

She wondered what had gotten into him, then decided not to over-think it. She shook his hand. "It was interesting getting to know you, too."

His laugh was full-bodied and sincere. "Have a nice trip, Shelly." He turned and walked down the aisle, taking a seat a few rows away.

Dumbfounded, she answered, "Thanks, Clay, you too." As she slid into an empty spot, she thought of how things had circled back to him on her way home, and wondered what else life had in store for her.

Part III

Chapter 32

THE AIRPLANE PULLED UP to the terminal in Salt Lake City, and soon the flight attendant announced the passengers could disembark from the plane. Exhausted from the long flight, Shelly waited for the other passengers to vie for the privilege of getting out first. She had already retrieved her carryon, which she clutched to her stomach nervously as she peered out the window. Her eyes followed the jet tracks in the sky going far, far away. She was back at the beginning, but totally different than before. At least, she felt different.

She couldn't believe she was home again already. Where had the year gone? Her mind replayed the events of the past few months, good and bad, and she wondered what was ahead of her. Finally she stood and walked out.

As she came down the escalator into the baggage claim area, she was attacked by her 'baby' sister Danyelle—who, at the age of sixteen, no longer appreciated the title—followed by her parents. She greeted and hugged, kissed and cried. She wasn't sure why she was crying, but the tears came, flowing down her cheeks as she held onto her mother for a long moment.

"It's so good to have you home again," her mother said with a hollow laugh. There were tears on her cheeks as well. "You look like you could use a nice, long nap."

"I sure could. I've barely slept in the past two days," Shelly answered.

Soon they had gathered all her luggage and loaded it into the car.

"Where is everyone else?" Shelly asked when she fastened her seat belt. She didn't expect them to be waiting at the airport, but wondered when she would see them.

"Lily, Curtis, and the kids will get here tomorrow. Kellie wanted to come, but she's messing with flowers for her wedding and she has to work this afternoon, so she'll see you tonight."

Shelly was excited to see all her siblings again. Christmas seemed like eons ago and the wedding plans, on top of her return home, promised to make this a crazy week.

"Have you had any luck with jobs yet?" her father asked as soon as he pulled out of the parking lot.

"I got an email from Salt Lake Community College before I left London. I have an interview with them Thursday." She'd been stuck at the airport for hours and had taken the time to check her inbox, thankful for the free airport wifi.

"Hey, that's great!" Her father beamed at her over his shoulder.

Danyelle peppered Shelly with questions about her trip, her visit to the lakes, and things she'd seen. When she finally had enough answers, she filled Shelly in on everything happening at Manti High. She told who was dating whom, who was gunning for the lead in the school musical—despite the fact it wouldn't be cast for two more weeks—and what she did at the party with her friends the previous night. After an hour or so, their mother asked Danyelle to settle down. Please.

Shelly smiled thinly. It was the best she could do in her weariness.

When she arrived home, there was a message on the answering machine from Katie. Though she wanted to talk to Katie again, Shelly asked her mom to take messages until morning. She was going to bed. Between the train trip, flights, layovers, and long drive home, she was ready to drop.

The familiarity of her childhood room wrapped around her as she sat in the growing darkness, her blinds turned to shut out as much light as possible. Exhaustion overtook her and she soon fell asleep.

❀ ❀ ❀

ROB STUFFED ANOTHER unopened letter from his father into the kitchen drawer and sighed. Leland was being very consistent this time, and Rob wasn't sure what to do about it. If the content of the five sealed letters that lay in the drawer was anything like the two he'd actually read, then he didn't want to read them. On the other hand, there was still a part of him—however tiny—that wanted to believe that this time his father really had changed, despite all of the previous times he had claimed he would, then failed.

The apartment was quiet, which meant Rhett was still at work. Rob was glad of that, as he could use some peace. He pulled leftover spaghetti from the fridge and dished some onto a plate, snagged a clean fork, and took it into the living room. Rhett always made gagging noises when he saw Rob eating cold leftovers, which was all the more reason Rob was glad to be alone.

He powered up his laptop and checked out the latest baseball stats before popping onto Facebook. An icon told him he had a private message waiting and he smiled when he saw the note from Shelly.

Rob, thanks for the heads-up on the job. I made it back to Utah yesterday and I have an interview for the job tomorrow. Wish me luck!

He wasn't sure what to think of his relationship with her. It felt like every time he turned around, she chose another guy over him. With the turmoil he was already dealing with because of Leland, he didn't think he had the strength to add the ups and downs of a relationship. He'd been relieved when her status on Facebook had changed to 'single' a few weeks before, but he still didn't want to jump into something right off. Two years was a long time and he was sure they had both changed.

Her note didn't mention getting together, so she must not be anxious to see him. He closed the window and shut down the computer. He had other things to worry about.

❀ ❀ ❀

SHELLY STOOD IN THE administration building at Salt Lake Community College, all applicable paperwork in hand for her interview. An older man with dark hair that was turning gray at the temples and a warm, friendly smile greeted her and ushered her through the door.

"Hello, Ms. Cox, we're glad you could come. My name is Frank Meyer," he said. Mr. Meyer's dark gray pin-stripe suit showed off his lanky frame, tall and awkward. "This is Polly Gates." The man pointed to the prim woman sitting at a long mahogany table. "It looks like you made it back from England all right."

"Yes, it was a long trip, but I expect to get my sleep patterns back under control sometime before Halloween." Shelly already felt more comfortable as her quip brought a chuckle from Mr. Meyer. She sat in a deep, brown leather chair. The room was well lit, but the furnishings were dark, giving it a calming feel. The air conditioning had been turned up, making the room too cold.

"Your résumé says you've been working on your master's degree. Did you finish it, then?"

"Yes." Shelly presented a copy of her transcript with a written statement from an advisor at Hull, saying everything had been completed. "I finished Cum Laude last week. I have a CD with my thesis on it, if you'd like to look it over." She handed him the CD.

"I've reviewed the outline you sent us on your thesis, and I was very impressed," Ms. Gates said. Shelly took a closer look at the forty-ish woman with honey blonde hair. Her ensemble was perfect; her emerald earrings matched the emerald suit with pearl buttons running down the front. She was more stand-offish, not offering a welcoming look like her colleague. Shelly found the detachment a bit intimidating. "If we hired you, we would need you to start almost immediately. Term starts in six days." Ms. Gates studied Shelly, a tiny frown tugging at her lips.

"Six days?" Shelly's chest constricted in alarm. Her head swam at the thought of getting everything ready in such a short time.

"Miss Cox, do you think you could handle a classroom? You look no older than the students," Ms. Gates asked.

"I did have to do presentations for my classes, and I'm very comfortable in front of groups as a general rule. I know I'll have to be strict if I don't want to be walked all over—believe me, I've thought about it quite a lot over the past six months," Shelly assured her, though her confidence was half manufactured. It was terrifying to think of standing in front of a class and being responsible for making sure they learned what was in the syllabus in a way that didn't put them to sleep. Shelly knew she could do it, but it still intimidated her. "Age is not necessarily an indication of ability to teach."

"That's true enough, but I'm sure you can understand our concern," Mr. Meyer said.

"Of course. And I appreciate you even giving me a chance for an interview when I'm certain you've been flooded with qualified applicants. All I can promise is that I'll do my best."

Mr. Meyer nodded his understanding. "We need to fill the spot as soon as possible. I know this is highly irregular, but how familiar are you with these syllabi? You wouldn't have to follow them to the letter, but it would give you somewhere to start." He extended the pages to Shelly.

A cursory glance told her she could make it, if she found her notes from classes and had the next week free from distractions to prepare. "I could handle this. Do you need these back?"

"No, we have extra copies. Take them home and look at it if you wish," Mr. Meyer said.

The rest of the interview went quite well and Shelly crossed her fingers that it would all work out.

❀ ❀ ❀

BEFORE SHE HEADED BACK to Ephraim that afternoon, Shelly stopped at the Department of Workforce Services to check for other jobs. The pickings were worse than slim. She could apply at Snow College and pray something opened up in the next year, but that didn't feel right, and the last thing she wanted to do was live at home and leech off her parents for months longer.

She also took a long look at the rentals available and checked out a few apartments in the city that were in her price range. She couldn't sign a contract yet, but if by some miracle she did get the job, she would only have days to move in and get ready for classes.

She thought about contacting Rob, seeing if he'd like to get together for dinner or something, but she didn't have the guts. It was easy to excuse her cowardice with the fact that she was needed at home for last-minute preparations for Kellie's wedding.

Promising herself she would call him next time she was in the area—whether she had a job then or not—she turned her car for home.

Chapter 33

THE CALL OFFERING SHELLY the job came on Monday and she spent the day scrambling to pack and sort all her belongings. Luckily, when she called the apartment complex with the studio apartment she'd liked, they said it was still available and she could move in that day.

Shelly hurried to tell Lily, to share the good news before she started repacking her things. Lily was thrilled. "I knew you'd get the job! Of course you'd be their top candidate."

"You're being very generous." Shelly hadn't been nearly that confident.

"No, I'm not. You've worked hard and learned everything you could. Now you get to benefit from your effort." Lily hugged her and then looked her in the eye. "Now, honestly, how much money do you have right now?"

Shelly looked away, embarrassed to admit the truth. "Not much."

"Do you need a loan to get into your apartment?"

This hadn't been why she had come to Lily, though the alternative was getting a loan from her parents. "I couldn't ask you to loan me more money—you already paid for my trip to England."

Lily leaned back against the kitchen table. "You made good use of that money by studying hard, seeing something of the world, and coming home more like the Shelly I remember—only better. You know we didn't miss a penny of it, and considering how much you did for me after John was arrested, Curtis and I both believe it was only what you were due."

"Your compensation for my support certainly had a high price tag," Shelly said drily.

"I know you'll pay back a loan for your apartment as soon as you can, and we're happy to help." Lily looked smug. "I already talked to Curtis about it, and he agrees. We knew you would get something out of town before you got desperate and started working at Kent's Market to start saving

196

again. Mom and Dad can't afford to loan you money, but we can, so let me know how much and we'll take care of it."

Tears came to Shelly's eyes and she hugged her sister, so grateful. "Thank you so much. You've always been so good to me."

"Of course I have. Always. As long as you only count the years since I went to college, and not the years before that, when it was my chief joy to torment you."

Laughing, Shelly agreed. "Right. Who would count *those* years?"

SHELLY WAITED UNTIL they were seated at dinner to tell her dad and younger sister about her imminent departure in the morning, her stress level was already about as high as she thought it could go, and she knew they wouldn't be happy about losing her again so soon. She had three classes on her first day, but was only teaching two courses. American Civilization and World History since 1500 would stretch and excite her, she knew. With only two days to prepare, however, she was terrified she'd make a fool of herself.

"You sure you don't want to hang out here and get a job at Snow College instead? Then you'd be close," her father suggested.

Shelly stood and walked over, wrapping her arms around him in a giant hug. "I love you, Dad. You're so funny sometimes." But she had to be honest. "I love this town, but it still holds too many ghosts for me. Being away for a year was great for helping me accept Jimmy's death. But this past week has been hard and I do need to branch out—besides, what are the odds that I'll get another teaching job in the next six months, if that? This is the perfect opportunity. I know I've only been back from England for a week, but it won't be months before you see me again—I'll be coming home a lot."

"You better. I might have to hogtie you and cart you home if you don't visit. It's been nice having you around." He held her close, always her rock.

Shelly returned to her seat. She focused on Danyelle, wanting to change the subject. "So, how are things coming for the school paper, madam editor?"

"Swimmingly. We put out our first edition next week. I'll mail you a copy. Riley is talking about doing an exposé on what's really in the chow mein." Danyelle took on a serious look, as if this were a very important topic, and then laughed, her curly brown hair bouncing. She was, as usual, bright, happy, and ready for fun.

Shelly's eyes prickled at the thought of leaving again so soon, but she knew it was time. She promised herself a visit home again soon. Since she had no Friday classes, she did have a whole slew of lovely three-day weekends coming up.

SHELLY HAD LEARNED when she spoke with Mr. Meyer that she would have five classes, which made her a full-time teacher. She would be incredibly busy. Every time she thought of standing in front of all those students and teaching them, her stomach formed knots. She knew she could do it, but was terrified of screwing up.

Since she'd lived in a tiny dorm in college, she didn't have dishes or any of the things she needed for an apartment, but she figured that was what second-hand stores were for.

She reached her apartment, signed paperwork and paid, and emptied everything from her car before noon. She would unpack later—by Friday at the latest. Then she went to campus to tie up loose ends and find her classrooms so she wouldn't get lost and be late on the first day of class.

She picked out a cell phone downtown, signed a contract, and wished desperately for the one she'd had in England—it had far more options and abilities than she could afford on this one, but it wasn't compatible with her carrier here. Next, she called her contact at the Taylorsville Redwood campus. She was happy when she arrived to find Ms. Campbell's office quickly and that the instructor was waiting for her. "Hi, I'm Shelly Cox. I'm taking over Mr. Temple's classes."

A middle-aged redhead greeted her with a smile. "Oh yes, I'm so glad to meet you. Did you have any trouble finding my office?" Minute smile lines framed her eyes and mouth, and a Bostonian accent accompanied the words.

"No. The campus map was great. I'm still reeling from everything that has to be done by the time my first class starts though."

Ms. Campbell chuckled. "I'm sure you are. Have you taught much before?" She pushed her chair back from the desk and the papers piled on top of it. Then she answered her own question before Shelly had a chance to respond. "You're so young, I don't imagine you have."

"You're right. This is the first for me, but I'll handle it. At least I only have one day of class before the weekend, so there'll be time to prepare for Monday."

"Mr. Temple had the office at the end of the hall. Frank asked me to let you use it and show you around. Here's your key."

"Thanks, Ms. Campbell."

"None of that. Please call me Judy. All my students do." She eyed Shelly. "Though you might appreciate the distance of using your last name with students. At least until you've got a few more years under your belt."

"I had thought of that. I'm sure many of my students will be older than me. Is there anything I should know?"

"Other than not to eat the macaroni and cheese casserole at the cafeteria, not really. If you've been studying at Hull, I'm sure you're well prepared."

Shelly wished she were as confident about that. If only she had a little more time, she wouldn't worry so much.

Her office was the size of a closet with just enough room to squeeze in a desk, two chairs, and a couple of tall, skinny book cases. She was grateful the books she'd shipped back from England had arrived on Monday, so she'd have something to put on the empty shelves.

Next she went by human resources to fill out her W-4 and other forms. Then she stopped by the accounting office.

She had waffled over whether she should track Rob down the first day or not, but she did want to thank him for telling her about the job—otherwise, she might have spent the next several months working the checkout counter at Kent's Market. The manager had offered Shelly her old job back, and while she was grateful for the offer, she was happy she hadn't had to take it.

She smiled when she entered the accounting office and found Rob hunched over his work, muttering something. "Hey, Rob, I see you still talk to yourself." She remembered how many times she'd come upon him at the school library or in the common areas of the dorm, him bent over his book and muttering. Oh, he was a gorgeous man. In the seconds it took for him to look up and react, she looked her fill. She had convinced herself over the past months that she had imagined how handsome he was with his big brown eyes, olive skin and dark hair.

He looked at her and his face lit up with a smile. Better and better. "Shelly. What are you doing here?"

She felt a jolt when their eyes met and had to steady herself for a second before responding. "I've been hired. Imagine me, teaching a class full of students."

"Easily. Congratulations! You didn't tell me you got the job." He stood from his desk and walked toward her.

"I found out yesterday, and I've been running like crazy ever since." She accepted his hug. "I wondered if you'd like to grab something to eat tonight. I'll have to buy sometime to say thanks—not tonight, of course. I need a paycheck before I start buying for an additional person."

He chuckled. "I'm sure I'll want to eat in a few weeks just as much as I want to tonight." He turned to the guy at the next desk and introduced her. "Shelly, this is Stu. Stu, this is Shelly Cox, the newest history professor."

"Instructor," Shelly corrected. "I think you have to have a PhD to qualify as a professor."

"Regardless."

"You hardly look old enough to teach college," Stu said as he came over and shook her hand.

"I guess I have one of those faces," Shelly answered.

"Liar. She's brilliant, actually, and a hard worker. She ought to just be finishing up her bachelor's."

"He exaggerates."

"Not true." Rob changed the subject. "I get off at five. If you'd like, I can swing by your place and pick you up. Unless you'll still be here on campus."

"No. I've got plenty of errands to run. I can be home by a quarter after, if that works for you." Shelly felt suddenly nervous. She grabbed a stack of sticky notes from the desktop and scribbled her address and new cell phone number. She probably should have set the date for the next day instead—there was simply too much to do before bedtime—but she was glad for the chance to get to know him again—to see if the spark and sizzle she felt in his presence would last once they got reacquainted. She handed the note to him. "Here. You can give me a ring if you're running late."

"I will." He smiled broadly and she felt his eyes on her as she said goodbye and left the office.

Shelly swung by the bookstore, then made a beeline for the second-hand store to pick up a few necessities for her apartment.

Chapter 34

SHELLY WAS CARRYING the last load of purchases into her studio apartment when Rob arrived. He stood in the doorway and checked out her mostly empty place. "Wow. You've gone minimalist." He looked behind the door, "Are you hiding another room where you're keeping everything?"

She felt herself flush. "My cousin Rich said he'd help me move the furniture in when I find some, but I haven't had time to pick anything out."

"So I noticed." He walked over and poked through the bags of kitchen stuff she'd set on the cupboard, and glanced at her pitifully small stack of personal belongings. "It looks like you haven't had time to pick up much of anything yet, though I'm impressed by the fact that you bought actual dishes, and not just paper plates."

She rolled her eyes at him. "Paper plates! Please, I think not."

"Have you bought any food yet?" He opened the fridge and found the loaf of homemade bread, jar of homemade jam, and two sticks of margarine she'd brought with her.

"I have a few canned things in the boxes over there. I'm not completely foodless."

He walked back to her and leaned against the counter. "How about after I feed you, we go grocery shopping, too?"

"After you feed me?"

"You didn't actually think I would let you go Dutch, did you?"

"I didn't want to assume." Her breath caught at the warmth in his voice and she felt her cheeks heat. "It probably wouldn't kill me to do more shopping while we're out."

"Good. I could stand to pick up a few things myself." He sauntered back to the door and motioned for her to precede him.

They stopped at a Mexican restaurant for dinner. Once they had their food and were seated, Shelly took a long moment to study Rob. She could sense an underlying tension between them, something that pulled at her since the first time they'd met three years earlier. Unless she was very much mistaken, he felt it too.

"What?" he asked when he looked up from adding hot sauce to his tacos.

"I wondered what happened to you and your girlfriend. Lindsey, wasn't it? I thought your roommate said you were engaged."

"She seemed to think so too," he mumbled.

"Do I not want to ask?" She didn't want to rush things between them, but she was encouraged by the fact that he appeared unattached.

"Some other time, maybe." He took a deep breath and turned the conversation. "So you're teaching history, huh? I thought maybe you'd decide to stay and work on a PhD. Or maybe get married." This last bit was said with an air of disinterest—too much to be believable.

"I thought maybe I needed a break from school before continuing with my PhD. But then, here I am." She flashed him an ironic smile. "And maybe, like your failed relationship, mine ought to be tabled for another day. Suffice it to say, it didn't work out."

He studied her for a moment before asking, "Are you all right?"

She shrugged. "My heart's not broken, if that's what you mean." She twiddled her fork through her food. "I do care for him a lot, but it wasn't meant to be. So I'm scrambling to put my life in some sort of order in record time. I'm up for the challenge."

"I know you are."

They lapsed into talk of current events, their families, and the latest news from friends—less personal topics that were easier with their strained relationship. This kept them going through dinner, grocery shopping, and the return trip to her place. As he brought in the last load of her groceries, he looked around again. "Surely a college instructor can afford bigger digs than these."

She chuckled. "I have a six-month lease. I figure it'll give me time to save for a car of my own, since Danyelle's whining about me commandeering the extra one she's been using. I also need to pay back the money I had to borrow from Lily and Curtis to get into this place, and to get my feet under me. By then I'll be ready to move into something somewhat, um, not so miniscule."

"I should think so. How big is it?" he asked as he looked around the studio. There was a tiny bathroom in the corner that stole space from the neighboring apartment. "Would you say six hundred square feet, or is that being generous?"

"Five-fifty with the bathroom and closet, actually. That number might include the porch as well. The landlord didn't say so, but I have my suspicions." She slid her milk and eggs into the fridge. "Are you still in the apartment off of seventy-sixth?"

"Yeah, my roommate got married, though, so Rhett's living with me."

"Fun. I'd like to see him again, talk about England. I'm already getting homesick for my friends and the lush greenness."

"What do you miss most—the steamy, hot oppression, or the cold winter wind that nearly drives right through you?" He leaned against the cupboard, his hand on a box of cereal, his eyes intent on hers.

"It never got hot in Hull—I don't think it hit eighty degrees once, it's too far north for that. Even the cold wasn't that bad most of the time. It almost never freezes there in the winter, but I was chilled half of the time anyway. I'm enjoying the heat right now."

That made him smile. "You never were much for the cold."

Mesmerized by his brown eyes, and feeling a tug of longing to be close to him, emotionally, she stepped closer to him. "No."

They stood facing each other, tension winding up between them, neither moving to cross the foot that separated them. She could hear the muffled sounds of the neighbor's television and the hum of the fridge. The sweet ache of hope, fear, and longing grew in her chest and she wanted to step closer, but didn't dare.

After a long moment, he blinked and looked away, moving back. "I ought to go."

"Yeah." Her throat felt thick and tears rose, but she managed to hold them at bay.

"I'll see you again soon?"

She smiled, though she feared it looked forced. "You have my number. You mind if I call for an extra hand to move in some furniture?"

"No, I'd be happy to help. Call anytime." He took a couple more steps without turning away from her, but he was already at the door.

"Thanks for dinner. It was great seeing you again."

He nodded. "Welcome home."

They stared at each other for several more seconds before he said goodbye and pivoted, disappearing through the door.

Shelly wished she had a chair to fall into, but she didn't, so she leaned against the counter instead.

Was it awkward because he knows I still have feelings for him, and he doesn't anymore, or does he feel like I do? She didn't have an answer. With a sigh, she turned and began unloading the groceries. When she finished, she would have to make up a bed on the air mattress her parents had loaned her. She made a mental note to search for a hide-a-bed sofa the next day.

⚜ ⚜ ⚜

SHELLY WAS THRILLED to find a sofa that wasn't horrifically ugly, or completely out of her price range after searching four stores. Since it had monster purple flowers mixed in with bright red ones, she figured it only qualified at *terribly* ugly rather than *horrifically*. Rich came up from Orem with his truck to transport the sofa, the small, dilapidated dresser, and the tiny table and mismatched chairs she had purchased for her apartment—all for under a hundred dollars. She was a master budgeter.

"Yeah, that's pretty clear," Rhett said when Shelly told him how little she'd paid. He and Rob had been happy to help unload the furniture at her apartment. "I'm surprised they didn't pay *you* to take the couch. It's hideous."

"Yes, but several steps down from horrible, don't you think?" she asked

He shook his head and worked with Rob to lift the old dresser into the truck bed next to the sofa. "If you say so."

"It's no worse than the one we unloaded at your sister's place a couple years back," Rob said to Shelly.

"No, that was far worse. Of course, she covered it almost immediately. I'll have to look around for an extra sheet or something." Shelly was already considering her options.

"I suggest a dark one. Those flowers would shine through a white sheet like a ruddy beacon," Rhett said.

"Quit bagging on my furniture."

"Shelly, if you don't want people to make fun of it," Rich suggested, "Get better taste."

Though she was thoroughly enjoying the banter as she watched Rich tie down her purchases, she crossed her arms over her chest and frowned. "It's not lack of good taste that's the problem. It's lack of funds for decent furniture, and the unwillingness to sleep on the floor for any longer. My back was not happy with me when I woke up this morning."

"You got me there. I wouldn't be all that excited about sleeping on the floor, either," Rhett said. "So, have you heard from anyone in England?"

"El and I have written a couple times. Homesick yet?" she asked.

"Oh, yeah. I'm already planning a trip back in a year or so."

"Why don't you ride back to your place with us so you and Rhett can talk about how homesick you are," Rob suggested to Shelly.

"I'll follow you," Rich agreed as he tied the last knot.

Shelly climbed into the car and talked about all the people she and Rhett knew on the way back to her apartment.

When everything was unloaded from the truck twenty minutes later, Rob and Rhett made their excuses and took off, though Rob did glance back over his shoulder. Shelly watched them go, still trying to decide how she felt about all the changes in her life.

"You haven't forgotten him."

She turned in surprise and looked at Rich. "What?"

"He's the one you dated at Utah State, right?" His signature slow, grin curved onto his lips. The Louisiana drawl that often disappeared now returned in force. "Don't be too surprised that I know. I do hear Lily and Denise talk. Lily didn't give any details—at least not while I was around—but I got the feeling you dated Rob pretty regularly. I imagine it put you in a tight spot when Jimmy came home."

And this is why Rich is Lily's favorite cousin, he pays attention and remembers details. Shelly nodded, grateful to have someone to talk with. "It was awkward—and so was introducing him to Brad this summer. We could have used a machete to cut through the tension."

"He was important to you." Rich studied her. "Still is."

She nodded again. "Right now, I'm trying not to think about it too hard. I'm mixed up and confused over things with Brad, and I don't want to jump into anything else too quickly."

"That's a good idea. Take your time. There's no hurry." He stood and gave her a hug. "I better get home or Denise will wonder what's taking me so long."

"Thanks for your help."

"Anytime. Denise wants you to come for dinner on your birthday. She'll probably insist you bring that boy with you." He slid his hand in his pocket and retrieved his keys.

"Rhett and I have only ever been friends. I don't know where you get these ideas from."

He smiled. "You can bring him too, if you'd like. I'll have Denise call and insist on it." With a wave goodbye, he headed out the door.

Shelly watched him leave, then plopped back on her sofa, thrilled to have one—regardless of how ugly it was.

Chapter 35

THURSDAYS, SHELLY TAUGHT three classes. She had studied the first few chapters in each book, reviewed her class notes, poured over other professors' syllabi, and pieced something together that she thought might work well enough.

Half an hour before class started, she had her stack of reference papers in the classroom. She was checking over them again when the students began filing in. She could have sworn there were twice as many faces in the room as on the class roster, but a quick head count proved her wrong. She saw several older students, and plenty who were probably her own age.

She stood in front of the class and took a deep breath to calm her shaking hands. Her hair was held back from her face in a single French braid and she adjusted her dark gray wool dress suit. It had been the most professional matronly outfit she owned. She had desperately wanted to give off an air of authority. Now she wondered if she would sweat through it before class ended—and she had two more classes to go before her lunch break.

"Hello, my name is Shelly Cox, and I'll be teaching History 1500 this semester." She spoke loudly and crisply, adding a touch of an English accent to her voice and formality in her word choice to assert her authority. She gave a couple sentences of background on herself, explained her grading system, and then turned to an overview of the class.

She felt the lecture went off fairly well, and only tripped over her own words a few times. When a couple of guys winked at her, she wondered if they were trying to fluster her. She managed to keep a straight face and her mind on topic.

By the end of the morning, she had a better idea of what to expect from her classes, and a very bad headache. After a quick lunch from the brown bag she'd packed that morning, she started revising the syllabus until she decided she needed to go home, grateful to have survived the day.

❀ ❀ ❀

THE NEXT MORNING, SHELLY was back at the office early and plugging away, despite the fact that she didn't have any classes—if she stayed home she would have been distracted by everything that needed to be done, and she needed to focus on preparing for the following week of class.

She finished the syllabi, scheduled her office hours, and made copies for each class the next week. Energized by the challenge that lay before her and all she had already accomplished, she decided to take her lunch outside to eat on the grass.

"What are you doing out here in the sun instead of slaving away in your office?" Rob's voice asked when she was seated with her back against a tree trunk.

Shelly looked up and smiled when she saw him stop in front of her. "I thought I'd take a lunch break. You could join me."

"I just finished eating, actually, but I have some time before I have to get back to work." He settled on the grass beside her. "So, how have your classes been?"

"I taught three yesterday. I was terrified and thought I'd make a fool of myself during the second class—I totally froze up when I looked at this huge group of mile-tall basketball players. But I carried it off—knock on wood."

"I'm sure you did fine." He nodded and a smile crept across his face. "I would've liked to see you up there laying down the law."

"Too bad you missed it. It would probably give you harassment material to last years." She opened the wrapping on her sandwich. "On second thought, maybe that's as well."

He smiled as she took a large bite of ham on whole wheat.

full Circle

❀ ❀ ❀

MONDAY AFTERNOON, SHELLY worked on her lessons for the next day. After endless hours trying to re-familiarize herself with the specific class content enough to teach it, and preparing questions for the upcoming quizzes and tests, she still felt behind. She hoped she would get the hang of this before too long.

Someone knocked on the door. It wasn't her office hours, but she called out, "Come in."

"Is this a bad time?" Rob asked, poking his head into the room and looking around the tiny space. "Wow, this is a nice office. I wish mine were this big."

"Very funny. Have a seat, there's almost enough room for your legs between the chair and the desk. I was working on my lessons." Shelly saved the file and slid the laptop back on her desk, grateful for an excuse to take a break. She felt a tiny jolt of pleasure at having him track her down.

"I heard some students talking about you in the library this afternoon." Rob sat in the extra chair, stretching out his legs to the side of the desk.

"Was it, 'That witchy professor Miss Cox is going to run me into the grave.'?"

"No." He laughed.

"Hmm, pity. So what did they have to say about me?" She sank back into her seat expectantly, all her attention turned toward Rob. She didn't want to have her students describe her that way, but at least having that kind of reputation would demand respect instead of the curious interest a couple of the guys were broadcasting.

"One guy thought you were awful to come in and make the class harder than he expected. He signed up for the original professor, hoping the class would be easy. The other guy told him to buck up and take it. He thinks you're cute."

Just what I need. That's bound to simplify my job. Not! "That's nice," she responded instead. "So, did you come down here to tell me the latest gossip, or is there something else to which I owe this pleasure?"

"Actually, Rhett's the ward music director in our singles ward, and he wondered if the two of us would do a duet in sacrament meeting in a couple of weeks."

It wasn't a date, but she wouldn't complain. Singing with Rob was one of her favorite things. "Really? It's been ages since we sang together. I'm honored he thought of us."

"I guess he has something in mind and he offered to accompany us, so we'll need to get together with him."

"That sounds great. My schedule's open other than my Wednesday evening classes."

"All right." Rob stood to leave. "I better go. I'm on break and need to get back. I'll let Rhett know and call you when I've checked his work schedule."

She almost let him go, then made herself stop him before he left. "Wait. I, uh, Rich and Denise are having a dinner tomorrow night at their house. They asked me to invite you and Rhett to come." Shelly kicked herself as soon as the words slipped out. That was the least enthusiastic dinner invitation she'd ever heard. "I meant to call earlier to ask you."

His eyebrows lifted. "Your cousin is asking *us?*" He pulled up his calendar on his phone and smiled. "Oh, wait, it's your birthday tomorrow. This is a *birthday* dinner."

"Yes." She flushed slightly and wondered why on earth, after the way they had split, he still had her birthday on his calendar. "I can't believe you remember that. I don't want a lot of fuss—definitely don't feel like you have to bring a gift—but I'd like it if you two could come. Maybe we could practice our song before we eat. They have a piano—Denise doesn't play at all but Rich insists their kids will—and I know she'd enjoy hearing us sing."

He smiled and she felt her heart tumble to the floor as the past two years of distance fell away. She was a goner. How had she ever fooled herself into thinking she could love Brad when she still felt like this for Rob?

"I'd love that. I'll check with Rhett. What time do you want us over?"

She dragged her thoughts back to the conversation. "Denise said six-thirty, but they live in Orem, so we should ride down together. Let me know what Rhett says and we'll coordinate rides."

"All right." He winked and left the office.

She settled back into her chair and thought about all the times they'd sung together in college. It seemed like decades since then. A quiver spread in her stomach and she returned to entering scores in the computer.

Chapter 36

THE NEXT DAY WHEN SHELLY got out of class, she had a message on her cell phone. "Hey, this is Rob. I talked to Rhett about tonight. If you can call me when you get this, I'm at extension 2043, or call me on my cell. I should be available pretty much all day. Bye."

"Hi, Rob, it's Shelly," she said when he picked up in his office a minute later.

"Hi. Happy birthday."

She felt herself blush and was grateful he couldn't see her. "Thanks. You said Rhett has the music?"

"Yeah, and he said he could meet us at your place at six. He's looking forward to it. He's bringing some British biscuits he picked up at a specialty store. Biscuits? He's back in America—why doesn't he call them cookies?"

Shelly laughed. "If you talk to him again, tell him I'm counting on them."

After work, Rob met Shelly at her apartment. "Rhett's running a minute behind. Are you ready?"

"Sure, let me shut down this computer. I've been grading papers for hours." She grimaced as she moved to the table where she had the laptop set up.

His fingers brushed her shoulder. "Have you been getting enough rest? You look tired."

She turned to him, knowing her face had been pale with dark smudges under her eyes when she'd looked in the mirror earlier. "I am tired. I've

212

been working like crazy, trying to get quizzes ready and checked, and preparing lessons and tests. And I've been settling in here." She let out a deep breath and smiled. "I'm excited to have this chance to sing with you. I needed a break."

"You're a work-a-holic." He studied her face "When was the last time you got out to do something fun?"

"I went running Friday evening and again last night, but I haven't been out like I used to. Between letting myself get lazy and the extra altitude, not to mention the drier air, the run about killed me." She knew her smile was unconvincing. "I'll have to get used to all that again."

Rhett arrived with a package of Biscoff, which Shelly had been craving since her return to the states, and they took his car to Denise's.

They pulled up at Denise's home early, and after Shelly hugged her cousins and cooed and hugged their little boys, she introduced them to Rob and Rhett.

"I'm sorry," Denise said when the introductions were finished, "dinner will be at least half an hour late. The boys have been little monsters today and I'm running behind." She tucked chin-length hair behind her ear and grabbed her toddler as he made a break for the sidewalk.

"No problem," Shelly reassured her. "We can work on the song now, if you'd like, or we can help in the kitchen."

"I'd love to hear your song practice—it would be good for the piano to get some normal use." She sent her husband a pointed look, but he smiled blithely, apparently unaffected by her remark.

Shelly and Rob settled at the piano. Rhett left them to warm up together while he ran back to the car for the music he'd left there. Shelly noticed it took him an abnormally long time to return.

Rhett came in the door several minutes later. "Sorry it took so long. Natalie called, saying she left a couple of her books in my car and has to have them for the first day of class tomorrow. I don't know what she wants me to do about it." He pulled out the music as he griped. "Here's the song."

Neither of them were familiar with the music, so Rhett ran through their parts quickly before they sang it together. Their voices blended in perfect harmony—most of the time. There were a few times when they had to stop and review the notes again since neither of them had heard the song before. Shelly enjoyed the easy camaraderie with both men as well as their playful banter.

They stopped when Denise announced dinner was ready. "We'll have to try again next week. It'll give me time to work on that rough spot in the second ending," Rhett said as he packed the music into his school backpack.

Shelly lifted her eyebrows. She didn't think he had a rough patch in the song anywhere, never mind at that section, but she supposed he might have noticed something she didn't.

Dinner was wonderful, and they were cutting the birthday cake, a tall, round chocolate cake with bountiful amounts of chocolate frosting in waves all over the exterior, when the doorbell rang. Rich answered it and brought Craig Sorenson back into the room with him. "Shelly, you have a visitor."

"Craig, what are you doing here?" Shelly greeted Jimmy's younger brother with a hug. She hadn't seen him since Christmas and found it was less difficult, emotionally, now than before.

"Our moms apparently thought you needed a few things, this being your birthday and all. This is for you." He handed her a large box, but must have seen her confusion since he explained, "Your mom said you'd be here. I was headed to Logan, and they asked if I'd drop it by on the way."

"That was so sweet of them, and it's good to see you!" She paused as she had a thought. "Hold on. Rhett, didn't you say you had some things of Natalie's?"

"Yeah."

"Do you have her address?" When Rhett nodded, she turned back to Craig. "You wouldn't mind doing us one more favor, would you? Their sister lives in Logan, and she left some books in Rhett's car over the weekend."

Craig nodded, always game to lend a helping hand if he could. "I'd be happy to take them by."

"Great, but first, you have to join us for cake and ice cream." Denise picked up the knife and cut him a slice of cake before he could respond.

"If you insist." Craig grinned at her, dimples appearing in his cheeks.

Shelly felt a small ache of longing at the sight of Craig, so much like his older brother. She was surprised, though, that the pain had diminished. She would always love Jimmy, but she was finally ready to let him go.

She used eating the cake as an excuse to ponder that odd tidbit for the next few minutes while the others talked around her. She caught Rob's concerned look, but smiled in return. Everything was fine. More fine than she'd once thought it could ever be again.

Rhett wrote down Natalie's address while Craig demolished the large slice of cake.

When Craig left twenty minutes later, package in hand, Rob turned to Shelly and nudged her with his elbow. "Are you sure about that guy? I mean, that's my sister we're talking about."

Shelly chuckled at his protective behavior. "Trust me. He's Jimmy's little brother. He's perfectly safe. If he and my baby sister weren't so completely different, I'd hook them up just to keep him around. Besides, it's not like they're going on a date. It's only a package delivery."

SHELLY, ROB, AND RHETT got together to practice twice more the next week, meeting at the LDS Institute of Religion near the Taylorsville campus. Rob's mellow tenor blended nicely with Shelly's soprano. She wondered if they needed to practice that much, but Rhett insisted and she enjoyed the break from real life, so she didn't comment on it. She justified that she hadn't done any real singing in ages and needed to get her voice back in order.

Then there was the added benefit of spending time with Rob again. They had settled down to their old friendship easily enough. But then sometimes she glanced over and caught him gazing at her with a look in his eyes that made her heart pound and fingers tremble as she turned back to the pages in front of them. It was that warm, tingly heart-pounding that made the start of relationships so much fun. She didn't know if he would make a move, or if she would need to do it instead, but, in the meantime, she enjoyed the fun of anticipation.

ROB SAVED THE FILE he was working on and leaned back in his chair at work. The pay period had ended and he'd spent the morning verifying timecards and preparing the batch to print checks. He needed to get up and move before his eyes crossed.

"Hey, I'm going to the cafeteria. You interested?" he asked Stu. He wanted to call Shelly to see if she could meet him, but didn't want to push things too fast. He remembered all too well how it had shattered him when she dumped him the first time. Rob sensed her hesitation and didn't want to put himself on the line like that again. He could be patient and wait for her to make some kind of move—something undeniable. They had slid seamlessly into The Friend Zone after her return, and he was afraid trying to break out of it would damage their relationship before they were both ready to move forward.

"I still can't figure out how you can eat there," Stu said.

"It's better than my own food." Rob's phone rang. "Accounting, this is Rob."

"Hi, this is your dad." The voice was hesitant and not very loud.

Rob didn't answer for a long second as a hundred disappointments rolled over him at the sound of Leland's voice. It took a moment before he could draw a breath. "Leland. What do you need?" *And can't you take a hint?*

"I wondered if you wanted to get some lunch with me."

Rob wasn't about to open that door again. "I already ate."

"It's not even noon yet," his father pointed out.

"Late breakfast. Big one." Rob picked up the pen from the desk and tapped it against his yellow legal pad.

"What about tonight?"

"I have plans. I gotta go—we're swamped. Talk to you later." Rob hung up, not caring that he'd been rude. He scowled at the pen in his hand and jammed it back in the desk organizer. One great mood spoiled in less than twenty seconds. That had to be a record.

"We aren't *that* busy, and you said you were going for lunch," Stu pointed out. Obviously he'd overheard the conversation. "What was that all about?"

Rob pushed himself from his chair. "Nothing." He walked toward the cafeteria.

He knew he shouldn't have lied to Leland, but he didn't feel bad about it, either. His father had never been there for him growing up, and Rob saw no reason to roll over and beg for whatever handouts the man would give him now.

His mind was still on the phone call when he reached the checkout stand in the cafeteria. He felt a tap on his shoulder.

"I called your name. You must have been in another world," Shelly said when he turned toward her.

He blinked and brought himself back to the present. "Sorry, I had some things on my mind."

"Must have. Your scowl was enough to scare half the people around you." She smiled, teasing him, and he felt himself relax.

"You must not have been too scared—you still talked to me."

Her smile broadened. "Yeah, you can't scare me. I know there's a marshmallow on the other side of that frown."

"Don't be too sure of that. Not today." He took his change from the girl sitting at the register and waited for Shelly to pay. Maybe it was a good thing they'd run into each other. He needed something to take his mind off Leland and she tended to suck up a hundred percent of his concentration when she was around.

They made their way to a table in the back. "You want to talk about it, or are you planning to brood all day?" she asked after a long moment.

He laughed slightly at her forwardness, then found himself talking about it, though he hadn't planned on it. "I got a call from Leland today."

"Leland?" She looked puzzled.

"My birth father."

She stuck a straw in her cup. "I didn't think you were in touch with him."

"I haven't been. A few months ago he started writing me and leaving messages on my answering machine. A few minutes ago, he called me here. Again."

"What does he want?"

"To recapture lost time. As if that would even be possible." He opened the can of soda on his tray. "The man ignored my existence for decades, and now he wants to be best buds?"

"That's nuts." Shelly shook her head. "Still, you think maybe he's realized how bad he screwed up? Maybe he's decided to try and make it right. Or maybe there's something going on you should know about."

"You can't take back the past." Rob's voice deepened and he stared down at his food. "Anything he has to say will be too little, too late. Anyway, my day was going great before he called. What's new with you?" He met her gaze, determined not to waste their time together talking about Leland. Rob could see from the way her brows lowered and she grimaced that she didn't want to let it go, so he was relieved when she allowed the change of subject.

"Nothing much—just correcting papers and preparing lessons. I got an email from my old roommate, El, this morning, though. She's all settled into her job and doing well." She took a sip from her drink and played with her fork. "I miss her."

Rob covered her hand with his on the tabletop. "I'm sure you do." When she lifted her gaze to his, he felt the magnetic pull between them and wished he dared lean over and kiss her. He reminded himself to be patient as he squeezed her hand and pulled back.

He chased her once, and he wasn't going to rush her again. He hoped.

Chapter 37

SUNDAY ARRIVED AND THEY performed their duet. Shelly was relieved when they had no trouble with the notes and she felt the Spirit strongly, especially since seeing Rob in a white shirt and tie again made her mouth grow dry and her heart race. Then she realized he did that to her regardless of how he was dressed.

Rhett walked over to them after sacrament meeting, a petite brunette at his side. "Wow, you two sing like you were *made* for each other."

He gestured to the girl beside him. "This is Marnie. She's in charge of music for the stake-sponsored firesides."

"I'm pleased to meet you," Shelly told her. She eyed Rhett, unsure how to react to his pointed comment.

"Me too," Rob said as he shook Marnie's hand.

She grinned broadly—or as broadly as someone that tiny could manage. "You don't know how happy I am to meet you two. I'm impressed. We're having a fireside in a couple weeks and I wondered if you'd be willing to sing a duet for us."

"I'd be happy to. How about you, Shelly?" Rob asked.

More rehearsals with Rob? Absolutely! "Yeah, I could probably squeeze the time in for practice," she joked. "I'd love to. Do you have any particular song in mind?"

"I have a couple that might go with the theme..."

Rhett offered to play for them, and they arranged times to meet before the fireside. When Shelly glanced between the brothers, it was obvious Rob

219

also saw what Rhett was doing, though Rhett pretended to be totally oblivious.

❀ ❀ ❀

AFTER PRACTICE A FEW days later, Rhett took off almost immediately, but Rob and Shelly lingered around the piano at the Institute building, talking and laughing for over an hour. They stopped for dinner at a burger place around the corner and it started to rain while they ate. Ready to leave, they stood in the breezeway for a minute, looking at the downpour. The pavement shone in the lamplight as a heavy rain filled the gutters and pooled in the low spots in the street. "Wow, it's really coming down," she said.

"Yeah. It can't last long at this rate, this is Utah." He nudged her with his elbow.

She stared out as lightning streaked through the sky several miles away. The downpour made her nostalgic. "I miss the rain. It's so beautiful, wild and untamed."

"I know you always loved it. All those storms you got in England didn't change your mind?" She turned and caught him watching her. He glanced down at the floor and smiled mischievously. "That's fortunate."

"What is?"

"You're wearing tennis shoes instead of dress shoes." Before Shelly had a chance to protest, he pulled her into the open with the sky pouring over their heads.

She laughed. "Rob, you're crazy."

He simply tugged on her arm, pulled her onto the blacktop, and ran with her to an empty corner of the parking lot where they splashed in the puddles. Rob slipped and landed on his rear end in water eight inches deep, soaked to the skin.

Shelly laughed some more, feeling lighter than she had in ages. She reached out to help him up, but he pulled her down beside him instead. He broke her fall, maneuvering her onto his lap instead of the hard blacktop. She tipped back her head and lifted her face to the rain, enjoying the feel, even though it was cold. It felt great to be out, goofing off like this for a change, even though she was soaked and growing very cold.

Rob laughed and she looked into his eyes. The closeness, the exhilaration of the moment, came together and she found his arms circling her waist and hers sliding around his neck, pulling them closer. They stared at each other for a long moment as the swell of emotion and electricity between them increased and she had a sudden memory of their last kiss, so long ago.

She longed for that and leaned in, closing her eyes as his lips brushed against her cheeks, her chin, her forehead. She melted into the sweetness of the moment, soaking up the feel of his arms around her, the softness of his lips on her skin, nearly able to ignore that she was dripping wet and shivering. She had been waiting for this moment for so long.

When his mouth finally touched hers, she felt her heart expand and her pulse race in counterpoint to the beat of the raindrops pelting their heads. The kiss lingered as they threw themselves into it, dissolving in the moment, in each other. Eventually he drew away and she caught her breath, opening her eyes to stare into his. It hadn't been like that with Brad or Jimmy. Nothing like that. It had only ever been like that with him.

The thought had her flying from his arms, the beauty of their first kiss in so long disintegrating. She couldn't shake the guilt and confusion she felt—guilt because she'd never been honest with either him or Jimmy about her feelings for Rob, confusion because she'd trusted Brad, but he hadn't been honest with her, and she should have seen all of the signs in the first place. She'd thought she knew Brad, knew him as well or better than she now knew Rob, but she hadn't, she'd been wrong to trust him. Could she trust anyone like that again?

Though she knew that last thought was ridiculous, and Rob had always been honest with her, Shelly couldn't shake the feeling that she wasn't ready for this. Not yet.

She didn't know what to do when he looked up at her. Darkness obscured his face and she couldn't read his expression. "I...Shelly, I'm—"

She held up a hand as she tried to regain her breath. She couldn't take it if he apologized, or even if he wanted an explanation for her actions. "Please, don't." Her breathing caught slightly as she tried to put it all back together. "Don't say you're sorry. I'm not. But I'm not ready for this. I thought I was—I want it so much—but I need more time." She hurried to her car, fighting to pull the keys from her damp jeans, and climbed in, not looking back.

221

full Circle

WHEN HE REACHED HIS apartment, Rob was still confused. Utterly. She needed more time? Granted, she'd only been back in the country a little over a month, but it wasn't like he'd proposed. He hadn't actually asked for anything. What did she think he wanted from her?

What *did* he want from her?

He plodded his way up the walk, his shoes squishing with water, rivulets of water running from his hair onto his face and he brushed the hair back—apparently it was time for a haircut.

Part of the problem he had with Lindsey was that he didn't take the time to stop and consider his feelings—he had just jumped in and hoped it turned out okay. So maybe he needed to pause and consider. He headed up the stairs, his feet ringing on the metal.

The whole dream, he realized.

Rob paused there with one foot on a higher step. He wanted everything from the picket fence to the houseful of kids, walks in the dusk and long evenings together after a tough day. She obviously wasn't ready to give him that yet. Was he willing to wait, to hope once again that things would work out? He'd been in pain the past several months while she dated Brad, not sure if she'd come home so he'd have another shot at making it work with her. How patient could he be, now that she was available?

If she still loved Brad, why was she in Utah instead of planning a wedding? Had he dumped her? She'd denied that her heart had been broken. So what held her back?

He took his time covering the rest of the stairs to his floor. It wasn't as though he could be any wetter, and the fall storm felt good on his shoulders, even if it was cold. He played with the keys in his hand, finding the one for his apartment, then looked up, noticing a man standing up on the balcony near his door.

The complex had lights near the stairs, but they were a distance away, and it was impossible to tell who the man was in the dark. Since Rhett was at work, Rob knew it couldn't be him.

When he reached the top floor, the man still watched him. "Can I help you?" Rob asked.

222

"I've been waiting for you. Did you have a date?"

Rob peered closer before he realized who it was. His worry about being accosted vanished, but his heart hardened. The tension grew in his shoulders as he took a calming breath of cold fall air. This was the last thing he needed tonight. "Leland. I have a life, you know. How long have you been standing here?" His father looked older than Rob expected.

His brown hair had big streaks of gray running through it and was wet. His formerly gaunt face had filled out some since he'd last seen his son, but Rob knew that often happened when you were off the drugs for a while. Leland was a bit shorter than Rob and had a stockier build, but Rob recognized the parts of his face they had in common. He'd hated those features many times over the years.

"About an hour. I figured I could wait until you made it home. I haven't been able to pin you down to talk, and I wanted to see you." Leland shuffled his feet, and buried his head and shoulders further into his jacket when the wind picked up and blew the rain sideways.

Rob looked at the man who had fathered, then mostly ignored, him, noting the new wrinkles around his eyes. He looked tired—tired and desperate. Rob wasn't sure what to think. He didn't have the strength to deal with everything. "Now you've seen me. You must have other things to do."

Leland shook his head. "Nothing as important as this." He fidgeted slightly on the doorstep where he was mostly sheltered from the rain. "I know you don't want to see me, and I can't blame you..."

Rob shoved his hands into his pockets and planted his feet. "Then why are you here, Leland? What's the deal? You come make nice and Grandpa gives you some money to live on—to smoke away? Then you can disappear again for a few years? Or maybe you need to soothe your guilt a bit. It never seemed to be a problem before, but maybe you've grown a conscience." He shrugged, though anger burned in his chest. "All of the forgotten Christmases and broken promises shouldn't matter anymore because you've *changed* this time."

Rob gestured with his hands, wanting to hit something, but forcing himself to hold it in. "You think you can make a few friendly gestures, play your father trump card, and I'll decide everything's all better. Then you can walk away and not think of me again until your guilt kicks in after a couple of years? Sorry, I'm not five anymore, and I don't want to go through all of this again." He shivered slightly, but it wasn't the cold that bothered him. Leland had left Rob's life in shambles on more than one occasion.

"It's not like that. I've made a lot of changes in my life. I know I have so much to make up to you. I'm just asking for a chance. I'm your father." This last sentence was said in a low voice, almost begging.

Rob sighed and ran a hand through his hair. "You've made your effort, and I'm not interested. It's a little too late to start playing dad again. I've got one already. He knows what the title means, and he earned it by being there for me every day." He pulled his keys out of his pocket again and stepped toward the door. "Now, excuse me. It's raining out here."

Leland watched him put the key in the lock, but when it clicked, he put a hand on Rob's arm. "Son... please, give me a few minutes."

Rob's chin trembled slightly, enough to disgust himself. "Ten years ago I would've jumped for a few minutes of your time. Go try your line on someone else." He pushed the door open and stepped inside, shut it tightly, and flipped the lock.

He dropped his dripping jacket on a kitchen chair and walked into the bathroom to clean up. It had been eight years since Leland had last tried to go through the motions of being a dad. Eight very long and eventful years, with only the barest acknowledgment of their relationship. Rob had written him off long ago. He would never be fooled again.

Chapter 38

WEDNESDAY EVENING, SHELLY settled at her computer to do research for an upcoming class. It had been a long day and she was still distracted with thoughts about Rob's kiss in the rain and the feelings it had raised in her. The problem had made it difficult for her to focus on her lectures, and now all she wanted was to settle into a tub of hot water up to her chin and read a novel. Unfortunately, her itty bitty shower stall in the coat closet that claimed to be a bathroom was not up to the task, so she'd pulled out her hide-a-bed, grabbed a bag of chocolate chip cookies from the freezer, and tried to immerse herself in her work.

Despite her need to focus on work, she was happy when a chat window popped up and El messaged her.

Hey, you available for a Skype conversation?

Sure, it's been ages since we had a good gab. Shelly wrote back.

Two minutes later, she was looking at El's face on the screen, smiling with excitement. "Hey, we should've done this ages ago."

"No kidding." El pushed a lock of hair behind her ear. "We haven't talked for a while. What's going on?"

"Stacks and stacks of paperwork, research, correcting. I'm having a blast." Shelly found she meant it. Despite the stresses of her job, she enjoyed her work, if only because she was able to study history every day and share it with others.

"You're such a geek. Hey, wait! Are those your famous chocolate chip cookies?"

"Best on the planet. Sorry. I know you're seriously jealous now." Shelly took another bite, exaggerating her enjoyment.

"You're so evil!"

"I try. What are you up to? Dating anyone new?"

"I've gone out with this guy named Seth a few times. He seems nice. How about you?" El took a sip from a paper cup with a green tea shop logo on the side.

"Same old, same old."

"So you're seeing Rob again and desperately in love?"

"What makes you say that?" *Surely I'm not that easy to read.*

El's look turned sly. "You have seen him recently, haven't you?"

Shelly took a big bite of cookie and chewed to prolong the suspense. "I've seen quite a bit of him, actually. We haven't been on any dates." She added this because El was obviously excited by the news. "But we've been singing together again, so we've met for practices and an occasional meal." She felt her cheeks heat and wondered if El would be able to see she was blushing from the video feed.

"Girl plus boy, plus activity, equals date, Shelly." She pointed at the camera. "Ah, and you're turning red. That must mean something."

Okay, so the feed is great both directions. "Last night after practice, we went out for dinner, then we ended up playing in the rain in the parking lot."

"I love that. And then what?"

She remembered it vividly. "We fell into a puddle—well, he fell, then he pulled me down with him." Shelly savored the memory, the rightness of being in his arms again, and felt the guilt follow close behind. "He pulled me close and kissed me and it felt so perfect, so right. It was everything I could have wanted. Then I felt guilty, and I don't know why."

Shelly looked at El, so grateful for a chance to talk face-to-face, even if it was through a computer screen. "I thought I was over all this. That after my experience with the locket, I wouldn't feel guilty about Jimmy again. It's not like I didn't kiss Rob when I was 'waiting' for Jimmy. And I kissed your brother more than once. Yet, that moment with Rob brought more guilt than all the other kisses we'd ever shared, combined." She buried her fingers in her hair and tugged, the pain it caused nothing compared to that burning through her chest. "It was only compounded by the way I felt for him the whole time I dated Brad."

El nodded, apparently unsurprised. "That's because you love Rob."

It took several long seconds before Shelly could answer that. "Yes. And I think, I really do, that we have a future." She knew they could, but if she couldn't even talk to him about her feelings, her confusion, then she wasn't ready to face a relationship, and she didn't want to make mistakes this time. She had already hurt him too much.

El smiled expectantly and waited for Shelly to continue, as she so often did.

Shelly was glad to unload her thoughts. "I keep thinking of that evening two years ago. The night was bright, the stars shone like tiny lamps in the sky, and the moon was full. Rob told me that when he looked in the future, he could only see me by his side. We had this amazing kiss, soaking in every moment. Then I told him in no uncertain terms that I was marrying Jimmy and couldn't be with him." She pressed her fist to her stomach, feeling the agony of pain growing there.

"I shouldn't have let him kiss me that night if I knew I couldn't marry him." She wanted to stand and walk to the window, but instead she just looked at it, and at the tiny block of stars she could see there. "I never told him what a near thing it was for me, how very close I came to telling *him* yes instead of Jimmy. It would have been cruel, and I didn't want to hurt him any more."

"You were sure about marrying Jimmy?" El asked.

"I prayed about it a dozen times, and the answer was always yes, marry Jimmy. And then there was the accident, and I was left wondering why I had gotten so many confirmations through prayer when he was just going to..." Tears sprang to her eyes and she wiped them away. "The worst part was that I was working my way up to telling him how serious things had gotten with Rob. Right there in the car, in the minutes leading up to the wreck, I was preparing to let him know that Rob and I had been much more than buddies.

"I felt guilty and sneaky and like I'd betrayed Jimmy. He knew I'd gone out with Rob a few times, but had no idea I still had feelings for him. I never planned to see Rob again, but I wanted Jimmy to know, so we could start off with a clean slate. And then he died and I never told him."

She grabbed another cookie and took a bite, needing the sugar rush and chocolate boost. "My life would've been totally different if I'd accepted

Rob instead. Would that have been better? Would it have made more sense?" And then there was the guilt she felt that Jimmy had died in the first place, knowing he wouldn't have been in that canyon if she hadn't insisted on the trip. It had taken a long time to give up that guilt. At least, she'd thought she'd gotten past it, but perhaps a bit of it lingered after all.

"Did it ever occur to you," El asked after a long pause, "that maybe you were supposed to agree to marry Jimmy because he wasn't going to make it to the wedding? This way, he didn't die bitter about the end of your relationship. He died every bit as in love with you as he was before. You had the life-changing experience as *my* roommate last year, which you totally can't feel guilty about loving because where would you be without me in your life?" she grinned. "Now you want to be with Rob so badly it hurts, but you feel guilty about that. Sounds to me like your healing isn't quite done. Don't let him get away, though. I like that guy."

Shelly wiped her face again, and El did the same. "I'll have to think about it. I believe Jimmy's happy for me, that he would be glad about me and Rob."

"I think that's true." El played with an empty candy wrapper. "Is that the problem between you and Rob, then?"

"I wish it were." Shelly readjusted the computer on her lap and leaned back against her pillows. "The other part was my guilt over still carrying those feelings for Rob when I started dating Brad. I thought Rob was engaged—that was why I decided it was time to move on and see other people." She covered her face with her hands and rubbed her eyes. "This is going to sound bad, and you're welcome to be mad at me, but I think I started seeing Brad because I wanted to forget Rob. But I couldn't. Man, sometimes I hate myself."

"You seemed to be making an honest effort with Brad."

"I did—that's the thing. I kept trying to push Rob aside, to keep my feelings for him from interfering with my relationship with your brother. I did fairly well, I thought, until Rob showed up in our ward."

El smiled. "Yes, I saw what a struggle that was for you. You worked hard not to offend Rob, yet not doing anything that would give Brad reason to worry. Except that every time you looked at Rob, your eyes said the words you didn't say."

Shelly groaned and leaned her forehead against her palms. "You never told me it was that bad. I thought I was being reasonable, balanced and totally okay."

"You failed, utterly." El gave a Gallic shrug and unwrapped a piece of chocolate, popping it into her mouth. "I hoped I was wrong when you kept dating Brad, but apparently not."

"No wonder Brad acted like a jealous git. He was totally justified." Shelly rolled her neck and shook it off—for now. That was more for her to consider as she thought about the situation with Rob. She turned the conversation, anxious to hear all the latest news, and settled in for a good chat.

❀ ❀ ❀

THE SONG PRACTICE the next week was all business—get in, get out. The tension between Shelly and Rob had never been higher, and he had no idea what to do about it.

After the last practice when the brothers walked out to their cars, Rhett turned to Rob in the parking lot. "You know, if you don't make a move for her soon, I might—she's pretty great."

Rob's thoughts had been on Shelly, but it was still disorienting to have Rhett bring her up. "What?"

"Come on, I know you're interested. I mean, you were so crazy about her when you two were at USU, you talked about her all the time—enough I still heard about her on my mission *in another country*. Why don't you take her out sometime? Like on a *date*—a real date, not... whatever it is you've been doing. Pretending you're just friends or something."

It wasn't that Rob hadn't thought of it himself, but Shelly's words in the rainstorm kept him from feeling safe in asking her out. "I don't think she's ready to date again yet." He turned and walked to his car.

"You'll never know if you don't at least try," Rhett called to him.

Sometimes Rob hated it when his little brother gave good advice. He supposed he would never know if he didn't try. Whatever was going on was fixable, right? But that wouldn't happen unless he made it happen.

Chapter 39

A FEW EVENINGS AFTER THEY performed at the fireside, Shelly looked up to find Rob at her office door.

"Hey, Shelly, how are your classes going?"

She tensed slightly, surprised by his sudden appearance and feeling the awkwardness between them as strongly as when he had been in England. It didn't help that it was the first time they'd been alone since their kiss. "They're coming along. I'm getting more on top of things. Now if I could only feel grown-up enough to be teaching a college class."

"I'm sure you're doing fine. You seem to succeed at everything you try." He picked up a paperclip from the edge of her desk and fidgeted with it.

"Not true. Have you ever seen me bowl? I'm terrible at it, and I've played a lot of games in my quest for, well, not sucking."

He smiled slightly at her words, but didn't meet her gaze. The paperclip started to lose its shape. "Shelly, about the other night..."

"Don't. Please don't apologize." Her voice was low and she stared at her computer screen. "I don't know if I could take it."

There was a brief pause before he answered. "I won't then, I'm only sorry about it because it made you uncomfortable, but... Are we okay?"

Relieved that he didn't regret the kiss, despite the way she had torn out of there, she turned and caught his gaze. "I hope so. I'd hate to mess things up with you again. Everything's more complicated right now than it used to be. Don't run away yet—I'm hoping to get my head on straight soon."

He nodded, though he didn't look as though he understood. "Things have been a little crazy for me lately, with the end-of-quarter work."

"I know how that goes. Just trying to get settled into my classes and doing the research has been nuts."

"But you said you're on top of it now, right?"

"Pretty much. I'm doing research for next week instead of tomorrow. That's a nice change."

He nodded.

They sat there for a long moment, as though not quite sure what else to say. Shelly saw a picture of Lily's family on the wall and had an idea. "I have some pictures from college I dug out of a box this week. Maybe sometime we could drink hot chocolate and talk about the good old days." It was a nice hybrid activity between dating and friendship that might make things less awkward between them.

"The good old days when we were both working, going to school full-time, and involved in so many extracurriculars, we barely had time to sleep?" he asked.

"You got it."

His shoulders visibly relaxed. "As long as your homemade hot cocoa and cookies are included in the deal, I'd love to. What if we grabbed some dinner and did that tonight? No one's waiting for me back home except for my fish."

She had forgotten about his aquarium, and how he had always been playing with new fish and equipment for it. "You and your fish. How many are there now?" She collected her things and he took her stack of papers from her as he walked her out to her car.

On the way, they launched into a discussion about the angelfish and bottom feeders and what he'd done with his tank in the past couple of years. He wasn't supposed to even have one in the dorms, but had managed to keep a small one around, anyway.

After she dropped him at his own vehicle, he grabbed some burgers and they met at her apartment. They poured over old scrapbooks at her dining table as Shelly heated water on the stove. She was glad she had put away the hide-a-bed that morning. It wasn't too awkward hanging out together in her apartment kitchen, but if the bed had still been out, it would definitely have been uncomfortable. There were some images she would rather not put in his head.

"Oh, remember this hike? It was for family home evening." She leaned over his shoulder, pointing him out in the group photo, remembering how care-free and excited they were.

"Yes, I look like a drowned rat. I made Dan pay later." He grinned over at her, their eyes catching for a long moment before he looked back at the page.

Shelly was grateful for something to do with her hands as she finished up the cocoa and poured it into large mugs. She wasn't sure what to think, and her hands fumbled with the canning jar where she kept her secret recipe.

Another long moment of silence passed between them, but it wasn't uncomfortable at all. Eventually she broke it. "So, you hear from your... biological dad lately?"

Rob scowled into his empty cup. "Yeah. He was waiting in the rain when I got home the other day. He said he'd been there for an hour."

She blinked. "Wow, he must have really wanted to talk to you."

"Whatever. He was probably hoping for a loan or something. Anyway, I let him know I wasn't interested and sent him on his way. I hope that's the end of it." His expression didn't quite agree, and Shelly wondered for a moment if he meant what he'd said, or if part of him still longed for the relationship they had never had.

She considered, trying to decide if she should respond or keep her thoughts to herself. "If he was willing to wait half the night in the rain, maybe he has something to say that's worth hearing."

Rob looked back at her, scowling even deeper. "You have no idea..." He bit the words off and shook his head. "He's done this too many times and he always disappears again. I won't get pulled in by his charm one more time. I'm through with him." He picked up another cookie from the zippered bag lying open on the table in front of him, but looked up when her hand slid across his.

"That doesn't sound like the Rob I know. Your dad made mistakes, yes—"

"I know, turn the other cheek and all that." He sighed and flipped his hand over to capture her fingers. She squeezed his hand back, hoping to encourage him to tell her what was going on. There were so many things they never discussed when they dated before. His dad was one of them.

He took a fortifying breath. "My parents were married kinda quickly, barely out of high school, because my mom got pregnant with me. The marriage only lasted a year, then they split and I rarely saw him growing up."

She nodded. She'd picked that much up from previous conversations.

"What I didn't tell you is he's a druggie. Mom didn't realize it when they first started dating, and by the time she knew that he was using, they were practically at the altar. She was young and in love and she thought she could change him." He grimaced.

"Of course that didn't happen, and they started arguing about his drug use. She hated it and demanded he quit. He wouldn't, but he didn't want to be nagged, either, so he walked out. He left a nineteen-year-old girl who had no skills or ability to get a real job, with a tiny baby and no way to make a living. He paid child support a few times, but she was pretty much on her own. She moved back in with her parents, who helped her during the day while she got a job to try to support us. That's where she met Marc."

"Rhett and Natalie's dad?" Shelly asked.

Rob nodded, his expression softening as he continued the story. He and Marc were close and often did things together. "He's been a father to all of us. Leland came and went in my life, showing up when it suited him. He promised he'd take me to the fair when I was five, then got plastered and forgot. He apologized when he saw me again a few months later at my birthday. He promised me a Nintendo for Christmas one year, then I didn't see him again until spring."

When Shelly opened her mouth to speak, Rob shook his head and pressed on. "I didn't see him at all from when I was ten until I turned twelve. I guess he was in treatment for his addiction before I saw him again. That was a great visit, actually, the best one I remember. He came by several times over the next few weeks and we hung out. It was almost like we were really father and son—a dream come true. Then he started using drugs again and disappeared."

He dropped her hand and grabbed the empty mugs, taking them to the sink and rinsing them as he spoke. "Back then, I figured he was a loser by choice. No one had made him take that first puff, inject the first vein—he did it of his own free will and he continued doing it because the high was more important than I was." He rubbed his hand over his chest, making Shelly think his heart must still ache. She didn't think she could handle discussing it as calmly as he did. She rose and approached him.

He startled slightly when her hand slid onto his shoulder from behind. He looked at her face and after a moment, continued on. "He came to my birthday party when I was fifteen. The word was he'd cleaned up, was doing better, so I gave it a chance—I wanted him there so badly—but he was totally high. He embarrassed me in front of all my friends. I didn't talk to him for over a year after that, even when he tried.

"Then, when I was eighteen, he kept coming around, over and over. He took me to a couple of baseball games, a day at Lagoon, an occasional pizza. He swore he was done with drugs. He was clean and he wasn't going back to it. We talked about my hopes and dreams, made plans for the future... I—" his voice cracked and he took a moment to regroup and get his emotions under control. "I'd never seen him doing so well for so long. I started to believe him, to be glad he'd finally realized that I needed him, to build trust again.

"It about crushed me when I realized he'd slipped again. I told him I didn't want to see him anymore." Rob swallowed and let out a low breath. "I didn't see him again until he showed up on my doorstep last week. It's been eight years and he acted as though I should open my arms in welcome." He swallowed hard, but his voice didn't crack with the emotions she could see flashing across his face. "I can't do it anymore. It's not worth the effort, not when I know it'll end the same way someday."

"Rob." She didn't know what to say. He'd given the simplest answer when she asked him about his dad before. She'd sensed pain beneath that, but hadn't pushed. Now she understood and she hurt for him.

"If it hadn't been for Marc, I probably would've ended up a wreck. Fortunately, he loved me like one of his own kids; there's never been an issue of who was biologically related. And when Leland messed with my head and then walked away, Marc was always there for me, ready to deal with my anger and frustration. Considering letting Leland back into my life after all of that feels like I'm betraying Marc."

Rob turned to face her, and she met his gaze, holding it for a long moment. He stepped closer and she stopped breathing completely. When he reached out and ran his fingertips over her cheek, she was sure he would kiss her. She wanted it, but didn't let herself kiss him when he didn't make the move. Though she wanted to offer him comfort, she was afraid kissing now, when their emotions were so strong, would end up in far more than kissing, and that would be a Very Bad Idea.

234

They stood like that for a long moment before he pulled back and turned away. "I probably ought to go."

The breath rushed from her chest and she felt her heart start beating again, pounding. Had it stopped before? "Right." She turned and took a step closer to the sink, grasping the edge with both hands as she tried to get her emotions back under control. She needed some time to think, even if her lips still tingled in anticipation of the kiss that wasn't going to happen.

"Thanks for asking me to stay. I think maybe I needed to say some of that." He came to stand behind her, though he didn't touch her.

"You're welcome. I was happy to listen. I needed to talk, too," Shelly admitted.

He moved away to put his jacket back on, then watched her for a long moment from the other side of the room. "Thanks for the hot cocoa—it's the best I ever tasted. Like always."

"You're welcome. Come back sometime and maybe I'll let you try it again." She managed a weak smile.

There was a pause. "I wondered if you'd like to go out with me. Like, on a real date. There's a new play at the Desert Star Theater. We could grab dinner there."

She smiled, glad the weirdness between them the past little while wouldn't be an insurmountable hurdle and he was still willing to keep trying. "I think I'd like that."

"Great. I'll pick you up at six on Friday?"

"That'll be perfect."

"Well, goodnight." He moved his hand to the doorknob.

"Goodnight. Drive carefully."

"I will." He opened the door and left.

Shelly stepped over to her window and watched him get in his car and drive away. She reminded herself that she wanted her independence, at least for a while. Whatever may or may not happen down the road was another deal entirely.

She hoped that future could include Rob.

Chapter 40

LATER THAT EVENING ROB sat at the dining table in his apartment, fiddling with a blue plastic ring from around the milk jug, sliding it back and forth across the worn wood veneer thinking about the conversation with Shelly.

He glanced up to where Rhett had set his letters from Leland. Another had come that day, and Rhett apparently felt it was his duty to pull them out and read off the postmark dates on them—making his point clear—that Leland was making a firm effort to reach out to Rob on his son's terms.

Rhett caught Rob's gaze. "You ought to at least read them, don't you think?"

"No, I don't. If I did, I would have." Rob looked away and took another bite of his Lucky Charms.

"What if he has something worth saying?"

Rob turned away, staring out the window at the falling snow while he finished his now-soggy cereal. "He never does. It's all song and dance with Leland. You know that. You saw how many times he yanked my chain, then walked away. I don't need him." He didn't mind Rhett pilfering from his cupboards or his nagging about whose turn it was to do the dishes—not much. His nagging Rob about his relationships with Leland and Shelly was growing old, though. Wasn't he doing the best he could to get through everything right now?

"True, you don't. You're grown up, independent. Why would you need someone like him? He's only your father, after all."

"Sperm donor," Rob corrected.

236

"Right you are; sperm donor." Rhett's voice was nauseatingly agreeable, and held a touch of British edge to it, though Rob wasn't sure if it was one of those times where he did it on purpose or on accident. "Let's keep this all in perspective. He's not important at all." Rhett paused, studying his brother's face for a moment, then added in an offhanded voice, "But then, it makes me wonder why you'd bother to keep seven letters from him if you have no intention of reading them, ever. I mean, a sperm donor doesn't deserve the consideration, and you don't need to hear anything he has to say."

"Look, Rhett, your meddling in my relationship with Shelly is bad enough. Can't you be happy with that?" Carrying around the uncertainty and questions was wearing him down.

"Your relationship with her... no, I can't. You know why? Because you all but ignore the fact that you have one. If you're not careful, some weasel will win her by default and you'll be stuck alone, staring at a stack of letters that reaches the ceiling."

"For your information, we have a date Friday night. Now go away. I'd rather be miserable alone than miserable with you." Rob glared at Rhett. "Don't you have homework?"

"Nothing is as important to me as your happiness." Rhett pressed a hand to his chest, his face serious. Meanwhile, he inched his way toward the front door, a glint in his eye. "I'm just going to borrow this for a while." He snatched Rob's coat from the rack by the door and took off. It was an old ruse, one they'd used since boyhood, and which had ended in more than a few playful tussles and innumerable bruises over the years.

Though Rob had been inclined to wallow, he took the bait instead and abandoned the soggy mess in the bottom of his bowl. "You better run." He dashed out the door and down the stairs as Rhett made his getaway. Rob had always been a bit taller, a bit faster, and it worked to his advantage as he chased Rhett, then tackled him halfway to the parking lot. They fell onto the grass, which sported an inch of late-fall snow. They rolled around, wrestling in the snow and rubbing it in each other's faces. Rhett had Rob's coat on, so by the time they stopped, sitting in the snow, and breathing heavily from the exertion, Rob was freezing. At least he felt better, and it hadn't devolved into a real fight.

"I better get inside," Rob said as he looked across the dark lawn, and mentally checked for sore spots that would turn to bruises. He thought he might have gotten away without too many this time, and felt refreshed after the tussle, some of his anxiety worn off.

"You'll be a human popsicle soon. You have snow in your hair," Rhett pointed out.

"So do you."

"At least I had the sense to put on a coat."

Rob laughed despite himself. "I'd go on another round with you for that comment, but I'm too cold. Go find someone else to bug." Rob stood and brushed himself off. He returned to the apartment, which wasn't too warm either, since he'd left the door ajar.

"It's too late for me to visit anyone interesting," Rhett said from behind him.

"Then go sleep, or study in your room where I can forget you exist." He wasn't upset with Rhett anymore, but he didn't want to risk a resumption of the topics that had caused the stress the first time.

"Read the letters. They might help," Rhett called before he disappeared into his room.

"Drop dead, Rhett." Rob leaned back against the outside door, staring at the pile of letters. He figured that when he had as many letters as he'd sent Leland while he was on his mission, he might bother reading them. Counting the two he'd opened before he started sticking them in the drawer, Rob figured he had about ninety-five left to go.

Deciding he had more immediate concerns, he walked toward the shower. He needed to get warm.

FRIDAY AFTERNOON WHILE Shelly corrected the last papers for her classes, she looked up and saw a notice that she had a private message on Facebook. She signed in and found a message from Clay Fuller. She paused for a moment. He hadn't friended her, and she had no intention of accepting if he did, but she could read his note. With some trepidation, she clicked on it.

Shelly,

I hope you read this and don't just delete it—I have a lot of things to say to you. Don't worry that I'll make a nuisance of myself again. There was no excuse for the way I acted last year and I want to apologize. Please read this to the end before you hit delete.

I admit I was angry when you sent the missionaries over that night. That was NOT in my plans. You see, though what I said was true—you do have a glow about you that intrigued me—I was not strictly honest about why I wanted to spend time with you. Of course, you realized that. Anyway, I thought if I worked on you long enough, I'd find your breaking point—I realize now how stupid I was. Your values were too important to give up for a berk like me.

Anyway, when the missionaries came, they gave me a Book of Mormon and I tossed it in the garbage. After I talked to you that night, I pulled it out and set it on my desk. I didn't know why, I just couldn't bin it. It sat on my desk for the rest of the summer and when it was time to move home, I almost threw it away again. Instead I put it in my bags and brought it home. I never opened the book, and didn't plan to read it. I started working in Albany last month. When I unpacked my bags and put things away from my flat in England, I found the book again. On impulse, I opened it and read the note on the fly leaf:

Yes, you wrote the inscription, inviting me to read the book and pray about it. It surprised me that your simple words could make such an impression, but they did. I want you to know that I took those words to heart, and I read. A few weeks ago, I found the missionaries in the phone book and set up an appointment. I decided today to be baptized. I wanted you to know that the good-for-nothing skirt-chaser finally gets it, and to thank you for being so hard-to-get that I had to learn more about you. You've made a huge difference in my life.

—Clay Fuller

Shelly stared at the message in wonder. This was the last thing she ever expected. She took a deep breath, then started typing a reply.

Clay, thanks for the letter. I'm glad you finally found what it was you were looking for. The gospel is so precious to me. It has gotten me through more trials than I even care to dwell on and buoys me up through every-day life. It has helped me...

Suddenly she realized that so many of her questions had been answered. In the previous months, she had learned more about herself than she realized.

...to figure out who I really am and given me direction. I don't think I realized its power to heal until now. You are one wild and crazy guy. I hope you find strength to help you in the transition to a different way of living. Whatever else happens, I hope you always remember that the Lord loves you and will help you through any difficulties you face.

Shelly

When she reread the letter and knew it was what she wanted to say, she sent it and then got up, taking a walk around the building to clear her head. Shelly wondered if Rhett had given Clay that particular Book of Mormon on purpose, or if it just happened to be the next one on the stack her young adults group had signed and donated to them earlier. She'd have to ask.

Chapter 41

SHELLY RAN HER FINGERS through her hair again, waiting anxiously for Rob to arrive. She'd been surprised when he'd asked her out, not expecting that on the heels of their discussion. Excitement zinged through her now as she looked ahead to the date.

She took a deep breath and forced a smile before opening the door when the bell rang. It took all her effort to keep her mouth from dropping open. Sure, she'd seen him dressed up lots of times, but he looked better than ever. The soft green and brown of his sweater turned his brown eyes almost hazel, and his smile was devastating.

"Hi," he said, looking her over. She had curled her hair and pulled it away from her face with only a twisty strand curling down her cheek, and knew she looked nice in her jade dress. Still, it was nice to see the approval in his eyes.

"Hi." Her mouth felt dry and she found herself wetting her lips as she grabbed her purse. "You're right on time."

"You know how I am about punctuality." He lifted her jacket to help her with it. "You used to know nearly all my habits."

"That's right. I'm afraid I've forgotten some of them. You'll have to reacquaint me." Shelly slipped into the jacket and accepted the hand he held out to her.

"Then it's past time I did."

The air between them crackled like bubble wrap in the hands of a five-year-old as they drove to the restaurant. They kept the conversation centered

241

on work and discussion of their mutual friends, but it sounded stilted, even to Shelly's ears. This was make-or-break night. If it didn't go anywhere now, their future was negligible. She was surprised her hands didn't shake.

The waitress sat them at a corner table and told them the evening's specials. After a short moment, they both placed their orders and turned back to face each other. "So, I got an interesting email today." Shelly played with the edge of her napkin, rolling and unrolling it.

"Yeah? What was it?" Rob sat back in his seat while his eyes studied her.

"You remember the guy I sent Rhett to visit while we were in England?"

His brow furrowed and then his face brightened from the memory. "The one who kept bothering you to go out with him?" Rob took a sip of his water and smiled at the waitress when she brought their sodas.

"Yes. He sent me a message through Facebook today." For the first time that evening, she began to calm. She still couldn't believe what she'd read that afternoon. "The Book of Mormon Rhett gave him? He finally read it. He called the missionaries, and he's getting baptized."

"You're kidding? Are you surprised?"

"Beyond shocked. I would have thought Pluto would crash into the sun before he even gave it a second glance. It's unbelievable." She shook her head and settled into the seat. "Remind me to tell Rhett when I see him next."

Dinner was lovely and the play as hilarious as indicated, with plenty of melodrama and interaction from the audience. Shelly found herself wishing the evening didn't have to end when they pulled in front of her apartment building. Rob helped her from the car and then walked her to the door. The strange awareness she always felt in his presence clung to them as they walked in silence with the moon shining down on them and a dog barking in the background.

"I really enjoyed the show," Shelly said. "Thanks for taking me."

"You're welcome. I'd heard good things about it."

What stars could be seen through the city lights hung in the sky, bigger than life. The unseasonably early snow from the previous day had mostly melted in the early November sun, leaving small puddles on the asphalt. "What a beautiful night," he observed, looking at the stillness all around them.

"Would you like to come in for some hot cocoa?" Shelly asked as they approached her doorway.

Rob hesitated. "Yeah, I think I would."

Several minutes later as she handed Rob a steaming cup and sat next to him on the couch, he asked, "So, what is it with you and hot chocolate? We seem to have it a lot. More often than we did in college."

"I didn't have a kitchen in college," she said with a laugh, then paused to consider his point. "I guess it's because my roommates in England always sat down and had coffee or tea and talked in the evening. It was a big social thing. I kind of got into the habit."

"Well, it's a delicious habit anyway." His gaze caught on something across the room and he got up and walked over to a large silver framed photo collage. "Is this new?"

"Yeah, I've been putting it together for a while, but I just hung it yesterday. You'll probably recognize some of the people." She pointed out people they knew in college, and roommates he'd met when he was in England the previous spring.

"Hey, where did you get this picture of me?" He pointed to one outside their old apartment buildings, where he stood with an old roommate.

"You posed for it, silly. Don't you remember?" she asked. "Just before Larry left on his mission at the end of the summer."

"Right, it seems like forever ago."

It had been a while. Did she dare bring up the past now when he'd been so unwilling to discuss it before? Would it sour the great evening they had been enjoying? She decided to risk it. "You and Lindsey dated for quite a while, didn't you?"

"Yeah. Nine or ten months."

He didn't close up on her or look away, so she decided to push on. "Do you mind saying how you ended up single when you were rumored to be engaged?" They still hadn't gotten around to discussing their individual relationship failures.

"That rumor came straight from Lindsey." Irony filled his voice. He blew across the top of the navy blue mug with the Utah State University symbol on it and the steam spiraling off of it danced away. "I wasn't sure why everyone thought we were already engaged, but didn't worry about it at first. Then February rolled around and I started thinking that since Lindsey and I had been dating for nearly a year, and she was pushing for marriage, maybe I should move in that direction. I know, I'm totally lame."

He took a sip of his cocoa and stared down at the table instead of meeting her eyes. "I had it planned, what I was going to do and everything. I went to the mall to buy the ring, but once I got there, I found I couldn't. She wasn't the one whose face kept appearing when I looked into my future." His lips twisted in a wry smile. "We'll say she didn't take it well."

His gaze lifted to hers and Shelly wondered if he was implying what she thought he was, but she wasn't ready to discuss it yet, or the fact that she'd had a similar experience. She wasn't quite finished battling her own demons.

"Your turn," he said when she didn't respond. "What happened with you and Brad?"

That question brought her fully back to reality and she turned back to him. "For the Fourth of July he took me to the beach and we roasted hotdogs and marshmallows and watched the sunset—it was as close to fireworks as we could get—then he told me he wanted to marry me."

His brows lifted. "But you didn't want that."

"No, I did." She saw the surprise in his eyes, and pushed on. "I wanted to say yes, but I asked for time to think it over, to be sure. When I finished praying and after a trip to the temple, I realized I couldn't marry him."

Rob nodded as he took another sip of hot cocoa, watching her. "That must have been so difficult, for both of you." His eyes roamed over her face and connected with hers. "A guy doesn't fall for a girl like you without falling completely." His gaze skittered away again.

She swallowed hard. Somehow the conversation wasn't as weird as she'd expected it to be. "I later learned he'd been drinking all along, but hiding it from me." She still felt heartache about that. "I'd mentioned how I felt about all the drinking everyone did, and he'd agreed with me, and about how it destroys your self-control and drives away the Spirit, but he still went drinking with his buddies, lying to cover it." She looked across her cup at the picture of her family on the wall standing in front of the temple on the day Lily and Curtis were married. "It's just as well we didn't get engaged, because it would have been awful to find out later."

"I know what you mean." He nodded in agreement.

"But it still shocked me." Shelly remembered how she had all but run from her apartment, then filling the rest of the summer with trips to different areas to stay out of his way. Maybe, also, to keep from admitting to herself that her motives for wanting to marry him in the first place hadn't been the right ones. Had it been a different kind of denial than she'd used about Jimmy's death? She couldn't be sure, but she did know the worries and fears that had drawn her away after her kiss with Rob in the rainstorm no longer haunted her. "It took me longer than I expected to deal with the jumbled emotions I felt then."

She met his gaze. "I don't want you to confuse my freak-out the other day with disinterest. That was fully about my own issues, and not because I wasn't happy to be kissing you." She felt herself flush—she wasn't entirely comfortable being so direct with him, though the last thing she wanted was to leave him wondering about them.

"Thanks for explaining." He let go of his mug and reached out to brush her fingers with his own before pulling his hand back. "I could probably use some time myself. Things with Leland are so crazy, I'm never sure if I'm thinking straight or just reacting."

He stood again and returned to the picture frame, looking as if he wished he hadn't brought up his father. "And there's the man." He pointed out a shot of Jimmy in his mission suit.

She didn't have to walk over to the frame to know who was in the photo—she could spot him from much further away than that. "Yeah, there he is." Shelly was surprised to find only a gentle warmth and sadness in her chest when she thought of Jimmy without the sharp regret or desperate grief she used to feel. She glanced over at Rob. The timing had been wrong before. Maybe it would be right now.

Rob looked at Jimmy again and pursed his lips. "You got the easy decision over with early. The rest of life is for the tough ones."

Shelly's throat closed off as she realized what he was talking about. Did he really think that? Then she realized, of course he did. It wasn't as though she let him know the truth back then. The truth would have made it harder for him to accept, she had been sure of it. And the last thing she'd needed at the time was for him to try to change her mind when she was already struggling with the decision. She shook her head again and managed to speak through the remaining airway. "Not easy."

He looked back at her, his eyes narrowing. "What?"

Her mouth had never felt so dry, but she knew she had to tell him—it was past time. She carefully set down her cup and walked over to him. She could have sworn her apartment wasn't more than fifteen feet in any direction, but it seemed so far this time. "It wasn't easy choosing Jimmy. It may have looked like it—I worked very hard at making it look like it was so you could have a clean break—but it wasn't." She crossed her arms over her stomach and stared at her shoes. "I prayed about it for weeks after we talked." She wet her lips and forced herself to look him in the face. "I second-guessed so many times. I knew what I'd felt, but I hated the idea of losing you. It made me feel like such a jerk."

Rob brushed his fingertips down her cheek, then slid his hand into the hair at the nape of her neck, warm and gentle, and pulled her to him. His lips were tentative at first, not like their final kiss two years before. They brushed hers once, twice, and finally pressed more firmly. Shelly felt the emotions rising inside her—she wasn't wrong about pursuing this relationship. She knew it.

Their kiss on that fateful night had been spectacular, almost desperate as she had known it would be the last for them and wanted to make the most of it, all while he was trying to convince her that they should be together.

This time she didn't have those worries, hoping this was only a beginning. The kiss lingered as she pulled him closer, leaned into it, let her mind spin away for a time as her hand came up to grasp his sweater. Then she slid back enough that they could see each other. She wondered if she looked as off-balance as she felt as she watched a grin spread across his face.

Shelly smiled and took a deep breath. "Wow." The guilt pang didn't appear this time and she felt relief that they could finally move forward.

"Yeah, wow." They stood for a long moment, looking at each other as they calmed their racing hearts. "Shelly, I—" His expression changed and he put some space between them, balling his hands at his side. "I want to promise you all kinds of amazing things right now, but I don't want to rush this." He must have seen the confusion and disappointment in her eyes because he let out a low breath and pulled her into a hug, resting his chin on her head. "This is too important to mess up, so I want to give it a little time."

She nodded that she understood.

When he left a couple minutes later, Shelly wondered if they were finally going to make those last few steps. She was ready.

Chapter 42

ROB OPENED HIS DOOR to get the newspaper the next morning and found a shoe-box sized package sitting on his doorstep. His name was scrawled across the top, though there was no address and it obviously hadn't been mailed. He was surprised at how light it was when he picked it up. It didn't take long to slit the tape and pull back the cardboard flaps. It was crammed full of white envelopes, each with a date in the right-hand corner.

He sat heavily in the nearby chair and pulled out a stack. He sorted through them, noticing the envelopes were in order and there was a number along with Leland's name in the upper left-hand corner. The dates were each about a week apart, and the first one was shortly after his mission had started. A look at the last envelope proved the writing had continued months after his mission ended—there had to be a hundred of them, maybe more. Leland had written him back all that time? Why hadn't he mailed them? Rob was dumbfounded, but nowhere near ready to deal with it.

He stood and glanced through the newspaper, unable to pay much attention to what he was reading, and munched his way through a bowlful of cereal. Rob kept staring at the brown box of envelopes as he ate, torn over whether to read them or finally throw them out. Wishing Rhett hadn't gone home for the weekend but was around for a game of one-on-one, he turned to his usual coping mechanism and cleaned up the kitchen and living room.

He cleaned out the refrigerator again, scrubbed the bathroom, and vacuumed, and still the pile of mail taunted him. Finally he grabbed the seven letters from the kitchen drawer and filed them in order behind the others in the box. But he couldn't bring himself to open one.

Needing to get out of the house, he made a list and left the taunting mail. All day he ran errands, shopped for food, worked out at the gym, and washed loads of laundry while the box sat on the kitchen table. Rob had decided that when Leland had written enough letters to make up for the ones he hadn't replied to, he would open them and consider trusting again. He'd never believed it was possible, though. Now he had to decide if he was going to follow through with the promise he'd made only to himself, or ignore everything else.

The entire day passed and that night he lay in bed unable to sleep.

The clock ticked beside him as he stared at the shadows on the ceiling. He looked at the clock at 11:30, then 12:09, and again at 1:34, but didn't think he'd even dozed.

It was after three o'clock when he returned to the kitchen. His bare feet rapidly cooled on the vinyl floor, but he ignored that. Rob flipped on the ceiling light and considered the box before reaching in and plucking out the first letter, dated three weeks after he entered the Missionary Training Center.

He pulled out a chair, scraping it across the yellow vinyl flooring, and sat, staring at the paper in his hands. There wasn't a time in his life that he could remember being so messed up about a piece of mail, but he had the feeling this was a step that couldn't be taken back. Once he started reading the letters, things might never be the same again. There was a chance, however slim, that one of these letters would contain something that would make it possible, inevitable even, that he find a way to forgive Leland, and he wasn't sure if he wanted to do that.

If Leland had taken the time to write back... The thought thrilled and terrified Rob. Afraid to hope, he stared at the cheap white paper for another long moment before turning it over and ripping open the flap.

His eyes slid over the words, but hardly picked up more than a few scattered phrases, and he forced himself to start again.

Dear Robert,

You're probably wondering why you haven't heard from me in nearly a year. I don't have an excuse. Your letters the past two weeks have been like manna. Mom and Dad brought them to me, I could have you write me directly, but I admit, I'm ashamed and don't want you to know where I am. Better for you to think I don't care than have the shame to bear, too. The truth is, several months ago I was traveling in Wyoming when I had a little accident. No, not a little accident—a major accident.

Yes, I was high.

You're probably disgusted with me. I don't blame you. I'm disgusted with myself. I hit a car and a little girl ended up in the hospital. It was my fault—I was reckless and stupid. I'm told there wasn't much news coverage since no one was killed, but I didn't bother trying to get out of jail on bail. I deserve to be here and I was sick of being the person I'd become. I hoped my time here would help me re-evaluate.

The days pass slowly and I'm forced to accept that I nearly destroyed a life. I can never fix what I've done, because the child spent months in and out of doctors' offices. When I think that it could have been you, that you could have been hurt by my carelessness, it scares me.

Your letters are so upbeat, despite the fact that I know you must hate me. I can hardly believe you bothered to write once, never mind twice, and say you'll write weekly. I've decided to do the same, though I can't bear for you to know the truth, not now when I have nothing better to offer you. I'll be here for at least two and a half years. I'm a drug addict, and spent the first few months here dealing with my withdrawals. I hope by the time I get to see you again that I'll be stronger, better. I know I never told you, and I certainly never acted like it, but I've always been proud of you and the decisions you've made.

Dad

Rob read the letter again and again. He had his answer, he guessed. Now he knew where his—where *Leland* had been. Knew why he hadn't seen or heard from him in years.

Suddenly he felt tired, so tired he knew he needed to sleep. He stood and returned the letter to the envelope, then filed it at the back of the box. One down, more than a hundred to go. He didn't know if he was ready to let Leland back into his life, but he felt like he was at least taking a step in the right direction—wherever that may lead.

DINNER AT DENISE'S the next day was a casual affair, and boasted enough food to feed twice the number in attendance. Shelly had brought Rob with her and they turned on an NBA game after they ate. Beyond the blaring of the pre-game, Shelly heard the soft strains of piano coming from the parlor. She'd seen Rob head in that direction a few minute earlier.

Denise nudged Shelly. "So, what's up with Romeo? He was awfully quiet tonight."

Shelly paused for a moment, trying to decide if she should say anything about it. "His dad rematerialized in his life and he's struggling over it." She didn't need to explain more than that, not to Denise. After everything Denise had been through, she could read between the lines.

"Ahh. You think he'd be upset if I talked to him?"

Shelly bit her lip and looked at her cousin's wife. Denise had always had a great listening ear, and she'd been through her own birth-family reunion a few years earlier. Though Shelly would usually be hesitant about interfering this way, something tonight told her it would be fine. "I think he could use it."

❀ ❀ ❀

ROB SAT AT THE PIANO, picking out a hymn, when Denise joined him. "Mind if I bug you?"

He looked back at her in surprise. He hadn't heard her approach. "No, you're welcome. Did you want to use the piano? Am I making too much noise for the TV?"

Denise laughed. "Heavens no, I wouldn't know where to start. I can't even play Chopsticks." Still, she settled on the bench beside him.

He gave her an incredulous look. "Come on, even a music dunce can play Chopsticks."

"Not me. Guess I'm below the level of dunce."

"I'll show you." Rob walked her through the simple steps, and soon had Denise initiated on the piano. "Now you can tell everyone that you play." He played a quick, but fancy, scale up the keys.

Denise laughed again. "You make that look so easy."

"It is after a few thousand hours of practice. You want to learn Peter, Peter, Pumpkin Eater?"

"Sure, then I can be more than a one-hit wonder."

Denise followed him through the motions and he relaxed, enjoying the company. Soon she changed the subject. "You know, I never had a chance for music lessons when I was little, and by the time my family adopted me, I was way too angry and stubborn to learn."

He didn't know many details about her childhood. "Shelly mentioned you were in foster care as a kid."

"Yes. Abuse and neglect—lots of neglect. My mom always made big promises when she was sober, but as soon as she started to drink again, or shoot up, she'd forget it all. She never did clean up. Not really. I was glad I made my peace with her when I did. It's been almost six years since I found her again, and she's still got years left in prison before they'll release her." She pursed her lips and stared at her hands. "I'm not sure she'll live that long."

"Are you close now?" Rob picked out another tune on the keyboard with his right hand, but focused on the conversation. His hands had played this so many times, he didn't need to think about.

"No. We're in touch, but I don't think we'll ever be close. That's the thing about a reunion with a parent. Sometimes it works and sometimes it doesn't. It's not easy—not for anyone. Too often the reunion doesn't go well, the pain is too deep, and they never work things out. Even then, though, the people I've spoken to are almost always glad they tried."

"Why?" Rob's hand stilled on the keyboard. "If it turns out badly, why would they be glad they tried?"

Denise tucked her short, dark hair behind her ear and focused on his face, as if she wanted him to understand. "People aren't perfect. Some of the people I know who've had an unsuccessful reunion were able to realize they weren't responsible for their parent's or child's problems. Some were glad they made the effort, even though it didn't work because it allowed them to release the guilt. My reunion didn't turn out all stars and rainbows with my mom, but we came to an understanding and I found peace—that was something I didn't think would ever be possible." She ran her fingers along the keys, as if caressing them, though Rob doubted she was paying attention to her hand.

"After all, I was able to ask my questions, even if I didn't like some of the answers I received. I got closure, and she's thrilled to be given updates on her grandkids. Eventually, with a lot of prayer and an understanding husband, I was able to accept that my mother's problems were her own and had nothing to do with how loveable I am."

Rob dropped his hands from the keyboard and allowed them to clench and unclench in his lap. "So she never really changed. Do you think she still might?"

"It's hard to know. If she lives long enough, after so many years in prison, she may be able to stay away from chemical assistance. Or she may find an easy outlet after only a couple of weeks—it's her favorite means of escape. All I can do is pray things will work out. I'm happier now because I pushed through that barrier. I'm not saying that if she were released tomorrow that I'd have her move in with me, but at least we have some kind of relationship now, and that's important. I set the rules for our relationship, which keeps things healthy. But at least we have a relationship now, and that's been good for me."

"How long did that take you to get to that point? To give her a chance when she had let you down over and over?"

She smiled and shook her head, tucking a strand of her short brown hair behind her ear. "Longer than I like to admit. And it started with just a crack in the door—a teeny, tiny one. That's what I needed, though. Thankfully, a tiny crack doesn't have to let in a whole flood."

Neither of them said anything for a long moment as Rob considered that.

Rich brought the crying baby to Denise. "Sorry to disturb you, she's ready for some dinner."

Denise took the squalling infant, but looked over at Rob, "You good?"

"Yeah."

"All right. The game starts soon—you'll want to come out and see my brother play before too long. He's promised me a good game."

"I will." Rob sat thinking about her words for a long while before Shelly checked on him, and he joined them for the basketball game. He'd have to mull over Denise's words more later.

Chapter 43

"HEY, SHELLY." ROB'S VOICE came through the telephone line as she entered scores on the computer.

She smiled. It had been a couple of days since they'd spoken last. "Rob, how're things going?"

"Pretty well. I'm sorry I haven't called before now. I should have. You've been on my mind."

Shelly reigned in the butterflies that popped into her chest. They hadn't gotten together since dinner with Denise, but she wanted to give him space to digest whatever her cousin had said. "Same here. We did say we needed some time before we discussed everything, didn't we? It's been a few days. I think we have a lot to talk about, once you're ready."

"I'm working on that, but for now, I have another request to make."

"What's that?" Shelly entered the quiz score on her spreadsheet.

"Our ward back home is doing a special program for its seventy-fifth anniversary in a couple weeks, and they asked if Rhett and I would do a song. I wondered if you were up to another duet."

"Always with you. When is it?" She sat back in her chair and twirled the pen in her fingers. So it wasn't another date, but it was something that would put them together again. The question was, would he have called otherwise?

"The weekend before Thanksgiving. It's a Saturday night, and my mom said she'd love to have you for the whole weekend."

Shelly looked at her calendar and grinned. "Isn't that the weekend of *your* birthday?"

He cleared his throat. "Um, yeah. Look, you don't have to come if you don't want to."

"I'd love to. Do we have the music?"

"Rhett's got something in mind. The thing is, he only has tonight open to practice. The rest of the week he works until too late. Are you available?"

"Absolutely."

❀ ❀ ❀

SHELLY WALKED INTO THE Durrant household a week and a half later, only to be hit by chaos. Natalie called down the stairs to her mom about some dress she'd left behind but couldn't find. Michelle, who was two years older than Rhett, was herding two toddlers from the kitchen. Their sixteen-year-old cousin Brie, who'd been staying with the family since August, trailed up from the basement with a couple of giggling friends.

"Sorry about the pandemonium," Mrs. Durrant said when they found her in the kitchen. "Just a typical family reunion."

Shelly laughed. "I know what you're talking about. I have three sisters myself, and things can get a bit crazy when everyone's home."

"Mom, have you seen my rhinestones?" Natalie asked as she entered the kitchen.

"Are you sure you didn't take them with you for that dance with Craig?"

Natalie let out a frustrated huff. "Right. I'll have to find something else."

She was almost out of the room when Shelly put a hand on her arm to stop her as the words clicked in her mind. "Wait, my Craig? Craig Sorenson?"

"Your Craig?" Natalie glanced to where her brothers were still focused on cookies, then wiggled her eyebrows and continued in a lower voice. "I would say he was *my* Craig." She smirked and slipped out of the room.

A trill of happiness ran through Shelly's chest at the thought. If she married Rob and Natalie ended up with Craig, he *would* be the little brother she'd always expected him to be, and she'd love that. She pushed that thought aside. She was getting ahead of herself.

The afternoon that followed was little better in the chaos department.

As she checked her hair in the mirror at the church that evening, Shelly wondered if she would have the unending energy to keep up with everything the way Rob's mom did.

The seventy-fifth anniversary of their ward proved to be quite an event. The old brick building swelled with hundreds of excited people, most of whom had spent the last few decades living elsewhere. One enthusiastic woman, a complete stranger, grabbed Shelly by the hand and started saying how nice it was to see her again. It had been so long, hadn't it? Shelly smiled and nodded. "Yeah," she whispered under her breath as she slipped away a moment later. "The preexistence was a long time ago."

After winding her way to the back of the auditorium, grateful the ward was currently meeting in the stake center so the building could accommodate the ever-growing crowd, Shelly spotted Rob and Rhett. "Thank goodness. If I have one more person ask me when I lived here, or try to tell me they remembered teaching me in nursery, I'll scream," she said as she joined them.

Rob laughed and slid an arm around her waist. "But you were so cute and cuddly back then—and everyone knows you were the brightest of your group. You could pick the red ball from the lineup every time. Of course, it helped that it had Strawberry Shortcake on it."

She poked him gently in the side. "You better watch it, young man. I'll introduce you to that nursery leader and leave you to suffer her recounting the exploits of every dark-haired toddler she's ever known."

He laughed and held up a hand in a defensive gesture. "I give. You ready to do this?"

"I've sung to crowds before." She tipped her head teasingly. "As long as you don't hog the microphone, we'll be fine."

"I don't hog the microphone."

"Every time." But she softened the words with a kiss on his cheek. It wasn't true, anyway—most of the time.

Rob didn't get a chance to continue in his self-defense as the spokesperson for the event called the crowd to order.

Their duet was first on the docket, and Shelly soon found herself standing in front of the mic with Rob. A hush came over the crowd as Rhett began to play. All eyes were on them. The song spoke of God's love for His children, of how even the lowliest was engraved on the palms of Christ's hands. The love and spirit that invaded the room swamped Shelly's chest. Christ knew her. He knew her trials, her worries. He knew how she struggled over the difficulties she and Rob faced in their relationship. By the time she sang the final lines, her heart was bursting with love she felt from the words.

He knows my heart like no one can. I'm not alone.

Rob led her off the stand in the cultural hall and slid an arm around her. "Are you all right?"

Shelly wiped at a tear trickling down her cheek and smiled. "Yeah, I'm fine. Better than fine."

❀ ❀ ❀

THE NEXT DAY AFTER CHURCH, as soon as lunch was over and presents had been opened, Marc walked into the room and set a package big enough for a basketball in Rob's lap. Shelly watched Rob look at it questioningly, read something on top, and then his face hardened. "When did this get here?"

"Friday afternoon. I mentioned to his mom that you'd be home today." His mother walked over and sat on the armrest of his chair, setting a hand on Rob's shoulder. Everyone waited in silence for a long moment watching him eye the package. "Are you going to open it?"

He nodded his head slowly. "I will, eventually. I'm... not quite ready yet." He looked over at Shelly and caught her puzzled look. "Leland."

She nodded and watched him walk out the front door. Through the window, she saw him put it in his car. He hesitated slightly as he set it on the seat, then locked the door again and walked back to the house.

"I thought for a moment there that he would throw it out," Natalie said.

"He's working on it, give him a break and I'll keep nudging him along if needed," Rhett said.

Marc took Rob's chair, so Shelly waved Rob over, and he sat in the empty spot next to her on the sofa. He sat rigidly next to her, and she slid a hand into his. She asked him, in a low voice, "Are you okay?"

He nodded, and relaxed after a few minutes under her touch. Eventually he joined the rest of the family in their banter.

She hoped Rhett was right and Rob was adjusting his way of thinking after all.

LATER, WHILE THE WOMEN were in the kitchen preparing a birthday dinner, Rob found Marc watching the game. "Do you have a minute?"

Marc glanced up. "Yeah, let's go into my office."

When they sat a moment later in the brown-paneled room, shelves full of books lined up behind the scuffed desk, the noise in the house shut out, Rob fidgeted in his seat. "I... Did you know Leland's been sending me letters?"

Marc folded his hands over his stomach. "Yeah. Do you read them?"

"Not at first. Well, I did read the first two, then threw them away, even angrier than before. After that I refused to read them. I kept a stack in my drawer. I told myself when he sent as many unanswered letters to me as I had to him, I'd open them." He looked into Marc's eyes, but found understanding rather than censure there. "I was hurt, angry. I felt giving him a chance was almost like turning my back on you."

Marc smiled in understanding—he'd always been one of the most loving and perceptive people Rob had ever known. "You shouldn't feel that way. I know you love me, that you've been happy in our home. Just because you're in touch with him again, if you decide you're ready to be in touch with him, doesn't lessen our relationship." Marc ran a hand over his thinning hair and let out a breath. "Rob, Leland came to us almost a year ago and asked if we'd hate him if he tried to talk to you again, and asked how you would take it. I admit, in the past I have hated the sight of him, knowing he'd make promises to you and take off again. But this time I felt a difference in him. I actually believed him."

Rob wasn't sure if he'd been trying to get absolution for letting his bitterness melt away, or if he'd hoped for an excuse to keep Leland at arm's length. Either way, the main thing he felt now was disbelief. "How? How can you believe him? How can I ever believe him? How can I learn to trust someone who never told me the truth before? Not once."

Marc obviously wasn't surprised by the fury in Rob's questions, but remained calm. "I don't know how to tell you that, but if you decide to open

257

those letters, I won't feel like you're turning your back on me. You need to feel whole. Letting Leland back into your life doesn't have to be a huge commitment. It *can* be if you want. He can be your other dad, invited to your children's blessings and birthday parties. Or you can just keep in touch; have dinner a couple of times a year—whatever works for you. The fact is, you'll need to make peace with him someday, and the sooner, the better for you."

Yeah, yeah, the old forgive and forget line. Does he really believe it's the answer? "So, I should give in now and invite him to hurt me again?"

"I didn't say that. If you expect to be hurt again, you'll still be miserable."

That got Rob's back up. "I'm not miserable."

Marc took a deep breath and picked up a glass paperweight one of the girls had given him for Christmas years earlier. He turned his eyes back to Rob, but juggled the piece of glass back and forth between his hands. "Bad choice of words. Forgiveness isn't nearly so much for him as it is for you. You need to understand that his actions had nothing to do with you, not in his head. He wasn't out to hurt you. Leland never got joy from causing you pain.

"What he did was purely selfish. His not writing you had to do with his past and his problems, and was not because he didn't love you—as much as he was capable of it."

Rob calmed and rested his head on the back of the seat, closing his eyes. "You know, he did write me while I was on my mission, but he never sent them to me. He left a whole box of letters on my doorstep a couple weeks back. I finally started reading them. I've read them all now. I think they were sincerely written, but everything he said to me in the past was sincere too, and it wasn't enough. I don't want to forgive him, even though I know I should. I don't know how to forgive him without setting myself up to be hurt."

"It can be a long process, son, but you'll get there. Six months ago, you would have tossed the present in the trash can instead of taking it to the car. Baby steps are fine, as long as they are moving in the right direction. Give yourself more time."

Rob decided Marc was right—he just hated the thought of the stress that would show up along the way.

258

Chapter 44

ON THE RIDE HOME that night, the small box and what it represented took up a big portion of Rob's thoughts, though none of them mentioned it. He dropped Rhett by their apartment and continued to Shelly's when she finally brought the subject up again. "Have you heard much from Leland lately?"

Rob wet his lips and kept his eye firmly on the road while he decided how ready he was to talk about it. Without realizing he'd come to a decision, he heard himself answer. "Not much... and yes." He laughed slightly and tried again. "I received another package from him a couple of weeks ago. It was full of letters, letters he wrote me while I was on my mission, but never sent. I've been reading a little each day, but it's been hard."

Her voice was soft when she spoke, and she set her hand lightly on his arm. "What, exactly, has been hard about it? Forgiving him enough to listen?"

The thought hit Rob and he shook his head. He stopped at a red light and lifted both hands to his face, rubbing it as the thoughts ran through him. It made so much sense. He shook his head as the light turned green, and allowed an ironic smile. "*Not* forgiving him, actually. I've been trying to stay angry, and with every letter it got harder. I don't want to let it go." They turned a corner and he pulled in front of her apartment building.

He looked over at her as she clutched her purse in her lap. "What kind of person am I? He's been through his own nightmare, and I can say that it doesn't affect anyone but me when I'm mad, but that's not true. The worst

259

part is, I feel part of me wants to forgive him and move on, and another part never wants to forgive—not ever. I could let this go and have a normal life, with or without him, but I can't seem to release the anger."

"I understand that better than you might think," Shelly's voice turned tentative and she looked at him as if uncertain about whether or not to speak. "I was angry with Jimmy for leaving me, angry with the Lord for taking him, and angry with myself for asking him to go home on the route we took. I didn't want to let go of the hurt and anger." Rob sent her an incredulous look. "I know, by the time I saw you last winter I was doing much better, but you should have seen me that whole year after the accident. It felt somehow *wrong* to go on and be happy when Jimmy was gone."

"Do you think he'd want you to be miserable?" Rob asked.

"No, he wouldn't. Realizing that was part of the healing process for me." Shelly reached out and touched his face. "Let me know if you ever need to talk. I'm always willing to listen."

He brushed his lips over hers and nodded. "I'll remember that."

She smiled softly and got out of the car. Rob watched her walk to her apartment and let herself in before pulling back onto the road. He had a lot to think about.

❀ ❀ ❀

ROB SAT ON HIS BED that night with the package in front of him. It had been thirty minutes since he dropped Shelly off and he still stared at the box. Marc's words had been so much like Denise's that he hadn't been able to ignore them. Forgiveness was for Rob, not for Leland. He didn't have to trust Leland much in order to see what changes the man had made. But Rob needed to learn to trust if he was going to make a relationship work with Shelly. There was nothing he wanted more than that.

Leland seemed sincere—even Marc thought so. Slowly Rob unwrapped the gift, setting the card to the side. He paused for a long moment in shock after pulling back the wrapping to show the box. A Nintendo video game console, complete with Super Mario and Duck Hunt, plus a few others he was less familiar with from his youth, and the various paddles and controllers for the different games. It was an ancient console—the one that was around when Rob was a kid and wanted his first game machine.

260

His fingers shook as he opened the card.

Rob, I know I'm about eighteen years late. I hope you'll forgive me.
Leland

He couldn't believe Leland had remembered. Tears began to flow and Rob set his head in both hands as he finally released his anger and the pain that had accumulated over the years. This was the first promise Leland had ever fulfilled—even if it was late. Maybe he *was* ready to change.

When Rob was back in control of himself, he wiped his face and placed the gift on the empty plant shelf where he'd see it every time he passed. He knelt by his bed to pray.

THE COMPUTERS HUMMED around him and Rob smiled as he finished the morning's work. He loved the precision of numbers, the way they always made sense and added up to the same thing every time. It gave order to his life, even when things were out of whack.

He pulled up his email and was sending a message to the payroll office when someone appeared in his office door. He looked up, and the smile slid off his face. Rob forced it back on again and looked into a pair of dark eyes. "Hey, Leland. What's going on?"

He saw the man swallow and force a smile of his own. "I was in the area and wondered if you've had lunch yet."

Rob was tempted to refuse, but found himself unable to—he wanted to see if that narrow bridge his father had been trying to build between them could hold any weight. "I haven't. You buyin'?" His smile became a bit more real when Leland showed his relief.

"Yeah. Nothing fancy, I was thinking of a burger. Is this a good time for you?"

"Yeah." Rob finished writing his short note and sent the file, then closed down his email. He stood and grabbed his coat from the nearby rack.

Rob tugged his coat lapels up to protect his neck from the wind as they walked outside. The wind had picked up and pummeled them both as they headed to a local restaurant. The silence stretched long and awkward between them, but Rob wasn't sure how to start a conversation.

"I thought for sure you'd tell me no," Leland finally said.

"I considered it, but I decided it was time I let you talk, and not just write letters." Rob shifted in his coat, trying to find a warmer pocket, and wished he had something to do with his hands. He needed to fidget.

"Why did you come?" Leland asked.

Rob shrugged. "Your letters. Not so much the ones you've been writing lately, though I appreciate them. Mostly the ones from prison." He snuck a glance at Leland before pushing on. "You know, I used to lie in my bed at night after writing you—because I had to write you, it was mission rules—and wonder what was so wrong with me that you couldn't write back." Writing those letters was one of the hardest things he'd ever done.

"That wasn't it at all,"

"I know that now. And maybe you were right. Maybe I wasn't ready to accept what you'd been through." He hoped he was ready now. He longed for a better relationship with his father than they had managed in the past.

On his terms while he tested it out.

"I was starting to worry you would never reach this point."

"A few weeks ago I would have told you it would never happen. Your letters made a big difference." Rob's nose stung with cold by the time they reached the restaurant. They ordered their lunches and found a table in the corner away from other customers.

They talked about Rob's work, Leland's parents, and the previous night's football game before circling back to more personal topics.

"What have you been up to? Dating anyone new?" Leland asked as Rob started eating.

Rob tilted his head. "I'm not sure how to answer that one. If you mean someone besides Lindsey, who I was dating last year, then yes. But Shelly and I dated before, back when we were in college." He knew Leland had heard about his relationship with Lindsey last winter. From what he'd heard, Leland's parents kept their son up on the latest happenings.

"Is this the girl your mom thought you were going to marry a couple years ago, or was that someone else?"

Rob looked up in surprise. "I guess you've been in the loop more than I realized."

"I've tried. You know, I had intended to keep in touch with you, to make our last meeting the first of many. But it seems my good intentions never made it very far. I've been clean seven years now, though, and I'm not going back." His face was set in determination and Rob wondered how many other times Leland had made the same declaration and failed. It had been seven years, though.

Leland explained. "I can see your mind working. I know I've told you the same thing before, that I was determined, that I wasn't going to slip up anymore. But I never made it a year before, hardly ever a month. Part of the reason it took me so long to contact you was because I wanted to be sure. I didn't want to fail you again."

Rob looked away when he saw the tears forming in Leland's eyes, and felt the familiar sting in his own. It didn't take much to pull back the emotion, to steady himself. "I'm not sure I'm ready to trust you yet, Leland."

"I don't blame you. We can take things one step at a time, if you're willing. I have most Mondays off. Maybe we can try getting together again next Monday."

Rob took a final swallow of his soda and crumpled up the empty hamburger wrapper. "Give me a call. We'll see how this goes."

"Maybe you can introduce me to your girl. Is she pretty?" Leland asked.

Rob smiled to himself, thinking of Shelly standing in the falling snow after their latest date. She wasn't super-model beautiful, but he couldn't imagine wanting anything more. "Very pretty, and the smartest person I know. She could run circles around me if she wanted to."

"She sounds like a keeper." Leland stood and collected the trash from the table top.

Rob nodded to himself. "She is."

As they left the restaurant, Rob felt more settled than he'd been in a long time—about Leland, of course, but also about Shelly. If he could find a way to meet his father in neutral territory and forge a new relationship, he was ready to step forward with Shelly as well. He just needed to figure out how to let her know.

Chapter 45

SHELLY LAUGHED AS ROB took her up the stairs to the Clark Planetarium. "Cool. I wondered what you meant when you said we were going star-gazing in the middle of the afternoon."

"It's too cold at night right now, so I thought this would be the next best thing."

"Do they have Aggie ice cream, too?" She well remembered nights when they'd walked across the campus lawns to the creamery, then sat on the grass to enjoy their treats under the stars.

"I'm afraid not. We'll have to track some down another day." He took her coat and slung it and his over one arm.

Shelly was fascinated by all the exhibits. She hadn't been to the planetarium since grade school, and everything had changed. They checked their weights on several planets and learned more about meteorites and the rotation of the earth. They learned about Mars and telescopes, how solid rocket motors work, and how the new solar panels on the roof allowed star power to run the exhibits at the planetarium.

Finally, he pulled her into the Hansen Dome for the film *The Ultimate Universe*. Rob led her to the back corner of the theater, away from all of the other patrons. Shelly marveled as 3-D images of galaxies flowed over the screen. They whispered comments about the show and partway through, Rob pulled her close and pressed his lips to hers.

"Are you enjoying yourself?" he asked.

"Yes." The dim light flickered across their faces and she felt a buzz of excitement. He'd been different today, with an undercurrent of anticipation. She wondered what was going on.

Then he lifted her hand and put something into it. A small box that was covered in velvet.

The air backed up in her throat as he leaned closer, whispering to her. "Last time I made a lot of mistakes, so I thought I'd try again. Only better this time."

Shelly sucked in a breath. "Really?" Her voice came out high-pitched and tinny. She didn't look at the box in her hand, didn't want to tear her eyes from his face.

He reached out and brushed the hair back from her face, trailing his thumb down the soft contours of her cheekbone. "When I see a star-strewn sky, I can't help but think of eternity. And the only woman I've ever been able to see with me in eternity is you."

Shelly didn't look away from Rob's face. She didn't know what to say, so she was grateful when he didn't give her a chance to respond.

"You've heard that before, I know. So let me try this again." His Adam's apple bobbed as he swallowed. "Shelly Cox, I've loved you for over three years. We've taken some twisted paths to get back here, but I've never loved anyone else as much as I love you. You make me want to be better. Will you marry me?"

She thought her heart would beat out of her chest, it was expanding so much. She didn't have any hesitation this time. "Yes, there's nothing I'd like more."

Rob took the box from her hand and opened it. He pulled out an oval diamond large enough to make her blink. "It's a little bigger than I could have afforded a couple years ago."

Shelly let Rob slide it onto her finger, then crooked her finger to keep it on as she threw her arms around his neck and kissed him. "As if that ever mattered to me. Yes, I'll marry you." She kissed him again as the credits rolled and people began to shift in their seats.

He tipped his forehead against hers and looked into her eyes. "I feel as if I waited my whole life for you."

"That would mean life was nearly done." She pressed another quick kiss to his mouth. "Our life has just begun."

Excerpt for Blank Slate

BY HEATHER JUSTESEN

Chapter One

Laura looked out the bus window at the rain, which grew worse every minute, and said yet another silent prayer that all would be well. She finished the text message to her sister on her cell phone. She listened to the hum of women chatting nearby, and more specifically, to the two women talking in the seats in front of her.

"And here's one with my brother's family—isn't his son cute? I just adore him—and the one next to it is me and my fiancé."

That comment drew Laura's attention and she craned her neck to see the picture Adrianna, the woman she had met just that morning, held up for the silver-haired woman seated beside her. She felt a yearning in her chest as she saw the happiness on their faces, then scolded herself. Of course the picture was happy—no one carried around photos of people scowling. "He's beautiful," Laura said.

Adrianna looked back and smiled at her.

The comment could have applied equally well to any of those pictured—but it was the baby boy who charmed Laura. While her sister Sandra and best girl friends had all married early and started families, Laura seemed no closer to the goal at twenty-seven than she had been at nineteen. She felt a twinge of jealousy every time Sandra, announced another pregnancy—and she just had child number four. A lot of the people Laura worked with were still single and happy with their freedom, but she couldn't help wishing for something more.

"What are you doing back there?" Adrianna asked, peering over the seat.

Laura closed the message and passed up her phone. "It's my electronic brain. I swear I'd never be able to keep track of things without it. Between church meetings and the fall school booster club schedule I'm always a bit distracted."

Adrianna looked at it and shook her head. "My brother has something similar but I've never been able to run the thing. I'm strictly a day planner woman. I have a cell phone, but I'm not really great at remembering to charge it." She scrolled through the menu, but looked lost. "Do you have Solitaire on here?"

"Of course." Grinning, Laura set up a game for Adrianna. "Mind if I take a closer look at your pictures? Where were they taken?"

"My parents have this waterfall and pond in their yard. It's the perfect backdrop." Adrianna handed back her wallet and flipped to the next photo, which showed her with her fiancé. "When Brock and I got engaged last spring, we and my brother's family went out for a visit. It was really nice. After decades of living in the city, my parents packed it all up a few years back and moved to Nebraska. Though their store keeps them plenty busy, Mom says she likes the slower pace there. After all the years she spent getting me into the symphony circuit, she claimed she needed a change. Their house already had the stream; they just shifted things around to make the waterfall."

"It's beautiful. They must really enjoy it." Laura glanced up as the bus swerved slightly and again she hoped everything would be all right. There were an unusually large number of cars on the road tonight, a fact she couldn't miss as the driver sat directly in front of Adrianna's seat. Laura returned to studying the picture. She knew from asking earlier in the trip that Adrianna was two years younger than herself and was getting married in a little over a month to a symphonic conductor. Studying the picture only emphasized how much she and Laura looked alike.

It wasn't just in their dark hair and eyes, height and build, but they could be sisters—maybe even twins. They both had oval faces with high cheekbones and rounded noses, though Adrianna's was slightly thinner. Their eyes were dark brown, and both wore their hair long, but Laura's was down to her waist—several inches longer than Adrianna's. It was no wonder they'd been mistaken for each other throughout the women's retreat to St. Louis.

The only noticeable feature that differed for them was the scar that ran along the underside of Laura's right jaw—a remnant of a Little League softball game. No doubt Adrianna's life on the symphony circuit meant she also lacked the numerous other minor scars scattered around Laura's body—

267

reminders of her many trips to the ER as a kid and some visits that were not so distant.

Laura looked up when the woman seated next to Adrianna flipped the light off over them. Her gaze was drawn out the window when something large and dark flipped in front of a pair of headlights. She felt her fingers grasp tightly on the wallet in her hand as the bus driver called out for everyone to brace themselves.

She clenched her eyes as a large white vehicle that had been heading north-bound on the other side of the freeway slammed into the charter bus. As Laura was thrown from her seat, she heard the sounds of metal ripping, windows exploding, and screaming women before everything went blank.

Gavin worked on a permit for a new home he and his partner, Jake, had just contracted to build—an event that was becoming more regular in their growing business. Though he could handle office work and the endless stream of forms contracting required, he'd much rather have been on the job hanging sheetrock or installing windows. He rubbed his eyes and double-checked the numbers. He couldn't afford any mistakes on this form. If they were going to get the client into his new home on time, this plan had to be approved in the city planning meeting the next day.

Holding back a groan as he shifted in his seat, he tried not to think of the football game he would have to watch by DVR or of his grumbling stomach. If he focused on the paperwork for another thirty minutes, he would be able to enjoy his leftover pizza and game with a clear conscience. He pulled out his cell phone and dialed his partner to clarify a detail on the contract. "Hey, Jake," he said when his partner answered. "I had a couple of questions."

"Adrianna's been in an accident," Jake's voice said in a rush, jarring Gavin from his work. "Now's not a good time."

Gavin immediately hit save and stood from his computer. "Where is she? What happened?" He was fond of Jake's little sister, and worried for his friend.

"I got a call from St. Joseph Medical Center in Kansas City. Her bus crashed."

"I'll meet you there." Gavin pulled his keys from his pocket as he hurried out.

Hours passed while Gavin sat with Jake and his wife, Megan, in the waiting room. He flipped through ancient muscle car magazines and listened to the clipped footsteps of hospital staff hurrying past the door. Jake turned on a local news station for a while but other than the forty-five seconds the reporters spent on the accident, no one listened to the television.

The doctors hadn't let them see Jake's sister yet because she was in surgery. It sounded like she'd been banged up almost past the point of recognition. Since they'd grown up down the street from each other, Adrianna had always been part of Gavin's world, if only on the fringes. Her life as a well-known piano soloist was light years away from his world of cement and 2x4s.

Jake, on the other hand, had been Gavin's closest friend for over two decades. When there was trouble, they were always there for each other, so he waited. Midnight came and went, and still there was no word.

The clock ticked and the cushions on the seats seemed to thin by the moment. Other patients' families came and went while the three of them continued to count the ticks of the clock. Though Gavin tried to get Jake and Megan to eat something, neither had seemed interested. When he grabbed food for them anyway, Jake finished his almost absentmindedly. Megan mostly picked at hers while she verbally reviewed good memories with her sister-in-law, interspersing her chatter with worries and fears.

Jake took turns sharing memories with his wife and talking with Gavin about the construction jobs they were handling. He cracked his knuckles every ten minutes, a nervous habit he'd had for as long as Gavin had known him. Finally, they all dropped into silence and waited while the clock hands slowly rotated around its face.

When sleep dragged at Gavin and he wondered if he'd be able to pull himself out of bed when the alarm went off in four hours, a woman in a white lab jacket entered the room. "Jacob Mueller?"

Jake and Megan jumped to their feet. Gavin rose more slowly, stiff from sitting so long.

"I'm Jake. Do you have news about Adrianna?"

"We've finished the first round of surgeries."

"The first round?" Jake looked stunned. When Megan reached out and rubbed a comforting hand over her husband's back, Gavin shoved his fists in his pockets. He felt supremely useless. He saw the mixed relief and worry on Jake's face and wished there were something he could do to help.

"There will be more if she recovers, but she needs to get stronger before we finish the basic plastic surgery. She was really beaten up. It's a miracle she lived at all with the amount of damage the accident caused. They had to restart her heart several times before we got her to the operating table."

Jake turned ashen at the news. "*If* she recovers?"

The brunette removed a pair of glasses and slid them into the front pocket of her lab coat. "She has an amazing will to live or she wouldn't have made it this far. I have to warn you though; it might be a while before she wakes. She was unconscious when she came in, and she may remain in a coma for some time. The surgery went well but it'll be touch and go for a while yet."

"For how long?"

Gavin wondered if Jake would be able to stay upright and stepped closer, taking his friend by an elbow. Jake leaned against him.

"There's no way to know." The doctor looked solemn. "I think her chances of recovery are at least fifty-fifty, but it's a waiting game for now. Come with me."

A few minutes later, the three of them arrived at the room where Adrianna lay. She would be moved to the ICU in a while.

Gavin had never seen her looking so vulnerable before—not since she was in elementary school. No, he told himself, not even then. Weak was not a word one generally used to describe Adrianna Mueller. Her face was swathed in bandages, her hair had been cut short, nearly to the nape of her neck in some places, and she was deathly still despite the beeping noises and flashing lights of the machines all around her. A lump filled his throat as he wondered if he'd ever see her laughing brown eyes again.

Buy Blank Slate from Amazon, Barnes & Noble and other retailers.

Acknowledgements

This story was actually the first one I ever started back in January 2000 and woke me up to the fact that I was a writer (I know, you'd think that I would have figured it out before then, but alas, with some things I can be somewhat stupider than your average chicken—and having raised chickens, I say this with good authority.) The process of getting from there to here has been long, with far, far more versions than I want to think of again. As with nearly every author's first book, this would have been totally unpublishable in its earliest format, but thanks to multiple edits, sixteen years, and lots of writing and learning in between on other projects, it's now publishable.

There were a lot of people along the road who helped me get to this place, first and foremost among them, my husband, who always believed in me—even when I was writing my first draft in a notebook because we couldn't afford a computer yet.

I also need to thank my critique group: Tristi Pinkston, Keith Fisher, Nichole Giles and Kim Job who helped me refine this once I finally figured out how to make the story work, as well as Randy McNeely who Brit-picked it for me and Maria Hoagland who read it to make sure the story flow worked.

More thanks to my amazing grammar ladies Diana Shanks, Brooke Heaton, Kayla Batty, Shelley Carr, Lori Banister, Jenn Booth, Tamika Featherstone, Cathy Jeppsen, Alison Foito, and Julia Lance for catching those last-minute typos and inconsistencies.

Thank thanks to all of my readers who have stayed with me and given me the courage to make it through twenty-five books now. You all are the best!

About the Author

HEATHER JUSTESEN has been reading romance for as long as she can remember and has been publishing in the genre since 2009. She has written more than two-dozen books. When she's not dreaming up new stories to write, or helping out with her community garden, she enjoys playing with her dogs and cat, cake decorating, trying new jewelry designs, and hanging out with her husband.

Learn more about her at her website and sign up for her newsletter at http://heatherjustesen.com/ follow her Facebook fan page http://www.facebook.com/pages/Heather-Justesen/273141090197?fref=ts or her blog http://heatherjustesen.blogspot.com/

Made in the USA
Columbia, SC
06 April 2024

34065118R00167